Giahem's
Talons

Katharine E. Wibell

Phaesporia Press

i

Giahem's Talons

Printed in the United States of America.

First Edition September 2019

Visit us on the Web! KatharineWibellBooks.com

Phaesporia Press

ISBN-13: 978-0-9983779-6-4

DEDICATION

To April, for without you my first series would not be where it is today.

CONTENTS

SPECIAL THANKS

To April Wells-Hayes, my editor; to Karen Wibell, who served as reader and preserved my sanity; to the Madison Writers Group, who encouraged and supported me during this process; and OliviaProDesign for the cover.

And I tip my hat to all those who told the stories that became the myths and legends that I read while growing up—and still do.

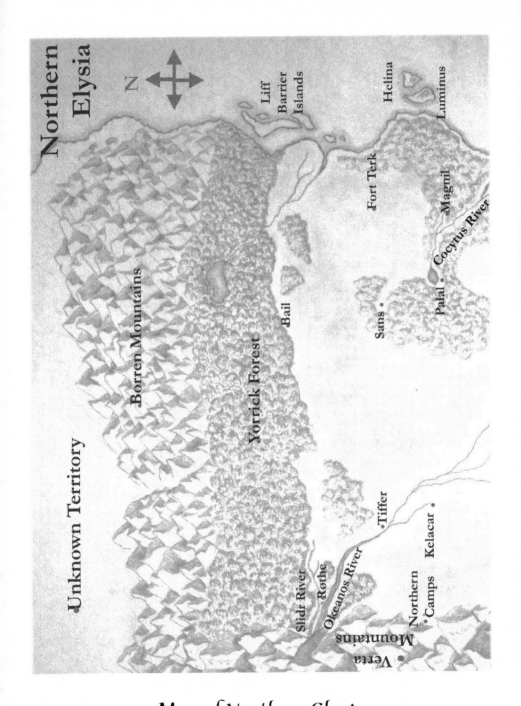

Map of Northern Elysia

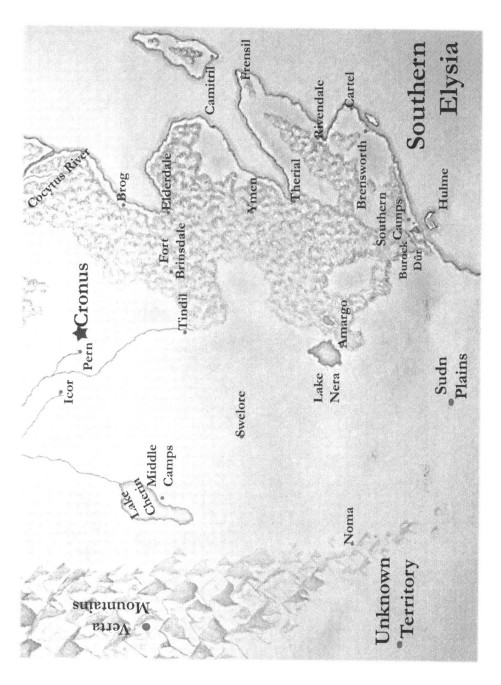

Map of Southern Elysia

GIAHEM'S TALONS

PART 1

Prologue

Darkness was their ally, like a vigilant brother always watching, always protecting. In the shadows, they lurked as silently as the ghosts they helped to create. Even when the thin eye of the moon was swallowed by the massing clouds, they could see as clearly as the giant night cats that lurked in these mountains. A decision was to be made, and soon.

At last, the one for whom they waited manifested out of the blackness. After a silent greeting, he observed the cargo in the middle of the clearing.

A low moan emerged. Too early, they all knew.

Another moan accompanied a few feeble movements.

One of the black-clad figures, taller than the rest, approached. A long needle was withdrawn from a hidden pouch; flesh was pierced in a move as quick as a viper's strike. The bound and blindfolded captive immediately went limp. Stepping back, the tall figure avoided the oozing liquid from the captive's reopened wounds. Blood might be smelled miles away. Caution must be taken.

A soft glimmer of starlight sifted through the ragged clouds as the sack covering the captive's head was removed. Long auburn locks streaked with blond tumbled over a face not yet marred by an abundance of years. Bare-chested, the prisoner's skin, which should have been pale, was deeply tinted and freckled by sunlight. His horsehide pants identified his origin.

"You were ordered to kill any that crossed the borders." This was the voice of authority.

"He is different from the rest," responded the tall one.

"He is human like the others. Same build, same look, same garb. Kill him, or I will." A glint of silver could be seen in the speaker's hands.

"No! Wait! He possessed something. Something you will want to see."

An item was brought forth, a bow that appeared to be made of gold but was far too light to be of that metal. Even the bowstring appeared to be formed from threads of spun gold. More extraordinary, the bow produced and disseminated warmth when touched. The weapon was unsurpassed in its strange, unnatural beauty. Each part of its workmanship vied for the observer's attention.

The clouds parted, and the silvery light above met the golden glow below. In the illuminating moonlight, the leader raised the bow so all could see the strange runes incised upon the weapon's handle.

The gleam of the runes was reflected in the black depths of their leader's eyes.

"Do you understand the meaning of this?" he demanded.

The others remained silent.

"The end of our age has arrived."

Chapter 1

One Prayer Answered

She had survived.

But why? She was responsible for every horrible thing that had occurred. Her mistakes were unforgivable. Unforgettable.

When the tunnel opening collapsed, countless stones had beaten down on her and her comrades. Terribly cut and bruised, she should have died in that granite tomb. Yet after the rumbling and cracking of shifting rock had subsided, she had heard voices calling out to her, "Lluava! Lluava Kargen!"

Lluava ignored her gloomy recollections. With her uninjured eye, she scanned the slow-moving caravan. A half-dozen Obsidian Guards, wearing black, skin-tight uniforms that revealed only their eyes, led the way on midnight-black steeds. Known as Shadows, their attire and accoutrements suited these elite warriors, who were rarely talked of and less often seen. Despite the futility of it all, they continued to pursue their single purpose: to defend and protect the king. Their leader, Regin, was determined that all would not be lost. Foolish man.

Upon their arrival at stables hidden in the forest, the rest of the party had been given mounts. Their trek had been harrowing, through miles of subterranean tunnels in which they had circumnavigated pits and ancient booby-traps. Head Councilman Themis had actually shown signs of delight once they emerged deep in the forest, far away from Cronus, the capital they had been forced to abandon. Themis blamed Lluava for all of this. He should. Hadn't she been the reason for their downfall?

Shouldn't everyone hate her? Byron claimed he didn't, but he was one of the first friends she had made upon being drafted into military service. They had become friends despite the fact that he was a human and she was a Theriomorph, who looked human but possessed the ability to change into an animal form. Together, she and Byron had seen friends die, castles and towns destroyed, allies betrayed. He assured her that it wasn't her fault; she had been so focused on defeating the Raiders' army that she had not recognized the other evil lurking in their midst. Many others had made the same mistake.

So shouldn't Byron loathe her as well? Byron, along with all humans, had been forced to flee when all went to hell. Those who remained were being hunted down and killed. However, Talos, Byron's military partner, had chosen to remain in Cronus to ensure the safety of his wife. Although Rosalyn was pregnant and unable to travel, Talos believed they would be safe because they were Theriomorphs.

Lluava should have stayed in Cronus. After all, she was a Theriomorph, she—

"Drink some water," Byron commanded as he thrust a water pouch into Lluava's hand. "If you are going to continue to refuse to eat, at least drink this."

Pursing her cracked lips, she stared at the pouch as a single droplet fell onto her horse's dark mane.

"There is no honor if both of you die."

Lluava choked back a tearless sob.

"Drink."

Tilting the pouch back, Lluava allowed the cool liquid to stream down her throat. Then, gagging, she spat half of it back up. Byron looked disappointed as she handed the pouch back to him. Clicking his spurs, he prompted his horse into a trot.

There would be no honor if she died through self-enforced starvation, that was true. However, it was not honor but penance Lluava sought—a way to atone for everything. What did Byron know? It was quite possible that Talos was safe and sound. High Priestess Yena had decreed that any Theriomorph who chose to follow her would be accepted into the new order. Talos would know what to say and do to ensure that he and Rosalyn would not be harmed. Byron's partner was fortunate. Hers was not.

Lluava remembered her partner's name being shouted along with hers after the tunnel's collapse. Varren had pulled her into his embrace, using his body as a shield, when the stone ceiling gave way. He had sacrificed himself to save her.

She had been pulled from the rubble first. Badly bruised and beaten, she remembered being laid on the ground while others dug through the rocks to recover their king. When Varren was removed, he was so still, so very still, that Lluava thought he had been killed.

Regin informed them that Varren was in a coma. At first, this was considered a blessing, but as the days passed, it began to seem more like a curse. If Varren did not awaken soon, he might not awaken at all.

Several days ago, Head Councilman Themis had shouted at her, "This is all your fault!"

She wondered if Head Councilman was still the right title, as all the human council members had been slaughtered in Cronus, their carcasses left in the very chairs they had so often frequented. Themis had narrowly escaped the same fate. And now, the last surviving councilman was still defending a king who might be dying and a kingdom that was overrun. Pathetic and sad.

"I know," Lluava had acknowledged. He was right.

"I advised against allowing that rabble through our doors. I begged that the armory not be opened to them. I warned that those decisions were grave mistakes."

"You were right."

"You invited the Outlanders here," seethed Themis. "You defended them. You assisted in their plan to overtake Elysia, our kingdom. You are one of them!"

"Enough!" roared Regin. "Whatever Lluava's hand in this, she will be punished accordingly in due time. Nonetheless, there is no reason to accuse her in terms of race. Being a Theriomorph does not mean that you are on the side of the Outlanders."

Lluava had waited for Themis to call her *monster, beast, animal,* but no other words were voiced. He strode off to the stretcher that carried Varren—his godson, Lluava's partner, their king. Instead, it was Regin who affirmed, "You *will* be punished accordingly."

She might be perceived as a villain, but others were the true villains. The Raiders, certainly. For example, Thad, Varren's childhood friend, and his Theriomorph partner, Horus, had been captured by the enemy early in the war. Horus had been brutally tortured and disfigured; he had died saving Lluava. Thad, for some unknown reason, had not been physically harmed. The torture he'd endured was mental. He refused to speak of it. In truth, he rarely spoke at all. He traveled with them, always mumbling incoherently near Varren's stretcher.

Yet the enemy was not always so obvious. Why had she trusted Yena? Because Yena was a high priestess of the old faith, her father's religion? Because they were both Theriomorphs? Or maybe, just maybe, because they were both Incarn? The term soured in Lluava's mouth. *Incarn.* Vessels created by the gods for them to inhabit, to use as they wished, and to mark with their own animal forms. Was Yena operating independently, or did her actions imply that the gods wanted to destroy all humans?

Lluava had not wanted to harm her human friends, especially Varren. Yet she had. Themis was right to have disliked her. Her decisions had resulted in monstrous events.

Looking back at the forested path, she envisioned the silhouette of Cronus in the distance. At the capital, Elysia was being destroyed by two different enemies: Theriomorph Outlanders, led by Yena, and the human Raiders, who were led by some brutish man Lluava had not met and perhaps never would.

Was Elysia truly lost? With the infrastructure of their government all but destroyed and no stronghold yet claimed, Lluava's sorry band of survivors had become refugees, fleeing their birth home. Wherever Regin was taking them, it was far away from Cronus.

"I have ruined everything."

No one contested her statement; perhaps they were too far ahead to hear it. What did it matter? Did she want sympathy? No. She watched as Varren's stretcher was pulled by his would-be mount; Regin held the horse's reins. At twenty-one, Varren's features had taken on a look of someone much older. Yet neither his soft, loose ringlets of dark hair nor the lips that could turn into a brilliant smile had changed. Under those closed eyelids were his ever-kind blue eyes. Still, he lay unmoving, and she was responsible.

The heat of anger no longer exploded inside her, forcing her to shift into her dual form, a white tigress. Instead, she was filled with self-loathing. Why had she allowed Hyrax and the other Guardians to convince her to pursue some ancient prophecy? This secret society had manipulated her, an unwilling Incarn, just as the High Council had manipulated Varren's grandfather. She should have known bad things would follow, but she was eighteen and foolish.

Up ahead, Varren's pallid face looked desiccated. Like hers, his lips were chapped. Like hers, his body was silently screaming for nourishment. Lluava would not eat until he awoke; if he died, she would die alongside him. That was fitting, was it not? Military partners leaving this life simultaneously?

How else could she handle the guilt of having placed Varren, the man she loved, in such a predicament? She still loved him, or at least she used to. Once, she had hungered to hear Varren say he would marry her. Now, she might never get that chance. Then again, did she actually want it? She was so confused, and Apex was responsible.

Apex. What had happened to him? Was he dead? Was he yet another victim of her mistakes? She could still hear his last scream on that horrible night. He had remained in the tunnel to give the others time to cross the narrow subterranean bridge and escape. Reaching the far side of the chasm, she had heard him shout her name as if imploring her to help. Turning, she had seen the massive silhouette of the Yorrick wolverine attacked by numerous Theriomorphs. Apex's scream had transformed into a thunderous roar so powerful that the entire cavern collapsed.

Lluava would have run to him had not Varren grabbed her at that moment. Her partner had thought only of her well-being. She was unworthy of either man.

"We are nearing Tindil's branch of the Okeanos River," Regin announced from up ahead. "We will make camp there tonight. This day is at its end."

Lluava was ready for all this to end. Her stomach cried out as her energy continued to diminish. It was a wonder that she could still sit upright in the saddle. Yet, she had survived a prolonged starvation period once before, imprisoned at Fort Brinsdale and left to die. But she hadn't died. Some had said it was unnatural. Had Theri—also known as Issaura, Goddess of War—intervened and kept her Incarn, Lluava, alive? Would the goddess do so again? If Lluava was being protected by the goddess, and Theri actually cared about her feelings, wouldn't Varren be well and Apex at her side?

Then again, Apex was Incarn to Ullr, Tyr, God of War. Maybe *his* god had kept him alive as well. But to what purpose? And was either she or Apex strong enough to overthrow Yena, Incarn of Crocotta, Queen of Gods? Would Yena punish Apex for helping Varren escape? Surely she wouldn't kill him. As Incarn, he would be too valuable. At least, that was what Lluava hoped.

"Let me help you dismount." Byron had come over to assist her. He understood how weak she was. It seemed he alone cared whether she lived or died on this journey. Byron's strong arms lowered her. His hands, callused from sword fighting, gripped her gently. When she stepped onto firm ground, she felt dizzy and her body swayed.

"Walk me over to Varren."

Lluava noted the sorrowful look on Byron's face as he assisted her to the king's stretcher. She sank to the ground and laid her head on Varren's chest. She listened to his heartbeat and felt the slight rise and fall of his rib cage.

"Please wake up," she quietly begged, holding his hand in hers. She ran her finger over his signet ring with its royal crest, a prostrate lion at the feet of a raven carrying an olive branch. Varren tended to fiddle with the ring when he was nervous. Lluava found that she missed his quirks, the sound of his voice, his assuring presence near her.

He seemed so distant now. His breath no longer smelled of rosemary and fennel but of something at the point of decay. His complexion hinted of yellow.

"Come back to me," she whispered in his ear.

Lluava had been angry with Varren for a long time. She blamed him for falling under Selene's control and considering matrimony, even though that hadn't been his fault. All Incarn had special abilities. Selene manipulated people, especially men; Yena foresaw glimpses of past and future events; Luka used trickery to his benefit. Of the five known Incarn, three recognized and exploited their gifts. Apex and Lluava had yet to identify their own.

And what of the other Incarn? There were twelve in all, one for each god in the pantheon. Apparently they resided outside of Elysia. Perhaps they were not even aware of what they really were. Lluava cared little for any of them. She cared even less for the gods.

Gently running her fingers through Varren's loose curls, Lluava wondered, Where was *his* god? Humans believed in only one god. Where was this all-powerful creator? Was he as heartless as the Theriomorphs' pantheon? If the human god cared, let him bring Varren back. Out of all of them, Varren was the one who needed to be saved.

"You have to let him go, Lluava."

Startled, she looked up at Byron through her platinum-blond hair, partially distorting her sight.

"I can't. I won't."

"You must let him go," Byron gently repeated as he bent down to lift her. "You need rest."

As Byron walked her to a blanket that he had spread on the ground, Lluava moaned, "I will never let him go."

Byron tucked her in just as her mother, Maessa, had done when Lluava was younger than her sister, Lamb. Mouse, her baby brother, would still be enjoying these simple pleasures. Her family would be asleep in their rundown farmhouse in Rivendale. That is, if Rivendale still existed and the war had not moved farther south.

Tilting her head to the side, Lluava glimpsed the Okeanos River sparkling in the moonlight through the trees. The sounds of lapping water soothed her. It had been more than half a year since she had lived and trained by the ocean.

Her pet raven, Onyx, alighted on her saddle bag, where he stood plucking out the entrails of some unfortunate lizard. What would the poor bird do when—if—she died? Fly away and join his feathered friends? Search for her after she was buried? Find another person to care for him?

Whispered words wafted to Lluava's ears as those huddled around the campfire conversed.

"I still think someone should watch her in case she runs."

"Look at her. She can barely stand."

"Can't you see that she is greatly pained by all this?"

"Good. She deserves pain. We should not trust her."

"Her weapons have been confiscated. She will not be harming anybody."

"Some refer to her as that pagan warrior goddess. She is dangerous."

"Not anymore."

Lluava tried to distract herself from the others' conversation, but her thoughts returned to what the men had said. They had taken Issaura's Claws, her weapons, after the cave-in. She remembered distinctly the Shadows pulling the golden weapons off her hands and tossing them into a travel sack. Her last memory, before she had lost consciousness, was her distorted reflection multiplied in the three curved, metallic blades of each claw.

The blades, in turn, were affixed to their specialized handles, akin to brass knuckles. She had received Issaura's Claws during her military training. Yet they were not like any weapon she had ever seen. They were a weapon made by a Theriomorph for a Theriomorph. They, too, had a special ability— they shifted with her to gild her foreclaws in hardened sheaths. A god's weapon. Apex and Yena also had gods' weapons that, though different in design, shifted with them as well.

Longing to have the Claws returned, Lluava curled into a shivering ball. The early spring was still snow laden, and the chilled air turned her breath into puffs of cloud. Cold had never been kind to her. Maybe she would freeze to death.

Soon her tormented dreams robbed her of the little rest she had gained. Muddled and confused, she dreamed that arrows with shafts as long as men skewered people together like the kabobs the traveling bandits had served. More projectiles flew past, pinning Theriomorph and human together, blood oozing from open mouths. Only Lluava was left standing among the bloodshed as an eagle keened high above.

Suddenly, Lluava was shaken awake.

"What's happened?" she croaked out, blinking away the realm of dreams.

Byron stood over her, his eyes wide.

"It's Varren, isn't it?" Lluava struggled to sit up. "Is he…?"

A tear slid down her blond-haired friend's bristly face. "He's awake."

Chapter 2

Sightless

Take me to him."

As Lluava struggled to rise, Byron lifted her up in a single, fluid movement. Was she really that weak? That light? Or had Byron always been that strong? With a whispered thanks, she quickly focused on Varren, who still lay on his stretcher. The entire camp encircled him, and her partner was shielded from her sight.

Themis was the first to take note of her approach. "You cannot possibly—" he began, but Regin cut him off.

"Let her through."

Several figures stepped back. Lluava half ran, half fell forward, landing on her knees as Varren struggled to raise his head and arms toward her. There was a moment when their eyes locked, green to blue, blue to green. Then, holding one another, they both began to sob. Neither cared whether their tears were happy, sad, or some other elusive, unexplained feeling. No words were needed. Neither apologies nor fears were voiced. They held each other tightly, more for emotional support than physical. Soon Varren's grip weakened, and he eased back down onto his stretcher.

"You both need rest," Regin stated. "There is too little time for that as it is."

"Wait," Varren rasped, his voice barely a whisper. "Let me look at her."

Lluava knelt as Varren lifted a hand to her face and tucked a swatch of her silvery hair behind her ear. Though his hand trembled, he succeeded in his gesture.

Onyx landed on Lluava's other shoulder and peered down at Varren with great interest, causing Varren to crack out a dry laugh. "You two look more alike every day."

9

Though his remark might not have been taken with such good humor in a different situation, Lluava chuffed playfully as she turned to observe her bird's scarred face and single dead eye.

"At least I should regain my sight," she said as she gently touched her swollen eyelids. Their tender mass had begun to subside, although the bruised skin was still painful.

"You are thin," Varren observed, his voice serious.

"Look who's talking," retorted Lluava.

"Both of you must recuperate," interjected Regin.

Lluava had forgotten that Regin still stood there. Though he was dressed like the other Shadows, Lluava could identify him by his build, eyes, and voice.

"Now, Your Majesty, please rest," he said.

Varren nodded. Another Obsidian Guard offered the king some broth to sip before he slept. Byron helped Lluava to her feet and returned with her to her sleeping area. At last, she could consent to rest.

***

The following morning seemed brighter, somehow—the sky bluer, the evergreens a deeper shade of green. Even the broth Byron gave her tasted good.

At Varren's side once more, Lluava could not help but grin down at the young man. He, too, looked better. "How did you sleep?" she asked

"As though I had not taken rest in a long while," Varren admitted. "Strange, is it not?"

"Regardless of your rest," the ever-watchful Regin interjected, "I must insist that you continue to travel upon your stretcher, at least until you are able to eat a heartier meal. I cannot afford to let you break your neck falling off your horse."

"I will follow your advice without complaint," replied the young king, who was still very weak.

Lluava gently squeezed his hands; they felt warmer today. "Where are we heading?" she asked.

"Far away. Far away. Far away from *them*," mumbled Thad, who had stood silently a few feet away throughout the couple's greeting. Although his eyes were cast downward, he was obviously listening to the conversations around him. Lluava gave the lordling a sidelong glance. Thad continued to shift his weight from side to side. He seemed to be getting worse. What had the Raiders done to him?

Regin, saddling his horse, replied to Lluava's question. "To the Verta Mountains."

Until now, Lluava had not cared where they were going, but her curiosity seemed to have awakened overnight. The Verta Mountains served as the spine of the kingdom. Somewhere within their peaks and valleys, far past Elysia's border, lay Leucrocotta, the hidden city of Theriomorph Outlanders, where High Priestess Yena ruled. Leucrocotta, the birthplace of so much of this misery. To be headed so near it caused a shiver to run down Lluava's spine, and the hairs on the back of her neck stood up.

Her discomfort grew as they traveled. Even though Lluava's body had begun to regain its strength and heal, as had Varren's, she could not shake the idea that more evil awaited her among the ever-growing, white-capped peaks. As they neared Lake Cherin, the largest landlocked body of water in the kingdom, Lluava hoped that they would seek refuge at the Middle Camps. Maybe that had been Regin's idea after all.

***

Unfortunately, her hopes were dashed upon the pebbly shores of the Cherin branch of the Okeanos River.

"Certainly, we leave her there. She can be held and tried at their leisure." Themis's voice seemed to cleave the calm of the deepening twilight. "We can leave *that* soldier with her as well."

Lluava had chosen to sleep away from the main caravan, though someone was always posted as sentry. This did not bother her. She understood that only Varren and Byron wanted her around. She strained to make out the words of the voices she overheard.

"I will send a Guard to scout the camps," Regin responded. "The inhabitants will not have been notified of the status of either Cronus or the second opposing army. If they still exist, they may prove useful. When did you last hear from their representatives?"

There was a long pause, for which Lluava surmised the reason: the High Council must have ignored and minimalized the war. Had Themis even kept in contact with the other training camps and forts? The Northern Camps had been destroyed when the Raiders attacked from the North with their Berserker Legion. The Southern Camps were barely functioning after their battles over the summer. Only Durog, the Theriomorph men's camp where Lluava had trained, still stood. Had the Middle Camps survived?

As the conversation resumed, Lluava was grateful for her hypersensitive hearing. Clearly, the humans believed she was out of earshot.

"We will continue to follow our prearranged plan. Cronus has fallen. You, as well as King Varren, know the protocol."

Varren spoke up, confirming Regin's statement. "The king and the head councilman will be taken to a safe refuge."

"Yes, yes," noted Themis. "But no others will be permitted. The point is to minimize the chance of an enemy discovering our sanctuary until we have overcome the crisis."

"The plan also states," Varren interjected, "that the High Council and royal family members are to be taken to several other hidden refuges for the duration of the crisis." His voice had almost returned to its former authoritative strength. "Head Councilman Themis and I are all who remain. And Thad—Thad is as close to me as any family member."

Lluava felt a twinge of jealousy as she listened to Varren.

"He comes with me. Moreover, we never envisioned a time when all human Cronians would be slaughtered. Byron will travel with us the entire way. Lluava also."

Themis cut in, sounding rather heated. "You know as well as I do, Your Majesty, where we are headed. No Theriomorph has ever, *EVER* crossed into that sanctuary. None are allowed. The Obsidian Guard will not stand for it!"

"Then, Themis," Varren sighed, "this is where we must part. Without my limited protection, Lluava will be hunted down by everyone. I will not leave her to die. She travels with us, or I stay with her."

"Noble words, my King," began Regin. "Yet Themis is correct: Theriomorphs are not welcome in that sanctuary. However, this is an extraordinary situation. The Lady Lluava will be brought with us, if only to ensure that you remain protected."

There was a moment's pause, as though Varren had been about to speak, but Regin continued. "She will come, but by a means of my choosing. She is a prisoner and will be tried accordingly for her actions, which resulted in the events leading to Cronus's fall."

Varren uttered an oath, but Regin went on, "Where we are going, even you, Your Majesty, will be out of your jurisdiction. If Lluava is found guilty, she will be punished, even if it means she must relinquish her life."

"And if I do not go with you?" Varren's question seemed to drip with poison.

"I'm sorry," said Regin. "That is not an option."

There was movement in the dark. Onyx cawed loudly and flew into the canopy. Before Lluava's still stiff body could react, she felt a sharp prick on her neck. The silhouette of a Shadow holding a long needle stood next to her. As she focused on the glinting metal, she felt her eyesight dim.

She was blind.

***

The days that passed were hard on Lluava. The cold had returned with all its former severity. Wind whipped and tugged at her riding hood, nearly buffeting her off her horse. Worst of all was her lack of sight. She was led like a child on a pony lest she trek off into the wilderness and freeze.

At first, Lluava had screamed when she lost her sight. She struck out, but a second needle prick caused the rest of her senses to relinquish their grasp. When she regained consciousness, she realized that she had been thrown across the back of what smelled like her mount and then strapped down like a sack. Moving sideways was horribly uncomfortable, and the ropes around her ankles and wrists cut deeply into her skin. Her vision had not returned.

The scent of rosemary and fennel alerted her that Varren was nearby. "Lluava. Please, do not struggle," her partner whispered. "Listen to me. Do not resist, and I will have them untie you."

"What's happening?" she questioned warily.

But Varren was gone. Was anybody near her? Who was watching her horse? Soon she sensed others arriving. Three, by the number of heartbeats; one was Varren.

He said, "They will untie you as long as you swear to behave for the rest of the journey."

"I will."

Cords were cut. She was helped onto her saddle.

***

In her darkened world, one day followed the next without change. As they traveled, the sunlight's thin warmth was soon lost to them. The chill intensified, as did the snow.

Lluava longed to talk with Varren. Would he understand what had happened to her in Tartarus? She had finally broken down the walls she had built against her own goddess, Theri/Issaura. Lluava had fought her inner darkness, that place where she lost conscious control, for a long time. She knew that Theri sought to manipulate her for an unknown purpose, and this terrified her.

Yet during her battle in Tartarus with Master Hon, the Outlander whose form was that of a massive white rhino, Lluava finally permitted—or, rather, accepted—her role as Incarn. She was more than a Theriomorph; she had been created so the goddess Theri could access and interact with the mortal world. In those moments of unification, Lluava had never felt more powerful and free. Although she was loath to admit it, the young woman was glad to have permitted the goddess entry. But should she do so again? Could Lluava give herself fully to the goddess whenever Issaura desired? Through Theri's acts, could Elysia actually be saved?

As Theri's Incarn, Lluava was deemed the savior of the Theriomorph race. Clearly, Yena believed that such a saving necessitated the eradication of the human race. Lluava was not so sure. If her gift as an Incarn was "to end war," could her willing unification with the goddess save Elysia? How? She did not know. She hoped Issaura did.

And what of the other part of the prophecy—that the child Lluava would conceive with Ullr's Incarn, Apex, would be the source of their salvation? She was to save her people by giving birth to the actual savior, Yena had told her. Through Lluava's life's blood would be born the one to rescue all Theriomorphs from the ultimate evil. That was what Yena had said. Yena. The one who had tricked her. The one who had taken over Cronus. Could Lluava believe anything the high priestess had told her?

Sighing, she shook her head to clear her thoughts. As long as they were traveling, she would be unable to discuss anything with Varren until they were safely at their destination. When would they arrive?

Eventually, Lluava realized she was being led down a slope. The decline was remarkably steep. Lluava gripped the mane of her horse, hoping she would not fall off. The horse's hooves clacked on stone. What had happened to the snow? Another horse trotted alongside her. Suddenly, someone shoved her head down. When she straightened up, she rammed her head into a ceiling. Stone. Were they in a cavern?

Down and down they descended. Finally, the clatter of hooves stopped, and Lluava was assisted from her horse. She felt Byron's strong, gentle hands leading her onward into the depths of what Lluava guessed was the earth. Where was Varren?

Several times, she stumbled on the stony ground. Once, she careened into a horse walking beside her; fortunately, the animal was less startled than she. Byron increased their pace. At least the cold had lessened.

More than once, the small caravan paused. Words were passed between voices she did not recognize, before they moved on. Eventually, the ground leveled out, and their horses were left behind. Byron helped her navigate turns and climb stairs. Up, up, up.

Finally, they stopped. Lluava's ears perceived a multitude of sounds. Most of the party seemed to trudge off in a different direction. She heard the movement of cartwheels, the swaying of ropes, and the clatter of...weapons? Lluava gave a start, but Byron told her, "All's well. Keep moving."

Easy for him to say. He could see. Just when she began to pant for lack of breath, Lluava was led into a chamber. She recognized the sound of keys and the clank of a lock, followed by the groan of a door opening.

"You can't be serious!" Byron exclaimed. "She doesn't deserve this."

Nobody responded.

"When King Varren sees what you are doing—"

Another needle bit into Lluava's neck. A low growl escaped her. She heard footsteps as several different people quickly moved away from her. The door slammed shut and was locked.

Byron's voice warned her, "Do not move, Lluava. Do not move at all. I will return with Varren. We will settle this."

Then Lluava was left alone.

Noises arose from the far side of her chamber. Should she investigate? From the worried tone of Byron's voice, she was to stand absolutely still. But why? What was making the noise? What was that...?

Random images swam in a colorless scene. Slowly they took shape and definition, then color exploded back into place. Her sight had returned! And, oh, she wished it hadn't.

Lluava was locked not in a chamber but in a cell fashioned for a villain. The space was of moderate size, yet the fearsome fact was that the far wall was not a wall at all; the fourth side was open. Bars were unnecessary. The edge of the floor ended in a sheer drop from a cliff's edge. Her cell was part of an enormous mountain cavern.

Creeping toward the edge, she craned her head to look at the vast, dark space. There was no opening except for what appeared to be air shafts high above. Scattered about the cavern walls at various levels were darker areas that indicated other openings. Were these also cells, like hers? All were vacant, as far as she could tell.

Light from sconces twinkled like fireflies; narrow troughs with burning oil illuminated other areas. Without their light, the entire space would be thrust into blackness. It was so dimly lit that even she had trouble seeing as much as she would have liked. Once more, she was thankful not to be human.

Near the edge, Lluava dropped to the floor on her stomach, stretched her head over the uneven ledge, and looked down. Although she could not tell how far it was to the ground, it was clearly far enough that she would not survive a fall.

The area below teemed with people, all dressed in shades of black. Lluava squinted to discern details. Most appeared to wear the garb of the Obsidian Guard, but a few pale heads were maskless and hoodless. How many were there? Hundreds? Thousands? And all in black.

With a start, Lluava realized where she had been taken. She was the first Theriomorph in history to be permitted into Erebos, the City of Shadows.

Chapter 3

Six Questions

Lluava would never leave Erebos. She realized that immediately. The Obsidian Guard would not permit a Theriomorph to leave who was even vaguely aware of their lair. But did that mean she would die?

Observing the ground so far below her, Lluava suddenly felt queasy. She pushed away from the ledge, rolled onto her back, and stared at the rocky ceiling above the massive hollow.

What did she know of this place? Any facts? No. Only hearsay, whispered suspicions. Little was known about the king's personal guardians—where they grew up, where they trained, or who deemed them ready to watch over the king.

Their sole duty was to protect Elysia's ruler. Founded during the Landon Wars, the Obsidian Guard had kept its secrets well. All that was known was that they lurked in dark spaces, listening, watching, constantly on alert for an attack. They were allowed no distractions—they never married, never fathered children. They were elite assassins, feared by all.

From time to time, over the years, there came a Call for Human Infants. Although females were seldom selected, every child under a certain age was tested by the Guard. The chosen children were brought to Erebos. In return, their families were bestowed with certain honors and compensation.

As Theriomorphs, Lluava and her siblings were not affected by the calls. Lluava's mother, Maessa, was secretly grateful that her children were safe from this forcible removal. Or had been until the draft.

There had been only one call during Lluava's memory. She had been young, and what she now remembered was extremely hazy. No one from her small town of Rivendale had been selected, so everyone went on with their lives as they always had.

Lluava had almost forgotten the tales told by human children who had seen the black-cloaked phantoms. The Obsidian Guard had seemed little more than myth until she accompanied Varren to the capital in the fall. Would she live out her life as a prisoner of the Guard in their hidden city?

A heavy key clanked in the aged lock.

"Varren!" Lluava exclaimed as she sat up.

However, it was not the young ruler who stepped through the darkened doorway but another Shadow. "The King cannot see you now," he stated solemnly. "Those who know you are not permitted to converse with you until after the trial. Everyone must be questioned separately. We want the most thorough and honest understanding of the events that occurred prior to the Fall."

Lluava's hands felt clammy. What would her friends say? How did they perceive what had happened? She should have talked to Varren on their journey.

"I am Jigo. If you need anything, ask for me."

As the guard turned to leave, Lluava stopped him. "Jigo," she began, barely able to make out the glint of his eyes as the man in black looked at her. "When will the trial take place?"

"Soon," he answered. "We do not like to keep prisoners here."

Instead of asking him her ever-multiplying questions, Lluava kept silent and watched Jigo disappear down the passageway. A second Shadow locked the door behind him.

In the gloom of Erebos, Lluava lost track of time. Once again consumed by her thoughts, she wondered what had happened to Onyx. The raven had traveled with her and would alight on her shoulder to nibble her hair or croon in her ears after she lost her sight. If the bird had noticed any difference in her, it was not apparent. Yet he had disappeared shortly before Lluava entered the underground lair.

Had he flown off on one of his daily hunts, only to return to nothing? Had he seen the little caravan disappear into the mountain range? Had he tried to follow? Poor, old, half-blind bird. Could he survive alone? A long life for a maimed creature in the wild was unlikely. Did Onyx have any chance at all? Did she?

Although Lluava was never treated with contempt, the Shadows followed a formal protocol. When food was brought to her—mildly flavored but hearty—no one struck up a conversation. No matter; she didn't really want to talk to anyone.

She spent most of her time peering over the ledge and watching the dark forms below move with a sort of precision. Shadows moved about one another quickly, spinning and turning as if locked in a dance, yet the clink of metal proved the movements to be more sinister. Was this the training ground? But it could not be, not entirely. Small groups would enter and depart through various openings at the ground level. There was a set pattern to their progression.

Once, Lluava had the sense she was being observed. Glancing up, she thought she saw a figure staring at her from another open-faced prison cell. She squinted to see better but could discern only an empty ledge. After that, the feeling of being watched never quite left her.

Finally, the time came when her gate was unlatched and Jigo told her to follow him. Unbound and virtually unguarded, she was steered down an unlit hall. Without even a small torch to light the way, blackness swallowed everything. Lluava's hyperactive senses were aroused, yet she struggled to distinguish what lay before them. Several times she grated her shoulder against the stone wall when the corridor veered off in another direction.

If she had so much trouble seeing, how could a human walk through these halls as if he were strolling around in the daylight? Could the Obsidian Guard actually see that well in the dark? Or had they memorized the layout of this place that well? Whatever the reason, why did they not use more lights? Why all this darkness and gloom?

"Over here," Jigo said as he led her into a chamber. At least this one had several sconces flickering around the perimeter. Three hoodless men sat at the back of the room on low stools. Regin was in the center, while two much older men flanked him. On the floor in front of them lay a woven mat. Regin motioned toward it.

"Take a seat," he commanded.

Lluava sat cross-legged on the mat and looked up at the men. These three figures would decide if she were to live or die.

Regin inclined his head. Streaks of silver in his short, groomed beard shone in the torchlight. "Lluava Kargen, daughter of Haliden Kargen. Theriomorph. You may begin wherever you see fit. I would advise you to leave out nothing, for even a small detail could alter our judgments. Tell us in your own words what occurred before the Fall of Cronus."

That was just what Lluava did. Keeping the secrets that High Priestess Yena had shared no longer mattered; the priestess had proved to be the enemy, just as the Guardians had, just like Councilman Hyrax. All their disclosures had been intended to manipulate her. It was time to expose them.

Lluava told the three Obsidian Guards what took place, beginning with Councilman Hyrax's admonition to leave Elysia and—with Apex's help—to seek other Incarn: their captivity in Leucrocotta, her return to Elysia to fight the Raiders, her discovery of Yena's treachery, and finally their flight from Cronus to save Varren's life. Although she felt that full honesty was called for, she did not share her feelings for Varren and Apex nor reveal what had occurred during her battle with Master Hon. Lluava finished by saying, "King Varren does not know most of this. He deserves to be told."

The trio of judges did not converse among themselves during Lluava's testimony. They sat silently, faces rigid, listening intently to every word, even when she spoke of the Incarn and the Guardians, the pantheon and the prophecy.

Once she had finished, Regin told her, "We have six questions. Answer them honestly. First, why did you encourage our king to permit the Outlanders within the walls of Cronus?"

Even though Lluava had just related all of this, she responded without hesitation. "I made an agreement with High Priestess Yena so she would send an army to aid Elysia in the war. I gave my word that our gates would be opened to her people. I keep my promises."

Regin spoke again. "Why did you advocate opening the royal armory to the Outlanders upon their arrival?"

"Since some Theriomorphs could fly, they arrived ahead of the land-traveling troops. However, Theriomorphs typically cannot carry weapons in their dual forms. When Ruire Thoth arrived with the winged troops, he needed weapons from the armory to help us fend off the Raiders' army. I backed his request. And they did help us withstand the Raiders."

When Lluava finished, she held her tongue. She could have argued that she didn't know the Outlanders would turn their weapons against the Elysians, that once the capital's stores were emptied, there would be little chance for the citizens to protect themselves. She could have admitted that she was terribly sorry. Yet what did any of that matter, after all those lives were lost?

The third question was asked. "Did you know or expect what the high priestess was planning?"

"No."

There was a long pause. The trio stared at Lluava as if waiting for her to retract her answer. Then Regin asked, "Do you believe you were specifically created by your gods to fulfill their will?"

"I believe everyone's will is his or her own."

"Do you believe you have special abilities?"

"I believe everyone has a special ability, whether to write beautiful ballads, dance with fluid grace, or engage in the art of warfare."

"Lluava Kargen," Regin began, "Do you believe *you* will end this war?"

"If it is in my power." Lluava considered each man individually. "Yes."

Regin glanced at the men beside him. Both nodded subtly. He turned back toward the defendant. "Lluava Kargen, we have heard your statement and the answers to our questions. Unless you wish to change or add anything, we have made our decision."

Already? Lluava's heart skipped a beat. Did they not want to deliberate? Had these men decided the outcome before they even heard her side? Was this her end?

"Those who aid enemies of the crown are sentenced to death. You did so." Regin's face was stern. "Yet your involvement in the events that led up to the Fall have been found to be unintentional. Regardless, you have shown poor judgment and have made choices that not only cost the lives of many but also risked the kingdom of Elysia."

19

The three men stared at her with unsympathetic eyes. Regin continued, "You will henceforth be stripped of your rank as corporal in the king's army, and you are barred from serving as future head of the High Council and military partner to the king."

The last phrase caused Lluava to inhale sharply. Momentarily speechless, she was unable to plead for a different verdict.

Regin finished his proclamation. "Though advised to discharge you from military service completely, you are an exceptionally skilled warrior. At a time when the king's allies are few, there is need for skill such as yours. Until required, you will remain here as ward of the Obsidian Guard."

"As your actions have been judged accordingly, you will be reassigned new quarters. However, you will be under Jigo's supervision during your stay at Erebos. Access is granted to the main chamber and to our meal hall. All other areas of the Dark are reserved for the Obsidian Guard alone; you are forbidden to enter them. Furthermore, you are not to shift into your dual form for any reason during your stay. Any attempt to do so will be deemed a hostile act, and you will be returned to and held in the cell in which you were originally placed. Remember, you will be treated as a guest only if you obey our directives."

Lluava could not hold back her question any longer. "Will I be able to see *him*?"

"That is up to King Varren." Something in Regin's tone forewarned her that Varren might not want to see her. "Jigo will take you to your room."

As Lluava was led through the pitch-black, winding corridors, she wondered if Varren actually blamed her. They had not talked about the Fall since he regained consciousness. Actually, little had been said between them. Their journey had been wearing, and they both needed to conserve their strength. Lluava thought these were the reasons for their rather quiet trek. Could it have been something else?

What did Varren think of her now? Would he feel differently about her when he found out what she had said during her trial? He had trusted her, and in doing so, had lost many of his people and possibly his kingdom. Suddenly, Lluava feared that nothing would be the same between them. Could it ever be?

Regin was right to remove her as Varren's military partner and future advisor. Once again, Lluava was overcome by grief for all the pain and suffering she had caused. Her eyes brimmed with tears. Wiping them away on her sleeve, she stumbled forward until she reached the bottom of the mound, what Regin had called the main chamber.

She looked up. From this perspective, the entire hollow seemed incomprehensibly huge. Was this what an ant felt like in its nest? A speck against a behemoth? Above, sporadic torchlight flickered like stars. Suddenly, Lluava felt unwelcome eyes on her.

"This way," motioned Jigo, once he noticed that Lluava had stopped. She hurriedly caught up with him.

Numerous Shadows swarmed about. But were they all Shadows? Lluava was unsure. Most wore the skin-tight, hooded and masked suits of the Obsidian Guard, yet cloaked old men shuffled alongside robed youths of varying ages. Twice Lluava thought she saw another female in the distance, but she was not certain. Everyone seemed to wear black except the teens, who wore dark brown. Nobody paid any attention to her. They all seemed preoccupied with their own duties.

Jigo led Lluava into a hallway on the opposite side of the cavern and up a single set of stairs before steering her to a small room. She heard flint sparking a candle, and the room took form. There was no bed, only another thin woven mat on the floor. A wooden block with a subtle indent was positioned at one end of the mat. An unlit sconce was affixed to the far wall. Underneath stood a very low table with quill, ink, and one unblemished scroll.

"Is that—?" Lluava started to ask, staring at the mat and block.

"Your bed. Yes," said Jigo. "We live simple, disciplined lives. It is quite late. I bid you a good sleep and will collect you for breakfast come morning."

As Jigo left, Lluava wondered how anyone could tell time without the light of sun, moon, or stars. Regardless, she tried to get comfortable on the mat and then placed her head in the cradle of the wooden block. Though less uncomfortable than she had expected, Lluava doubted she would get much sleep.

The hours slipped by and she wondered if, when day finally arrived, Varren would arrive with it. The young woman's desire to talk to her partner grew until it became a physical ache.

He would never be able to forgive her. How could he? To spare her feelings, Varren would lie and tell her everything was all right between them. He always tried to protect her. Yet the results of her decisions were unforgivable. How could he look at her, think of her, as he once had?

Lluava envisioned Varren's cool blue eyes, veiled by pain that she had caused, staring at her. She shuddered at the image. How ironic; all the work she had done, all the anguish she had endured to break Selene's hold over Varren had been ruined by none other than herself.

There was a knock at the door. Lluava sat up and rubbed her stiff neck. "Come in," she called, hoping and fearing it was Varren.

When the figure stepped into the room, Lluava leaped to her feet as if seeing a ghost, for that was what it felt like. Before her stood not only one of the rare female Shadows but also the Shadow acknowledged as Regin's second-in-command. The Shadow she had left in Cronus to bury the body of her slain handmaiden. The Shadow who had not escaped with them.

"Holly!" Lluava gasped out. "You're alive!"

Chapter 4

Onyx's Return

How?" questioned Lluava. "I was sure you were trapped in the castle."

"There was another route out of Tartarus," answered Holly. The Shadow pulled off her mask, revealing her waterfall of curls. "A less preferable one, but there were no other options."

"When did you get back?" Abruptly, Lluava remembered her manners. "I'm sorry. Take a seat...where you can."

Holly cracked a weary smile and sat on the floor across from Lluava. From this position, Lluava realized, the redheaded woman appeared close to her mother's age; strangely, though, she seemed more like an older sister.

"I arrived several hours ago. The journey was not an easy one."

Both women paused, trying to figure out what to say next. Holly began, "I have come bearing news you will want to hear." Lluava absentmindedly scooted closer to Holly as the older woman spoke. "After I laid June to rest, I found a number of humans, including the young lieutenant who is a friend of yours, and—"

"Vidrick! He's still alive?"

"Yes, as is the Theriomorph colonel, Ojewa."

"Thank the gods," Lluava whispered without realizing the implication of the words.

Holly's smile flickered again, then disappeared. "I showed them the way out of Cronus."

"How many made it?"

"In that group, thirty or so."

"Thirty," Lluava repeated, dismayed.

"The lieutenant led them south, away from the war. Ojewa stayed behind to try to save more humans before the rest were slaughtered. He is a good Theriomorph. Much like yourself."

"Yes," agreed Lluava as she fondly remembered the officer who had trained her. "He is very brave."

Did Holly know what horrors Lluava had accidentally caused? Lluava asked in a voice on the verge of breaking, "Do you know if my friends Talos or Rosalyn were among the thirty? And Apex?"

"Colonel Ojewa was the only Theriomorph among the group. I know not what happened to any of your race inside Cronus." Holly must have seen the look of pain on Lluava's face, for she added, "There is a chance that the colonel will find them and lead them out."

"What chance is there, really?" Lluava asked bitterly.

"A slim one at best."

Had she lost Apex for good? Was Talos's plan to protect Rosalyn and their unborn child working? Lluava's whole body was wracked with a physical pain. She clutched her stomach tightly.

"Have hope," Holly said tenderly as she stood to leave. "Without hope, there is no chance for the future."

"June…" Lluava said. Holly paused. "You knew her name. With hundreds of people working in the castle, you remembered hers. How?"

"I am an Obsidian Guard. We know everyone who resides within the castle's walls."

"True," Lluava acknowledged. "Yet there is more to it than that. You called her June, not Juniper, her real name. And I remember how you picked up her body. You knew her personally. Why else would you tend to one dead girl when so many other corpses littered the ground? June meant something to you. What?"

"June—Juniper—was my youngest sister. My biological sister. Our mother had a preference for botanical names." Holly had never shared personal details with or revealed her feelings to Lluava, but now her eyes misted over.

"I thought Shadows did not associate with their birth families."

"We are not permitted to make contact with them, that is true. Nonetheless, June was my sister."

"I'm sorry," Lluava blurted, far louder than necessary. Thinking of her own little sister, she felt wretched and unable to comprehend the loss Holly felt. "I'm sorry I could not protect her. I failed…." Lluava could not finish her sentence as her own tears began to well up. She turned away and stared at the floor.

"No," Holly affirmed, touching Lluava's shoulder gently. "The fault is mine alone. I asked the castle's head housekeeper to recruit June. I thought I was helping her. I wanted her to have a better life." Holly stepped away. "My mother was so very poor. She did whatever she could to make a coin. That was one reason why most of my siblings have different fathers. But things changed after I was chosen for the Guard."

Sighing, Holly replaced her hood. "After receiving the largest sum of money my mother had ever seen, she thought that since she had birthed one Guard, she could produce another. By the time my training ended and I was selected to serve in Cronus, my siblings had multiplied from five to eleven, including two sets of twins. With so many mouths to feed, my family had become more destitute, if that was possible."

"Although I could not rescue all of my siblings, I selected one to bring to the castle. June was young enough not to have been corrupted by my mother's way of life, yet she was old enough to prove useful. I foolishly believed that if I could save just one, I would have done my family some actual service." Holly's voice trailed off as she became thoughtful.

Lluava inquired apprehensively, "Your family. Did they live in Cronus?"

"Yes."

With that, Holly silently slipped out the door and into the darkness.

***

The next morning, or at least when Jigo proclaimed that morning had arrived, Lluava arose with a feeling of great discomfort. She was an outsider who had been brought to a place where she did not belong. Erebos was for humans only. Not a single Theriomorph before Lluava had trodden across its hollowed-out center. She would never have been permitted inside. Although her innocence had been proclaimed, she was stripped of her official positions, and she had no idea what to do.

Everywhere she looked, members of the Guard moved with determination. Most took no notice of her, while a few gave her questioning looks. Did they deem her an intruder? Certainly they knew who or what she was. Lluava needed something to take her mind off these thoughts, something to keep her away from roaming stares that only reminded her of the horror she had caused.

In one part of the mound's vast base, a number of teens were training with three-pronged sai, others with bō staffs. As Jigo was leading her through the gloom toward their meal hall, Lluava asked, "Will Issaura's Claws be returned to me, now that I am no longer deemed a threat?"

"They will. They are yours," acknowledged Jigo. "It is the *when* that is in question."

Lluava expected as much. "Then what am I to do here? I cannot train or aid in decision-making. I need a purpose. I don't want to sit in my room for days on end."

"You have traveled far and been through much," said Jigo. He showed her to a low table, where he and Lluava took a seat on more woven mats. "Take this time to recuperate."

Lluava could not help but worry about her friends in Elysia who were fighting for survival. Two boys about fourteen years old brought them plain porridge and goblets of water. They bowed first to Jigo and then to Lluava before turning to leave.

"Who are they?" Lluava asked as she blew on her first spoonful. The other conversation was clearly at an end.

"Some of our youngest acolytes," explained Jigo. He lowered his head and said a silent prayer to his god. Lluava waited awkwardly until her host was finished. For the first time, Jigo pulled off his mask, revealing a man in his early forties. His skin had an olive hue like Lluava's, though his long hair was dark, braided and coiled into a bun at the back of his head.

Taking a bite of porridge, Jigo continued, "During their training years, the acolytes assist in the various jobs that help Erebos function. This city is entirely self-sustaining. During each stage of training, the acolytes are assigned a new role. By the time they take part in the initiation exams, they are adept at all practical tasks—cooking, washing, growing crops, running messages. Although they begin training in the arts of war while young, that skill takes longer to attain."

Swallowing her mouthful, Lluava inquired, "Why do they need to learn all the ordinary tasks? Why not let them focus on training to fight, if they are going to serve and protect the king in the end?"

Jigo paused before responding. "Not every acolyte becomes an active Obsidian Guard. Only the best are chosen. The others are allotted jobs in which they will serve until they die, just as those who age out of active duty will return here and serve out the rest of their lives. We train the acolytes in all tasks to determine what they are best suited to do."

Now Lluava understood a bit better the plethora of people living in this dark abyss. None of the children brought to Erebos could leave. The Obsidian Guard would not risk others finding their hidden stronghold, nor allow anyone to reveal their secrets. To be chosen by the Guard entailed a lifelong obligation that could never be revoked.

Toward the end of their meal, a disturbance of black feathers manifested in the candlelit gloom, only to half crash, half perch on Lluava's shoulder.

"Onyx?" Lluava questioned excitedly. "How did you get in here?"

"I told you she was fine," Byron's voice permeated the dark. He entered the room along with Varren and Thad. "They wouldn't find fault with her."

Smiling, the broad-shouldered soldier sat down on one side of Lluava. "Everything is sorting itself out. Things can begin to get back to normal now."

"Not exactly." Byron's optimism only increased Lluava's uncertainty.

"What do you mean?" he asked, still jovial, as Varren and Thad found seats at the table. He ran his hand over his recently shaved head as if feeling the tips of his hacked-off blond hair.

"I'm no longer Varren's partner," Lluava stated. "Didn't you hear?"

"What?" Now, Byron was caught off guard.

"She is correct," admitted Varren.

Lluava could tell he was not about to appeal the verdict. Perhaps that was for the best. She knew she deserved to lose that privilege.

"But why?" Byron turned to Jigo, the only Guard at the table. "She did nothing wrong."

Before Jigo could answer, Lluava intervened, "It's for the best, Byron. Truly."

If Byron wanted to contest that judgment, he kept quiet. He seemed to understand that it was not his decision. Thad had not even acknowledged the conversation, and with both Varren and Lluava refusing to argue the point, why bother?

Varren, seated across from Byron, looked at Lluava with eyes full of turmoil. This must be hard for him, she thought. Varren was aware of the destruction that had resulted from her actions. What could he say to her now that the verdict had been rendered?

Onyx tugged at Lluava's silvery hair. "Stupid bird," she muttered under her breath, clearly unable to actually hate the creature. Thad's eyes flickered slightly.

"I had him captured for you," Varren acknowledged. "He must have been flying about the entryway for some time. When I heard a raven was out there, I had him netted and brought inside."

"That bird would not shut up," added Thad in an almost inaudible voice as the acolytes returned with steaming bowls of porridge for her friends. As if on cue, Onyx began to murmur in Lluava's ear. She scratched the bird's neck, and Onyx sidled away from her touch. Rude, she thought.

Studying the young king, Lluava wondered why he hadn't come to see her last night. If he had knowledge of the verdict, why hadn't he checked to see how she was doing? Didn't he care about her anymore? Did he hate her that much? If they had not met by chance, would he have sought her out? Would he ever love her again?

Unable to stomach her own answers to these questions, Lluava stood. "I'll be in my room."

"Are you all right?" Varren inquired suddenly.

No, you fool! she wanted to scream. Looking at his cool blue eyes, Lluava could not take it anymore. Why did he try so hard to be nice? Couldn't he just say what he was thinking?

She mustered a curt nod and waited for Jigo to accompany her; she wasn't sure she could find her way back. Jigo replaced his masked hood and nodded respectfully to the king before heading toward the door.

"Wait!"

Jigo immediately obeyed Varren's command, although Lluava took several more steps before consenting to stop.

"Can we have—?" Varren began to ask Jigo, but the Guard had already disappeared into the shadows. Varren peered after him as though trying to make sure they would not be overheard.

"Do you have something you wish to say?" Lluava asked hesitantly. Onyx shuffled on her shoulder.

"Yes." Varren moved toward her. "I know you must be upset, and I need to let you know why I have not countered those proclamations."

Not sure she wanted to hear the reason, Lluava remained silent.

"Many things have changed since the battle of Castle Alcazar, and I believe it is best that we take time to sort out *everything.*"

So, he did know. *Everything.* Lluava noticed how Varren's fingers toyed with his signet ring. "Too much happened, too quickly. We need time. I need time.

"For now, I must devise a counterattack aimed at both enemies. Elysia belongs to the people, to *me.* I cannot let anyone destroy her, so I will continue to fight. I will not give up on her. I could *never* give up on her, even if all seems lost.

"Lluava, you are still important to me, though it may not seem that way right now. I just…I just want you to know that the proclamations do not have to last forever."

She interjected sourly, "Just until we sort through things. Got it."

Spinning on her heel, Lluava fumbled her way back to her rooms, only getting lost four times.

Chapter 5

Kitchen Banter

Over the next few days, Lluava saw little of her friends, or anyone else for that matter. She chose to spend the majority of her time in her room, watching Onyx's lackluster antics in the faint hope of escaping her boredom.

If Varren needed time to sort things out before seeing her, she would not interfere. That was the best thing to do, right? Anyway, there was Thad. He had survived one hell only to be thrust into another. Thad needed Varren's care and support as much as Varren needed to protect and look after his childhood friend. At night, Lluava would often hear the sound of screams echoing down the corridor. It could only be Thad. Whatever nightmares ravaged his dreams were far more horrific than hers.

On the other hand, Byron had no reason to be distant. Yet he, too, seemed to prefer the king's presence to hers—the one who had let the enemy through the gates. This meant she was alone.

Being alone came easy to Lluava. She had grown up without friends her own age. Studying, caring for her younger siblings, and working on the farm had filled most of her time. She had disliked Rivendale's narrow-minded human children and had never yearned for their friendship.

Lluava had never thought she would need to rely on another. That is, until she met Varren. Nesting alongside her own self-loathing was her despair that he might never trust her again. Her longing to share every detail grew stronger. Certainly, he knew what she had said during her trial. Yet she wanted to tell him what had happened to her in Tartarus when she finally allowed Theri to control her. She wanted him to understand that he had been manipulated by Selene for her own selfish purposes. But Varren needed time,

28

and Lluava would give that to him. She owed him that.

Jigo checked on her often, even after she no longer needed him to lead her to the meal hall and washrooms. He was kind in a stoic way but never warm, never an actual friend. That designation was left to her scrappy raven, even though he snapped at her fingers when he pecked at bread crusts.

At the end of the first week, Lluava noticed the acolytes who worked in the meal hall struggling to clear tables before a new group of elders arrived to eat. Here was a way she might help. Stacking several ceramic dishes in her arms, she followed the last boy through a dark doorway at the back of the room.

The muggy kitchens lay behind it. Several older men were overseeing the food being prepared by a handful of youth. They glanced at Lluava questioningly, yet none said a word. Following the boys, she saw them drop their wares into several washtubs set up in a line near a side wall.

One small, dark-haired boy scrubbed furiously at a plate, arms deep in dingy suds. Taking a spot next to him, Lluava reached for a rag hanging from a peg and began to do the same. The boy, about seven years old and by far the youngest person she had seen in Erebos, looked over at Lluava. He raised an eyebrow and seemed to appraise her work. Drying off his plate, he pulled Lluava's from her hands.

At first, she thought this was a sign that she was unwanted. Then she realized that he was showing her how to properly wash the dishes—at least according to his standards.

"Thanks," Lluava said. The boy gave her a curt nod as he picked up a goblet. Sometime later, when her fingers were thoroughly pruney, she said to her quiet companion, "My name's Lluava Kargen."

"They call me Odel," the boy said as he studied her with his crystal-blue eyes. "You were not given permission to be back here." He nodded toward one of the elders, who was tasting the contents of a large cauldron. "Kido has been watching you closely."

A little concerned that she'd been unaware of others observing her, Lluava knew she had to expect it. They were called Shadows for a reason. "Will he kick me out?"

"Only time will tell," answered Odel.

Several hours later, the dirty dishware had slowed to a trickle and then stopped; all had been cleaned and stacked on the appropriate shelves.

"Maybe I'll see you tomorrow..." Lluava hesitantly remarked.

His smile was that of someone years older. He bowed to her, then to Kido, who stood near the door. Turning to the elder, Lluava tentatively inquired, "Tomorrow, then?"

Kido gave her no answer as she left the kitchen.

The following day, Lluava arrived early at her self-appointed job. Kido made no move to stop her as she assumed her position next to Odel. At first, she was kept distracted by learning the surprisingly detailed ritual of cleaning kitchen wares and memorizing where each item was kept. Yet the methodical scrubbing soon became automatic, and she could not stop herself from thinking about Varren and Apex.

Varren had always struggled with making choices. Lluava had come to realize that he avoided major decisions because he was so concerned about and afraid of the potential outcomes. What if they hurt others? What if people died?

Lluava and Talos had had to push the prince to take up his role as ruler of Elysia. So, it was ironic that Varren's fear of making a bad choice manifested in Lluava. It was *her* decisions that had caused harm, that had killed many. If only she had stopped to think about the consequences. Why—

Crack!

The dish in her hand shattered and sent numerous shards into the water. Lluava watched them sink under the murky bubbles.

"Here, take this." Odel passed Lluava a clean washcloth.

Noticing that her hand was bleeding, she allowed the boy to wrap her wound before the blood contaminated the water.

"I'll get someone to clean out the tub," noted the boy as he hurried to talk to one of the older and stronger acolytes. Everything was removed and replaced quickly.

Gesturing toward her hand, Odel told her, "I'll wash. You dry."

Quietly, Lluava switched positions and began her new task. Now the throbbing pain of her hand competed with the pain of not knowing whether Apex was alive or dead.

"Whatever is haunting you, you must let it go," Odel told Lluava as he handed her a dripping platter.

Wiping a tear with her sleeve, Lluava said in as kindly a tone as she could muster, "You don't know what I've seen."

"Here, we are taught not to linger in the past but to move toward the future."

Lluava regarded the boy as he continued to clean dish after dish. His loose curls hung low from the humidity trapped in the kitchen. He seemed to focus only on his work, never complaining or daydreaming of fonder things.

"I'm a Theriomorph, you know," stated Lluava. She was curious to see how the young boy would take this news.

"No."

This response startled Lluava. Odel continued as he stacked clean plates in Lluava's arms, "You are more than that. You should not minimize yourself with base descriptors. Nobody is just one thing or another. Each of us is more, and each of us is unique."

"How old are you?" Lluava asked, following the boy to some empty shelves.

Odel smiled. "Old enough to give my opinion."

"Ha! I like you, Odel," Lluava said as the boy began stacking dishes on a shelf. "I like you a lot."

For the rest of the afternoon, Lluava enjoyed the company of her new companion. She was awed by the child's profound statements and his thoughtfulness in the smallest of things.

"I have a pet raven."

All the excitement of childhood flickered in Odel's eyes.

"Would you like to meet him?" Lluava asked.

"I would if I did not have studies to attend to after this." Odel was clearly disappointed.

"I'll bring him tomorrow. I think he would like to leave the confines of my room."

That was exactly what Lluava did. To her complete surprise, Kido did not object to the black-feathered creature perching on Lluava's shoulder as she washed dishes. Odel was beside himself. The ringing of the child's laughter could be heard periodically through the kitchen door. Even the older acolytes, who were usually much more reserved, fed the raven scraps from their hands and let him tug clumps of their hair.

As Odel and Lluava left that night, she asked the old bird, "Do you like our new friend?"

Onyx fluttered over to the boy's shoulder and seemed to dance, bobbing and turning and making snapping noises with his beak. Pushing through the door, the pair burst out in giggles.

Lluava's laughter was cut short at the sight of Head Councilman Themis. He was seated at one of the long tables, where he was finishing the remnants of a long-drawn-out meal. As he stared back at her, she could have sworn she saw him raise an eyebrow, but a different angle proved her wrong.

"Themis," she acknowledged curtly as Onyx returned to her shoulder.

If the councilman was insulted at the deliberate omission of his title, he did not show it. Instead, the silver-haired man replied, "Lluava, where have you been keeping yourself?"

"I've found ways to avoid idling that are actually beneficial to those in this city." Lluava did not want to become ensnared in Themis's web of wordplay. She hoped he would be satisfied and let her leave.

He was not.

"Making friends, I see," he noted, as Odel slipped away silently. "You do realize the Obsidian Guard was founded to kill your race, don't you? It will be hard to make a true friend here. Word of advice: try not to get your hopes up too high."

"No worries," Lluava forced a smile. "What other friend do I need than you?"

"I'm an advisor," began the councilman as he sipped on some steeped tea. "That is what comes naturally to me. You," he said, as he sliced into his steak, allowing the juices to ooze out, "are a natural soldier and thus meant to take orders. When everyone keeps to what is natural, the world moves smoothly. You, more than most, should be aware of what happens when someone acts unnaturally. Soldiers are not meant to proffer new ideas or personal opinions, for that is when disaster strikes."

Lluava felt her inner heat rise. If it boiled over, she would shift into her dual form. How would Themis taste? Probably gamey and rotten. Lluava held her tongue.

"I must give you credit for your inner strength," Themis said as he took a bite of the steak. "I should find it hard to get up in the morning knowing that I was the cause of the destruction of all those innocent lives in the capital. I fear if I were in your shoes, I would consider ending everything. But then, you are much hardier emotionally than I."

Lluava's pupils narrowed like a housecat preparing for a kill. Quickly looking down, she heard Themis take another bite, chew slowly, then swallow.

"Well," he added, "I hope you do not continue to make yourself so scarce. I have barely seen you since our arrival."

Regaining some of her composure, Lluava looked back at the councilman. "Actually, I think I've *seen* more of you now than on my journey here."

"You always had a sense of humor," noted Themis as he wiped his lips on his personal handkerchief. "As long as one has a sense of humor, one's spirit is not completely broken."

"I'll keep that in mind," replied Lluava. "Now, I must excuse myself." She left before Themis had time to respond.

As she crossed the base of the mound, once again the hairs on the back of her neck stood erect. She scanned the area. The Shadows did not seem to be interested in her movements. Looking up, Lluava peered at each pockmarked indentation that represented a window portal or unused cell. The illusion of movement came only from the flickering of scattered firelight. She moved on.

***

That night, Lluava found it difficult to rest. Though her dreams of animals tearing apart human corpses had dissipated, her nightmares of Berserkers gutting person after person caused her to jerk awake in a sweat. After her fifth attempt, she splashed her face with water and decided to wait out the night. Only when Onyx pecked her clothes did she shake off her drowsiness and make her way to the kitchen.

"Not this time," she said to the raven as she placed him on his perch. Onyx cawed unhappily but did not fly after her. Maybe he had some intelligence after all.

Kido was waiting at the door when she arrived. His voice creaked like his bones when he walked. "Your service is no longer needed."

"Wha…wh…why?" Lluava blustered as she looked over Kido's narrow shoulder to see Odel's puzzled expression.

"We truly appreciate the help you gave." Bowing, Kido waited patiently until Lluava left of her own will.

Glancing at the slowly filling long tables, Lluava hissed, "Themis."

Once again, the councilman had found a way to strip her life of what little joy she could find. Charging out of the meal hall, Lluava spotted Themis walking with Varren, Byron, and Thad.

"You couldn't leave me alone, could you?" Lluava screamed as she rushed toward the councilman. "You had to take that away from me!"

Themis looked shocked. Clearly, he was a practiced liar. Lluava shoved the councilman hard enough that he stumbled to the ground.

"What is going on?" demanded Varren as he moved to intervene.

"None of your concern," snarled Lluava. She turned back to the councilman and snapped, "Why do you hate me so?"

"Calm down, Lluava." Varren's order was sharp. "Whatever the problem is, *we* will deal with this rationally." Turning toward all the watchful eyes, he assured them, "Everything is all right."

But it wasn't. As head councilman, Themis wielded immense power and abused it. He had purposely kept news of the war from old King Thor's ears. He had minimized the danger when he could have defended the kingdom by moving the Elysian forces into position. It was even rumored that he was responsible for several mysterious murders, including the girl Varren had gotten pregnant in his youth. Themis had deftly manipulated the enfeebled king until Varren, Thor's spirited grandson, ascended the throne upon the king's death. Moreover, Themis despised the Theriomorph race. Although he did not have the authority to destroy her people, he took great pleasure in persecuting the young woman. Themis was truly evil.

Lluava moved to attack.

Varren intervened. Grabbing Lluava's shoulder, he flipped her to the ground. If her old injury had not healed, her shoulder would have certainly been dislocated.

Releasing an enraged roar, Lluava struggled to contain the beast inside. "*There is no we*," she spat, rejecting Varren's extended hand.

Righting herself, she could see that the whole mound had become one black mass. As if the darkness had come to life, the black-suited Obsidian Guard all held their weapons at the ready, waiting for any sign that Lluava intended harm to their king. She backed away from Varren.

Looking at the shocked faces of Byron and Thad, Lluava turned away from her former military partner. "I will not stay away from the front lines much longer. The war needs to be won, and that will not happen inside this place."

Themis stated coldly, "She is unstable and needs serious help."

As Lluava turned to leave, she heard Thad repeat his earlier warning, "Keep away from them. The blue monsters. Far away."

***

Jigo met Lluava at her quarters. "You like to act without much thought."

"Themis deserved it," she snarled as she moved past the Guard.

"How so?" asked Jigo, following her inside.

"He hates me. Always has. He had me barred from working in the kitchen."

"Were you asked to work there?"

"No."

"Then why did you start?"

Lluava tried to explain, "They needed help, so I helped."

Jigo inclined his head thoughtfully. "Were you told why they released you?"

"They said…" Lluava realized how ridiculous this must sound to him. "They said that they did not need me anymore."

"Then what proof do you have that the high councilman influenced that decision?"

Sinking sulkily onto her mat, Lluava admitted, "None. I guess."

"I suggest that you keep to your room for a little while," noted Jigo. "I will bring you breakfast shortly."

"Ah…" griped Lluava after he left. "Why is everything so hard?" Then, staring at the far wall, she questioned aloud, "Apex, where are you?"

***

The day passed dreadfully slowly. After handing Jigo her dinner tray, Lluava curled up on her mat and tried to sleep. Her dreams took shape in new ways. She was in a forest. Slushy puddles of melting snow soaked into her shoes, yet she felt no cold. A rabbit hopped about not far out of reach, completely oblivious to Lluava's presence. Taking a moment to clean its long ears, the rabbit sat for a moment.

Suddenly, the creature bolted.

A new beast lunged into sight. This one's form matched Lluava's tigress in size. Long, metallic-bronze fur coated the Yorrick wolverine that sniffed at a reddened patch of snow before moving toward another drift. Apex was here before her! Somehow, she knew he was searching for her. All she had to do was call to him, but she had no voice.

She tried to run to him. He needed to see her. Yet something held her back. A thick, cold cord was wrapped around her throat, strangling her. Lluava clawed at the scaly mass.

The anaconda hissed into her ear, "He's mine."

Jerking awake, she gasped for breath. She felt the tightening pressure of a rope around her throat.

While Lluava had slept, she had been noosed and the cord pulled tight.

Chapter 6

Beyond the Plains

With a sudden, forceful jerk, Lluava careened sideways. The noose pulled her across the small room's floor until she slammed into the closed door.

She tried to yank the end of the cord free, feeling her face flush and pressure build in her head. Her fingers fumbled behind her, only to discover that the taut rope had slid under the small gap at the base of the door. Her assailant was on the other side.

Balling one hand into a fist, Lluava beat on the door; her other hand struggled to loosen the rope. She reached for the handle. As her sweaty fingers slipped on the metal, she realized that the door opened inward. Her own body was pinning it shut.

The world around her wavered. Without warning, she felt a second presence—that thing inside her—awaken, and she accepted the goddess's aid. As Lluava's inner fire blazed through her arms, her fingernails shifted into four-inch claws that easily severed the cord.

Gasping for air, the young woman rolled forward and crawled away from the door. Forcing herself up on shaky knees, she threw it open. Footsteps faded down the corridor. The discarded cord lay on the ground.

First stumbling, then running, Lluava determined not to let her attacker escape. She might not have Issaura's Claws, but she did have one deadly weapon: herself. Time to let the tigress out.

In mere seconds, Lluava would become a giant felid hunting down her prey. She permitted her inner heat to explode throughout her body. Just as her skin began to blister and bubble, she heard a woman shout, "Stop!"

Holly's sudden order jarred Lluava. She hesitated and retained her human form. Manifesting from the shadows, Holly appeared, fully dressed in her black bodysuit.

"Lluava, return to your quarters immediately!"

"I was just attacked!" Lluava tried to scream, but her bruised throat made the words almost inaudible.

Holly's green eyes observed Lluava's neck. "I'll go with you."

"What's…" Lluava began as her throat seared with pain, "going on?" She would have asked more, but her aching neck made her question shorter.

"If I only knew," Holly replied.

Lluava noticed that the female Guard held several throwing suns. What would Holly have done if Lluava had shifted? Would those suns have targeted her? Surely, Holly would have given her a chance to explain. Wouldn't she?

Returning to Lluava's room, the Shadow asked, "Do you know who that was? Can you sense anything?"

Had the situation been less serious, Lluava would have laughed at the naiveté of the human's grasp of Theriomorph capabilities. She could not risk allowing her senses to heighten. She took a deep breath and tried to scent the dissipating undertone of the assailant.

"Human, male," was all Lluava could identify. Unfortunately, that meant the person who wanted her dead could be almost anyone in Erebos.

Holly picked up the severed cord. Studying the would-be weapon, Lluava realized that it was not actually a rope but dingy strips of hide braided to create the long noose.

"I need to talk to Regin," Holly said, mainly to herself. "Stay here. I'll send someone to keep watch."

After Holly left, Lluava asked herself what would happen if the person Holly sent were the one who had tried to kill her. Any number of people might prefer her dead. Erebos was proving far too dangerous for her liking.

Shortly there was a knock at the door. Lluava half expected to see Jigo's garbed face; instead, when she opened the door, Byron's tired eyes smiled back at her. He handed her a warm cup of tea.

"To sooth your throat," he said as she took a seat on her mat.

Byron stood to one side of the door and tried not to yawn. "So, what's been going on with you lately?"

"That's not funny, Byron," Lluava said rather tersely. "If you cared, you would have been around."

Byron's posture tensed. "I don't understand you. What's going through your head?" The normally easygoing young man looked angry. "You have rebuffed everyone who cares about you since we arrived—Varren, Thad, me. You have become a sullen, moody, almost loathsome thing. Where is my friend? What happened to her?"

Lluava pointed a finger at her own chest. "*I'm* the problem? How is it that I'm at fault, when Varren practically told me to step out of his life?"

Refusing to cry, she continued, "I have been stripped of everything, *everything*, and then told to step aside by someone who matters so much to me. He told me to keep away!"

Tears sprang into her eyes, although now they were caused by the searing pain in her throat. She took a sip of the warm tea to ease the tenderness. The added honey was soothing.

Byron moved over to her and knelt down. "Don't you see that you are both hurting right now? You're not the only one who lost something. We all have. To get through this, we need each other more than ever."

"You," Lluava said in a milder tone, "should stop caring for me. All I caused—" She took another sip of tea to muffle her sob.

"Lluava," Byron began softly, "one must learn to live with the choices one makes. Yours were well meant, though they had poor consequences. You must not let the resulting tragedy consume you, or you will never allow yourself to make a decision that could prove beneficial." He gave her shoulder a quick squeeze. "But only you can stop torturing yourself."

As Byron stood up and readjusted his scabbard, Lluava pointed out, "You know you have not lost Talos. He's alive. I have faith."

"Perhaps," acknowledged her friend. "But I did lose my mother. She was still in Bail when the Raiders took the North."

"That was not your fault," said Lluava sympathetically as she stood up, half wondering if she should hug the young man.

"I've come to terms with that now, but over the winter it tore me apart. I regretted not bringing her with me when I came south. I had no idea that the Raiders would take the North so quickly."

"Why didn't you tell me any of this sooner? I could have...I don't know. I would have been there for you."

"When you hold yourself to blame to the point of self-loathing, you feel nobody can redeem your soul. As I said, only you can forgive yourself and eventually move on. I'll be outside if you need me."

As she lay down, Lluava pondered her friend's words. How could she not be upset about the Fall? Yet Byron was right. She was so focused on what had happened that she was not figuring out where to go from here. If she continued to wallow in her sorrow, she would be all but useless. She had to stop letting her emotions rule her thoughts, and think of her friends and her family instead of herself.

When sleep was not forthcoming, Lluava again sought out Byron. He was leaning against the wall outside her door, tired but vigilant. "Do you know who tried to kill me?"

"No. I think someone was captured, though," he acknowledged.

"Was it a Shadow?"

"I don't know, Lluava. I *do* know you need to try to sleep."

"One more question. How is Varren doing?"

"He misses you. Now, sleep."

Grudgingly, Lluava returned to her mat and eventually dozed for a time. She got up when Onyx started moving about. Somewhat less heavy-hearted now, Lluava called out, "Byron, I've decided to take your advice. I've—"

But Byron had been replaced by Jigo. "Your friend's shift ended. He is resting now."

For some reason, Jigo's presence startled her. Maybe it was the fact that he left no telltale odor; maybe it was because he was a male human, one whom Lluava did not fully trust. As far as she could recall, no Obsidian Guard ever gave off a scent. "Where's Holly?"

"I do not know of her current whereabouts," replied Jigo neutrally.

"What about Regin? I want to ask him something. It's important." If all Shadows were odorless, Lluava wondered, how would she know if one were about to attack her?

"The commander is a very busy man. I will inform him of your request for a meeting. Until then, remain in your quarters."

"What about my breakfast?"

"It will be brought to you shortly."

Was she under some sort of house arrest? Lluava did not like being confined in such a small space. Her phobia of being trapped began to resurface, and her heart began to pound.

Jigo seemed to sense her concern. "This is only a temporary arrangement."

Backing into her room, Lluava shut the door. If her assailant were one of the Guards, could it be Jigo? Yet, like the other Guards, he had no scent; moreover, she knew the distinct odor of each of the Elysian humans. But the odor she had picked up today was unknown to her. That meant it could not have been Themis, at least not directly.

Could the councilman have hired one of the Shadows to do his bidding? Could the Obsidian Guard be so easily swayed? Doubtful. But someone did try to assassinate her, and the Obsidian Guard's original purpose, after all, was to kill her kind.

***

That afternoon, Lluava received a welcome visitor. Holly called to her from the open doorway, "Lluava, come with me."

Jigo gave both women a small bow before moving off in a different direction. If he was curious about what was happening, he did not show it.

Lluava hurried behind the female Guard. As they wound through the network of corridors in the gloom, she tried to keep quiet, hoping that Holly would proffer the reason for this sudden excursion. Taking stairway after stairway, they made their way toward the topmost part of the mountain and at last stopped at a well-guarded door.

Turning to Lluava, Holly stated, "You weren't the only prisoner here."

So, she *had* been viewed as a prisoner, and maybe still was. Lluava watched curiously as Holly waved to the pair of Obsidian Guards standing watch. "Be wary," she warned them. Then, unlocking the heavy latch, Holly motioned Lluava to follow her inside.

Two more Guards stood at attention in a cell that mirrored the one that had originally held Lluava. This chamber, however, was positioned much higher up than hers, and its captive was male.

Behind the two Shadows, Lluava discerned a tall, lithe man kneeling on the ground. Shirtless, his sun-darkened, freckled skin was marred by old scars, though he could not have been much more than twenty. His long auburn hair, streaked with blond, hung raggedly over his face.

As soon as Lluava entered, the prisoner lurched forward. Instinct kicked in, and she vaulted sideways to move out of his path. She needn't have worried; the dart shot into the man's neck caused him to collapse to the ground within three strides.

Rubbing her skinned knee, Lluava stood and warily eyed the unconscious prisoner. His hide pants had been torn off up to mid-thigh. It was the same hide that had been used for the noose.

"Who is that," Lluava asked, "and why does he want me dead?"

"That is one of the nomads from beyond the Sudn Plains," explained Holly, her mouth turned down in displeasure. "He was captured entering Elysia through the Verta mountain range. He was hunting Theriomorphs."

Lluava knew all too well that bands of southern nomads had hunted and killed Theriomorphs since the goddess Theri bestowed upon a group of humans the ability to shift into the forms of animals. This newly created race carried her name: Theriomorphs. That was the myth Lluava had been told by her father and her grandfather. These nomadic humans were the original inhabitants of the continent.

With the arrival of Varren's ancestors, they were expelled from Elysia. The spears and longbows of the horse-riding people had been no match for Mandrun's invading soldiers, armed with broadswords and recurve bows. The nomads had taken refuge in the deserts and survived in pockets of oases. As a result, their hatred of both Theriomorphs and Elysians had grown stronger and more deeply ingrained with each generation.

Holly spoke again. "He must have seen you in the main chamber from this vantage point." She pointed to the cliff's edge. "He could have been watching you since you arrived."

The eyes, Lluava realized. He, not the Obsidian Guard, had been responsible for that feeling of eyes staring into her. She was the nomad's natural enemy. He wanted her dead for no other reason than that she was a Theriomorph.

At least she had discovered who her attacker was. Now that he was locked up and guarded, she could relax a little.

"Thank you for showing him to me," Lluava offered as she stepped out of the cell.

Tentatively descending the first flight of stairs, Lluava waited for Holly to lead the rest of the way back. As the female Shadow stepped in front of her, she warned, "I do not think you are safe."

"Do you believe that man can take down multiple Obsidian Guards?" Lluava questioned.

"It is not the prisoner who worries me," admitted Holly. "It is whoever released him from his cell."

Chapter 7

Gold Wings

Someone let him out? Lluava's worries rekindled.

"There were no signs of forced escape," explained Holly. "His door was barred from the outside. Someone released him and then re-latched the door.

"Why would anyone let him out?"

"To do exactly what he attempted," Holly answered. Her green eyes burned in the dark. "Whoever set him free knew he would first find and kill you. You were the target; the prisoner was just the chosen weapon."

Uneasy now, Lluava said, "Then the prisoner could try to kill me again."

"Precautionary measures are being taken. Several of the Guard will stand watch outside his cell at all times. But, Lluava," Holly warned, "until we discover who tried to orchestrate your murder, I cannot promise you will not be attacked by some other means."

Lluava nodded toward the top of the stairs. "Can you find a way to get that man to tell you who freed him?"

Holly motioned Lluava to follow her, as if she did not want to loiter in the stairwell longer than necessary. "I have never dealt with the nomadic tribes. I do know that they refuse to disclose information, no matter what means are used to encourage them."

"So, we have no way of knowing who was actually behind all this, and I am left with a target on my back." A low growl rumbled up Lluava's throat. She made no attempt to stop it.

"Your room will be watched from now on," responded Holly.

"What if one of *those* men is my would-be killer? What then?" the young woman demanded uneasily.

41

"Two Guards will be stationed at all times to prevent any attempts by either one. But you must stay on high alert."

"I appreciate you telling me all this," Lluava replied earnestly. After a few paces in silence, she spoke again. "Holly, you and I both know that I should not be in Erebos. I only came because it was supposed to be a refuge and, well, to make sure Varren came along. But I think it's time for me to leave. I am not safe here." Holly's pensive silence, Lluava knew, was her way of agreeing.

Once back in her room, Lluava knelt at the low table and began to strategize. Using the quill and ink provided, she wrote in Theriomorph script in case her attacker found her plans. Surely these humans, like most others, had never learned to read the ancient runes. Although Lluava's father had taught her a few basic characters before he died, it was only through the encouragement of Hyrax, the Guardian who had infiltrated the High Council, and through her own studies in Leucrocotta, that she had developed some proficiency. Unfortunately, all her ideas led to ends as dead as the language itself.

"On the positive side, I'm far less bored," she told Onyx fondly when the bird hopped down to inspect the scribbles of drying ink. His foot stepped on a still-wet character and left a line of four-toed footprints trailing off the page.

There was a knock at the door, and the lead Guard, Regin, entered. Once inside, he pulled off his masked hood and said, "I was informed you wish to leave Erebos."

Though mildly surprised, she should have expected Holly to tell her superior of Lluava's wishes. Had Holly told anyone else?

"Does Varren know?"

"Should he?"

"No," admitted Lluava. She knew the king would want to go with her.

"Sometimes the best decisions are the hardest to make," acknowledged Regin. He moved over to Onyx's perch, on which the raven had just alighted. "That is why I cannot allow you to leave without knowing what you intend to do next. Many here do not think you are trustworthy. Some believe you are working against us."

"I'm not; you know that," Lluava tried to reassure him. She stood up so quickly that the scroll fluttered off the table.

Regin bent down and picked up the parchment. "Yes. But others—" He broke off in mid-sentence as he looked at the runes. "You know how to read this language?"

"Yes," Lluava replied cautiously. Would this make him think she was a traitor? That she had been lying the whole time? That she was working with Yena? "It's to be expected that I, a Theriomorph, would want to learn to decipher my people's writing."

"Could you translate something for me if I showed you a piece of script?"

This request was not what she had expected. "Possibly," she said carefully.

After replacing his hood and opening the door, Regin told the outer Guards, "Lluava Kargen will accompany me for the remainder of the afternoon. Do not leave your posts until we return."

Once again, Lluava found herself being led all but blindly through corridors that snaked through the unlit underbelly of the mountain. This time, she was led below the main level to a chamber whose door was sealed by several large locks.

Pulling out a set of brass keys, Regin opened each lock in turn. He pushed the door inward and stepped into the blackness. Lluava heard a hiss, and torchlight flared.

Should she follow him? Before she could ask, Regin stepped back out of the room. In one hand he carried a torch, in the other a recurve bow. He carefully handed Lluava the golden weapon for her inspection. As soon as she held it, she realized that it was not real gold, for it was far too light. Stranger still, the weapon resonated with a warmth of its own. On its handle were runes, which she instantly identified.

"Where did this come from?" she asked sharply. At the same moment, Regin inquired, "Can you read them?"

With quickening heartbeat, she asked again, "Where did you get this?"

"What does it say, Lluava?" he countered.

She gave the metallic weapon a closer look and noted that the bowstring was made from the same golden element.

"The Wings of Giahem. This is a god's weapon. Just as are Issaura's Claws. Where did you find it? Regin, I need to know."

The head Guard looked at the bow with an expression both expectant and skeptical. "This weapon was in the possession of the prisoner with whom you have recently become acquainted."

"That should not be," stated Lluava as Regin returned the bow to the vault. "Those bandits use only longbows. Giahem's Wings were made for a Theriomorph owner."

"Is it impossible to consider that its rightful owner may have been slain by the nomadic tribes?" questioned Regin as he began to lock the heavy door. "They would kill any Theriomorph they found."

"Yes, it is," Lluava explained, "for the person who was meant to wield that weapon is Giahem's Incarn."

Regin looked doubtful, so Lluava quickly added, "I know you don't believe in the concept of Incarns or Theriomorph gods. But the man destined for that bow would be a powerful asset in this war. With that man, the Incarn of the King of the Gods, on our side…"

Lluava did not know how to make him understand. For most humans, the concept of the Incarn was far too pagan an idea for their liking. "All I'm saying is that if we can track down that weapon's true owner, we might find a great ally."

"Why wouldn't such a person, if he were alive, side with that false priestess, Yena?" questioned Regin. "You claim that Selene and Luka are Incarn, and they follow her. If your huntsman does the same, why would I risk bringing another enemy into our midst?"

Lluava considered his question. "He would be powerful, I promise you. Yena is searching for him as well as for the other Incarn; there is no way around that. Whether he is for us or against us, we must reach him first. And that means we need to find him."

What Regin would do, if he did anything at all, was uncertain, Lluava knew. If he believed her, then he must acknowledge the Theriomorph pantheon. On the other hand, doing nothing would give Yena time to gain more allies and weaken Varren's chances to reclaim the throne.

"How can you be sure such a man exists? That bow was tested and proven false."

"What do you mean?"

"The bow and string are of one solid material. Our best archer attempted to draw it, and the bow would not bend. The weapon was not designed for actual use but merely as a decorative symbol."

"If it cannot be used, then why did the prisoner carry it with him? Certainly he would not have relied upon a fake weapon."

"Unfortunately, our questioning of the nomad has proven fruitless. We have no rationale to explain why he was transporting this item or where he intended to take it."

"You could not get him to talk," Lluava began, just as an idea came to her. "But I can. I will need Giahem's Wings and Issaura's Claws."

***

Once she had finally convinced Regin, she still had to present her idea to a delegation of elders. Luckily, the head Guard backed her up, and the elders agreed to her plan.

Taking one last slow, deep breath, Lluava nodded to the Guards outside the prisoner's door before walking in, completely alone.

Regin waited in the corridor with Holly, Jigo, and a few other Shadows. They had weapons in hand in case things went badly for the young Theriomorph. Although Lluava hoped it wouldn't come to that, she was certain of one thing—the prisoner would try to take her life.

The captive was sitting down and staring over the edge of the cliff. He did not glance behind him to see who had entered until the door was shut and Lluava spoke.

"Is this yours?" she inquired, holding up Giahem's Wings.

The prisoner looked at her critically, then at the bow. He did not speak but slowly rose to his feet. Lluava felt herself tense in response, but she refused to show any sign of weakness. This man wanted her dead. She would not give him the opportunity.

"This weapon—is it yours?" she repeated.

No response save the glare of his fiery eyes.

"Do you know that this is a Theriomorph weapon? Do you know you are carrying something made by my people?"

Lluava's attempt to infuriate the nomad worked. The anger in the captive's eyes turned to hatred.

"That bow belongs to *my* family. *My* bloodline."

"No, it doesn't," countered Lluava. "This was meant for Theriomorphs. Who did you steal this from?"

"That weapon belongs to my family, beast," snarled the prisoner. "We would never use anything made by your kind." His spittle landed on the ground mere feet from Lluava.

"Well you have, and you do," replied Lluava. She pointed to the handle. "Do you see these marks? They're my people's writing."

"Those are gods' marks."

Ignoring the prisoner, Lluava read the runes aloud, "The Wings of Giahem."

"That is not what they say!" yelled the man. With an effort, he calmed himself. "They claim the weapon for the First."

"Who is the First?" Remembering that the nomads were also polytheistic, she asked, "One of your gods?"

The man clenched his bruised jaw. "That is no monster's weapon. It was made for my bloodline."

"If it's yours, prove it. Draw it back. Show me that you can wield it, and you can keep it." Placing the weapon on the floor, Lluava stepped away to allow the man room to approach.

For a moment, he did not move. Then he leaped forward with the power of a wild horse and picked up the bow. In one fluid movement, he drew the cord back to his face, aimed an invisible arrow at Lluava, and released the string with a twang.

"That's impossible," Lluava gasped out. Searching for an explanation, she could not hide her shock at the smirk on the prisoner's suntanned face. The bow was without a doubt one of the god's weapons designed for the Incarn. The human should not have been able to draw back the bow, especially when no others could. Even she had tried and failed.

"I don't understand," she murmured under her breath.

"This," the captive began as he stepped closer, proudly holding the bow, "does not belong to your kind, she-beast."

"If...if you would hand me the bow back for one moment, I want to test something," Lluava said. This was her last attempt to prove the bow's authenticity.

The man stepped forward to pass one end of the bow to Lluava's outstretched fingers but instead swung the metal device toward the side of her head. Lluava reacted too slowly. She stumbled on impact and managed to right herself just as she reached the edge of the cliff.

Turning quickly to face her attacker, she saw the captive swing the bow like a bō staff once again. As the second blow forced her to skid over the edge, Lluava shifted into her dual form.

Within seconds, her inner heat caused her flesh to bubble, as white and black fur sprouted out all over. The searing prick of an erupting tail, the taste of blood as old teeth dissolved and new ones burst forth, the snapping and tearing of muscles and bones breaking and realigning— all resulted in a large felid form exploding through her clothes. Bits of shredded cloth scattered as the tigress dug her claws into the stone. The grating sound quieted as she hung over the ledge. With one loud roar, Lluava hooked her rear paws against the rough stone wall and lunged back into the cell.

Clearly, the prisoner had not expected a white tigress to emerge from the young woman's transformation. He held his ground and waited for the feline to attack.

There was a click, and the door behind them swung open. Guards flooded into the small space. Lluava spied several blowguns and shouted, "Stop! This is between him and me!"

Regin waved the Shadows off.

Lluava approached the captive. The man swung the bow at her a third time, but her large paw swatted the weapon out of his hands.

"Kill me then, beast."

"I am not here for blood," growled Lluava. "Not yours, anyway." Stepping back, she asked the Guards, "A cloak? I've destroyed my clothes."

As she kept an eye on the prisoner, Lluava heard several people moving behind her. Soon, she was given one of the dark tunics worn by the acolytes.

"Leave us," Lluava said to Regin and the other Shadows.

"That is ill-advised."

"Then leave Holly. Please do not make me shift in front of everyone here." The men filed out after Regin gave his nod. "And Issaura's Claws."

The golden weapons were passed to Holly, and the head Guard stepped outside and shut the door. Shifting back, Lluava hastily dressed herself as Holly watched the captive. The bow, which had been reclaimed by the Guards, had been placed at Holly's feet.

Once dressed, Lluava slid one of Issaura's Claws over a hand. The touch of her weapon made her feel whole again—which was strange; she had not considered herself broken until that moment.

Turning back to the prisoner, she picked up Giahem's Wings with the other hand.

"Issaura's Claws are my weapons. Though they look odd, they were made for a Theriomorph like me." Lluava knew she needn't go into too much detail. "They are of the same metal as your bow, and if I am right, both weapons are gods' weapons, which means…" Lluava touched the two weapons together, and just as hers had done when touched to Ullr's Fangs, strange, rune-like designs appeared on each of them. And on her weapon, a name appeared: The Claws of Issaura.

Both Holly and the prisoner gasped. Lluava heard the door open and quickly separated the weapons, which reverted to their normal appearance. The captive continued to shake his head. "That cannot be. That *cannot* be."

"As I said," Lluava began as she handed Issaura's Claw back to Holly for safekeeping. "That bow is meant for a Theriomorph, a special Theriomorph. I need to know who."

"You are a witch and a monster," spat the prisoner. "You will not make me question my beliefs!"

"I don't want to, but—"

Before Lluava could finish her statement, the young man lunged at her, a fragment of rock grasped in his hand. Lluava raised the bow between them in defense, but it was Holly's sai positioned at the man's throat that halted his attack.

"Drop the rock," hissed Holly as she pressed the three-pointed weapon into his neck hard enough that droplets of blood began to ooze down. Regin and the others re-entered, but the nomad had already released the stone.

Lluava eyed the blood. Strange, she thought, and then asked, "Where were you born?"

"Your questioning is over," Regin stated. Lluava was ushered out. She picked up Issaura's Claws from where Holly had dropped them. When she tried to hand them back to Regin, the head Guard pronounced, "Keep them. They are yours."

Suddenly, Lluava was elated. But the feeling was short-lived, for she saw Regin removing Giahem's Wings.

"I told the prisoner he could keep the bow."

"You had no authority to do so," replied Regin.

"But I promised!"

"Something that was not yours to offer."

Though unhappy to be perceived a liar, Lluava was thrilled to have Issaura's Claws back in her possession. She held them tightly as Holly led her back to her quarters.

"You were right about his weapon and yours," noted the female Shadow. "They are special."

"But," Lluava said, "I just don't understand how he could use it. He was able to draw the bow back with such ease."

"Are you sure he is not one of you? Maybe he was raised to believe he was human."

"No. He is human," asserted Lluava. "Yet there is still an impression of Theriomorph about him, like a thumbprint on glass. I've never sensed anything like it before."

Chapter 8

Amargo Bound

"Yet he *is* human?" Holly questioned once more.

"Yes."

Pondering the strange essence that wafted from the captive, Lluava pressed on. "The bow he possessed. Have you examined it closely?"

I was only recently made aware of its existence."

Lluava wondered if Holly was offended that Regin had not taken her into his confidence, but the Shadow seemed as collected as ever.

"Did you notice how strong it is?"

"I know only that the captive has been able to bend it."

"Yes, yes. But how much power does one need to use a weapon like that?"

"The draw strength is far beyond the normal requirement. Are you insinuating that he is unnaturally strong? He was captured as easily as all the tribesmen who infiltrate Elysia."

"No. I wasn't about to go that far." Lluava hesitated as she tried to explain herself better. "I was thinking about the arrows. What arrow could match the power of that weapon? Any standard shaft would be too light. Or am I wrong?"

"The nomad was kept alive for reasons that I do not know. If that decision was based on the weapon he possesses, the knowledge he has, or the actions he took, Regin would know the answer." Holly paused, then added, "Those who are meant to wield weapons like yours have a greater purpose, do they not?"

"I believe so."

They had reached Lluava's quarters. The Guards stood at attention at the door. With a curt nod, Holly left the young woman for the night.

As Lluava drifted off to sleep, she wondered about the true owner of Giahem's Wings. Where was he? If she could convince him to fight on their side, could they defeat Yena and rescue the people inside Cronus's walls?

***

Lluava was in the castle's Grand Hall, the heart of Cronus. The smell of death and decay permeated everything. High Priestess Yena, garbed in her silver robes, sat on Varren's throne. The sultry Selene was seated at her right hand, the pallid Luka on her left. Selene's luminescent, sepia-hued fist clutched a bronze chain linked to a collar that encircled Apex's neck. In his wolverine form, the enormous bronze beast reclined complacently near Selene's manicured toes.

Lluava was confronted by faces of Leucrocottan Theriomorphs. A few she recognized, many she did not. Four unknown figures stood around her, guarding her, eyeing the bindings that tethered her hands behind her back and kept her from rising from her kneeling position.

She was on trial for her life. This she knew instantly, though she could not recall how she got there. Everyone was silent, as if waiting to hear her defend herself.

Glancing at Apex, Lluava silently hoped he would break free from Selene's grasp and come to her aid. But he seemed all too content where he was. He was the only one who took no notice of her and her plight.

Suddenly, to her horror Lluava realized that she would die just as the Elysian Theriomorph High Councilmen had died during the takeover of Cronus. One of her guards held an axe. If given the chance, he would cleave her head from her body in one stroke.

She had to run, but the rope bindings constricted her wrists. She had to fight back, but try as she might she could not shift. Without fang and claw, Lluava was helpless.

As the man with the axe stepped closer, there were four sharp, short sounds of *kee!* The cry of an eagle accompanied the four golden shafts that lodged themselves deep within the sternums of the men around her. As they collapsed outward like the unfurling petals of a flower, Lluava looked around for Giahem's Incarn, for it was certainly he who had saved her.

Yet the man who stepped before her was not a Theriomorph savior but the captive nomad, carrying Giahem's Wings. He stretched his arm toward her, and Lluava instantly realized she was unbound. As he assisted her to her feet, the nomad said, "As we promised."

Lluava awoke. She understood immediately the message within the dream. The nomad, though a human Outlander, was an essential participant in the upcoming game of life and death that would be played out as they marched on Cronus. Whatever plans Varren, Regin, and Themis were developing, the captive must be included. It was Lluava's job to ensure it.

Onyx fluttered down onto Lluava's chest and cocked his good eye to look her over. Had she wakened him from his slumber, or had he been observing her for a while? Regardless, Lluava could sense that morning had arrived, even though she lacked the ability to see the rising sun.

Clacking his beak, the black bird flew back to his perch. As soon as he alighted, there was a knock at her door.

Sitting up, Lluava called out, "Who is it?"

"It is I," came Varren's voice from beyond the wooden barrier.

"Come in," Lluava called as she quickly ran her fingers through her shoulder-length hair, trying to tame it.

The king's blue eyes sparkled with excitement as he entered the room. The long candle he held seemed to quiver with his pent-up energy. "I have come to tell you that we will be heading out tonight."

"So soon?" Although Lluava was not upset about the sudden departure from the dark underground abyss, she had not expected it.

"The decision was made a while ago, but we were advised to keep this information between those with whom we—" The sparkle left the young king's eyes. "I still trust you, Lluava. You know this."

Lluava thought his statement lacked earnestness. If he trusted her, he would not have allowed her status to be revoked. He would not have pushed her aside.

Sensing her doubt, Varren continued, "I wanted to tell you in person, since I believe you are, as I am, ready to join the rest of the realm."

"Where are we going?" Lluava inquired.

"South. To Amargo." He moved over to scratch the back of Onyx's head. Surprisingly, the bird permitted him that privilege. Varren continued, "Word was sent that the resistance has been massing there. An army is being formed, Lluava. They are waiting for their king to lead them. We will meet them within the next few weeks and together set our sights on liberating Cronus. It is time to make our last stand against those who wish to destroy our kingdom."

Lluava could clearly see that the young king firmly believed in this plan. "What then, Varren? Do you have a strategy for combating two opposing armies? Yena's followers hold Cronus, while the Raiders continue to ravage the rest of the kingdom. How many trained troops are ready to fight? Many of our soldiers have been slaughtered."

With a look of dismay at her apparent doubt of him, Varren countered, "Durog's legions from the Southern Camps who survived the battles by the sea, as well as the recruits from the Middle Camps, have assembled there. The soldiers at Swelore, along with those stationed at the Noma outpost, also await our arrival. In addition, many refugees that have fled south are willing to fight. We have an army—the largest one we have mustered since the attacks began last spring."

"And the plan?"

"That will be finalized once we are all united at Amargo. The commanding officers stationed there deserve to be included in the decision."

"So, who's going with you?"

"The Obsidian Guard, Head Councilman Themis, Byron, Thad, and you."

"You do realize that I am no longer your partner." The words nearly stuck in her throat.

"I know. But you are still an Elysian soldier."

Lluava pursed her lips at the unsatisfactory answer.

Varren started to raise his arm but held back. A glint of sadness flickered in his cool eyes. "I miss talking with you. I miss the way things once were."

"I do, too. But—" Suddenly, guilt for all the lost lives caused Lluava to choke up. "After what happened in the capital…that *can't* be forgiven."

Varren was all too solemn. "I know. I have told myself that ever since it happened. I don't deserve forgiveness, especially from you. I still cannot explain why I made those decisions, but I must live by their consequences."

"What are you talking about?" questioned Lluava, now clearly befuddled.

"Selene. The Clans. All the ludicrous proclamations I made when I should have been protecting my people." He looked at her as if expecting her censure. "I was given full authority over the kingdom, and I made a mockery of it."

"Uh—" Lluava gasped sharply. Did he really believe she was the victim of his indiscretions? Did he not realize what had been done to him? "Varren, that wasn't you."

"I wish I could believe that. But I made those choices. Disastrous choices."

"No, listen to me," Lluava began in earnest. "Selene has a special ability, a power of sorts. She can manipulate men. Hypnotize them, if you will. You were under her spell. Those choices you made were actually *hers*. She was controlling you. *You* are innocent."

"That's preposterous. Magic, mind control—those are nothing more than myth and legend. Something dreamed up in Yamir's fantasies."

"But they're not. Selene is an Incarn. She—" Lluava realized that Varren was unaware of so much. Upon her return last winter, she had not shared this information with him, for by then it was too late; he was already under Selene's spell. And there had been no time in the days preceding the Fall. Lluava had never explained. But why, she wondered, hadn't Regin divulged this information? Regardless, now Varren *had* to know.

"I haven't told you the real reason I went north with Apex," she began. After they had seated themselves on the floor mat, Lluava finally explained all that had occurred over the past months. She disclosed everything she had told Regin and the elders who had judged her, but because she still trusted Varren above all others, she shared more.

"When we were fleeing Tartarus, and I turned to kill the Theriomorph known as Master Hon, I finally allowed Theri to take over my body. I've never felt anything like that before—that amount of power resonating through me, that feeling of some all-knowing presence making my decisions, *our* decisions. There was no fear of death or pain. I knew, *we* knew, exactly what to do to kill him. And I did."

"I felt complete in my purpose. In that moment, I fully accepted my role as Incarn. Because of that experience, I believe that the enemy can be conquered. But I am afraid of what will happen if I give myself fully to Issaura. If I am an Incarn created exclusively for Theri's wishes, will I lose myself and become only her?" Lluava voiced this new fear that she had refused to acknowledge until now. "What if, once this is over, I cease to be?"

"No. No. No," Varren soothed as he pulled her into his reassuring embrace. "I have you now. I will always have you. I will never let anything take you away. Not Themis, not Yena, not some Theriomorph deity. I promise you this as I live and breathe."

Trembling, Lluava thought about what had happened between them. Varren had been hurting all this time, blaming himself for circumstances over which he had no control. He had thought Lluava was angry with him for his engagement to Selene, the imprisonment of Yamir, and his inability to defend the kingdom. She, in turn, had thought Varren was disgusted that she had placed her faith in Yena, abetting the evil that led to the Fall. If only they had found the strength to talk openly to one another earlier, these past few weeks would have been far more bearable.

Feeling stripped bare and emotionally raw, Lluava relished the comfort of Varren's embrace. She had missed him horribly. Even though they had been near one another for the past few months, neither had actually been *there*. Did that even make sense? There was a distance between them that each had helped create. But this invisible, intangible distance had finally been overcome.

As Lluava breathed in Varren's familiar scent of rosemary and fennel, she reacquainted herself with the rhythmic rise and fall of his chest. She turned to look at his compassionate face. Without a second thought, she reached up and pulled Varren's face down to hers. The kiss they shared held no awkwardness or reserve. Lips passionately roamed over lips, cheeks, and neck. Fingers curled around locks of hair; bodies pressed as close as two separate forms could.

As hands reached to pull clothes from flesh, the door swung wide. The pair turned, astonished by the figure who stared back at them. Themis pronounced sternly, "You were right."

Behind him, someone approached. Varren stood as Regin appeared. Themis chastised the young king, "You should know by now that the sole ruler cannot run off alone. Guards will be present at all times."

Regin stated coolly, "He never left our sight, as you can see. He *never* goes anywhere unseen." Whether this statement was meant to placate the disgruntled councilman or to warn the king, Lluava could not tell. Regardless, her time with Varren alone had ended.

"I do not mind protective eyes following my movements," declared Varren as he helped Lluava to her feet. "But that does not mean I do not deserve some privacy, especially while among close friends."

Themis's face was devoid of emotion, but Lluava felt he was seething with anger directed at her. The councilman said, "Privileges such as privacy are sacrificed when one becomes king."

Regin intervened, breaking the mounting tension. "Your Majesty, we need you to come and approve some last-minute decisions before this evening."

"Very well." Varren could not hide the disappointment in his voice. Turning, he kissed Lluava's hand, right in front of his godfather. The revulsion in Themis's eyes was quickly buried beneath an impersonal demeanor.

"Varren," Lluava whispered quickly. "There is a prisoner here, a nomad Outlander. He must come with us."

There was no need for the young king to press for more details. His eyes showed that he trusted her, that he always had. Without another word, the three men strode away.

A short while later, when Odel arrived bearing Lluava's breakfast, she wondered if she were becoming the most popular figure in Erebos.

"Kido allowed me to bring this to you…so I could say goodbye."

"Come in," she said, as Onyx flew past her to perch on Odel's shoulder. The boy smiled wide as the raven crooned into his ear.

While Odel placed the tray of food on the table, Lluava asked, "How have you been?"

His clear blue eyes were tinged with sadness. "Truthfully," Odel said as he pinched off a piece of toast for the bird, "a little bored. I clean, study, and sleep."

"That's not all bad," noted Lluava, taking a seat on the mat.

"But not exciting."

Lluava wondered if he had heard about the incident with the prisoner. She took a sip of lukewarm water. "Excitement is overrated."

Onyx tugged at Odel's dark, wavy hair. The boy didn't seem to mind, so Lluava allowed the raven to persist.

"I wish I was older," mused Odel. "Then I could go with you."

His words caused Lluava to remember all those who had been killed during the war, including young children like him. She quickly countered, "No. You do not." Realizing that she had sounded very harsh, she added, "Everyone has a purpose, Odel. This upcoming battle is not yours."

"What am I meant to do, then?"

The earnestness of his question was jarring. "I don't know. But you will find out when the time is right."

Odel seemed to accept this with that odd understanding of one older than his years. "Will I see you again?"

Lluava found she had to be honest with the boy. "I don't know. I hope so."

Moving Onyx onto his perch, Odel bowed formally, "Farewell, Lluava of the Theriomorphs."

"Goodbye, Odel of the Shadows."

As the boy left, Lluava felt a tear roll down her cheek. She let it slip down until it fell on the stone floor. With no more time spared for tears, she spent the rest of the day mentally preparing herself for what would come next.

***

Jigo's sharp knock alerted Lluava that the time to leave had arrived.

"Lluava Kargen, you are to follow me," Jigo said in a most formal and commanding manner. There was no need for him to speak to those stationed outside her door; they already knew the orders.

Onyx remained on Lluava's shoulder as she followed the Shadow toward the mound. Jigo didn't seem to mind the addition of the feathered creature. In fact, he seemed lost in thought. Instead of heading into the mound, Jigo led her up several flights of winding stairs. Suddenly, Lluava recognized where they were headed.

"Are you taking me to see the prisoner?"

"Regin said, if you can get the prisoner to come along on our journey, he can leave. But he is *your* responsibility. Which means you must be able to handle him."

Varren had to have requested this for her. However, the tone of Jigo's voice insinuated that no one believed she could convince the nomad to join his enemy on their venture. This way, Lluava realized that Regin would appear to obey the king's wishes, all the while planning to keep the prisoner locked up in Erebos. That is, unless she proved them wrong.

Jigo unlatched the door and waved her into the cell. Fortunately, she had Issaura's Claws on and was ready for the first sign of attack. The Shadow entered behind her to observe the encounter and be ready to intervene.

Scanning the chamber, Lluava knew something far worse had occurred than failure to persuade the nomad to leave. The cell was empty. The captive had been released once again.

Chapter 9

Grudging Agreements

"Find him!" Jigo ordered the befuddled Guards standing by the door. His sai were in his hands before he even spoke.

"You're going to kill him, aren't you?" shouted Lluava before Jigo disappeared into the darkness.

"He has left us no choice!" flung back the Shadow. Then he was gone.

Lluava's mind raced. What could she do? Her dream had held a message, one she believed. This prisoner would play an important role in the future. If the Obsidian Guard killed the nomad, what then? Did the outcome of the war hinge on one individual? That was ludicrous, right? Maybe. But she could not take the chance.

How could she find the captive before the Shadows did? This was the Guards' home. They knew every tunnel and alcove, and they could see in the darkness. Lluava's night vision was limited, and she could barely blunder around. Where would the prisoner have—?

The sound of minuscule stone fragments falling onto the lip of the ledge caught her attention. Lluava turned to the cliffside opening. Slowly inching toward the sheer drop, she peered into the chasm of the mound. A few flickering sconces caused dark forms to dance on the rock. The only other movement resulted from the Obsidian Guard traversing the ground below.

A few more fragments tumbled down onto Lluava's platinum-blond hair. Onyx croaked in annoyance. She turned her gaze upward and caught sight of the nomad as he climbed the sheer rock face. He was heading toward a darkened opening high above him.

So he hadn't been released—he was escaping! He was scaling the cliff, seeking a way out of the mound. Could she reach the man before the

Shadows spotted him? Several throwing suns in his flesh would certainly cause him to lose his grip and plummet to his death.

Lluava ran into the corridor, where she paused for a moment to scan the gloom. She had to find the stairs. Retracing her steps, she quickly found the stairwell. Bounding up several steps at a time, Lluava guessed which level to try.

Please let me be right, she silently prayed to no particular deity.

Estimating where the opening might be, Lluava hurried to a closed cell. Yanking on the door, she found it locked. There was no time to hesitate. She slashed at the wood around the lock with Issaura's Claws. The beams splintered, and she kicked the door in.

At the edge of the cell's ledge, she scanned the cliff face below and saw the nomad only inches away. Not far below him, several Shadows were easily scaling the cliff in pursuit of the escapee. They were experienced rock climbers. More Shadows appeared at other openings, their weapons glinting in the torchlight.

Pulling off one of the Claws, Lluava reached down and shouted, "Take my hand! Hurry!"

Onyx fluttered from her shoulder angrily and circled about inside the cell. The captive looked up and scowled. Lluava didn't care. "Come on!"

The prisoner edged sideways, changing direction. Was he trying to find another way out?

Eyeing the glimmers of the throwing suns, Lluava demanded, "Take my hand, you fool! They are going to kill you!"

Whether it was the earnestness in her voice or his dire situation, the nomad hoisted himself up and grabbed Lluava's forearm. She struggled to keep her feet braced against the rock floor lest she fall over the ledge. With one long heave, they both collapsed in the cell.

Before she had a chance to catch her breath, Lluava felt her throat constrict as the nomad's arm wrapped around her neck, choking her. She tried to fight back, but to no avail.

Should she shift? If she did, would the goddess take over? Would Issaura kill him? Time was running out.

Lluava raked her Clawed hand across the back of her attacker. The nomad cried out and struggled to maintain his hold on her. Taking advantage of his weakened grip, she tore free.

Both jumped to their feet. Lluava could see the blind hatred emanating from his eyes. If he charged her, one or both of them could be propelled over the ledge. This man would throw his life away to kill her, a Theriomorph, his sworn enemy. He would not stop. She realized he would continue to attack her until one or both of them were dead.

At that moment, a trio of Shadows burst through the shattered door. The captive sprang at her discarded weapon. With a low growl, Lluava shifted. In mere seconds, she became a white tigress with gilded claws on one forepaw. She reached him just as he grabbed for the other Claw.

Lluava batted the man with her large paw. He slammed into a stone wall and collapsed. Then she leaped over his fallen body to protect him. With an enormous roar, Lluava warned off the Shadows.

"Nobody touches him. He is *my* ward," she snarled.

One of the Shadows silently slipped away, while the other two stood watch over this peculiar and rather disagreeable scene until Regin arrived. He appeared unsurprised at the scene.

Lluava reminded the head Guard, "You promised that if I could persuade the prisoner to come, he would travel with us to Amargo. As you can see, he will not be arguing that point."

They both knew this was not what Regin had meant. For now, the nomad would cause no more problems.

"Very well," consented Regin grudgingly. "He can come, but you are responsible for him. If I see any sign that you are unable to control him, he will be executed immediately."

"I have your word, then?" Lluava waited.

A long breath later, Regin said, "You have my word."

***

Lluava was blindfolded, along with Byron, Thad, and Themis, as the rather large band of Obsidian Guard left Erebos. Later, she was helped onto a horse and instructed to keep the black cloth over her eyes until permitted otherwise. Onyx clutched her shoulder tightly and snapped at the Guard who tied the blindfold. Lluava couldn't help but smile.

She had been forced to place her trust in Regin. Would he keep his word? He had promised the nomad would be released into her care once they were far enough away from Erebos that none would ever find the hidden lair again.

She hoped the captive was traveling with them, but her blindfold prevented her from verifying Regin's honesty. They were warned to be quiet because night cats and other wild creatures were in the area. The day passed with only murmured whispers and low talk breaking the silence.

Next evening, Varren said, "You can take your blindfold off. It is time for us to make camp."

The king had been by her side the entire time; despite her blindfold, they had talked incessantly, in hushed voices, about anything that came to mind.

Removing the cloth, she impatiently looked around. They were in a grove of scattered pines. Several Shadows had lit a cooking fire and were spitting the game they had caught that day. Scanning the area, Lluava breathed a sigh of relief when she saw the prisoner, bound and gagged, strapped and flung sideways over a horse like a sack of flour. Varren had told her he was there, but seeing the nomad with her own eyes eased her mind.

The captive's blindfold had been removed, and the burning glare she received caused her to shake her head. If the nomad was going to be of any help, he must come to terms with working alongside a Theriomorph.

"He is going to be trouble," Varren warned. "Is he so important that you are willing to take this risk?"

"I think so," replied Lluava. She knew Varren did not fully understand her reasoning, so she added, "I have to do this."

"I will support you," the young king assured her, "unless he causes harm to anyone. That is where I draw the line."

Lluava gripped the Claws tightly. "I won't let him."

Did the prisoner know who she was speaking with and what they were talking about? The hatred in his hazel eyes seemed to make them gleam more brightly. Lluava moved toward the cooking fire and left the captive on his horse.

Hopefully, he'll calm down, she mused to herself; at the very least, restrain himself. She kept him in sight as the evening progressed until she felt sorry for the tired equine.

With Byron's assistance, she carefully lowered the nomad onto the ground at the base of one of the many large pines that had grown in defiance of the inhospitable mountain climate.

Lluava was knotting the ends of the rope she had wrapped three times around both prisoner and trunk. "Almost done," she said from behind the base of the tree. Her cold fingers fumbled with the bindings.

There was a crack, followed by a short string of curses. Leaping around the tree, she saw Byron holding his bleeding nose as the prisoner sat glaring, wrists and ankles still firmly tied together.

"He clouted me with his elbow," Byron admitted reluctantly.

Behind him, Jigo called, "What's going on over there?"

Lluava gave Byron a pleading look, and the young soldier replied, "Just a small accident on my part."

Crisis averted, Lluava quietly said to her friend, "You sure you're all right?"

"Yeah," snorted Byron as he continued to pinch his nose. "I expect to break it at some point in my life, but not this way."

"I don't think its broken," Lluava said as she examined him. "Come on, let's get you some food." She ushered Byron away from her ward. "It'll make you feel better."

Nodding, Byron asked, "What about him?"

"Let him miss a few meals and see how willing he is to attack those watching over him," she said in a half snarl. Byron looked dubious as he led the way to the roasting arctic hare that crackled on the spit.

Over the following days, their journey was both cold and slow. The snow-laden ground was beginning to thaw, and it took much more effort for boots and hooves to slog through the slush. At some point, they re-entered Elysia, and their trek picked up speed.

Lluava waited a full three days before offering her ward any sustenance other than water. On her first attempt, he snapped at her fingers as soon as she removed the gag, and then began to yell. Hurriedly, Lluava shoved the grimy cloth back into his mouth and tightened the ends around his auburn hair. The next day, she tried again.

"If you keep quiet," she offered, "I have a bowl of porridge for you to eat." She removed the gag. "There are dangerous beasts about, and I will not allow you to summon them."

This time, the prisoner seemed more compliant, whether due to hunger, weakness, or pain from the saddle sores on his torso. He was still forced to ride his mount strapped down sideways. With wrists bound before him, he carefully lifted the bowl to his lips and allowed the food to slide into his mouth.

"See how much better it is when you work with—" Lluava was not allowed to finish her statement, for the ceramic bowl was flung at her face and broke against her jaw.

"The seven hells!" she roared out before containing her hot fury. "I have a right mind to knock you unconscious again," she snarled, then took a final breath. "Luckily for you, I can be forgiving."

Carefully bending down, Lluava collected the half-buried shards of the bowl from the snow. Tasting blood, she hurried away before she changed her mind and allowed her inner tigress to teach her ward a harder lesson.

"How are you and your prisoner faring?" Themis asked, feigning interest. Lluava knew he could clearly see the bruise flowering on the side of her face and the cut above her lip.

"As well as you expected, I'm sure." Lluava forced a smile.

Varren must have overheard their exchange. "I cannot make you two like one another," he inserted, "but I can command that you treat each other respectfully for the remainder of our journey."

"As you wish," was their mutual reply.

The following morning, with Byron at her side Lluava fed the prisoner some more gruel. This time, he ate without balking, although Byron kept his hand on the hilt of his sword the entire time.

"Much better," remarked Lluava. "See how nice it is when we get along?"

For once, her ward did not scowl. Lluava said, "To show you how happy I am that we have a sort of understanding, I will allow you to ride upright today. I'm sure your saddle sores are far from comfortable." She nodded at the red marks on his bare chest. Though wrapped in a thick blanket during the journey, the Obsidian Guard had refused to allow the prisoner any spare clothing.

Arms bound, the man was helped onto a mount. Lluava took his horse's reins and led it behind her to make sure it maintained a steady pace. The horse was very docile and content to stay in step with hers. The morning progressed with little to note until her ward's mount abruptly sprang away from the caravan.

Lluava looked around in shock. The nomad had shoved the halter over his mount's head. No longer tethered to Lluava, he was kicking the horse's flanks to drive the animal into a frantic gallop.

"Stop!" Lluava cried out as she spurred her horse into a gallop as well. Behind her, shouts were heard, including Regin's urgent command, "Not you, Your Majesty!"

All Lluava could do was keep her eyes on the escaping captive. The blanket blew off and nearly collided with her, but she veered away just in time. The nomad was an expert horseman and used his strong legs to steered his mount exactly where he wanted to go. To stay in pursuit, Lluava had to tug reins and dig her heels in. Pine branches slapped at her, and several times she was nearly knocked off her horse. The nomad was heading straight toward a heavier stand of trees and would use them as cover.

She had to reach him. If he escaped, the Obsidian Guard would hunt him down. If she did not bring him back herself, he would die.

Up ahead, Lluava watched the nomad's horse rear as it tried to spin around. From the thicket emerged several dozen figures wearing horned helmets and heavy furs. A band of Raiders charged the pair of them, crossbows raised and ready to shoot.

Chapter 10

Oldest of Enemies

Hurriedly turning her own steed, Lluava shouted, "This way!"
She steered her mount to the left while the nomad spurred his to
the right. Damn him, she thought angrily and altered her own
course. Heavy, square-headed quarrels from the Raiders' crossbows streaked
through the air and threatened to cut her mission short.

As the bulkily clad men raced after them, so did a half dozen or more
Shadows. Some of the Obsidian Guard had indeed followed the escaping
captive. Now the opposing sides met with a clatter of weapons and the cries
of enraged men.

Lluava did not stop to assist them. She had to herd the prisoner back to
the others. But at what risk? In doing so, would she lead the enemy to Varren?
How many marauders were hiding in the woods? Who outnumbered whom?
Certainly, the Raiders would be no match for the Guard.

Onyx cawed angrily from above. What use was that bird if it alerted the
Raiders to her whereabouts? Before she could shout at the raven, Onyx dove
down in a blur of black feathers—straight for the nomad's eyes. Instinctively,
the man raised his arms to protect his face, thereby throwing himself off
balance. His mount slowed.

Now was her chance. Lluava leaped from her horse and pulled the
nomad from his. There was a moment when bodies, horses, and hooves
collided with the ground. She found herself struggling to control the
thrashing prisoner.

"By the Twelve, stop or you'll kill us both!"

The nomad stopped resisting. "You know nothing of the Twelve, savage."

Lluava ignored the insult. "If you want to hate savages," she said disdainfully, "then hate the Raiders who attacked us. They are the true enemy. For everyone, including your people."

Jerking the man to his feet, Lluava did not care that the Claws grazed his reddening flesh. The cold would soon turn him white, possibly even blue. Maybe it would be better to let him freeze.

"Come on," Lluava said. She pulled him forward while scanning for their horses. One stood nearby; the other was out of sight. Just as the nomad began to follow her, a piercing scream caused the pair to freeze in their tracks.

"Vor's kingdom!" the nomad exclaimed after the horse's scream died. Lluava recognized the bastard name for the goddess Nott. Did his gods mirror her own pantheon? Of all the gods to call upon, the goddess of death was the last she would have expected.

She knew the nomadic tribes viewed harming a horse without due cause as a sin. Their steeds provided transportation, means of protection, and above all, survival.

"Keep moving," Lluava ordered. The pair headed toward the remaining steed, which was now trotting skittishly in circles.

Before they could reach the horse, a large, dark object hurtled into Lluava and knocked her down. She gasped and shoved a horse's severed head off her chest. Beside her, the nomad stood stock-still. His eyes widened at the figure approaching them. The man, who wore an enormous horned helmet, towered over them. From his gore-splattered face, bloodshot eyes glowered. With a terrible, guttural roar, the Raider lifted a battle-axe far heavier than a normal man could wield.

"Run!" Lluava coughed out as she struggled to her feet. The nomad continued to stare in horror at the formidable giant. The odor of tainted smoke wafted in the air. "Run!" Lluava's voice was louder now. She yanked the captive hard and shouted, "RUN!"

This time, the nomad did not hesitate. He darted ahead of her on his strong legs as they desperately tried to evade the behemoth charging after them. They had no choice but to head back toward the main fray. If they were to survive, they needed the Shadows alongside them.

Black bodysuits whipped around the more cumbersome fur-laden marauders. Many Raiders were clearly in pain, while others lay as corpses on the ground. One or two Shadows had been killed, but their superior agility and skill had prevented a worse outcome. It was hard to tell one Shadow from another, but Lluava thought she recognized Jigo.

"Behind us!" Lluava alerted the Guard of their arrival and the monstrous assailant on their heels. She did not look around when she heard the sputtering coughs of several Raiders hacked down by the giant's axe. His drug-induced rage caused an uncontrollable urge to kill, and anyone who got in the way of his objective was at risk, friend or foe. The nomad glanced back. Whatever he saw caused him to blanch.

A Guard moved in front of Lluava and shouted, "Duck!"

She barely had time to comply with Regin's order when a set of four throwing suns whirled over her head and embedded themselves in the behemoth. Stumbling, Lluava continued forward, for she knew the monster behind her would not be stopped by injuries such as those.

Regin stood his ground.

Although it was a heroic move, Lluava knew it meant certain death for him. The head Shadow had never dealt with such an enemy. With a growl, Lluava knocked Regin aside and shifted into white tigress form.

Several of the Guard had moved to attack the behemoth while others kept warily away, for their sai would be of no advantage. Regin's throwing suns were embedded in the brute's chest and left arm, but the Raider took no notice of his injuries.

Lluava knew that since he had smoked his drug, only decapitation, the destruction of his heart, or bleeding out would kill the monster.

"Aim for his head!" she roared as she lunged toward the lumbering beast. Her gilded foreclaws caught the fur cloak that covered his arm and dug in deeply to tear at his flesh. She had to knock his helmet off, for neither throwing sun nor naginata could penetrate its metal. Trying to bat at the large horns that branched to either side, she lost her grip as the giant jolted sideways.

On the ground, Lluava felt the bloodshot eyes bore into her. The brute swung his axe upward just as a Shadow's chigiriki shredded a large section of flesh and bone at the behemoth's jawline.

She scrambled to her feet as the sickening thunk of the axe cleaved the poor Shadow in two, splattering blood and entrails. The giant turned back to Lluava. The roots of several remaining teeth were exposed in his ruined face. "Theri," he sputtered.

Hearing that name caused the thing inside her to stir. Should she let the goddess out? Would she be able to tell friend from foe? Or would she be no different from this monster, who focused solely on slaughter and annihilation?

She crouched, anticipating attack, snarling ferociously. Feinting a strike, Lluava swiped at the axe. Several more throwing suns clattered against the metal helmet, leaving small dents. The last one slashed the man's throat.

With no time to rejoice, Lluava leaped out of the way of the swinging blade. Though the giant's death was imminent, he would try to take others with him to his hell. The behemoth blundered forward, his axe dealing damage with every strike.

With a roar, Lluava threw her full body weight at the Raider, hoping to knock him down. Somehow the man held his ground. He dropped the axe and moved to grab her. At the same time, Lluava stood up on her rear legs and bit into the spewing neck. Her canines crunched on bone. The villain's body finally went limp.

Suddenly, the enormous corpse fell on top of her, and pain shot into her underbelly. Lluava cried out, "Get him off me!"

The taste of blood in her mouth and the piercing sensation in her gut acted as a trigger. Her sight began to waver. No, she thought. Not now. The time is not right.

Other figures approached. Fortunately, they were Shadows, who commenced to free Lluava from her fleshy prison. Once on her feet, she scanned the carnage. The entire party of Raiders had been slain, along with seven Shadows. Several other Obsidian Guard were injured as well; one was Jigo. His shoulder bore a deep cut where the giant's axe had caught him.

"How badly are you hurt?" he asked her brusquely.

Examining her body, Lluava realized that the throwing sun embedded in the behemoth must also have dug into her striped torso. "Not terribly," she muttered, trying to hide her fury at what had just occurred. A few stitches were nothing, all things considered.

The real problem was that now her ward would no longer be under her protection. She only wanted him to be shown a little mercy. Hoping the head Shadow would be just, Lluava cautioned the others, "The prisoner will not be harmed without Regin's direct command."

The nomad stood nearby. He held a small knife in his bound hands but dropped it as the Guards moved toward him. Plodding up to the captive, Lluava sniffed the fear emanating from his body. Her whiskers and nostrils flared.

"What was that demon?" the nomad asked her as he was led away.

"That was a Berserker. They are the enemy."

She watched as the nomad, deep in the horror of his own thoughts, followed the Guard in silence.

Jigo seemed to appear out of nowhere. He nodded toward the head Shadow. "You know that Regin will sentence the nomad to die because of his escape attempt."

"Yes," Lluava admitted dejectedly, "but it should be done mercifully and not in a moment of rage."

Jigo inclined his head subtly as Regin approached. The leader of the Obsidian Guard ordered, "Take the prisoner back to the others, and set up camp. Holly will be in charge until I return." He looked at Lluava intently. Eyes flashing, he chose several of the Guard. "You will come with me. We must make sure there are no more Raiders." Without another word, the small band of Shadows dispersed to ensure their king's safety.

The trek took the better part of an hour. Everyone was cautious, and some of the injured struggled to keep pace. Their tracks were all too visible in the snow. Lluava hoped they would not be followed. Since Berserkers traveled in trios, two others must be nearby.

Her tail twitched agitatedly the entire time, an instinctual reflex she could not control. That the Raiders were this far south did not bode well for their caravan. For all they knew, they were in the middle of enemy territory.

What did this mean for Cronus and Yena? Could the Raiders have finally breached the walls of the capital? That wouldn't be the worst thing, would it? If the Raiders slew Yena and her Outlanders, there would be one fewer enemy and one fewer army for Varren to face. But what about Apex? What of Talos and Rosalyn? Had they been killed? Would they be killed?

Varren and Holly greeted the weary survivors on their return. It was evident from the expression on their faces that the two had been informed of everything. Had they heard the skirmish? Had the Shadows alerted them about the enemy?

The injured were treated with what limited medical supplies they had. Lluava was handed a blanket under which to shift, and a new set of black clothes. Though they were a size too large, she did not mind, for this new issue was made of Endun, the Theriomorph material that changed with them. Had Holly brought them for her on purpose? While someone stitched up Jigo's shoulder, another Shadow handed Lluava a clean cloth and a bowl of water. Stifling a cry of pain, she dabbed the cuts on her torso, three in all.

Varren spoke with each of the wounded. Lluava knew he could not show favoritism, but she noticed the worried looks he cast her way.

"I've been through worse," she said as she lifted her shirt to expose a long, dull scar. "Remember?"

"All too well," he added. "That is one debt I hope to be able to repay."

Suddenly, Lluava felt sick. "As do I," she replied. Her thoughts returned once again to Apex.

The nomad was tied to the trunk of a tree to await judgment. But first, the dead had to be dealt with. It was customary for the Shadows to burn their dead, but with the enemy afoot, they would have to be left where they fell. None of the Obsidian Guard would put their king at undue risk.

Next, the conversation shifted to the prisoner. Lluava stepped forward and began, "If I may—"

Themis interrupted her. "Whatever you wish to say, take note: you have no authority at this council."

"I know," Lluava remarked as courteously as she could. "All I ask is that whatever means of death you decide for the nomad, let it be quick and without unnecessary pain."

"You choose to extend the prisoner mercy?" Varren questioned. Lluava could clearly tell he was proud of her. "Even though he would not have done the same for you?"

"Yes."

"He is the enemy of us all," reminded Themis. "He would kill anyone who lives within Elysia's borders."

"But," Lluava brazenly interjected, "if I, as a Theriomorph, the nomad's sworn enemy, older than the Mandrun line's rule—"

"Remarks like that—" Themis began in a calm voice tinged with poison.

Several Shadows' eyes flashed in warning and disdain.

Lluava continued unabashed, "Wish mercy on him—"

"Your advisory role has been stripped," reminded Holly sternly.

Raising her voice, Lluava finished, "Then why shouldn't you?" She did not flinch under the angered eyes of those insulted by her insubordinate behavior. She added, "That is all."

Stepping away, she left the others to deliberate. Knowing Varren, she hoped the plea for mercy would appeal to him. Since they were now in Elysia, he would make the final decision. The prisoner's attempt to flee had resulted in many deaths and a number of injuries. The nomad would have to die.

Lluava walked over to the captive and sat down on a fallen tree trunk nearby. The man still seemed shaken.

"I told you," she began when the captive looked in her direction, "that I was not a monster." Pausing, she thought about the past year and amended, "Well, I am not the only one."

"In my religion," the nomad began, giving Lluava a start, "the gods never meant their ability to be given to your ancestors. The gift was condemned, although it was too late to take it back. The Messenger came down from the heavens with a command from the First. The command was that it was the duty of humans to slay anyone with the god's gift.

"You and your race were wrongly created by the gods. But that thing—" the nomad's eyes momentarily glazed over. "That monster was not made by the gods. That thing is an abomination. That thing is a sacrilege."

Lluava regarded her distorted reflection in the Claws. "I don't know how that thing came to be. I do know where he comes from, and there are more."

"They will destroy everything?" questioned the nomad.

"Yes."

Looking over at the men who were deciding his fate, the prisoner admitted, "My father called me Aquila, after my family's totem. It means *eagle*."

"In my religion," Lluava said thoughtfully, "the bow you possessed was forged for the king of our gods, Giahem. His dual form is the eagle. The weapon is fitting for you."

In the following silence, Lluava brooded. Could she have been wrong about Aquila? She had to have been. His death would be proof. There were no such things as signs; no greater power spoke to her in riddled dreams. She was not Yena, who had the gift of foresight and prophecy. All Lluava had done was prolong the inevitable. The nomad was going to die. Now more deaths were on her hands and his.

Shaking his blond-streaked auburn hair to clear his sight, Aquila stated solemnly, "Their decision has been made."

He was right. The group of men was heading in their direction. Varren's grave features did not indicate whether Lluava's plea had had any effect.

"I, King Varren Mandrun, true ruler of Elysia, order the prisoner bound before me to die by a shot to the neck with a poisoned dart. The venom it possesses will send the prisoner quickly into the realm of the afterlife."

Holly stepped up with blowdart in hand.

At least it will be painless, thought Lluava as she stepped away. She did not wish to see any more lives taken.

A horn trumpeted solemnly, followed by the steady thrum of war drums.

"Raiders," Holly pronounced. The execution was forgotten. "Everyone protect our king!"

"Gather your weapons," ordered Varren simultaneously. "The war is upon us."

Lluava moved to Varren's side. She might not be his military partner, but as an Elysian soldier, she would guard Varren until her last breath was drawn.

"They have to be a mile away," said Byron as he cocked his head to listen to the odious sound.

"They may be," noted Jigo. "But look there."

Two enormous figures had appeared on the far side of the camp. Each stood close to eight feet tall. One held a massive spiked mace; the other, a gigantic maul. Berserkers had found their camp. Death was sure to follow.

Chapter 11

Unbound

God save me!" Thad cried out. The look of terror on his face would have affected even the most stoic heart. Behind the Berserkers, a new army of Raiders awaited. Like hunters releasing their hounds, they stood behind the pair of approaching monstrosities.

Next to the king, Holly gave a nod, and the Obsidian Guard charged. Once again, the skill and prowess of the swift-moving Shadows brought down many a Raider with relative ease. The Berserkers were a different story. The Guard swarmed the giants like ants to invasive locusts. Even so, both Berserkers forced their way forward, step by giant step.

Holly and a score of Shadows moved into a protective ring around Varren. Defending the king was their ultimate mission. Lluava and Byron did the same. Even Themis pulled a long dagger from under his cloak.

"Please, Varren, we have to run," implored Thad. His hands trembled along with his voice. "I can't...I can't...not again..."

Varren attempted to sooth his oldest friend. "Stay by my side. I will not let them take you."

Thad's body shook, and Varren cast a worried glance in Lluava's direction. Their friend, once a proud warrior, had been reduced to a fragile shell of himself.

"We need to get to the horses," advised Byron. "They are our best chance to get away."

Lluava would have agreed with her blond friend, but the route to their mounts was blocked by two rabid behemoths and a mass of ragged marauders.

"Give the Shadows a chance," Lluava insisted as she nodded toward the mayhem. Already a number of Raiders lay dying. Unfortunately, the Guards' ability to conceal themselves in shadow was useless in the bright daylight. Without darkness, their gift of surprise was stripped away, leaving them vulnerable.

"No time! Move!" shouted Varren just as the pair of Berserkers picked up speed and barreled straight toward the king. As Varren ran, most of the main circle of Guard followed in position, while a few slipped away to defend their young ruler.

As more Raiders appeared, Varren halted. "We have to fight. All of us. Together."

The Guard split and formed a defensive line, but this defense was quickly breached. The Berserkers were undeterred.

"Free me!" screamed Aquila, thrashing in his restraints. "I can help!"

Lluava ignored the nomad's pleas as the first Berserker's mace crushed the legs of the Shadow to her left. She needed to focus to stay alive.

"Together!"

Varren's voice resounded in her ears, and they both charged. She understood exactly what he planned to do. She leaped for the leather buckles fastening the Berserker's thick hide breastplate and sliced through them with the Claws. Varren thrust his sword at the giant's exposed chest.

Their attacker swung his massive mace at the king. Lluava had to protect him. To give Varren time to back away, she shifted and grappled with the arm wielding the deadly weapon. The giant's intended blow was so powerful that the tigress was almost hurled to the ground. He grabbed the scruff of her neck with his free hand to pull the enraged feline off.

The Berserker's grip was fierce; her hide was being pulled from her musculature. She had to escape his grasp. Twisting, she bit the wrist of his right hand, shattering it. With one final crunch, she released the giant's arm, which still held the mace. Like the blades of a windmill, Lluava was flung to the ground while the mace and mutilated arm followed her arc to pummel the life out of her.

The sound of metal ripping through muscle and bone followed. Varren had severed the Berserker's wrist; the hand lay on the ground, still clutching the mace. With a grunt of annoyance, the brute turned to face the king.

Lluava struggled to rise. Though badly bruised, all her limbs functioned. So much blood had been spilled that the ground itself was slippery.

A Shadow threw a sai into the monster's lower back as Varren attempted to strike from the front. In the midst of the fray stood Thad, frozen; he would not move, even to give Varren a better angle of attack. Instead, the king positioned himself in front of his friend to shield him.

Even disregarding the young man's bad leg, Lluava mused, Thad was a dangerous liability and would certainly pose a risk to Varren as long as the king tried to protect him. But what could they do? Certainly not leave him to his nightmares. It would be more merciful to kill him.

Snarling at the vile thought, the tigress raked the ground with her gilded claws. Had that idea been hers or the goddess's? How, Lluava wondered, could she ever entertain the thought of allowing a friend to die? Regardless, something had to be done about Thad.

Once again, Aquila shouted, "Lluava! Set me free!"

Lluava swung around. The second Berserker was heading toward the bound nomad. Aquila was easy prey. If he could not escape, he would be killed. She had to release him, even if it meant she never saw him again. No person deserved to die without a fight. As more Shadows came to their king's aid, Lluava caught Varren's attention. "The captive—"

Without hesitation, Varren replied, "Go!"

Missing a weapon and a hand, the Berserker who had attacked them was no match for the five Shadows that descended upon him. For the moment, Varren was safe. But would he approve her action to free her ward? Did he realize what she was going to do, or did he think she was going to defend the prisoner?

Racing ahead of the second Berserker, Lluava began to sever the nomad's bindings with her gilded claws. She had freed his wrists and was almost finished with his ankle bindings when Aquila shouted, "Behind you!"

The giant was almost at the tree. Tufts of red hair stuck out from under the massive helmet. Throwing suns peppered his left arm and shoulder. Snarling, Lluava leapt to the man's side, feinting strikes to draw his attention. Aquila would have to fend for himself. She hoped no Raider would slay him before she could untether him from the tree.

Varren was at the center of the skirmish. He and several of the Guard were trying to protect the all-but-useless Thad. Although the king was defending his friend, others were not as concerned for the lordling. Lluava would have assisted but for her own gigantic problem.

The Berserker's maul whooshed over Lluava's head, so low that she felt the sting when it contacted her erect ears. Leaping back, she had to bat at the sword of a neighboring Raider. This smaller brute's underbite exposed cavity-infested lower teeth and a tattoo on his lower lip. The crooked incisors oozed slaver; the odor of decay offended Lluava's nose.

The Raider lunged at her at lightning speed. The thin rapier looked fragile in the man's hands, but he handled it with deadly skill. Instead of combating this enemy with her metal-infused claws, Lluava employed a defensive strategy. With the approaching Berserker closing in behind her and the Raider attacking from the front, Lluava—grateful for her Endun clothing—shifted into human form just as the giant swung the maul at the tigress. Aided by her smaller human form, she leaped out of the way to reveal the Raider behind her. The deadly maul took down its new mark.

Crumpling to the blood-spattered ground, the smaller Raider met his end. Lluava, on the other hand, still had to survive to fight. With the Berserker fixated on killing her, she was forced to turn and run.

All around her, fur-garbed men fought those in black. The clatter of metal resounded above all other noise. Onyx cried from above, while dark-winged birds gathered hungrily in the neighboring trees.

She saw Varren struggling with a Raider; Byron hacking his way toward his king; Thad on his knees, sobbing; the growing shadow of the giant gaining on her.

The thing inside her stirred as her internal heat rose. Skidding on her heels, Lluava veered away sharply. From the sound of the lumbering feet, the Berserker was still on her tail. Maybe she should—

Suddenly, she fell flat on her face. A dying Raider had grasped her ankle. Glancing around, Lluava saw the Berserker only steps away. "Let go!" she cried as she kicked at the Raider. He released her, his head popping like a cherry when the Berserker stomped on his skull.

Issaura's Claws, though strong, would not be able to deflect the blow from the Berserker's large maul. There was no time for her to get away. Even Theri would not be able to help.

There was a scream.

The Berserker kept his eyes locked on Lluava's.

Aquila's sword dripped with the giant's blood as the behemoth fell to his knees. Both tendons severed, the monster would not rise again. Lluava moved into action as the nomad knocked off the Berserker's horned helmet. Lurching at the giant's face, Lluava drove both of Issaura's Claws deep into his skull. The great opponent was no more.

In the hour that followed, the rest of the Raiders either fled or were slain. Once their giants were dead, the attempt to kill Elysia's king failed.

The survivors had a moment to take a breath. At first, Lluava did not see Themis among them. Maybe the gods had been merciful and rid the world of the head councilman. Scanning the area once more, however, she recognized him. Although his dagger was bloody, he sported only a tear in his sleeve.

"Nott's lair," Lluava cursed under her breath as she kicked a crossbow out of the cold hands of a Raider corpse.

"I want the numbers of the dead as well as the injured," Varren ordered the Obsidian Guard next to him. "Also, every salvageable weapon needs to be gathered and brought with us. The people gathering at Amargo might have use for them."

Several of the Guard followed the king's command. The rest took a moment to revel in the fact that they had survived. As Themis wiped off his dagger, he asked pointedly, "Who freed our prisoner?"

"I—" Lluava began to confront Themis but suddenly stopped. Aquila was standing nearby. She had not fully cut him loose. How had he escaped his bindings?

When no one spoke up, Themis said, "I suggest we search him."

Varren nodded, and a pair of Shadows approached the nomad. Aquila had discarded the sword he had acquired during the battle, but tucked into one of his boots was a ceramic shard.

"What's this?" Themis asked as the shard was presented to the king. "Looks like a bit of a pot or bowl."

Lluava flushed. "I broke a bowl near him a while back. I thought I had gathered all the fragments."

"It seems you missed one," noted Themis. Though the tone of his voice was not insulting, Lluava knew he reveled in her mistake. "You enabled the prisoner to arm himself."

"It's not a weapon," Lluava pointed out.

"No," commented Varren unhappily, "but if it was sharp enough for him to cut the ropes, it is sharp enough to kill."

"Your Majesty,"—Themis looked directly at his godson—"this adds to the charges against him. His execution must take place immediately."

Glancing at Aquila, Lluava saw that the nomad was not about to run. She spoke up on her ward's behalf. "He had it, true, but he did no harm with it, nor did he use it to escape."

"Do you really believe," argued Themis, "that the captive would not have used the shard if given the chance?"

"He saved my life!"

"He can't be trusted."

"Enough!" Varren rarely raised his voice; doing so now caused the others to fall silent. "Lluava, he may have saved your life, but I cannot be certain he did not act merely out of self-preservation. In times such as these, that must be considered."

"What, then? Kill him?" Using this to divert their attention, Lluava spoke out. She did not care whether people thought her impertinent. "I assumed you needed every fighting man you could find to retake Elysia. Two armies oppose us. How do you plan to defeat them? I do not believe we can take on both."

Varren was silent. Several Guards edged closer to her. She knew she had overstepped the boundaries of acceptable behavior, but Varren raised his hand and held the Shadows off. Lluava realized that he was waiting to see if she had anything more to say.

"I think," she began as she warily eyed those in black, "that we must take a stand before it is too late. The longer we wait to come up with a viable plan, the more opportunity we give them to tear us apart, piece by piece, until we are nothing."

When Lluava had finished, Varren asked, "Anyone else? If you want to have your say, now is the time."

Byron spoke up. "Though I do agree that the longer we wait, the greater the chance we offer the enemies to destroy us, I know that we first need a plan. We cannot run at them blindly swinging our swords." He looked at

Lluava apologetically. "If there were only one enemy, I would have more hope. But there are two. If only they would destroy each other..." Byron sighed and shook his head.

"Plans can and will be made once we are all gathered at Amargo." Themis spoke with confidence. "For anything to work, we must act as one."

Varren was clearly not listening to Themis's council. Suddenly the king asked, "What if there *were* only one enemy? Then our chances for success would grow. How could they not?"

"Your Majesty—" Themis broke in but was waved silent.

Varren weighed his words carefully. "The leader of the Outlander army, High Priestess Yena, has some sort of fascination with Lluava. She desires to have Lluava at her side. I believe that we could use that to our advantage." Varren turned to face Lluava as if speaking to her alone. "The Outlanders *will* kill the Raiders for us."

Chapter 12

Rise!

Haven't they been doing that?" questioned Byron. "Have they not been fighting one another since we fled?"

Varren considered the question. "Yes and no. They have been fighting; of that I am certain. But I assume that as long as Yena holds Cronus, she would focus on defensive tactics. If I were her, I would save my resources and minimize the loss of my troops until I could successfully defeat the Raiders. Who knows? Perhaps she hopes that the Raiders will slay all of us for her."

"If the Outlanders are protected by Cronus's walls," Byron asked, "why would they risk an offensive strike on the Raiders in the open?

"Faith." Varren studied the skeptical expressions of those about him. "The Outlanders are extremely religious and follow the Old Ways. This is why the high priestess is their leader. They also believe that certain Theriomorphs serve as hosts for their gods." Varren glanced at Lluava. "Yena seeks Lluava's support because she believes that Lluava is one such host."

Themis scoffed. Varren was unperturbed. "Come now," he went on. "We know that in the pagan religion it was foretold that the goddess Issaura would return to Earth to save the Theriomorph race. The Outlanders believe that Lluava is Issaura—or, rather, the host for that goddess—and will lead them to victory. If Lluava exploits that faith, she could persuade the Outlanders to rise and follow her. She could lead their army into a full-on battle with the Raiders."

"They will lose," Thad's voice rasped out. His wide eyes turned quickly downward.

"Perhaps," concurred Varren. "But the Raiders' army would still be weakened. That is when we would attack. We can win this war." Varren's voice rose confidently. "We *can* win this war."

"I am loath to ask," Themis interjected, "but how do you know that Lluava would not be swayed by her own people? How do we know we are not empowering yet another future usurper of the throne?"

"Your lack of faith in Elysians concerns me, Themis," Varren admitted earnestly.

"My grandfather, may his soul rest in peace..." Varren began.

The others echoed, "Rest in peace."

"My grandfather decreed that both humans and Theriomorphs were Elysians. They will be treated equally. We are one people united under one king. Lluava will not be swayed by the Outlanders, for she is not an Outlander but an Elysian. Lluava is a soldier of the Elysian army and will fulfill her duty to her king."

Varren paused, but no one disputed him. "Once Lluava has done her part, we will attack what is left of both our enemies and then turn our sights on Cronus. Elysia will be ours again."

"As you say," Themis bowed graciously to his monarch.

Without lifting his head, Thad muttered to himself, "The blue monsters will kill everyone."

"If I am to be sent back into that nest of vipers," began Lluava as a low rumble reverberated in her throat, "then the nomad comes with me."

"The prisoner is to be executed," countered Themis. "Anyway, he would be killed on the spot by those Outlanders, since he is human."

"Exactly." For once Lluava agreed with the head councilman. "He can either die here, now, or at the capital. If he will die either way, why not give him a chance at redemption? He might be able to aid our endeavors."

Aquila gave her an understanding look. There was no trace of hatred in his eyes, only a genuine determination. "I will fight for the she-tiger."

Varren raised an eyebrow. "Will you, now? Even if she be your mortal enemy?"

"She *is* my mortal enemy," responded Aquila briskly. "And will always be so, as ordained by the gods." Nodding toward a Berserker corpse, he said, "That is not god made. That, and any like it, are an abomination in the sight of the mighty Twelve. They must all be destroyed and the natural order restored."

Themis clearly opposed this scenario, but Varren had another question. "The Berserkers, though large in stature, are mortal just as we are. What, then, other than a god or gods, could create them?"

"Evil," replied Aquila.

Varren ran his fingers through his wavy hair. "What would you do if I released you?"

Aquila regarded the king. "I would hunt down the vile things and kill each one I find with a shot from my bow."

"One shot each?"

"I never miss."

"And what if you do? What if you are captured?"

"I will take my own life, for no other deserves to do so."

"I do not believe that you would come to Lluava's aid if she were in peril. I think you would leave her to die. But," Varren spoke slowly and clearly, "what I do believe is that you truly want to destroy the Berserkers. You are being honest about that."

"The gods," replied Aquila lowering his blond-streaked head in a sign of respect, "will smile upon any who take up their cause."

Themis pulled out a handkerchief and wiped sweat from his brow. "As much as I wish one could change one's behavior, the prisoner has proven himself to be wild. And Lluava has not demonstrated that she is capable of controlling the captive. He could slit her throat the first night out. We would not want *that*."

"Lluava is far more capable than you think, Head Councilman," responded Varren. "The nomad will accompany her. And you should all remember," he said, looking at Holly, "that we are in Elysia, and *I* have supremacy here.

"Now, we must depart and make camp elsewhere. We cannot risk staying in this location any longer. Evil *is* about."

***

Before Lluava went to bed, she found an opportunity to talk to Varren alone. There was rarely a moment when the king was out of the Shadows' sight and hearing.

Sensing her worry, Varren motioned her to sit next to him on the blanket. "Sit down. Please." Once she was beside him, Varren asked, "What is on your mind?"

"I have no idea how to get Yena's followers to side with me. I'm not sure that's even possible."

Varren gave her a hard look, then grimaced. "Yena wants something from you. Maybe that is the bargaining chip. Maybe that is what is needed for the Outlanders to follow you, for Elysia to survive."

Lluava felt bile claw its way into her throat. "She wants Ullr's child—a child conceived by me. How could you bear that? How could I?"

Remorse was clear in the young king's voice. "Elysia is dying. It is my duty to save her. Even if..." Varren hesitated. "I will not command you to pursue that path, but I must make you aware of the sacrifices we all must be willing to make so that our home, our people, can survive. Elysia must live on, whatever it takes. You must persuade the Outlanders. You can do this, Lluava," Varren spoke softly. "I know you can."

The thought of bearing a child that she did not want was sickening. Yet if Varren could accept this in order to protect Elysia, shouldn't she?

"I will do my best." She reached for his hand.

"That is all I ask," he replied as he gently clasped hers in return.

Lluava tried to suppress her fear of the journey ahead. In a tone drained of emotion, she said, "I might die."

Varren sat in silence, staring at the small campfire. Lluava whispered, "If this is our last time together, I have something to ask of you."

"Name it, and it shall be yours." He leaned in to hear.

"I would like—"

Before she could form the words, Varren leaned toward her and kissed her. This was one wish he could grant. Lluava pulled him close to her in return. The fire crackled, but the warmth she felt was not from the flames.

"*Caw?*"

Onyx alighted before the pair and cocked his good eye as if to get a better look at their embrace. Their sense of seclusion shattered, Lluava stood and bade Varren good night.

Walking past Thad's bed, she heard him mumble, "Better to be dead than in their grip."

Lluava soon realized that sleep would offer no comfort. Her dreams never did…

***

There it was. The sound that caused her stomach to churn. The one she wanted to find and destroy. But where was the source?

"Lluava," the husky voice began, almost teasing—the one who made that horrid sound. Looking about, all she could see was black.

"It is time."

Lluava reached ahead of her. Her hands—no, her paws—clawed at the blackness. The speaker was out of sight and out of reach.

"Rise," rasped a second female voice. This one, harsher, was unknown to Lluava's ears. There was a sense of urgency.

The first female purred, "Your destiny is nigh. It will find you, and so will I. You cannot hide."

"Rise!" the second voice cried, cracking.

"We, the Incarn, await you," decreed the first voice, then burst into a peal of laughter, one that rose and fell in that horrid sound Lluava hated over all others. The laugh of the hyena. The laughter of Yena.

"RISE!"

Onyx was screaming above her head, fluttering about in a panic, as she awoke violently from her nightmare.

Lluava threw a handful of slushy snow at the bird; she had to quiet him before a throwing sun did. Shadows were patrolling the camp, and the bird was a nuisance. All else was quiet.

She checked about her. Everything was as it should be—except that Thad was no longer in his bed.

As her senses heightened, the world seemed to brighten, even in the

77

night. Thad knelt next to Varren, who was propped up on an elbow. The two were talking. She could hear their conversation.

"...better to die than to go back there. Better to die than be at their mercy. The blue monsters. Blue monsters..." Thad sounded so pitiful.

"I told you," Varren responded, "I will not let them harm you. You will stay at Amargo and not return with me to Cronus. You will be safe."

Thad shuddered. Varren reached out and hugged him. "You are my brother. I love you." He kissed his friend's forehead.

"Love is mercy," replied Thad, quoting scripture from the humans' religion.

"Yes."

"Mercy."

Suddenly, Thad's hands were at Varren's throat. Lluava sprang from her bed with weapons at hand, just as a wall of living night swarmed about the pair. Varren coughed as he struggled to push Thad away. "No one harm him! He is sick. Sick, I say!"

The Obsidian Guard, weapons drawn, were ready to end Thad's misery. There was no need. Varren had pushed Thad to his side and pinned his friend to the ground.

"Thad, Thadius, listen to me," Varren tried to calm his crazed comrade. "They will not get you. You are safe. Safe."

Lluava stood in the midst of the Guard and watched the exaggerated rise and fall of Thad's chest finally lessen.

"He is better now, see?" Varren said to the Obsidian Guard, though his eyes never left his friend. "He will be all right."

Aquila was the only one still abed. He had watched the strange ordeal without interest. Although Thad was an immediate threat, other Shadows had kept their eyes steadily on the captive.

"Thad will have to be monitored, Your Majesty," Holly said as Varren held his friend down.

"Yes," agreed Varren, "but not harmed."

Thad's eyes stayed shut, though they rolled about under his lids.

"Mercy," he murmured almost inaudibly.

A Guard helped Varren to his feet. Byron moved to assist Thad. Though unwilling to right himself, Thad was pulled to his feet easily enough. Though his eyes remained closed, a tear slid down one pale cheek.

"It will be okay now, Thadius," Byron said. But Thad collapsed on the ground. As Byron shrugged at Lluava, she noticed something glinting in Thad's boot.

In that moment, she understood. Thad would try to kill Varren again; he believed that death was the most merciful way out of their predicament. A kindness, an act of love. Even held at bay, how many times might he attempt to slay the king? Varren would do his best to protect his friend even though it meant risking his own life. That's who Varren was. He would do the same for her. But she could not allow him to make that mistake.

Just as Thad righted himself, Lluava shoved Issaura's Claws into his back. Spitting blood, their distraught companion lost all strength of body and collapsed into her arms. A small knife fell from his hand to the ground.

"No!" Varren shouted. Unable to look at the horror on the king's face, Lluava stared into Thad's blanched one. "Love is mercy," he coughed out. "Better to die than—"

"What have you done?" Varren screamed as a Guard pulled the Claw from the body. In death, a smile brought peace to Thad's features.

"*What did you do?*"

Lluava had murdered the king's oldest friend. Her relationship with Varren would never be the same. She was known as a warrior, a killer of enemies. But now she would be known as a murderer. That's the kind of person *she* was.

Chapter 13

The Lion's Enemy

"God, no!"

Varren rushed to the Shadow who had retrieved Thad's body.

Lluava stepped aside. To save the king's life, she had murdered his best friend, but there would be no forgiveness. She had destroyed whatever chance she and Varren might have had for happiness together. There had been no other way.

"Thad!" Varren cried as he gently laid the body on the ground. He lifted Thad's dusty-blond head to his chest.

Slipping away, Lluava quietly gathered her gear. She did not want to wait any longer. As she listened to the heartbreak in Varren's cries, her heart shattered with his. A tear slid down her cheek, and she quickly wiped it away. She did not deserve to cry.

Lluava motioned to Aquila, who seemed to understand her intentions. Together, they swiftly saddled a pair of horses. The Shadows watched, yet no one attempted to dissuade them.

"What about food?" Aquila asked.

"You can hunt, can't you?" Lluava replied harshly. She could not tarry any longer. The very essence of her being implored her to leave immediately.

"'Course," huffed the nomad as he swung onto his mount with ease.

Just as Lluava climbed onto hers, a solitary figure approached. It was Holly. She positioned herself in front of their horses. Would she try to stop them? Was it Lluava's turn to be punished for what she had done?

"You did the right thing." Holly's statement refuted Lluava's fears.

Gritting her teeth in an attempt to hold back tears, Lluava nodded. She knew her words would drown in salty rivers flowing down her cheeks.

Holly continued, "To reach Cronus, you will need to use every resource at your disposal. Take these." She handed Lluava a set of daggers, obviously confiscated from the slain Raiders, and a leather pouch containing a set of throwing suns.

"They are light and will not burden you too much. And this." Holly lifted Giahem's Wings, the glimmering golden bow, and handed it to Lluava. Though Aquila would have happily accepted it, the nomad seemed content simply to have it near him again. Lluava knew that feeling. She gripped Issaura's Claws tightly once everything was packed.

"I have no arrows for you," acknowledged Holly. "But when you get to Cronus, there is a cache stored in the vaults. Go there first."

"What about Regin?" Lluava knew he would surely disagree with Holly's decision.

Holly chose not to respond. Then, without wishing them farewell, she disappeared into the darkness.

Onyx fluttered onto Lluava's shoulder, his favorite position on long journeys, and crooned softly in her ear. Glancing back at the camp one final time, Lluava's gaze lingered on the silhouettes of the two figures huddled on the ground.

"Winds picking up. Might storm soon," Aquila noted as his horse pawed anxiously at the ground.

"No," refuted Lluava. "The storm has already arrived." She kicked her horse, and the pair rode off to the north and the awaiting enemy.

***

Through the night and all the next day, Lluava kept up a fast pace, trying to distance herself from the pain; yet it remained and would, she knew, for some time. Pain and heartbreak had become second nature. Was it really worth it to fight on? Should she just give up? They had so little chance of success. Something, surely, drove her to continue. But to what end?

The sky birthed clouds as dark as her mood until the heavens grew dim. Lluava claimed that the overcast gloom compelled her to make camp early, yet it was her exhaustion, both emotional as well as physical, that forced her to dismount.

Aquila kept his word and made no attempt to flee. Moreover, he kept pace with Lluava and even roused her when she almost fell asleep on her slowing steed. After that incident, she realized that she should be on her guard. The nomad could have killed her. Although they had a common enemy, he was by no means her friend.

Why had she brought him along? Her certainty that the nomad served some greater purpose had dwindled to almost nothing. She was a fool to believe in prophecy, to believe that greater powers communed with those on the mortal plane.

Yet wasn't she herself the instrument of a goddess?

Fine; so she had been chosen for some larger purpose, but Aquila had not. He was human and certainly not Incarn. And she now possessed Giahem's Wings. Could he be any help without the weapon? Why had she felt so sure that he would prove valuable? She was his enemy. Didn't that make him hers?

How could she trust him? Glancing sideways, Lluava saw Aquila gazing at the golden bow slung over her shoulder. How could she risk sleeping near him? He could take the weapon and run—or worse, kill her where she lay. Something had to be done.

"I must tie you up tonight," stated Lluava matter-of-factly.

"Why would I kill you now, when I could have before?"

So he had thought about it. This knowledge unsettled her even more. "I need insurance, since you have tried to harm me in the past."

"As do I. My people have a saying: A hungry lion is always your enemy. You have not eaten, she-tiger. You haven't fed all day."

"We can hunt tomorrow during our journey," she told him. It was a partial lie, for how could she trust him with any weapon? Rubbing her neck, she remembered what he was capable of doing with only a few strips of hide.

Aquila looked at her dubiously.

"I will not eat you. I'm not *that* hungry." Lluava added in a teasing manner, "And you're probably too gamy for my liking."

Though the nomad did not look amused, she did not sense the fear of death about him. Yet he was still hesitant.

"What?" she asked. "I will need you to keep watch for part of the night. So I do trust you, in a way."

"If I'm tied up, what do you expect me to do if the enemy appears?"

"Wake me."

Thankfully, Lluava did not have to resort to threats. Aquila grudgingly allowed her to tie his wrists and ankles. Then, settling himself next to his saddle pack, he said, "I'll take first watch." Before she could protest, he added, "You almost fell off your horse. You need sleep, now."

Tentatively, Lluava lay down on her saddle blanket after tucking the Wings beneath it. She turned to face him and forced her eyes shut, gripping her weapons tightly. Though she tried to keep her ears on alert, she was soon pulled into a haze of dark dreams.

A sudden nudge awoke her, and she lurched to her feet. Aquila hopped back to escape the swinging Claws.

"I'm sorry," Lluava said as she blinked away her mental fog. "Is it time already?"

"Yes. Unless you want me to keep watch the entire night."

"No. You sleep. It's my turn."

The night passed peacefully. Was that a cricket she heard? Had the weather warmed up enough for nymphs to become adults? Her breath no longer puffed out in milky bursts. Soon, trees would bud and leaves unfurl. For now, all Lluava could see was the sky sluggishly brightening as the sun fought to shine through the layer of clouds.

Aquila awoke on his own. Lluava had already saddled her horse when he asked, "Am I to stay bound?"

The idea would be a pleasing one, but Lluava untethered the nomad. And so the day began with little conversation between them, until Aquila halted his horse and pointed.

"Deer. Five of them."

Studying the imprints in the muddy earth, Lluava noted how fresh they were. Allowing her senses to heighten, she imagined the strong, gamy smell of fresh venison. Her mouth began to water.

"I require a knife," Aquila said as he rubbed his wrists. "To hunt, of course."

"Of course," Lluava responded hesitantly as she reluctantly handed over one of the blades.

Quickly, Aquila broke off a branch and began to strip it of leaves and twigs. "Lead the way," he said as he began whittling the tip into a point.

"After you," Lluava rebutted. She needed to keep both eyes on the nomad. He shrugged and allowed his horse to mosey after the whitetails.

Aquila used his spear skillfully; by dinnertime, the two were feasting on his catch. Even without the Wings, he could hunt with great accuracy. Lluava wanted to acknowledge his help but could not bring herself to voice the words. Instead, she kept her praise to herself and wondered if she should ask him to relinquish his new weapon.

As she approached him, he seemed to realize her intentions. "Tying me up again?"

"Unfortunately, yes."

The next several days passed in a mix of strained silences, occasional hunts, and uncomfortable sleeping shifts. The wind arose in harsh gusts, while the chill in the air refused to abate. Though the predicted storm never fully manifested, all nature seemed to be building to something fierce.

Then one day, they both exclaimed, "We are being tracked!" They blinked at their unanimous statement.

"When did you notice?" Lluava asked, hoping that she had known before him. Yet her answer never came. Instead, a long, solemn howl cleft the silence like a double-edged sword.

"Wolves," Aquila snarled as his horse shied sideways.

"No." She paused, sensing something else. "Theriomorphs." Moving her own steed close to Aquila's, she added, "Give me your wrists. I need to tie them."

"You don't know whether they are friend or foe," he hissed. "I am not about to relinquish my best source of defense."

"They are Theriomorphs," Lluava reaffirmed. "Which means that whether you are for or against Elysia, you will be viewed as their enemy. If they see you are my captive, they might allow you to live."

Aquila continued to glare at her.

Lluava implored, "Do not die today out of foolish pride."

He thrust his hands at her. Quickly binding the nomad, Lluava sensed an incoming blow to her face. Too late. The sharp kick knocked her off her horse and onto the thawing ground. Ears ringing, spitting out blood, she lurched to her feet. Aquila was gone. His horse remained next to hers, whickering.

Lluava had just enough time to clamber onto her mount before a pack of fifteen snarling canids burst from the underbrush. Struggling to keep her horse under control, she scanned the battle-scarred wolves. Aquila's abandoned mount ran, maddened, in panicked circles. Though the wolves were in rough shape, they clearly had a good bit of fight still left in them.

"Theri," a voice growled out. Lluava turned toward a large black male. "You are still alive."

"Derrick!" Lluava cried out and half fell off her horse as she moved toward the shifting creature. As soon as the young woman reached him, she embraced her dark-skinned friend. "I haven't seen you since—"

"You saved our lives," added the young soldier. "If only we could have done the same for you. If I had known you were not right behind us, I would have come back. You know this."

"Yes." Lluava gave his arm a quick squeeze.

Nodding toward the other horse, Derrick inquired, "Where is your companion?" Sniffing the air, he added, "There is a definite odor of…"

"One of the nomads from the south. He is gone now."

"Don't tell me they are attacking us, too."

"No. He is the only one in Elysia that I am aware of. He is not a threat," reassured Lluava.

"Things are going to get quite interesting," Derrick muttered to himself. Many of his men had already shifted. Two of them were holding the reins of the horses.

"The nomad is under my protection," Lluava hurriedly explained. "Leave him be."

"Oh, I am *sure* he is," noted Derrick as he glanced at Lluava's split lip. "Where are you coming from?"

"South." Lluava was happy to alert them. "Varren is alive and well. He is traveling with the Obsidian Guard to Amargo, where an army is amassing. He will take back his kingdom. You should go there. He will have great need of you."

"King Varren? Alive?" Derrick seemed more surprised than pleased at the news. "The gods are with him, then."

"One can hope," acknowledged Lluava, trying not to praise the divine.

"Why aren't you with him?"

"You know me," Lluava said vaguely. "I have a plan in the works. But truly, Varren has need of you."

"Well, there is a bit of an issue," admitted Derrick as he signaled one of his men. The redhead let loose a howl as Derrick went on, "We aren't working alone anymore."

Lluava's stomach knotted. "Who are you working with?"

The sound of hundreds of hoofbeats was heard by Lluava's heightening senses. The stench of sweat and men stung her nose. Her pupils narrowed automatically. Had Derrick turned, joining forces with Yena and the Outlanders? If so, she had just revealed the king's plans to the enemy.

But this was Derrick. They had trained together in the Southern Camps. He had proven himself a true Elysian. Moreover, he had always been one of Varren's most ardent supporters. He would not betray his country. He would never become a mercenary.

The thrum of approaching riders was growing. Lluava's mouth began to dry out. "Who are you with?"

Suddenly, a throng of riders galloped into sight and encircled them. Shouting and yipping with excitement, they snapped whips in the air and raised their spears. Lluava recognized one man as he broke away from the ring and approached.

Yamir smiled at her and said, "The Clans are happy to see that you are well, Theri."

Chapter 14

Crane and Lift

Lluava was momentarily at a loss for words.

Derrick barked out a laugh. "After our escape, Yamir led us to his family." He nodded toward the clansmen. "We have been living among them ever since."

"Hospitable hosts, I hope," Yamir teased as he slid off his horse.

"No better kind," joshed Derrick. Lluava had never seen the young man in such amiable spirits. His fierce and stoic view of the war had always made him appear a bit hard-hearted. Now, however, Derrick seemed unusually relaxed despite the situation.

Yamir's smile had also returned. Lluava had thought she'd never see that smile again. He resembled the youth who had antagonized the officers in the camps far more than he did the war-weary young man beaten down before the Fall. He still spiked his hair in his stylized fashion, but now his ruddy skin was decorated with many piercings as well as a small tattoo on his arm. With shredded fringes on his clothes, he looked every inch the clansman. Any sign of the Elysian soldier was gone. He had even donned an Endun outfit made of fragmented pieces of stolen cloth that was much the same as the garb his people wore.

Looking past Lluava, Yamir said, "Father, see who has returned to us."

Lluava spun around and spotted the leader of the Cloven-Hoofed Clan. At first, she thought he looked thinner, yet at second glance the rolls of fat appeared the same as before. Father's grin revealed a new golden tooth. When he spoke, the long, thin strands of facial hair that sprouted from each corner of his mouth rippled in the air along with his second and third chin. "Lluava, it seems ya can never be away from us fa' too long. I knew m' good looks were getting to ya."

With a grin, she shook her head and said, "I can't believe you all are alive and well."

"Oh, we are more than that," admitted Yamir. His oval-shaped eyes sparkled. "Every clan has come together. The Razor Back, the Silver Tongue, the Tri-Gilled, and all the others. A treaty between us has been made—grudgingly, mind you, but one where we all fight with a singular purpose. We are not going to be forced from our homeland by marauders from beyond the sea."

"How many are you?"

Father nodded at Yamir, who was one of the few in the clan who could count. "Three thousand fighting men. Another six if you want to add those willing to lay down their lives."

Lluava breathed excitedly, "That's amazing."

Derrick entered the conversation. "Lluava was just telling me that there is an army forming in Amargo to take back the kingdom." His words caught their attention. "She says that King Varren will lead them, and our help would be welcomed."

Yamir spat on the ground, and several others did the same. "To the seven hells with King Varren."

"He's your friend!" Lluava exclaimed aghast.

"He decreed that my people were to be slaughtered," Yamir retorted icily.

"That wasn't him. I told you that was Selene's doing. He had no—"

"Because of his decree, 672 good men, women, and children were slain. Their blood is on his hands. He is a butcher, just as is the Raiders' king."

Lluava couldn't breathe. She had not realized that the decree had taken so many lives before it was revoked. But Yamir needed to understand that his friend and king had been manipulated; he had not been himself.

"That man," began Father, "ate food at our table, slept under our tents, received our protection. He then had th' audacity of turnin' on us."

Though spoken much more calmly than Yamir, Father's rage was unquestionable. Derrick pressed a hand on Lluava's shoulder as a warning. So, they would be of no help to Varren's cause. What did that mean for the kingdom?

"We'll speak of th' young tyrant no more t'night. Instead, let us rejoice that a true friend has returned. Come, Lluava, let's break bread t'gether."

She hesitated but realized that her refusal would be perceived as ill-mannered and disrespectful. "I would be ever so pleased to partake of your hospitality."

As they headed toward the clans' camp, Lluava grew anxious. This break in her journey was not welcome, yet she felt forced to stay for supper that evening. Although her growing saddle sores rejoiced at their temporary reprieve and the sound of children's laughter was refreshing, her sense of peril grew.

Yamir had declared himself Varren's enemy, as had Father. Would they try to prevent Varren's return to the throne? Surely, Yamir would not want to kill the young king! These thoughts made Lluava's stomach queasy.

She waited near the wagon cages that had once held a sorry menagerie of performing animals. Now, they were only hollow shells. Was this what Cronus had become?

When supper was announced, Lluava made her way to the seat of honor, on a low bench at Father's right hand. Yamir was seated on his left. Derrick sat nearby with his brethren and half howled with laughter when some joke was told. All around the circle, clansmen talked and bickered and carried on; they did not seem concerned about the enemy in their homeland. Yet this façade would easily crumble if even a whisper of the Raiders' presence came to their ears.

After the third course of food was presented (on mismatched platters and serving ware), Father changed the direction of the conversation. "Why have ya come this way? Alone? Derrick mentioned ya are working on a plan of sorts."

Suddenly the honeyed wine seemed to cling to the inside of her throat, and Lluava coughed up the golden liquid. Father waited patiently for a response. She had to be careful. "I'm heading back to Cronus."

"The capital is overrun by th' Raiders. Ya should stay w' us where it is far safer."

"I wish I could, but I must be off in the morning."

"What's in Cronus, Lluava?" Yamir asked, beyond Father's shoulder.

She had to tell them something. Did Yamir even know about the Outlanders and the Fall? "I am seeking help to fight the Raiders."

Father guffawed. "The only thing that far north are traitors and th' sea brutes."

Although she wished to leave it at that, Lluava's hand was forced by Yamir.

"Lluava would never head into enemy territory without due cause," he said. Then her friend's eyes widened. "If Varren's in the south, something has happened to Cronus. The king would never have willingly left his throne."

Lluava felt a multitude of eyes upon her. "I let an army of Theriomorphs enter the capital, a group of Outlanders that I had met over the winter. They hold Cronus now. They follow the Old Ways, and their leader, a high priestess of Crocotta, turned on us and killed every human they found. We fled—the few of us that could. Talos and Rosalyn were left. I don't know if they escaped or not. The loss of the capital was my fault. I am doing what I can to undo that wrong."

"You said they were killing humans," began Yamir. "Talos and Rosalyn are not human."

At least he still cared about those friends; if only he viewed Varren in a better light. "I know. That's why Talos chose to stay. He said they would pledge allegiance to Yena, the priestess, in order to ensure their immediate safety."

"Why would he do that?" Yamir asked, as Derrick and his group moved closer to the conversation.

"Because Rosalyn is pregnant. They did not want to risk the child."

There was no time to be elated by such news. Derrick inquired, "So you are going back? For another rescue mission?"

"Not exactly," admitted Lluava. "Even if I found them and got them out, where would they go? Where is it safe? Our kingdom has fallen apart. There is no refuge. Not until all this fighting ends."

"What, then?" Yamir asked. Next to him, Father quietly listened.

"In order to defeat the Raiders, we need an army of massive proportions. Varren does not have that. Yena does not have that. But together, we would have a chance. I am going to Cronus to give Yena's people what they want if they will agree to join with Varren's troops and combat the Raiders."

"And what *do* they want?" Father asked.

Lluava felt all the others' eyes bore into her. "Me."

Some who overheard laughed, yet not one who knew Lluava made a sound until she explained. "They believe in the Old Ways. They believe that I am a host for Issaura, her Incarn, for her second coming. They believe that I will bear a child that will lead them into a better future. Because of this, they want me."

"Are you the one?" Derrick asked. His seriousness had returned.

"I think so."

Men's whispers fluttered around the camp like the wings of bats. Interest in Lluava spread like wildfire.

"You would turn yourself over to someone you view as an enemy?" Yamir was appalled. His belief in her was unquestioning, as was his faith in the pantheon. "You would give them that power?"

"I have to." Yamir looked displeased, but Lluava continued. "I have to try to make things right. The Raiders cannot win."

"That is for certain," snarled Derrick. His men were standing behind him. "We are coming with you."

"As is the Cloven-Hoofed Clan," Father announced. Then, taking a moment to stand up, he boomed, "Tomorrow, the Cloven-Hoofed Clan rides for Cronus to join the Theriomorph army!"

At a nearby campfire, an elderly man stood up and shouted, "As will the Silver Tongues!"

"And the Tri-Gills!" exclaimed a third.

Soon, every clan leader had proclaimed that they would join Yena's people.

Lluava beheld the hooting and hollering men. Had she just given Yena the army she needed? Had she destroyed Varren's chance to regain Elysia?

***

When morning's light encroached on the night's sky, the clans were ready to ride out. All of them. From the elderly to the newborn, all were prepared to make the journey. Lluava attempted to dissuade the men. "You need to know that we will most likely face the Berserker Legion. They are gigantic men that have inhuman properties. They—"

"We are well aware of the Berserkers," said Father sullenly. "They have slaughtered fellow clansmen and reduced our numbers."

"Then why risk your families? Fighting men, I understand, but them..."
Lluava gestured to the wagons that were already lined up.

"They cannot be abandoned. With our fighting men gone, what
protection would they have against enemies of any sort?"

So they came. All of them. Close to fifteen thousand strong. The slower
speed of this large a caravan would almost double the days it would take to
travel to the capital.

"You could leave them," Derrick whispered to her one night. His men
seemed unusually prepared for some anticipated order.

"They would follow, regardless," said Lluava as she scanned the circled wagons.

"They could get you killed," Derrick stated coldly. His dark skin barely
reflected the sliver of moonlight. "They make you an easy target."

"I could die either way. And they are my friends."

"Would you rather your friends die or yourself?"

"I would prefer all to live." Lluava let loose a large sigh. "At least now,
we are more attractive to Yena."

Derrick looked pleased at her response. He stared at the cloud-filled sky
that was strangling the moon. "It's as if the storm were waiting for the right
moment to break. Strange."

Stranger still was the shape hurtling down at them from above.

"Watch out!" Lluava yelled, as she pushed Derrick aside. She had seen too
many projectiles impale people. However, this one was different. Instead of the
expectant crash, there was not a sound when the object landed. Long and thin,
this was no spear or crossbow bolt. This was a sarus crane, standing erect.

"Ruire Thoth?" asked Lluava, for he was the only Theriomorph she had
met with that particular avian form.

The crane's sharp eyes seemed to quickly assess the number of clansmen
gathering around them. Shifting, the strong, wiry man replied, "Theri."

"You know that is not my name," Lluava retorted.

The kohl eyeliner made Thoth's eyes appear even fiercer. "You now
know that it is. Nevertheless, I have not come to bicker but to warn. You
must not continue to Cronus. It is not safe."

"Will ya refuse to let us in ya gates?" Father questioned. "We are
Theriomorphs come to serve our people."

"I know your intentions," noted Thoth as he adjusted the purple wrap
that covered many of the intricate tattoos on his torso. "You must cease your
journey immediately."

Lluava had to force herself not to fidget. Of course, Yena would have
been watching them in her mysterious pool of black water. Did she know the
real reason Lluava was coming to Cronus? Did Thoth?

"Do ya not want our help?" Father asked. "Even though we ride with
the Incarn of Issaura?"

Thoth glanced back in Lluava's direction. "The more reason for you to turn around. The Ocean Men have *real* monsters. *They* will kill you. All of you."

"Monsters?"

"What are you talking about?"

These and other questions were shouted by the crowd. With one sharp gesture of his hand, Thoth restored silence. "Their monsters are far worse than their bear-men."

"Bear-men? You mean the Berserkers. What else could there be?" questioned Yamir.

Lluava knew what he was thinking. There could not possibly be anything worse than those oversized brutes.

"The Ocean Men have something else with them. Though human in appearance, they are not. They cannot be." Thoth paused to look in the direction of the capital. "We thought we knew the enemy. We were wrong. We have entombed ourselves behind the walls. There is no escape for us."

"Then how did you?" Lluava asked dubiously. Certainly, this was just a ploy to keep her away from the Outlanders. "Escape, I mean. If you flew away, why can't others?"

Pulling aside his wrap, Thoth exposed the broken shaft of an arrow protruding under the inked rune for honor on his chest. "I doubt that I will be returning to Cronus."

"Find a healer," a Razor Back clansman shouted.

"Somebody get Grandmother," ordered Father.

Thoth ignored those scrambling to help him. "I was sent to ensure that you and your army would not meet the same fate as ours. You are too important to our future, Theri."

"Why would the high priestess send you, the Ruire, the ruler of the Outlander people, if she knew you would surely die?" Lluava questioned.

"Would you have believed this warning from anyone else other than the high priestess?"

The faces of Apex, Talos, and Rosalyn appeared in Lluava's mind. If Yena's people would die, so would they. "Return to Cronus," Lluava affirmed. Her voice was deadly calm. "They have medicine that can save you. You know this to be true. At the very least, try."

Thoth considered her thoughtfully. Their relationship had always been one of distrust.

"If you make it," she said, "tell Yena to ready the lift at the rear of the city. We will arrive soon."

Chapter 15

Murder Is Great

Addressing them all, Lluava explained, "There is a lift designed to deliver goods directly to the markets in Cronus. It is large enough to hoist several wagonloads of people at a time. It is our best option to enter the capital without encountering the Raiders' army positioned at the main gate."

"But the lift was badly damaged when you helped me escape," Yamir reminded her.

Looking directly at Thoth, Lluava affirmed, "That's true. So it must be repaired immediately."

The Ruire's expression did not change. "*She* told me what you would say; she said to tell you, if you must come, do not approach Cronus until the new moon has passed and word has been received. Any sooner will mean certain destruction for those who follow you."

"How could she—?" Derrick began, but Lluava waved him silent.

Although Yamir did not question Yena's ability, he was not happy with the plan. "That's three days from now. We could arrive tomorrow if we pushed ourselves."

Father scanned his people. "A rest would be much appreciated. I have no issue with caution."

"Nor do I," admitted Lluava. "But on the night after the new moon, we *will* be at Cronus."

"High Priestess Yena will be waiting," said Thoth. He shifted and flew off without delay.

Lluava hoped he would survive the journey back. If he did not, or if the lift was not repaired, how many would die seeking entry into the capital?

"That was strangely easy," noted Yamir as he spat on his hand to re-twist a spike of hair. "I would suspect foul play."

"Yena needs to keep me alive. She will do everything in her power, even if it places her own people at risk, to ensure this. Thoth might not like me, but he knows that I am essential to the high priestess's cause. The lift will be ready."

At least, that is what she hoped. If Yena ever doubted the young woman's value or questioned the prophecy, Lluava and the clansmen could be left to die unaided at the hands of the Raiders.

Turning away from the direction of the capital, she said, "We must fortify our camp."

The clan leaders did not rebuke her, even though she had no right to command them. Then again, it was a simple order.

"What's on your mind?" Derrick inquired, which was quite unlike him.

Lluava shared her troublesome thoughts. "I'm wondering how we are going to get all these people inside Cronus."

The question worried her. She gestured at the numerous unhitched wagons. Restless children were jumping from their wheeled homes to stretch their legs at no less than full sprints on the ground. The elderly were helped off the wagons; some were carried to blanketed seats on the cold earth near newly made cooking fires. There were enough people to populate a small town. All believed that safety would be found behind Cronus's high walls.

"We aren't," Derrick answered.

Appalled, Lluava looked at the dark-skinned soldier.

Grunting, Derrick grimly explained, "You must prepare yourself, Lluava. Even if the gods smile on us, there is no way that a migration this large will escape the enemy's notice. We will be discovered, if we haven't been already. We will pay for this with many lives."

"But...if we..." Lluava stammered, unsure what to say.

"People are going to die. Even you, Incarn of Theri, cannot prevent that. All we can do is try to minimize our losses, many though they may be." Derrick patted her shoulder solemnly before heading off to see his fellow comrades.

Onyx, who had been patrolling the terrain, alighted on Lluava's other shoulder. He muttered into her ear, which did not help the gnawing pain now tormenting her stomach.

"What am I to do, Onyx?" Lluava questioned as she continued to observe the clansmen's activities.

Snapping his beak, Onyx cocked his good eye up to the nearby trees. Small, dark silhouettes of the raven's kin clustered above. They seemed to be watching the camp hungrily.

She shivered.

That night, rest abandoned Lluava. Giant forms lurked in the corners of her smoke-shrouded dreams. A face—no, just a broad nose with flaring nostrils—inhaled the dark-stained air deeply. Now a beard and hair the color of blackening blood framed emerging features. Though not real, they seemed as harsh as a sea storm that consumes a fleet in a blink of an eye. Eyes. The eyes held a flame that resembled a fire found only in the seven hells. These searching eyes bored through Lluava as if she were no more than a ghost or a vanishing zephyr.

The head turned on a neck pulsing with black veins. With each pulse, Lluava felt her own pulse beat in time with it. Thump. Thump. Her heart strained to match the other's. Thump. Thump. The beating grew more rapid. Thump, thump. Her heart was racing now, confined by the fear that tethered it to the monstrous figure before her. Thump-thump. Thump-thump.

She could hear the salt-encrusted lips crack as they parted. "Murder is great."

Jerking awake, Lluava gasped, "What?"

A pair of startled clansmen jumped in surprise at her sudden movement. One pointed to the flocks of crows in the early morning sky. "I said, 'th' murder's a great many.'"

Under the cloud-choked sun, the massing crows joined with groups of ravens and numerous buzzards. The heralds of death were circling above the future victims.

"We need to leave," Lluava said to no one in particular. Wiping the chilled sweat from her brow, she tied her unkempt hair into a knot at the base of her neck. Then she found Father's wagon and called to him, "We must head to Cronus immediately."

There was a fit of hacking and coughing before the mammoth man climbed out of the covered wagon. "What is it ya said?"

"We need to leave as soon as possible."

"I thought th' agreement was that we wait a bit." Father hacked again and spat out a wad of phlegm.

"We are a target here. The longer we wait, the more likely we will be found."

"What of th' lift? Ya think it will be ready 'n time?"

"We need to chance it."

From a neighboring wagon, Yamir called out, "What's happening?"

"Ya friend here says we should leave now," alerted Father. Then, returning to the prior conversation, he asked, "What ya know, Lluava?"

"Something is coming for us. Something big."

Father furrowed his brow. He harrumphed once, then twice. Although he waved Yamir over to help him off the wagon, his massive weight still caused him to land heavily. The thin strands of facial hair twitched agitatedly as he shuffled about. "What chance will we 'ave if we can't get over the wall?"

"What chance would we have if we were discovered here?" Lluava knew Father was not appeased. "I can't really explain why I feel that we must push forward. Something inside me is telling me so."

"You sure that's not just fear?" questioned Yamir earnestly.

Father's voice boomed out, though not intentionally, "Theriomorphs all 'ave a special ability, Lluava. Th' not as special as ya' select Incarn, I suppose, we still 'ave a natural instinct. It's said that humans once were much th' same. But they lost this gift as they began to rely less on the land and to live more in towns and cities. Heeding this sixth sense 'as kept our species alive on more than one occasion. It is a privilege that not many choose to benefit from nowadays. But when we do listen to it..." Father looked out over the sprawling camp. His features changed, and he growled out, "We will head toward Cronus come noon."

Yamir looked vexed. He bent over and spoke directly into Lluava's ear. "Since I know you won't, I will pray to the gods that you are not wrong."

Above them, the caws and sharp cries of the winged scavengers grew louder.

**

With the sun directly overhead, the wagon train began to slowly lurch northward. Lluava rode near the front, for she could not stand the grumblings of the unhappy crowd. Derrick plodded next to her in his wolf form. Lluava's horse, though accustomed to his scent, continued to eye the canine warily.

"You don't agree with this, do you?" Lluava asked. Though none had rebuked her, she was aware that many were displeased by the sudden departure.

"Actually, I do," acknowledged the black wolf. "Look at them." He nodded toward the sky. The massing flock of birds flew about in no particular order. "They are a screeching alarm that we are here. We need to keep moving."

Lluava shivered again. "Do you think the Raiders know about us yet?"

"I have sent my troop members on perimeter patrols. They will scout out and alert us if an enemy approaches."

"Let's hope we don't hear a warning howl anytime soon."

Lluava peered back at Yamir. He looked fierce with all his metallic piercings sparkling in the light. The gauges he had wedged in his ears were made of long canine teeth, and his bare chest sported a painted pattern associated with the warriors of his clan.

"What happened to him, Derrick?"

"I heard that Father might make him his heir."

"That's amazing. I wonder why he has not told me yet?"

"You do realize what that means?" questioned Derrick as he snapped at a biting fly. The spring temperature was warming enough for insects to appear.

Lluava thought for a moment. "That he will command the Cloven-Hoofed Clan and assume the role of Father for his people."

Derrick huffed, "A people who are the sworn enemy of the Mandrun line. If he accepts that role, he must permanently separate himself from Elysian society. He will never be allowed at court, at the capital, or in any city. He will denounce the monarchy, the government, and the very structure of our kingdom. In many ways, he will represent everything you have been fighting against."

Could Yamir really embody all of that? Lluava shook her head. He is just angry. Until he has had time to let go of some of his blind hatred, he will never be able to understand and accept the truth about the recent past.

Derrick seemed to read her thoughts. "Some people cannot let go of their anger. It becomes part of them."

Lluava thought of Aquila. The nomad had pushed aside his hatred of her. He had been willing to help them in the war—that is, until Lluava said she would have to rebind him against his better judgment. She was wrong to have asked that of him. Anyway, he was gone now. Find your way home, Aquila. Get far, far away from this place. Evil *is* all about.

***

When the great walls of Cronus came into view, the large caravan went on high alert. Many of the clans' finest warriors joined Derrick's men in protecting the perimeter. With the flocks of carrion-eaters close behind, they anticipated an attack. Wagons that contained children, the elderly, or the infirm were positioned in the middle of the train, while those carrying able-bodied people were on either end so they could protect their weaker clan members.

The extreme tension caused many to jump whenever they heard a twig snap or saw a shadow move in the strengthening breeze. For the last several days, the wind had never died down completely; it waited as patiently as a night cat about to ambush its prey. Now, the air stirred with activity. People whispered that it was a sign some higher power watched their progress, although they questioned for whose benefit.

Derrick kept pace with Lluava whenever he was not on patrol. She enjoyed his company, since she had neither Varren nor Apex by her side. Slowly, the walls of the capital rose above them like a titan. She noted how the spiderwebbing trails of red lichen and blue-gray moss had begun to grow like veins and arteries over the ancient stone backdrop.

Gesturing to the left, Lluava said, "The lifts are a little farther that way."

"It seems that our welcoming party is ready," responded the large wolf as he spied the distant faces peering over the parapets. A few figures scurried around, while others watched, transfixed by the sight of the approaching caravan.

Thoth must have made it back safely. Why else would Yena's men not sound an alarm? They were expecting them. Lluava had been right to make the clans leave, although she knew it was neither instinct nor her goddess's guidance that had led her to make that choice. Fear, no matter what source, could also help at times. Safety was in sight.

A rider approached from the rear. Yamir reigned in his horse on the other side of Derrick. "This was a mistake. Something is not right." Yamir's obvious apprehension ran counter to everything she had been thinking. Beads of sweat peppered his ruddy brow. "If the crane said that the Raiders would kill anyone that attempted to leave Cronus, why did they allow us to get so close to the capital? Don't say it's because they don't know we are here."

Lluava looked worriedly over at Derrick. He, too, seemed caught off guard.

It was Derrick who stated what they now all understood. "We have walked into a trap."

"Alert everyone to head to the lift as quickly as possible," commanded Lluava as the hairs on the back of her neck began to rise.

Yamir wheeled his horse around and spurred it on to spread the word. As Derrick turned to assist with the notification, the echo of a wolf howl reverberated from the right rear.

"The Raiders are approaching," snarled the lupine. "I'll help defend."

But before he could run off, another howl burst forth, this time from the left. Then another from up ahead.

"We are surrounded," growled Derrick.

The lifts were in sight. Lluava exclaimed, "We have to prevent them from cutting us off!" Turning, she shouted to those behind her, "Everyone, to the lift!"

No one questioned the young woman's command. The cracking of cart whips and the whickering of spurred horses confirmed that her order was being followed. Charging forth, Lluava and Derrick raced ahead in hopes of preventing the enemy from reaching their target first. More howls pierced the once-quiet spring day. They were accompanied by the beating of war drums and the cawing of excited crows.

Reaching the base of the lift, Lluava leaped from her horse with Issaura's Claws at the ready. She did not care if the frightened beast bolted; her only concern was to see if the lift was in working order.

Above her, the large platform stood frozen in its position at the top of the wall.

"We're here!" Lluava shouted above the growing din. "Lower the lift! Lower the lift!"

Where was everybody? Atop the wall, not a figure moved. The lift lay immobile above them.

"Somebody lower the lift!" Lluava screamed.

Nearby, Onyx attacked a crow, plucking tail feathers out of his smaller kin. The crow cawed out in panic, flapping wildly, trying to escape.

With each exasperated caw, Lluava recalled the terrifying voice from her dream: "Murder. Murder! Murder is great!"

Chapter 16

Ring of Fire

The first wagon arrived, and still the lift had not moved. Just out of sight, the enemy was encroaching. The clansmen were trapped in an ambush of their own design.

"Get ready to fight," snarled Derrick, baring his sharp teeth. His raised hackles made him look even larger.

A horn blasted. The Raiders were nearly upon them.

"Where is your lift?" demanded Father as he lowered himself from his wagon.

Yamir stood next to him, scowling fiercely. Lluava knew this was exactly what she had feared. From a pouch about his waist, he pulled out several long porcupine quills. The sharp barbs were ready for him to expertly throw into their fleshy targets.

From the wagons, a baby squalled, increasing the tension unbearably as its mother tried to silence it. Then long, inhuman shadows, cast on the ground by the horned helmets of three gigantic forms, emerged from the forest-lined road. Behind them, a line of Raiders held their weapons at the ready.

Lluava glanced down at her distorted reflections in the Claws. Each Claw's three curved blades reflected a different fragment of her face. She watched her pupils narrow into sharp, javelin-like slits; she felt the cool metal counter the boiling heat in her core as it spread to her extremities. Shifting, Lluava raked the earth with her gilded foreclaws and let out a deafening roar.

The central Berserker removed the war hammer strapped to his back. His companions followed suit with battle-axe and mace. They approached slowly, dragging their weapons lazily behind them. Lluava could smell the drug-tainted smoke from their breaths. Her muzzle crinkled in disgust.

A heavy groan, like that of a man adjusting an injury to seek some relief, came from above. Risking a glance, Lluava saw the lift lurch slightly before it slowly began to make its way to the base of the wall.

More wagons arrived, and Lluava growled, "Get the families onto the lift—the children and those unable to fight!"

Several men responded to the order and began to organize the first group. Lluava had to turn her attention back to the enemy. A line of clansmen, their war paint showing, lined up just behind Lluava and her two friends.

"Ready?" Derrick snarled.

Yamir echoed, "Ready."

With a quasi-bestial roar, Lluava shouted, "Charge!"

The Berserkers did not run toward them. Instead, they strolled at a leisurely pace until the clansmen were within swinging range. Lluava and her friends slowed to avoid the first strike, but others were not as fortunate. A Berserker's mace ripped flesh and bone from the first pair of clansmen that met his weapon. A stunted scream was heard from the victim of the axe.

The tigress leaped at the arm wielding the war hammer, while the black wolf rushed behind the brute, hoping to tear his Achilles tendons. Once grounded and disarmed, the Berserker would not pose as great a threat. This tactic had worked before. Would it work again?

Yamir's dual form, a porcupine, was not as quick-footed as the others, so he stayed in human form, where his throwing quills could do their damage. These small projectiles whistled past Lluava's ears; one even brushed against her sensory whiskers. Their targets were the charging second line of Raiders; several collapsed as Yamir's quills pierced their eye sockets or jugulars.

Lluava's foreclaws sank into the Berserker's thick leather arm brace. As she stood on her hind legs to wrestle him down, she felt his massive free hand grip her rear leg to pull her off. His steady tug caused Lluava's grip to loosen. She gave one huge jerk, and the brace tore free of his arm. The tigress tumbled to the ground, claws still embedded in the leather casing. Before she had time to lash out, the giant dropped his war hammer and grabbed the feline by the nape of her neck.

Tightening his two-handed grip, the Berserker hoisted her off the ground and tried to pull her apart. It felt like being tortured on a rack. The helpless animal kicked and slashed at the Berserker's face. Her claws knocked off his helmet, sending it clattering to the ground. Lluava's muscles and tendons were stretched taut. She could do little more than emit a high-pitched scream. No aid would come from her friends, who were engaged in desperate battles of their own.

From the corner of her eye, she saw Father shift into a giant walrus. The beast bellowed and stabbed at oncoming Raiders with his huge tusks, protecting the first group of his people as they slowly lurched upward on the overburdened lift.

A sharp pain erupted in Lluava's side as a muscle tore. Uselessly, she kicked out again. Every groove she carved in the Berserker's chest bled unnoticed. She was being ripped apart in this monstrosity's huge hands.

Something stirred inside her; the goddess was waking. Was it time to release her? Looking into the bloodshot eyes of her would-be killer, she saw little humanity left unsuppressed by the drug. She was nothing more than a hindrance to his sole objective, slaughter. Suddenly his blue eyes glazed over.

Before his lifeless hands dropped her, Lluava had only a moment to marvel at the handmade arrow shaft that had bored into the Berserker's huge skull. She landed on her side and barely managed to scramble out of the way before the mammoth corpse collapsed. Two other arrows repelled attackers, allowing her a chance to regroup.

Who was her savior? Lluava could not tell where the arrows came from. Archers atop the wall shot projectiles taken from the stockpiles in the royal armory; the arrows that had saved her were hand-cut, and tipped only with the hewn points of the wooden shafts.

Her thanks would have to wait. More Raiders circled the tigress, attempting to stab her with their rapiers. They were five to her one, yet she knew they were all doomed. Did they?

Color began to drain from Lluava's vision; only crimson dared stand out against the blue-green-tinted world as that thing inside her, her second self, took over. She no longer had control of her body, yet she could still sense every inch of herself. Her mind acquired a surreal clarity, and she knew instantly what needed to be done to slay all who opposed her.

As if manipulated by an invisible puppeteer, the tigress attacked. Her body moved fluidly; tooth and claw hit every mark. Lluava could visualize every action of those around her moments before they actually occurred. She countered them with ease. The Raiders were felled in a calculated order that was not of her design.

With five corpses at her feet, Lluava turned to the rest of the battle. The second Berserker was dead, but the third, his clothing splattered with bits of brain and blood, continued to ravage the clansmen.

The ring of defenders shrank as some were killed and others hoisted to safety. The lift was descending again, but far too slowly. Four rope ladders, made up of multiple smaller ones knotted end to end, now hung down from the parapets. Although those in Cronus were doing what they could to help, Lluava knew it wasn't enough.

On one of the wagons, Yamir and another clansman were busy. A few others of their clan distracted several attackers to give them time to complete their mysterious work. Close by, Derrick rabidly ripped into a Raider who kept striking the wolf with a dagger.

Lluava ran in the direction of her lupine friend. Grabbing the foul-tasting Raider in her great maw by the back of his shoulder, she pulled the screaming man back into the woods. A clansman rushed up to assist Derrick to the lift, a trail of blood in their wake.

Spitting out a mouthful of remains from the body on the ground in front of her, Lluava bounded to the final Berserker. He was pulling his mace out of what she assumed was an elder's body. Void of emotion, the behemoth looked at her and grunted, "Theri."

Feeling no fear or anger or pain, the tigress vaulted forward, her gilded claws clashing with the spiked weapon. As before, she knew exactly when the Berserker would gasp his final, gurgling breath. She was oddly aware of everything around her; yet at the same time it seemed as if she and this gigantic enemy were the only living things that existed. Then it was over.

As arrows flew down and various weapons whirred about them, Lluava continued her choreographed dance of destruction. Her white fur now tinted red, Lluava shook off the hellish droplets and moved to where she was needed next.

The ring of wagons separating the Raiders and the clansmen suddenly burst into a scorching wall of flame. Yamir! He had created a line of defense. Another load of refugees neared the top of the wall, but there were still too many clansmen waiting to ascend. As the battle inched closer to the circle of fire, Raiders began to shoot crossbow bolts at the lift's ropes. One hit its mark and snapped a few cords.

Defenders atop the wall continued their counter-fire. A Raider with a crossbow was struck down next to Lluava. She somehow knew to move in a strange, unpredictable pattern as another wave of arrows struck the battlefield. No projectile touched her.

The Raiders were quickly outnumbering the remaining clansmen. The enemy archers began to shoot at those riding the lifts. One bolt hit a far deadlier mark, and the rope holding one corner of the platform snapped. Those on the lift clung to any hold they could find as the device struggled to hoist them to safety. Several unlucky ones fell off as the platform shifted to an angle. Far too high, they died at the feet of their kin.

Panic.

The truce between clans was broken; the men at the base of the lift began fighting one another to clamber up one of the rope ladders. A Tri-Gill stabbed a Razor Back. A member of the Saw Tooth Clan grabbed the leg of a Silver Tongue above him on a ladder, causing the man to fall. The enemy used the disarray to their advantage and easily targeted the terrified clansmen.

The warriors on the field retreated in wild disorder. Many risked horrid burns as they ran through the flames to reach the ladders. Above them, the survivors on the lift scrambled off with the assistance of the Outlanders.

As Lluava charged a Raider attempting to rearm his crossbow, screams erupted at the wall. One of the ladders had come apart at its knotted connections. The remaining ladders appeared secure, for the moment.

The tigress took down a marauder by slashing at his thick-bearded throat. He would not shoot another helpless victim. Nearby, a second Raider took aim at her. Before he could draw his bow, he collapsed from one of those makeshift arrows. This time, Lluava saw the shooter—Aquila.

As soon as she spotted him, a strange understanding took over. In the final moments before Lluava was released from her connection with the goddess, she knew she had to protect him.

"Head to the ladders!" Lluava shouted at the nomad as her vision and senses abruptly returned to normal. "We need to get to safety."

"How?" questioned Aquila as he loosed several more shots. His targets collapsed in unnatural heaps. "The fire is too big."

He was right. The wall of flames crackled threateningly. Lluava could feel the intense heat even at this distance. Behind them, more Raiders were emerging from the forest.

"Climb onto my back," she said, crouching low.

With her living cargo clinging to her fur, Lluava loped along the line of fire. Ahead, she spotted an abandoned wagon whose axle had broken, leaving it dipping down at the front. It was the lowest point and their best bet for entry.

Getting a running start, the tigress leaped into the flames. Her rear paws had to spring off the front of the wagon to make sure they landed clear of the trailing sparks. Her scorched feet stung. Blisters would appear on her pads before long. Fortunately, Aquila was unhurt, though he slapped at an ember burning a tiny hole in his shorts.

The crowd of clansmen was packed close together. Everyone was at odds and fighting for the chance to clamber to safety. Father was still on the ground in his dual form. His tusks were tipped with the blood of Raiders. Seeing Lluava, he bellowed, "Let Theri through! Let the Incarn pass!"

Despite their palpable fear, the throng moved aside to allow the blood-smeared tigress and her companion to pass. At the base of a ladder, a man from a clan Lluava could not identify refused to give up his spot in line. Lluava would have been patient, but a second figure punched the man first, so hard that he crumpled to the ground, unconscious.

Cursing, the second man spat at the collapsed party. "She is our savior!"

Without hesitating, Lluava shifted to human form. "Aquila, you go first."

Quick as a monkey, he began to climb. Lluava followed, inches below his heels.

The sounds of crackling erupted as one of the burning wagons collapsed in upon itself, while another's timber began to fall outward. She risked a glance over her shoulder and saw that the Raiders were using these gaps in the fire line as entry points, hacking their way into the inner circle.

Father defended his people mightily; however, the flood of opponents was too great.

"No!" Lluava screamed, as a Raider thrust his lance into the clan leader's side. In spite of the wound, Father drove his tusk deep into the enemy's chest.

Unable to remove the corpse, Father bellowed his death cry as he was butchered by a swarm of seafaring men.

A crossbow bolt grazed Lluava's thigh before shattering against the stone wall. Above her, Aquila shouted, "Move, she-tiger!"

Fighting back the burning tears, Lluava hoisted herself over the parapet and collapsed onto its walkway. She could hear the screams of those still trapped at the base of the wall. Male and female, young and old—corralled like sheep, they stood no chance.

"They're on the ladders!" cried an Outlander as he shot his longbow. Next to him, Aquila took aim with his strung sapling.

"Cut them down! All of them!"

Lluava recognized the stoic, rumbling voice of Ammit. The tall man with leathery skin stared down at the chaos, his wide mouth pursed. Two Outlanders followed his command immediately and brought axes to the top of the ladders.

"Stop!" Lluava shouted as she hobbled behind them, but it was too late. Looking through an embrasure, she saw everything in what felt like slow motion. The rope ladders were severed. The ascending climbers' faces were struck with fear as they fell into the inferno. Their drawn-out screams grew silent. Those still alive at the base of the wall lost hope.

"Murderer!" Lluava shouted as she turned on Ammit. The man made no move as she approached. "You killed them all!" she cried out in hysterical sobs. "Somebody, lower the lift! Lower the lift!"

No one moved.

"It is done," Ammit said, turning to look at her. He calmly clasped his hands behind his back.

Shaking with rage, Lluava wanted nothing more than to attack the man before her. Instead, she said, "There were so many more we could have saved! You have condemned them to death!"

Ammit simply replied, "The enemy were climbing the ladders. They could not be permitted to reach the top."

Taking a ragged breath, Lluava implored, "They're all going to die."

"They were already dead," came a voice from behind her.

Lluava turned slowly and beheld High Priestess Yena. She was dressed in a silver Endun bodysuit. Her cropped gray hair shone bright against polished skin of the blackest hue. Yena's all-but-white irises looked kindly at Lluava, as a mother does when about to teach her daughter a difficult lesson. The priestess's thick, smoky voice continued, "You were warned of this. Yet you did not listen. They died because of you."

Chapter 17

The Jackal in the Room

Sinking to her knees, Lluava struggled to understand. She heard her own ragged breath but not the hysterical shouts and barked orders. Tears blurred her vision, and she couldn't focus. She was unaware of the figures strapping large, lidded vessels onto the damaged lift. Nor did she notice the Outlanders restraining Aquila at Ammit's command. She barely registered the lift plummeting to the ground when the ropes were severed.

The colossal booming of explosions and a towering column of fire blasting to the top of the wall jarred Lluava to her senses. The screams from below were silenced.

Yena contemplated the billowing smoke. "*I* am merciful."

Lluava was unable to say or do anything. Her body felt frozen as she watched the high priestess turn and leave. Until Ammit ordered, "Throw the human over the wall."

"I wouldn't do that," said Lluava quietly. Rising on shaky legs, she limped over to the Theriomorphs who struggled to restrain Aquila. She positioned one of Issaura's Claws under a restrainer's jaw.

"Release him."

Nearby, Ammit stared at her, his face emotionless. "Humans are not allowed inside New Rhadamanthus."

"He is an exception," hissed Lluava as she pressed the Claw into the man's flesh. Beads of blood dripped down the golden weapon. The restrainer stiffened.

"There are no exceptions."

"The high priestess will want the nomad alive. Where is she?"

Yena had already left for the castle. Something had to be done to save Aquila. Growling at Ammit, Lluava threatened, "Kill him now, and you will deal with *her* repercussions."

The young woman waited in deadly seriousness, daring anyone to doubt her. The priestess was too far away to be easily summoned. If Lluava's claim was true, Aquila could not be killed at the wall.

"High Priestess Yena *will* want him alive, I assure you."

"Take the human to the Judgment Hall," Ammit ordered, then spoke directly to Lluava. "The high priestess will decide his fate."

Lluava chose not to look over the wall during the prolonged trek to the stairs; she knew the sight would haunt her forever. Moving slowly on her blistered feet, she agonized, wondering how in the seven hells she could convince the high priestess to give Aquila amnesty. Her leverage was gone; Giahem's Wings had been left in Father's wagon. If the bow survived the fire, it would surely be seized by the Raiders.

By the time they arrived at the castle, she still had not come up with a solution. Aquila never looked at her. This was good, for she was certain her face would alert him to the futility of his situation.

The Judgment Hall was the renamed Grand Hall, the former royal throne room. Entering, Lluava half expected to see Varren seated upon the tall, ornate chair. But a new ruling power held Cronus, and Yena was its head.

From her vantage point on the dais, the high priestess watched them enter. The chamber's raised seating had once held the stern faces of the High Council in life and their rotting corpses in death. Now, a new panel of judges waited. Robed in black and sporting their gruesome obsidian masks, the Guardians, like evil effigies, rigidly observed those entering.

Yet this mattered little to Lluava, for it was those perched on the minor thrones to either side of Yena who drew her attention. The Incarn had replaced the royal family. The twins, Luka and Selene, exchanged a knowing glance, while Apex appeared unconcerned.

Apex was alive!

Lluava had always hoped this was true, but his final, echoing cry to her in Tartarus's cavern had sounded like his last. But he was alive and even looked well. Everything was the same: the stubble on his face, his dark hair that gleamed like copper in the sunlight, his fierce golden eyes flecked with red. He was alive. And seated next to Selene.

A low rumble began in Lluava's throat. Selene, the seductress, appeared more desirable than ever. Her gown dipped so low that her two perfect blessings almost broke free of the laced bodice. Her coppery skin complemented the rouge on her lips and the gemstones tucked into her luscious locks.

Lluava wanted to snap those slender shoulders, choke the woman with the silver teardrop necklace nestled above her breasts. There had been a time when Lluava was embarrassed by her unfeminine body and yearned to look more like Selene. Now, she was proud of her own sinewy form, her power and strength. She was a warrior and looked nothing like the epitome of feminine beauty—but she had no need to use trickery and enchantments to force men to love her.

Ammit knelt at the base of the dais and began to speak. His words were lost to Lluava's ears as she continued to stare at Apex. He was constantly glancing at Selene, and the pair would lock eyes for a drawn-out moment. Lluava instantly recognized what was occurring: Apex was under Selene's spell.

Anger flamed up within Lluava, but this time it *was* tinged with jealousy. Why did Selene covet the men she loved? Wait—did she actually love Apex? That would be impossible if she were still in love with Varren. Or could someone actually love two people at the same time? Regardless, Lluava was certain Selene knew what she was doing. This seduction was meant to hurt Lluava, and it was succeeding.

"What have you to say, Lluava?"

Blinking, Lluava looked at Yena, who was patiently waiting for her response. "C…Can you repeat the question?"

"Why is the human's life of value?"

"Because," Lluava fumbled, "he was in possession of Giahem's Wings."

Yena looked sharply over at Aquila, who was being forced to kneel, then back at Lluava. "Where is Giahem's Wings?"

Lluava felt a bead of sweat roll down her face. Aquila's life would be determined by her answer, and the answer was not what Yena wanted to hear. "It is—"

"Here!" Yamir's voice rang out from the back of the room. Lifting up the golden weapon, the clansman was allowed to approach the base of the dais to deposit the bow.

Moving fluidly, Yena descended the steps to pick up the weapon. As she inspected it, Yamir took a moment to gather himself. From his tear-streaked face, Lluava knew he had seen what had happened to Father and the others who lost their lives at the wall.

"Lluava was storing the bow in one of our wagons. I saw it as I was rigging them to burn and knew it was important." He gazed at Issaura's Claws. "I made sure that it reached the top of the wall."

The twins leaned down to get a better look. Pale and gangly, Luka appeared nothing like his adopted sister. His dark hair was speckled with white. Both watched intently as Yena attempted to pull back the golden string, to no avail. She handed it to Ammit, but the strong, muscular man could not budge the gleaming twine.

"This is indeed Giahem's Wings," said Yena once the bow was back in her possession. "It has been returned to us." She stroked the smooth side until she reached the runes on the handle. "Yet my question remains. Why is the human's life of value?"

Now that the high priestess had authenticated the bow, Lluava roared out, "Because he can wield it!"

A Guardian's muffled voice was heard. "Impossible."

"Please. Let him show you," Lluava implored, yet still Aquila was not released. "High Priestess, if he can wield a god's weapon, that must mean something. Shouldn't it?"

Yena nodded. The captive was allowed to slowly approach and take hold of the bow. In a single smooth movement, Aquila drew the string back and released it. The resounding, low-pitched twang echoed around the room like rumbling thunder.

The high priestess moved close to the nomad. Her eyes studied his every feature, pausing at the line of crusting blood on his tanned forehead. Then she quickly turned about, ascended her throne, and stated nonchalantly, "The human will live."

Lluava released a sigh of relief as Yena continued, "Assign the human and the rest of our new guests quarters, and provide them food and medicine."

Unabashed, Aquila spoke out. "I want to stay with the she-tiger."

This was certainly unexpected. Until recently, the nomad had sworn to kill Lluava. Fortunately, the high priestess was not upset by the human's disrespectful attitude. A slight smile appeared at the corner of her mouth. "As you wish."

Before Lluava could retreat to her former rooms, Yena's voice broke out again. "I have one more question. Why have you returned, Incarn of Theri?"

Lluava needed a reason, and not the real one, to offer the waiting priestess. "As you said, I am the Incarn of Theri. I cannot deny that. As an Incarn, my place is alongside you and the other Incarn. I cannot abandon the Theriomorphs who fight here. I have a responsibility, a duty, one I was created for. I must fulfill it now."

Understanding that the best lies come from truth, Lluava looked around at the Guardians. None moved or spoke. "I left during the uprising in order to get Varren to safety. You know that. I also believe that you were aware of my affection for him. He was my military partner and my friend. You may not agree with my actions, but I could not watch my friend die, even if it would have been better for my race. That was a selfishness I fully admit to and will continue to defend. Yet, after helping him escape, I realized that I could not abandon you. So, I have come back to help. You may not believe me, but I have come to finish this fight."

In a voice like the rustling of dry leaves, a Guardian inquired, "How can we trust you?"

"You may never find it in yourselves to trust me," acknowledged Lluava. "But I am here to defeat the Raiders. I have brought with me the clans, who still stand by the old faith, and Aquila, who can wield Giahem's Wings."

Whispered words fluttered up to the vaulted ceiling as the Guardians deliberated. Yena seemed to capture everything that was said. Finally, she lifted one ebony hand, silencing all. "Crocotta is the Mother Goddess. And what is a mother who cannot forgive a misguided child? Go to your chambers, Lluava. Rest. We will speak later."

Bowing slightly in feigned respect, Lluava slowly made her way to her rooms. Her seared feet throbbed with every step. Even though the Endun shoes covered her soles, Lluava could feel blisters. The leg grazed by the arrow only added to her pain.

Aquila followed her like a shadow. Neither one questioned why Yena had permitted the human to keep Giahem's Wings; a bow with no arrows was useless. The nomad clutched the weapon to his chest as if protecting something precious. This feeling Lluava understood; whenever she was separated from the Claws, she felt as if a part of her were missing. Was it the same for him?

She could sense Aquila's discomfort. His eyes were wide, and he seemed hyperalert. Suddenly, Lluava realized the nomad had never been in a city, much less a king's castle. The grandeur of scale and magnificence of furnishings must be overwhelming. She remembered the first time Cronus loomed up before her. The castle at its heart, with all its spires and towers, was unlike anything else in Elysia.

"It's this door," Lluava indicated. Stepping into the room, she allowed him a moment to take it all in. It was just as she remembered. The lovely sitting area filled much of the main room. The fireplace was already stacked with wood. Even Onyx's perch awaited the return of the raven. The bedroom was entered from the archway on the right. The emerald green curtains of the four-poster canopied bed were tied back to reveal a number of soft pillows and a down-filled comforter.

Aquila walked to the large glass doors on the far side of the room. He peered at the private balcony that overlooked much of Cronus. The doors had been fixed, its shattered glass mended, as if someone had expected Lluava's return.

"It's different, isn't it?" Lluava asked as she eased onto the velvety couch and gave her feet a reprieve.

"*Different* might not be the word."

She moved a pillow to the small of her back. "You know, you can put down the bow. You don't have to hold it forever.

"You would leave the Claws?" he asked warily.

Looking at the weapons still positioned over her knuckles, Lluava shook her head. "I guess not, for now."

"You are smart, then."

There was a knock. Luka poked his head inside. "Licking your wounds yet?" He smiled at Lluava, then eyed Aquila with obvious curiosity.

"What are you doing here, Luka?" asked Lluava. She could not push aside her suspicion that he had been sent to spy for Selene.

Stepping through the doorway, the young nobleman bowed low. "I come bearing gifts." He pulled out a vial of Idun, the Outlanders' medicine that healed even the most grievous of wounds. Tentatively, Lluava took the offering.

Luka appeared a bit hurt. "Come, now, Lluava. Have you lost all faith in me?" His eyes flashed to Aquila, who was watching the interchange intently. "In all honesty? I intercepted the healer who was coming your way. I felt I needed a good reason to see you."

Lluava observed Luka critically. After all, he was the Incarn for the trickster god, Shennue. Although he appeared to be honest, could she trust him? "Have a seat," she said, gesturing at one of the wing chairs.

Once he was comfortable, he continued. "I just want to say that I understand why you did what you did. I hold no blame. I was fond of Varren myself. Yet I am not what you call inherently brave. I loathe fighting." Luka looked over at Aquila, whose rigid presence could be felt in the room. The Incarn slowly peeled off his fashionable gloves and laid them in his lap. "You can see that I am not built for battle," he said, indicating his own lanky form, "like your friend, here." Aquila was certainly far more fit than Luka, although they were both probably the same height. "It's a wonder that I ever shoot my slingshot in the right direction. I mean—"

"Stop. I get it," Lluava said. "You love Selene. She's your sister. Even though she and I, you know…"

Luka smiled wickedly. "Are mortal enemies?"

Lluava couldn't help but laugh. "Yes. That we are."

"She's a snake. What can I say?" Luka continued to grin. "I just wanted to clear the air between us. I feel that I am still your friend, though you might not see it that way."

"Times have been challenging."

"Agreed," Luka stated before looking at the nomad once more. Then, leaning playfully toward Lluava, he asked, "Does he know how to relax?"

Laughing, Lluava acknowledged, "I don't actually know."

Though clearly not amused, Aquila did not appear insulted. He turned to inspect the light tapping sound coming from the balcony doors.

Opening one slightly, Onyx flew inside. The raven landed on the table near Lluava and ruffled his feathers so much that he seemed to puff up into a ball. He must have been searching for her since the chaos of the battle.

The humorous sight added to the ring of laughter between the pair of Theriomorphs; even Aquila's face broke into a slight smile. Onyx peered up with his good eye, uncertain what had just happened. Then, with an indignant *quork,* he began to preen his tail feathers.

Collecting himself, Luka wiped his tearing eyes with the corner of his handkerchief. "The main reason I wanted to see you tonight was to implore you not to get into any trouble with my dear sister."

"You don't want *me* to make trouble?" Lluava was insulted. "Me? Why, she tried to kill me!"

Luka threw his hands in the air in mock defense. "Selene was wrong. We both agree on this. But you really have a knack for getting yourself into unpleasant situations. Trust me, going head to head with my sister would not end well."

"For whom?" snarled Lluava. Onyx flew into the air and fluttered about before settling onto his perch.

"To be honest," Luka said, "you."

Lluava had to bite her tongue to keep from saying something foul. Luka used this to his advantage. "You have connected with your goddess."

"How did you know?"

"Sensed it as soon as I sat near you. This is good. Now, your special gift can manifest and begin to grow. But," he said before Lluava could chime in, "my sister is much stronger. Her gift has been growing rapidly. Please, this is a friendly warning. I don't want to see you hurt. Either of you."

Sinking lower on the couch, Lluava wondered what he meant. How could Selene's gift manifest even more? She already had the ability to control any male. Could she manipulate females, too? Or multiple people at once? There were so many questions, yet the one she asked was different.

"Why did Selene choose to seduce Apex?"

Luka seemed to struggle with his response, as one does when there is something loathsome to admit. "Why not? He is the ideal image of masculinity. A perfect counterpart for Selene, though a bit too hot-tempered for my taste."

"But he is a fellow Incarn."

"That is why you do not have to worry about him," countered Luka truthfully. He paused, toying with his frilled cuffs. "There are other men, you know. Men whom Selene would never bother you about."

Lluava knew she had given too much away. Luka had recognized her far-too-strong connection to both Apex and Varren. She needed him to believe she did not constantly think of one or the other. "Like who?"

"Well, for a start, me. Selene would never...could never...romance me," he said with a foolish grin, which caused Lluava to laugh. "Why, we would be the talk of the city. The kingdom, even!"

"We would be, at that," Lluava, equally playful, agreed. Despite the good humor, she could sense his affinity for her. Without hesitation, she used this to her advantage.

"Luka, do you know what happened to my friends Talos and Rosalyn? The soldier and his healer wife?"

"Yes. They are here in New Rhadamanthus. I can take you to them."

Chapter 18

Waiting

They're here in the castle!" exclaimed Lluava.

"Well, not exactly," Luka explained. "They have been relocated to the city. Most Theriomorphs who were living at court have been assigned other homes, in New Rhadamanthus."

"Why?" Lluava asked. Then, realizing the reason, she answered her own question ruefully, "Because Yena wants her own people close to her. Though the others might be Theriomorphs, they are also Elysians."

"A little oversimplified, but yes," concurred Luka. He tucked his handkerchief into his lapel before slipping his gloves back on.

"Take me to them," Lluava said excitedly. "But first…" She held up the vial of Idun. Swallowing two drops, she instantly gagged. Nauseated, the young woman bent her head low between her knees and tried not to throw up the putrid liquid.

"What did you do to her?" Aquila questioned as he leaped next to Luka threateningly.

"I'm fine," Lluava said as she struggled to keep from vomiting. "It's the medicine. Just give me a moment."

After a few more slow breaths, Lluava stood up. Tugging at her soiled, oversized clothes, she said, "Let me change into something a little more fitting. Then we're off."

As she put on a V-necked black Endun shirt with white pants identical to those issued to her in the training camps, she heard Luka talking to the nomad.

"I know you want to join us," Luka was saying, "but seeing that humans aren't looked upon kindly here, maybe you should consider staying in this room."

Returning to the main chamber, Lluava added, "I think I agree with

111

Luka. The high priestess has allowed you to live in the castle without confinement. You don't want to risk making her change her mind."

Clearly displeased, Aquila moved over to the glass doors. "I will stay with your bird."

Onyx ruffled his feathers and muttered contentedly.

If Aquila had been her friend, Lluava would have teasingly told him to behave himself, but he wasn't, so she left without another word.

***

In the main city, Luka led her through the labyrinth of households and shops. With no street wider than two passing carts nor any direct paths to places of importance, Cronus's convoluted plan had been designed to hinder attacks on the king. If the city's walls were ever breached or the sole gateway broken, the enemy would have to blunder through the city in a narrow line, making them easy targets for those protecting the capital.

The streets and alleyways were full of newly arrived Theriomorphs. Clansmen intermingled with locals. Healers, nurses, and a few doctors aided the injured. Other, more community-minded individuals assigned accommodations to the sudden influx of people.

Lluava was surprised at how quickly everyone was being organized. Food stands were open with the sole purpose of distributing goods to the hungry survivors. In lengthening lines, the clansmen stood patiently awaiting their shares. This was far from natural to them, yet with only occasional bickering, everyone seemed inclined to follow the new order.

Until Luka bumped into a member of the Razor Back Clan, a tribe known for hot temper. The clansman shoved Luka to the ground. Before Lluava could intervene, Luka rose and, with an apologetic look, handed the man a large apple as a sign of peace. The clansmen snatched the fruit from Luka's hand and sniffed it, his nose ring brushing against the deep red surface.

Making several small bows, Luka retreated next to Lluava. Tugging her sleeve, he said, "This way. Hurry."

She was dismayed by her friend's lack of backbone. "You shouldn't have been the one to apologize." A pained cry came from behind them. Without stopping, Lluava looked back and saw the clansmen spit out what must have been a tooth, while he stared baffled at the stone in his hand. Snickering, Luka hurried on.

"How did you do that?" asked Lluava as she moved a bit faster.

"Make him bite a stone?" Luka smiled slyly at his platinum-blond friend. "Selene's abilities haven't been the only ones to grow." He must have read Lluava's confused expression. "It's just an illusion, like a mirage. The more willing one is to believe in the illusion, the more real it becomes. In a desert, a stranded man wants water, so he sees an oasis. That man clearly was hungry. So, it was easy for him to see an apple and not a stone."

"I'm hungry," she said. "Though it was not given to me, I saw an apple, too."

Speaking to himself, Luka mused, "And they keep on growing."

As they made their way through the city, Lluava's thoughts were on the Incarn and their abilities. What benefit were these manifesting gifts if they were not meant for actual good? Yena could glimpse past, present, and future events using her gift of scrying, but she could not interact with those in the images she saw. Luka could create small illusions like the one she had just experienced, but how many could he do at one time? On that note, what about Selene? She could certainly get a single male to do her bidding. But unless she could control multiple people at once, what good was that?

Luka halted, and Lluava asked, "Why did we stop?"

In an overly exaggerated fashion, he placed a pale hand on top of her head and turned it to the side. There, standing on a doorstep, was Rosalyn, holding a bucket of odds and ends.

"Rosalyn?" Lluava questioned, surprised at her own lack of words.

Rosalyn turned slowly. Strands of raven-black hair had escaped her large bun and fell in front of her blue eyes. Her porcelain cheeks were slightly flushed. Her mouth opened wide.

"Lluava?" She shouted through the open door. "Talos! Talos, come quickly!"

The young women hurried toward each other. After a strong hug, Lluava stepped back. "Rosalyn, are you starting to show?"

Placing one delicate hand over her belly, Rosalyn beamed. "A little."

From out of the house came a golden-haired, well-dressed man. Talos said, "Gods be good!" He ran toward Lluava and swung her around. "I cannot believe you made it back! I mean, I can, but still."

"Well, here I am." Lluava grinned. Even her injuries felt momentarily better.

"Come inside," Rosalyn said. "Please."

Elated, Lluava remarked, "I have so much to tell you both."

Then, as Talos and Lluava moved toward the steps, they glanced at Luka.

"Act like I am not even here," Luka said as he stepped after them. Then, reading their unspoken conversation, he joked, "No trust? Fine. I will stay outside. After all, it's such a nice day." He looked at the cloud-burdened sky. Threatening a bad rain, the atmosphere was tense with pent-up energy. "Waiting…"

Lluava felt a little badly but knew Luka's presence would have stifled the conversation. Giving three-way hugs, she and her two friends began to catch each other up on the events of the past few months.

"You go first, please," Lluava said. Still physically tired from her stressful homecoming, she welcomed the brief respite.

Talos and Rosalyn took turns explaining their experiences, stopping only when Rosalyn made tea to ward off the unseasonable chill.

Talos took up the narrative. "Since your escape, Rosalyn and I have been doing our best to lie low. The high priestess has instigated many changes, including renaming the city New Rhadamanthus."

"I heard that," said Lluava as she tucked a footstool under her still-tender feet. "And that you were moved into the city."

"Those first days were horrifying," Rosalyn chimed in. "So many humans were killed. Their bodies were thrown over the walls and left to the wild animals and the Raiders. All Theriomorphs were called up to make our personal pledges to High Priestess Yena and the old faith. We were asked what our occupations were prior to the new order." Rosalyn looked at her husband and grasped his hand.

Lluava turned to Talos. "What did you say?"

"That my wife and I come from nobility and that I had enlisted when the Raiders began to attack."

"You told them the truth?"

"I could not risk a lie being discovered. I did say that the reason I enlisted was to protect the people I loved." He smiled at Rosalyn. "I was ordered to desist from fighting unless called upon. Since Rosalyn professed herself a healer, she was allowed to continue that work."

Rosalyn explained, "Along with the majority of the surviving nobility, Talos was assigned a new occupation. Everyone has to do his or her share here. Because Talos is well educated, he teaches some of the citywide mandatory classes. Do you want to explain?"

Nodding, Talos continued, "Everyone living inside the walls must participate in one of several reeducation classes pertaining to the old faith." Lluava remembered having to do the same in Leucrocotta. "Three four-hour sessions are offered daily. Every person must attend one of them, depending on which best fits their schedule. The high priestess seems to believe that she can reunite our race—one people, one culture, one realm, one religion—as we once were."

"Yena," Lluava interjected, "has a strong *belief* of how things should be."

"Yes. That is very clear," agreed Talos. "The ruire—her counterpart, as you know— demands a certain order. Everyone keeps busy schedules. We have little time for ourselves. I suspect he does this to prevent any uprisings."

"Is the ruire still Thoth?" questioned Lluava.

"I think that is his name."

"He is still alive? He delivered a personal message to me a few days ago but was badly injured. I wasn't sure he had survived."

Talos shrugged and Rosalyn replied, "I have not seen him in a week, but I do not have access to the sick ward inside the castle. The priestess uses her own healers for those who live there." Rosalyn hesitated, then looked at Talos, "Tell her about the attack."

Sensing Lluava's concern, he quickly explained, "Not long after the uprising, another wave of warriors from the Outlander army tried to enter Cronus. The second wave must have been held in reserve while Yena was capturing the city. When they arrived, they were all but demolished by the

Raiders, who were waiting outside the walls. Only a fraction of the Theriomorphs were able to enter Cronus." He paused, then added, "None of the surviving Cronians were involved in that skirmish."

Glancing at Rosalyn's belly, Lluava said, "I'm just glad you three are safe and sound."

Talos and Rosalyn smiled at each other. Then Talos asked, "How about you? How have you fared?"

Lluava understood that they wanted to know if Varren was still alive and if their king was planning anything to assist Elysia. She filled them in on all that had occurred since her flight with Varren into Tartarus, from her experience in Erebos to battling the Raiders alongside Yamir and Derrick. The young couple listened intently. Talos was relieved when he heard that his military partner, Byron, was still with their king. Lluava hoped that one day the two men would be partners once more, but that would depend on her completing her objective.

When she told them about Thad's demise, her friends' faces were grim, though to Lluava's surprise, Talos consoled her, saying that not everyone could be that strong, and Rosalyn agreed.

Lluava's voice dropped to a whisper as her story neared its end. "I need to persuade most if not all of the Theriomorphs to unite with me and fight the Raiders alongside Varren's army. We must crush them once and for all. Yet I cannot fulfill what Yena desires. It might not make sense, but even if Selene releases her hold on Apex, how could I have relations with him, when I still have feelings for Varren?"

Rosalyn and Talos exchanged a glance. They understood Lluava's caution. Luka, the Incarn of the trickster god Shennue and brother to Lluava's personal enemy, waited somewhere outside. As much as she wanted to, Lluava would never trust Luka; she could not risk him overhearing her true intentions.

Bending close, Talos gripped Lluava's shoulder firmly. "We are always on your side."

Rosalyn stood up. "Now, where did I set that bucket?" She scanned the room, retracing her previously distracted steps.

Talos explained, "It contains her medical supplies."

Looking quite confident, Rosalyn held up the wooden container. "You said Derrick was injured. What are we waiting for?"

Outside, they met the waiting Luka, who was obviously happy at the relief of his boredom and helped the trio track down the whereabouts of Derrick. The dark-skinned soldier had been placed in a special facility due to the severity of his stab wounds.

A former estate house had been converted to a makeshift hospital. Stripped of furniture and the frivolities of luxury, the large home accommodated the most seriously injured clansmen. When Rosalyn saw that only one doctor and three nurses were desperately trying to care for the wounded, she immediately offered her assistance. Lluava knew little about medical practices, and Talos had had no training at all. They were told to wait outside.

"I hope your friend will be well," consoled Luka.

"Thank you," Talos replied, and Lluava added, "We've known him for a while. He's a fighter. He can get through this."

Yet the image of Derrick bleeding profusely as he was assisted to safety remained in Lluava's mind. She could not deny the possibility that she might lose another friend that day. Taking seats on the building's stoop, the trio waited patiently for word from Rosalyn.

"What are you thinking about?" Lluava finally asked Talos, whose expression had grown distant.

"Waiting," the young man sighed. "Not just for this answer, but overall."

Luka, wanting to join in, asked, "Meaning what, exactly?"

"This waiting that the Raiders are forcing us to endure," began Talos. "I am trying to figure out if they are toying with us, working on their own strategy, or hoping to starve us out."

Furrowing her brow, Lluava said, "I don't understand."

"Since you left," Talos explained, "though the Raiders did cut down the Outlander reinforcements before they reached Cronus, there have been no attempts by the Raiders to breach the walls or the main gate of the city. We know they can find ways to scale the walls, since they have done so in the past."

"But they were never able to enter in numbers," Luka pointed out, proud that he knew something of military strategy.

"True. But they only need to send one of their Berserkers over the wall to open the gate from the inside. Then their army would be able to rush the city."

"And we would take them down in the streets," countered Lluava.

"We might be able to hold them off, but think about the damage they could do." Talos shook his head, sending his golden hair dancing. "Something is wrong. It is not that they have made an unsuccessful attempt, but that they have made no attempt at all. They are waiting. *We* are waiting. But for what? They must have some plan. I only wish I knew what it was."

Luka, catching on, agreed. "It's almost as if they were toying with us."

"Why else have they not attacked Cronus outright?"

"Do they think that they have already won?"

"Or do they *know*?"

Lluava broke into the men's debate. "It's impossible to know anything about the future." Having spoken, she realized that was not true. Yena had the gift of prophecy. She would never have allowed her people to be caught in such a large trap. Yet hadn't Thoth told Lluava just that? They were all doomed, he had said. She wondered if she should speak to the high priestess. She hated Yena—but what if there was a chance to turn the war?

Looking up, Lluava saw Yamir approaching. Although exhausted, he greeted Talos with a firm yet friendly embrace. As Talos and Yamir began catching up, she suddenly remembered another person supposedly able to see the future.

"Yamir," Lluava interrupted. "What happened to Grandmother? I know she had been traveling with us, but did she make it into Cronus?"

"New Rhadamanthus," Luka whispered.

Yamir looked wearily at her. "I don't know. I just came from getting a head count of the Cloven-Hoofed Clan. She is not among us."

Aghast, Lluava began, "You don't think—"

"No," countered Yamir. "Her wagon was not accounted for on the last day of travel. Some believe she knew what awaited us and that she left when we headed here." Seeing the distressed look on his friend's face, he added, "Don't worry. There is a good chance that Grandmother will outlive us all."

The conversation moved to other topics. The day continued to wane. Lluava finally turned to Luka with a yawn. "You really don't have to wait for us. I know Derrick isn't your friend."

"True," noted Luka. "But you are, so I will wait."

Lluava did not need to say how grateful she was; Luka already understood.

As time passed sluggishly, her yawning became uncontrollable. Luka studied the dark circles under the young woman's eyes. "Lluava, you really need to sleep. Have you eaten anything? You should be resting."

"No. I'm fine," she retorted, trying to blink away her exhaustion.

Talos added, "You should listen to him. Rosalyn's looking after Derrick. If you push yourself too much, you will be useless to us if an attack does occur on the city."

Grudgingly, Lluava consented to return to her rooms. Luka walked her back. Lanterns were being lit about the city. Above, clouds choked out any starlight. The moon's presence was obscured.

Entering her chamber, Lluava saw Aquila standing by the double doors to the balcony. She wondered if he had moved even once during the entire day. Although she yearned for bed, she noticed a tray of food left on a table. Taking a seat on the couch, she was readjusting her position when she felt something small and hard under her. The vial of Idun lay where she had discarded it earlier.

"Luka?" Lluava hoped her friend was still within earshot.

Luka's lanky form re-emerged from the doorway.

"I need you to do me a big favor, right away." Handing him the vial, she said, "Take this to Rosalyn. If I know Yena, she will save the reserves of Idun for the Outlanders. If Derrick is to survive, he will need this. Please."

Inclining his head slightly, Luka said, "It will be my pleasure. Now, rest, Lluava. You will need it."

Once he had left, Lluava began to hungrily eat her cold dinner. Watching from a distance, Aquila noted, "Your bird did not like the server."

"Onyx has always held his own opinions of people," replied Lluava as she sliced into a shank of lamb. The cut of meat was incredibly tender and well-seasoned. In the midst of stuffing a second roll into her mouth, she asked Aquila, "Do you want some?"

"The smell is foreign to me."

Taking that to mean no, Lluava finished her meal. Leaning back, she unfolded the cloth napkin to wipe her mouth, and something fluttered to the ground. Picking the item up, she inspected the white-tipped gray feather with its black stripe. Her whole body grew rigid.

Aquila had approached from behind. He must have sensed Lluava's change of mood and asked, "A warning?"

"No. A threat."

Chapter 19

Giahem's Talons

More problems were about to arise. The feather was proof. Feeling drained of all energy, Lluava sank down onto the couch.

"There is a Theriomorph here by the name of Maruny," she told Aquila. "Her dual form is the mockingbird." Lluava twirled the feather's quill between her thumb and forefinger and watched the white flash of the tip. "She believes that I killed her mate, Zeek, or at least that I let him die." Aquila's eyes bored into her, and Lluava quickly countered. "I didn't. I actually tried to save him, but Maruny will never accept the truth."

Old emotions refreshed themselves. Lluava took a long, shaky breath. "When I lived here before the Fall, I had a little handmaiden, a young servant girl, June. She was only nine years old. When Yena gave the order to butcher all humans, I knew I needed to make sure June got to safety." Lluava began to ramble. "We were running through the castle when Maruny found us. She grabbed hold of June and had a knife. She said she just wanted me to come with her. I would have…I was going to… in order to keep June safe. Then an Elysian soldier appeared. Maruny panicked, and…" Lluava silently raised a hand to touch her throat. "I held June while she died. I felt her slip away."

Tears rolled down Lluava's cheeks. "June died. Maruny lived. And now she wants me to know that she is still here and that she has not forgotten about Zeek."

"She wishes you harm?" Aquila asked. "I will not allow that."

"You might not have a choice," said Lluava, oddly grateful for the nomad's temporary turnaround.

"I will not allow outside harm to come your way." He was serious in tone and appearance. "I promise you that."

119

Maybe Aquila was genuinely concerned for her, or maybe just for his own life should Lluava be slain within this Theriomorph stronghold. But what did it matter? Turning away from him, she quickly wiped her face. "You need to have a weapon about you at all times. I'll get you a dagger or a sword, whichever you prefer."

"I want only my bow," Aquila replied. Giahem's Wings was still in his hand.

Lluava didn't argue. There is a special bond between a person and their weapon of choice. Knowing this, she said, "Then you're going to need some arrows."

***

After a long but fitful sleep, Lluava and Aquila took turns bathing and refreshing themselves. The nomad was awed by the various pools—hot, lukewarm, and iced—in the cathedral-sized washroom. After reassuring him that it was not witchcraft but underground hot springs that allowed the pools, Lluava left him to strip down and swim.

Returning to her room, she brushed her silvery hair. Her locks were finally growing out again. Though they were not nearly as long as they once had been, Lluava braided them in a way June had taught her.

Walking onto the balcony, Lluava scanned the lightening sky. The moon's waning crescent was hidden by a ceiling of clouds. How long ago was the night she had first stepped out onto this precipice beneath a full moon? Closing her eyes, she recalled the sensations she had experienced when Varren approached her and they shared their first kiss. She could still vividly remember the taste of his lips and his subtle scent, rosemary and fennel. That had been at the beginning of autumn, and now an overly cool spring had taken hold.

Opening her eyes slowly, she could see the awakening city below. The day would begin soon. She had much to do. There was no time to dwell on old fantasies or past romances. Turning around, Lluava was startled; a man stood by the balcony doors.

Apex appraised her coolly. "You're thinking about Varren."

Lluava gave a broken laugh and nodded.

Stiffly, Apex moved toward her. Close up, Lluava could see that his tired, bloodshot eyes struggled to focus. Somewhere deep inside, Apex was fighting Selene's grip and losing. Knowing that the one other man she cared for was being manipulated just as Varren once had been, Lluava laughed anew. Surely, she sounded like a mad person, but who cared? Apex—the huntsman, the Incarn of Ullr, God of War—was as helpless as a whimpering pup.

Still, her heart beat rapidly as she stood near him. She had to concentrate not to speak rapidly. "It's funny, you know?" Lluava did not wait for an answer. She knew this would be a one-sided conversation. "After all this," she gestured at Apex's state, "abandoning you to save Elysia's king, I ended up losing you both. Selene has you now."

In a voice as hollow as Lluava felt, Apex replied, "I love Selene."

"With the same passion as Varren did, I'm sure." Lluava stared at the tuft of chest hair that curled over Apex's bronze button-up shirt. He was groomed far too well, dressed far too nicely. She could not stop noticing Selene's influence all over him. Yet she could clearly remember the feeling of those chest hairs between her fingers as they kissed lustfully only a season ago.

"Well," Lluava said, bending close to the huntsman's ear, "I'll tell you a secret. Varren and I are never to be." These were the words Apex had yearned to hear, but there was no change in the huntsman's demeanor. Under Selene's control, all that was left was the shell of a man unable to think for himself.

"You know why?" Lluava asked, not caring that she might as well speak to empty air. "Because I killed Thad in front of him. Thad, his closest childhood friend. There was no going back after that. I did what I needed to do," she said confidently. "I made that choice to protect my king. And for that, I lost the man I loved."

She had always been able to express her darkest thoughts to Apex, her worst fears. In this, he was like Varren, or had been until the Fall of Cronus. "What makes this whole situation even more ironic is that just as I am coming to terms with that loss, I'm faced with another." Lluava reached up and placed her hand upon Apex's bristly jawline. "I've lost you as well."

Taking a stiff step back, Apex said coldly, "Selene wants me now. I am to go to her."

Lluava did not watch him leave. As she turned away, she said, "I guess I really am meant to embody Issaura, the virgin goddess, in *all* ways." Breaking down into a tear-filled bout of laughter, she felt all her emotions slowly drain away.

When she collected herself, Lluava felt less burdened. This was good. She needed to be fully focused when she and Aquila broke into the royal armory. The nomad needed arrows. She would get him the best.

Last night, they had made the decision to wait until morning. Unsure what challenges lay ahead, they knew they needed to be rested. Moreover, darkness, though protective in many ways, encouraged others to be hyperalert. Conducting a burglary in the light of day was unusual, though just as tricky to accomplish.

After Lluava had practically bribed Aquila to put on the Endun outfit that had been left with their breakfast trays, she and the nomad were ready to go. Lluava noticed Aquila's sneer as he looked down at his golden clothes.

"They're not *that* shiny," Lluava declared.

"They are of the barbarian material," he countered as he readjusted Giahem's Wings on his shoulder.

Trying not to be insulted, Lluava pointed out, "Well, those 'barbarian' clothes will help you blend in with the Theriomorphs. They might sense that you are not one of us, but at least you look the part." Raising a finger to shush Aquila's rebuke, she continued, "Think about our goal. We can't afford a mistake."

Lluava wondered if Yena's choice of color for Aquila's clothing was intentional. Was she trying to make him easier to spot? Few wore metallic shades. The only others she had seen were Yena and Apex. Or was she mocking the fact that he could wield the golden bow of Giahem?

Peeking around a corner, she risked a look at the armory's doors and quickly counted the guards: a half dozen. Stepping back out of sight, Lluava grumbled, "Rats. I was hoping there would be fewer."

"They are called vaults for a reason," said Aquila.

Was he trying to be humorous? Swallowing the rumble in her throat, Lluava knew this was no time to be funny. "We need a plan," she said, stating the obvious. "There are six men, all armed. They will hurt us, but we must not kill them. If we do, Yena will surely imprison us. And lastly, these aren't the vaults. That's an old term for the treasury."

"Then why are we here?"

Lluava was baffled by the nomad's question. Tying his long auburn hair into a bun, Aquila said, "Your human friend, the woman in black—she said that the vaults had many arrows."

"I think she meant the armory," countered Lluava. "The treasury would not hold weapons; it would store riches, gems, gold, and other prized possessions of the royal family. Unless the Mandrun line deemed a weapon to be of great value, they would store it in the armory. Six guards, and we have only Issaura's Claws." Rubbing her eyes, Lluava tried to think.

As she studied her golden weapons, she recalled the day she had received them. Berkley, the elderly healer, tailor, and inventor at the southern training camps, had worked hard to have Issaura's Claws removed from the royal treasury in order to bequeath them to her. If Issaura's Claws had been considered a treasure, might not other weapons?

"You know what?" Lluava asked. "I take it all back. You're right, Aquila. We should be searching in the treasury."

With their new objective, the pair wound their way to the treasury's entry. This time, there were only two guards. It appeared that riches were currently not as valuable as weapons.

"Much better," Lluava purred. As a third guard approached, she and Aquila ducked into an alcove and hid. The trio of Theriomorphs shared a brief conversation before all three rushed off in a different direction.

"We've got to go now," Lluava said excitedly.

"Isn't it a little odd?" Aquila questioned, always distrustful.

"Yes," Lluava acknowledged, "but it might be our only chance. Hurry." She ran to the doors. They were locked. The young woman pulled several oddly shaped pieces of metal from her pockets. "Time to pick a lock."

Lluava had watched others do this but had never done it herself. She struggled for several tense minutes while Aquila stood watch. Finally, he pushed her aside and began working the lock himself. His meticulous manner was far too slow for her liking.

"I think someone's coming," she said worriedly.

There was a click, and the door swung inward. They were inside the treasury! After quietly closing the door behind them, they breathed more comfortably. The massive collection that filled most of the large vault was an impressive sight, yet there seemed to be no actual organization to the place. In some sections, all the items clearly had been arranged with care. Jewelry hung on specialized stands; garments made of silk and other expensive materials were folded in neat stacks. In other areas, gold coins and gemstones were simply heaped in large piles. Rolled tapestries were in one corner, while a score or more crowns adorned the heads of manikins positioned near a line of extraordinary handcrafted furniture.

Picking up a coin, Aquila inspected the face of a deceased monarch. Then, tossing it back on the heap, he asked, "Do you see any arrows?"

"There's so much stuff. If any are here, who knows where they would be?"

Carefully working their way to the back of the room, the pair searched behind old shields, around the bases of life-sized sculptures, under ornate carpets. Soon, a strange pedestal caught Lluava's attention. On top was a one-of-a-kind rest for a missing item. Suddenly realizing what it was for, she slipped off Issaura's Claws and placed them onto the molded forms. The weapons stood erect, the sickle-shaped claws facing each other.

Aquila was clambering over a pile of coins. His movements caused a jade vase to slide down next to Lluava. Retrieving the Claws, she followed the nomad as he made his way to another pedestal, upon which rested a golden quiver with matching arrows.

Aquila pulled out one of the sharp projectiles. It was made of a single material, a material that matched his bow. He nocked it, pulled back the bow, and aimed at the ceiling. As soon as the two objects touched, beautiful designs manifested on the bow as well as the projectile's shaft. Runes formed on the arrow as well. Lluava knew what they said before she read them aloud: "The Talons of Giahem."

"Well done." A voice fractured the amazing moment. "You've found them already."

Aquila instantly aimed the bow at the robed man. He was about to shoot when Lluava called out, "Wait."

Pulling down his hood, Hyrax regarded the pair expectantly. He raised his hands in feigned defense. "I am glad that Giahem's Talons have found a fitting owner."

Aquila eyed Hyrax suspiciously, and with good reason. Lluava knew the former councilman was a Guardian. He had manipulated the Incarn to follow their supposed destinies. He sided with Yena and thus was an enemy of Varren.

Hyrax smiled innocently. The two white stripes running down his pointed black beard seemed to have widened since the last time Lluava saw him. White hair had even begun to sprout down the center of his scalp, yet his face looked the same.

"You knew we would come for Giahem's Talons," said Lluava as she tested her grip on the Claws. Why hadn't she noticed his distinctive perfume earlier? Then she realized that he wasn't wearing any; instead, the musk of badger was present. "You told the guards to leave. Why didn't you just give us the quiver? Why didn't you unlock the door?"

"There is a path that must be taken when dealing with the gifts of the gods. This is the way it was meant to be."

Lluava did not like that response. She might be the Incarn of Issaura, but she was also Lluava Kargen, a Theriomorph from the town of Rivendale, soldier for the Elysian Army, former military partner to the rightful king. She was so much more than a toy for her goddess.

"I do wonder how you discovered the Talons' whereabouts so quickly," said Hyrax, who continued to look kindly on the defensive pair. "You were told they were here. It wasn't Varren, for he never cared to dally among his family's spoils. He probably does not even know of the arrows' existence. Was it Regin? He always watched over the Talons with such interest."

"No," responded Lluava; she would not give Holly away. Nodding to Aquila, the pair lowered their weapons and headed for the treasury doors.

Motionless, Hyrax watched them pass. "I must warn you that the Obsidian Guards are not your friends, Lluava. They will kill a Theriomorph without a second thought, even you."

Lluava continued to zigzag through the chaos of the vault. Her neck hairs prickled at the Guardian's comments, but she refused to play his game. Hyrax continued, "All nomadic people were ordered killed upon entry into Elysia. The Obsidian Guard has never failed before, yet this nomad was allowed to live. Do you want to know why?"

Hating herself for doing so, Lluava stopped. Hyrax had baited a hook, and she was compelled to bite. The Guardian, noting her interest, added, "You said that the nomad was already in possession of Giahem's Wings. For that, he was kept alive, in accordance with one of the Obsidian Guards' most critical directives."

As Hyrax reached into his robes, Lluava prepared to strike out, but it was Aquila's harsh accent that said, "Not fast, beast-man." Giahem's Wings were trained upon the Guardian's every move.

At a respectfully slow speed, Hyrax produced a yellowed scroll and handed it to Lluava. With Aquila watching Hyrax, she unfurled the ancient parchment.

"As you can see," Hyrax began, "this scroll contains the original addendum that King Hammond issued to the members of the Obsidian Guard. Examining paragraph three of the seventh section, you will note that the king assigned a specific task to the Guard. They were to unite the full set of religious weapons of the Theriomorph race. Now, if you—"

"I can read," said Lluava tersely, cutting him off. Too soon, unfortunately.

Skimming down the scroll, she tried to understand what was written. The Code of Shadows used archaic rhetoric and a formulaic style; it seemed almost as if it were an entirely different language. Such phrases as "most valuable mission," "essential secrecy," and "never to repeat what is known" were interspersed with others: "weapon of unfathomable power," "knowledge to control must be retained," "to be wielded by dominant authority for the welfare of humankind." However, three words stood out: "twelve runed artifacts."

Disappointed in herself, Lluava lowered the scroll. "I don't understand what this is saying."

Though Hyrax certainly was aware that Lluava lacked knowledge of political rhetoric, he did not mock her. "Essentially, Regin had to keep the nomad alive. As an Obsidian Guard, it is his duty to gather all knowledge about the gods' weapons. During the Landon Wars, several of these were removed from the city temples of their respective gods and confiscated by the Mandrun line."

Lluava remembered that each Theriomorph city acted under the command of a ruire, their ruler, and the high priestess of their temple. Each city had a patron god or goddess. Twelve Theriomorph cities, twelve gods, and twelve weapons. Lluava listened intently to the Guardian's lecture.

"King Hammond understood that each weapon possessed great power, although the form of that power might forever be unknown. He wanted to gather all twelve weapons, believing that their united abilities would solidify the Mandrun rule over Elysia. The Obsidian Guard's mission, in part, was to fulfill this task.

"That is the true reason King Hammond decreed equality between the races. He thought that once the Theriomorphs accepted that they were citizens of his Elysia, they would produce the rest of the hidden relics. But the gods' weapons had been scattered, and Theriomorphs were never more than second-class citizens."

Hyrax took back the scroll and tucked it into his robe. "You see, the Obsidian Guard has never looked upon a Theriomorph in earnest friendship. But the Guard will do whatever it takes to discover and keep track of the gods' weapons. Now, that includes those who can wield them. The Guard will ensure that the Mandrun line controls the greatest weapon of all time, a unit comprising Incarn who will fight at the king's bidding for whatever purpose the crowned ruler deems fitting. I fear, Lluava, that you have been played once again."

Chapter 20

Rhadamanthus of Old

Y ou must never trust humans."

Hyrax's last words resounded in the vault.

Lluava countered confidently, "You're wrong." Her tone masked her growing trepidation. Even if the Guardian's words were in any way true, surely Holly had become her friend. They had been through too much, shared too much, especially sweet June. Holly had not only helped Lluava in the past but had also told her where to find Giahem's Talons. She was not merely manipulating Lluava into trusting the Guard, unless that was part of a larger plan—one that united arrows with bow and Aquila with the golden weapons.

But what if Holly really *had* played her, just as the High Council and the Guardians had? Needing to prove him wrong, Lluava said, "Varren would never use the Incarn as some massive weapon of war. He didn't even know we existed until recently. If he had been informed of his ancestor's plans, he would have revoked that addendum."

"This knowledge is only passed on when a new king is crowned. Special precautions were taken this time."

"What precautions?" Lluava asked just as Hyrax continued.

"If everything had gone smoothly, Varren would never have known about the Incarn."

Repeating her earlier question, Lluava asked again, "What precautions?"

"We were able to manage the kingdom and the king himself through the help of your fellow Incarn, Selene."

"*You* made her control Varren?" Lluava questioned, clearly shocked.

"We simply placed the idea before her. She did the rest."

"Then you're no different from the Obsidian Guard," snarled Lluava.

Hyrax nodded knowingly. "I do not blame you for feeling that way. Regardless, the Guardians have always done what was best for the Theriomorph race."

"What *you thought* was best." Lluava realized that the Guardians would not help defeat the Raiders in order to protect the kingdom of Elysia and return Varren to the throne. They were interested only in the Theriomorph people. Yet they had failed to protect their precious race. "Are you not ashamed for the deaths on your hands? Theriomorph deaths? If you influenced Selene, and she instigated the butchery of the clans, then you are responsible for all those lost lives."

"Gods work in mysterious ways, and so do we," responded Hyrax calmly. "I will admit that King Varren's decree shocked us as well, but it sparked a fire that incited the clans to join together to overthrow human rule once and for all. They might not have joined us otherwise. Regardless, the Theriomorph race is now united."

Hyrax paused thoughtfully. "I will not try to make you see it my way. In time, you will understand. However, I must inform you of an invitation from High Priestess Yena. She wants to share something with you and wishes you to meet with her in her quarters tonight."

If everyone around her was playing some invisible game, she would join in. At least now she was more aware. "Where are the high priestess's quarters?"

"She has taken up residence in a house near the temple."

This was a surprise. Lluava had fully expected Yena to have claimed the royal quarters as her own. In a strange way, she found she respected the priestess's choice. Lluava nodded as she and Aquila left Hyrax to his own devices.

"Will you go to the she-beast?" Aquila inquired.

Guessing his real question, Lluava responded, "You can't come with me."

He did not argue. However, he spent the rest of the day near the balcony doors, occasionally scratching Onyx's feathered head. At sunset, as Lluava left to meet Yena, he said softly, "May the Twelve watch over you."

***

The temple was an enormous structure with a columned, wraparound porch. Rising many stories higher than the surrounding buildings, it seemed to dare the saturated clouds to stroke its peaked roof. Ornate doors on a raised platform were reached by a great number of steps, each twice as high as those for daily use. When she saw Yena waiting outside a newer structure adjacent to the temple grounds that had once housed the human priest, she was thankful. At least she wouldn't have to climb up the steep steps.

"You knew I would come," Lluava said. Once again, she felt the restraint of her own personal fate.

Smiling pleasantly, Yena's timeless features glowed in the waning daylight. "Follow me, please," the high priestess said in her throaty voice. She turned and led the way to the temple.

Lluava had always been loath to enter a human church. Yet this had been a Theriomorph temple before Varren's ancestors arrived. It was also the only Theriomorph building left standing after the humans conquered the city that became Cronus. The other buildings had been leveled, their stone and wood repurposed to help construct the castle. The only other structures Lluava had seen like this one were the temple in Leucrocotta and the temple in Therial, which had been turned into a church. Clearly, her ancestors had been architecturally brilliant.

Yena led her through the two outer chambers into the back, where only an empty marble pedestal for a Theriomorph statue remained. Following Lluava's line of sight, the high priestess inquired, "Do you know the patron god that once ruled over this city?"

Shrugging, Lluava noted the vast size of the three-foot high base that measured ten feet on each side. "It couldn't be Crocotta, for hers is in the Verta Mountains."

"That leaves ten options."

"Eleven."

"Ten."

As Yena waved her forward, Lluava said, "I thought all the gods had patron cities."

"The entire pantheon had their own places of worship, but one god was never permitted either a temple or a city." Yena's fingers traced the mortar at the back of the room. As she did so, a dark crack seemed to fracture a large section. The priestess gave a slight push, and the door swung backward into darkness.

Yena's ghostly irises seemed to beam at Lluava. "This city is built on top of Rhadamanthus, where Giahem was the patron god."

"I thought..." Lluava stammered, "I thought the city was destroyed...that Tartarus...the royal dungeon...and this temple were all that remained of the original city." She did not mention the miles of booby-trapped tunnels stretching westward that had served as her escape route during the Fall.

"Rhadamanthus was destroyed, in most respects. Homes, shops, markets, and the coliseums were leveled. The temple was left, as you know. But that was only a fragment of the city. The rest was subterranean. Let me show you."

They entered the blackness. When the door resealed behind them, the walls began to glimmer. Soon, the strange light activated Lluava's hypersensitive night vision. She could see the corridors clearly, as if they were lit by sconces. She recalled the slimy, organic moss that illuminated Tartarus's inner depths. The same slime coated these ancient walls. Although Theriomorphs had used it for just this purpose, human eyes could not discern the mossy light. Humans would have stumbled around blindly, their limited vision of no help.

Fortunately, Lluava was not human. As she moved along the descending path into the first cavernous chamber, stones that had been perfectly hand cut to fit next to one another suddenly metamorphosed into brilliant mosaic murals. The entire room from ceiling to floor was decorated with the chipped gemstone imagery. Around each fragment, the glowing slime radiated.

"This... is...everything," Lluava breathed in awe as she began to recognize the stories the images depicted. "This is our religion."

"Yes," purred Yena. "Everything from the *Karmasana* to the *Virisinu* is portrayed on these walls. From our beginning to our end. Come. This way." Yena disappeared down the far hall.

Half paying attention to the high priestess's directions, Lluava tried to absorb all that she saw. This part of the subterranean infrastructure was nothing like the decrepit tunnels through which she had escaped several months ago. It was as if she were in a totally different city.

"Why is this all here, underground? Why bury such beauty?" Lluava did not understand.

"It was created to worship the one it was made for." Yena's answer was as mysterious as their surroundings.

Lluava passed the first mating ceremony between Giahem and Crocotta, walked alongside Issaura and Ullr riding in their chariots of moon and sun, crossed over Ucrin as he first took command of the sea. She stopped momentarily when she noticed the image of two figures, a man and a woman, connected at the spine. Their features looked similar, as one would expect with twins, yet distinctly different in accordance with their genders.

The high priestess moved alongside Lluava. "That is the transformation of the god Himeros into the goddess Frij. After Himeros raped Slypher, the Goddess of Earth, Giahem punished him. Himeros would spend the rest of his days as a female in order to better understand the wrong he had done. Frij would be eternally mated to Ucrin, who was as harsh as he could be gentle."

Knowing the story, Lluava added, "Slypher bore Himeros two children, the Twins: Suada, Goddess of Lust and Seduction, and Shennue, God of Mischief and Mayhem."

Yena nodded and they continued. Several times during their wanderings in Rhadamanthus, Lluava stopped long enough for a brief conversation with Yena about a specific tale of gods or heroes. Finally, the high priestess led her into an apparently insignificant room that was clearly dedicated to one goddess.

"Do you recognize her?" Yena inquired.

Lluava looked up at the raven-haired goddess with black eyes. Her face was grim, almost hollow, yet there was a supernatural beauty to her. Lluava replied confidently, "That is Nott, also known as Vor, the Goddess of Night, Death, Dreams, and the Underworld."

"And," Yena said, gesturing to the next depiction of Nott, who held a crying infant, "the mother of Theri."

Lluava walked around the room while Yena patiently waited by the final doorway. The entire chamber was indeed dedicated to a particular series of events. Lluava could see the golden eagle of Giahem meeting with Nott, and their love manifesting in the birth of their child. Then she saw the mood shifting to a darker one as Crocotta discovers her mate's betrayal; she attacks Nott and tears out one eye. The other eye is spared by Giahem, but to sooth his enraged mate, he is forced to condemn Nott to live in and rule forevermore over the underworld, both to protect her and to appease Crocotta.

"Is this what you wanted to show me?" Lluava asked as she traced the empty eye socket of the goddess. "What happens when a god must be punished?"

"No," countered Yena soothingly. "What I want you to see is in here, in the black mirror." She gestured for Lluava to enter the final room. This area was larger and contained a raised rectangular pool filled with thick, black liquid—the same liquid, Lluava remembered, that the high priestess used for scrying. Its still surface reflected the interior of the chamber almost like a mirror.

As soon as she entered the, Lluava's body grew heavy, her voice suppressed. Beside her, Yena began her throaty ritual. Nonverbal humming sounds rumbled from the high priestess's throat in a rhythm so obscure that Lluava barely recognized it. Yena appeared to glide up to the edge of the pool, where total darkness encapsulated the pair. Then, reaching into the liquid, she scooped up a handful, allowing the black fluid to run down her arm. The droplets left virtually no visible trail, for her flesh was almost the same shade. Ripples from the falling liquid spread until they reached all corners of the large pool.

The high priestess's voice took hold. "Crocotta, O magnanimous Queen of the Gods and all that lives, Prophetess, Matriarch of the Blessed, I have come to learn your will."

A low glow arose from the center of the pool.

"Bestow upon me, your servant, keeper of your word, the knowledge you wish to instill."

A vision began to take shape in the illuminated liquid. Lluava could finally move closer to the pool and observe the scene that unfolded. A presence, commanding and harsh, seemed to be the main focus. Lluava felt her skin prickle as the massive man, a Berserker, turned to face them. Her gasp was silenced in her throat. The Raider before her was the haunting man from her nightmare. He wore no helmet, unlike his fur-clad brethren, who circled around his gnarled alder throne. A wolf-hide cape with eternally snarling heads over both shoulders exposed little of the pulsing black veins about his neck. His eyes burned wickedly as two Berserkers dragged a prisoner before him—a man whom Lluava recognized.

Ambassador Alcove was thrown at the feet of the Berserkers' leader. Landing heavily on the ground, he spat out a mouthful of blood and bile. He looked wild, his hair and beard untrimmed, his clothing frayed and befouled, his body far too thin.

"Strip him of his cloak," the leader ordered. It was obvious that Alcove no longer merited a title.

The two guards pulled off the prisoner's garment, which was of similar design to the harsh man's cloak. Shivering, Alcove seemed meager compared to the Berserkers. Even so, he stood proudly, sunken-eyed, in front of his condemner.

Touching one of the snarling heads on his own cloak, the seated man pronounced in a harsh, guttural accent, "You are no longer worthy to wear the Garb. You do not have a drop of our blood in your veins. The disgrace you have brought upon us has confirmed my suspicions. You are tainted by your affinity with those beasts. Your authority is hereby revoked."

Alcove was led away without even a note of protest from his lips. In turn, an elderly man hobbled up to the throne. Pointing up at the gap in the clouds, he wearily said, "The omens favor us. Their fortress has indeed grown silent."

The man in the chair waved the elder away and then summoned a fellow Berserker. Lluava recognized Sweyn, the red-bearded prisoner of war who had been traded at the capital for Thad before the Fall. He had claimed he was invaluable to their military leader, the one Lluava supposed was seated in the chair. She wanted to slice off Sweyn's excuse for a nose.

Sweyn spoke up, unabashed. "Th' boy's pets be many."

Lluava's neck hairs rose as the seated figure touched a nub where a finger should have been. "If Mandrun thinks his monsters frighten us, he is wrong. We have *monsters* of our own."

The commander's voice became as dangerous and cold as a shard of ice. "Release them."

The pool returned to its prior nature, reflecting the strained faces of the two women. Yena spoke first. "These are the humans' brethren. They share the same ancestors. See how they treat one another. Feel the chill in their hearts."

"That may be true," Lluava agreed, now that she was able to speak again, "but the Mandruns renounced that kingdom centuries ago; they rejected their heritage. They are not like those men we just saw. I know you believe that we cannot trust any human, but consider this: With allies such as the Elysian humans, we would have the army we need to fight off the Raiders and their 'monsters.'

"I am not asking you to befriend humans but to use them to reach a mutual goal. Tell me the truth. Do you think we have any chance—*any*—to defeat the Raiders alone? I know you want to trust me, so I ask you to show me that I can trust you as well."

Just like the liquid in the pool, Yena's pale irises seemed to glow of their own accord. "After you slipped away with young Mandrun, I had a reserve army attack the Ocean Men. Our numbers were vast: great herds of reindeer, swarms of birds, packs of other wild things. Yet the giant ones, the—"

"Berserkers," Lluava interjected.

"Yes. Berserkers. They cut down many. By the time it was over, the ground was so saturated with blood that the water we drew from the wells was red. We retreated, and what was left of our army was brought inside these walls. Since then, I have tried twice to send word to Leucrocotta about our state; twice the Ocean Men returned our messengers—headless."

Just envisioning that battle made Lluava feel queasy. "Did Ruire Thoth make it back?"

Yena lowered her eyes. Something glinted on her cheek. Had she actually cared about Thoth? When the priestess looked up, her resolve had returned. "What you witnessed tonight is a message from Crocotta. This message has recurred every night since I took control of New Rhadamanthus. It is a warning of what is to come. The only other message I have received was a glimpse of the slaughter by the wall upon your arrival. That is why I sent Ruire Thoth to you. I wanted to warn you not to come. *You* are the catalyst of our race's salvation. Your life is important above all others."

Lluava felt something was still out of place. "The slaughter at the wall had nothing to do with the vision that you keep seeing. What do you make of this other one? If Crocotta keeps showing it to you, it must be important."

"I thought the two were linked. That was my error," admitted Yena. "Recall the scene with the Ocean Men. The sky, the part that was visible, had no moonlight. Yet the stars were observable. That only occurs during the new moon. I wanted you and the clansmen to wait until after this new moon passed, for fear that the battle by the wall was caused by the monsters referred to in the original message."

"Well, it wasn't," Lluava said sullenly, just before a new and horrifying thought came to her. "High Priestess, tonight is a new moon."

Chapter 21

The Chamber Above

After a moment of silence, the priestess said, "If this is the night when the monsters are released, I need you to be ready." Leaving the chamber, she added, "The morning may bring new challenges. Until then, rest is what you need."

As Lluava turned to follow Yena, she noted the crudely carved figure of a raven by the stone door. Although its purpose likely had been forgotten years ago, the image of the black raven in the black chamber, eternally guarding the black pool, was unsettling. Solemnly, Lluava left the underground city.

Before leaving the priestess, Lluava felt compelled to ask something of her. "The Raiders are our enemy and might have the strength to eradicate us," she began. "Yet they will do the same to the human Elysians. I have seen what happens to any who cross their path. Have you ever thought that maybe we were not meant to work alone? That maybe we were supposed to work together? Maybe *this* is what Crocotta is telling you?"

Yena listened patiently, though from her expression she was not enthralled by the idea. Yet with a new threat lurking in the mists, Lluava needed to take advantage of this opportunity.

Licking her dry lips, she explained, "In the Elysian military, each Theriomorph was partnered with a human. Military partners offset each other's weaknesses. We discovered that we were stronger when we worked together as one.

"What if our abilities could be strengthened by pairing them with the humans? What a force we would be! Although this partnership would be one of necessity, it need continue only long enough to ensure that our race will live on."

Yena gently rested her hand on Lluava's shoulder. "You were blessed with the ability to search for good in others. Unfortunately, that can blind you to their true nature. May your wisdom grow with the waxing of the moon, Incarn of Theri."

With a mood as gloomy as the sky outside, Lluava returned to her rooms. As she approached, she heard voices within. Yamir, perched on the arm of the couch, stood when he saw her enter.

"What are you doing here?" she inquired, happy to see a friendly face.

"Checking up on you and that bird of yours."

Onyx had always had an affinity for Yamir. The raven scooted along the back of the couch to get closer to the conversation. Aquila was sitting cross-legged by the unlit hearth. For the moment, he was not marveling over his new possessions.

Before she could speak, Yamir said, "Derrick's still bad. We don't know if he will pull through. That medicine helped, but not enough, I fear."

His wounds must be horrific if Idun had failed to heal them. Lluava was determined to ask for more. Yamir looked wretched. Knowing all the losses he had just endured, she could not bear to tell him about the trouble to come. Instead, she gave him her condolences for one in particular. "Yamir, about Father—"

"I'm going to go now, before it gets late," Yamir said, then quickly left the room. His sorrow left a clinging sense of dismay. Onyx stretched his neck out and tugged at the end of her sleeve. "I know he's upset," she said to the bird before turning to Aquila. "What were you two talking about before I arrived?"

When Aquila chose to ignore her question, Lluava wondered what a nomad and a clansman could have in common. Her curiosity would have to be left unsated for now.

Darkness was growing. Outside the windows, the moonless night prevailed.

***

The next morning, everything seemed well in Cronus. No word or whisper of an oncoming attack was heard. No nervous behavior by lookouts or guards was observed by those milling around the city. Maybe this new moon wasn't the one depicted in the black water last night. Maybe this day would be just like any other.

There was a knock at the door.

Without thinking, Lluava called, "Enter!" Still in her sleeping alcove, she quickly pulled a shirt over her head. From the sitting room, she heard a luscious voice comment, "Your rooms are just as I remembered them."

Lluava slid on Issaura's Claws before forcing herself to face Selene. The woman's pretty smile triggered the taste of bile in Lluava's mouth. The sepia-skinned Incarn gestured to the nearby chaise. "May I?"

Giving a curt nod, Lluava realized she was still awkwardly standing in the open entryway between her rooms. "What do you want, Selene?" she asked as she made herself move forward.

From his favorite position near the balcony's glass doors, Aquila was observing the strained interchange with an unusual level of interest. A blanket on the floor nearby suggested that he preferred to sleep near the balcony rather than on the couch. Onyx, on the other hand, was nowhere in sight. Maybe Aquila had let him out for a morning flight.

"I wanted to officially welcome you back. I hear my darling brother has already beaten me to this gesture several times over. Just the same, I am glad to see another familiar face. And your friend…" Selene's gaze found the nomad. "My, isn't he a handsome fellow."

Aquila, for the first time in their short acquaintanceship, looked bashful. His cheeks flushed, and he shifted uncomfortably for a moment until Selene looked away. "A shy one, is he not?"

"I assumed you were *with* Apex," Lluava struggled so not to hiss out the words.

"Who is really with whom?" mused the beautiful woman as she leaned against the chaise. The manner in which she so naturally sprawled over the piece of furniture was just as alluring as all her other gestures. "But, yes, Apex is my chosen partner."

"Who did the choosing?" Lluava asked before reprimanding herself for blatantly displaying her feelings.

Selene did not look offended. "I gathered there would still be a great deal of animosity between us. You must understand that I come here in earnest desire for friendship."

"Have you forgotten your attempt to bash my brains in?"

Selene appeared overcome with remorse. She sat up straight and clasped her hands before her as if begging for forgiveness. "I am *so* sorry for that. It was just a rush of emotions. Maddened by fear, you could say. Too much had occurred too quickly. I needed Varren, and you had been working to undermine me. I was angry. And people were dying. I was terrified." It was hard to follow Selene's rationale, since she was jumping between two entirely different lines of thought. "I sought only protection, as I always have. I had been working so hard to secure a place at court for myself and my brother that I forgot to consider the feelings of my friends."

Dropping her gaze, Selene admitted, "I have never been good at friendship. Well, not the female sort. I did not even consider that you had romantic inclinations toward Varren. Not until after I made my *claim*. You…you who were always so resilient and strong. So independent. I guess I saw you as a soldier, not another woman."

Selene sighed before continuing. "By then, what was I to do but carry on? I could not have released him. What would have happened if Varren realized what I had done? I would have been imprisoned or worse. And what of my brother? He would have been disgraced, ruined. He could not return home. Not to our father, who wanted him dead."

When Selene's sensual gaze looked up again, Lluava almost thought she saw the woman blinking back tears. "And I did have a true affection toward Varren. You *must* believe that."

"But you did not love him." Lluava's voice hardened like cold granite. "You would never have done that to him if it was real love."

"I was never blessed with the knowledge of love, other than that of my own brother," admitted Selene. "Perhaps my affections toward Varren were not as pure as yours, but I did need him. I really did. He would have provided Luka and me the security that we could never have received otherwise. And I would have done right by our race if I sat as queen on the throne."

Slowly, Selene resumed her prior position on the chaise as Lluava took a seat across from her. "If I had known about the high priestess and what was to come, I would not have clung so hard to keep Varren to myself. If I had *known* that the security I had been looking for would be attained by other means, I would have never approached the king. If I had been as brave on my own as you are, I would have withstood the pressure of the Guardians and what they made me do. That is the solemn truth."

Lluava was not sure how to react. Selene claimed she had only acted as she had in order to survive; she had done the best she could to take care of herself and her brother. Could she actually be less villainous than Lluava thought?

"If this is the case, what about Apex?"

Selene's eyes seemed to flash with an inner ferocity. "What of him? Well, I'll tell you. I realized that with everything that has occurred, I do need a strong figure by my side. And as the rites of our rekindled culture dictate, the female chooses her mate. I should not have taken Varren away from you; I know this now. So, I have chosen Apex. He is everything I need in a man." Suddenly her eyes grew wide. "Don't tell me your affections have shifted to Apex. That would be so devastating for us and our future ability to work together."

"You have him under your spell. Release him, for he has the right to refuse your claim."

Lluava's gaze seemed to be bound to Selene's, unable to break free. Selene looked innocently at her and said, "I do *not* know what you are talking about."

The lie seemed to weigh the air down, and Lluava felt herself struggle for breath as she tried to move, speak, even blink. The oppressive silence caused her mind to spin into a panic. She felt trapped in her own body, unable to control anything but thought.

Selene stood up, breaking eye contact. "Welcome back, Lluava," she said. Her tone, although melodious, was laced with a subtle venom. As she let herself out of the room, Lluava instantly knew she could move once more.

Still standing by the glass doors to the balcony, Aquila slowly turned to focus his gaze beyond the city walls, leaving Lluava to unravel all that had just occurred.

***

Later, Luka came to show Aquila around the castle. When asked to come along, Lluava bowed out, claiming that she needed to get some fresh air. Actually, she wanted to lessen the chance of bumping into Maruny or Selene. Before long, she found herself outside Talos and Rosalyn's lodgings. They welcomed her back quite happily.

"How's Derrick?" Lluava asked, after settling herself in the living area.

Rosalyn replied, "It is strange. In all honesty, he should not have lived with the wounds he suffered, yet he still fights on."

"Have you given him all the Idun I sent you?"

"Yes. Lluava, he was hemorrhaging so much internally, but that seemed to have stopped. His external afflictions are also showing signs of mending, but for now the healers are watching him closely. He is hovering between life and death. There is nothing the rest of us can do but wait and see."

"I hope he gets better soon," said Lluava. "I have reason to believe that things are going to get worse for us." She recounted to her friends last night's strange episode with the high priestess. Absentmindedly munching on the biscuits Rosalyn set out, Lluava said, "I don't know when Varren's army will arrive, but right now Yena will not agree to ally herself with any human. And with this new threat, if these so-called monsters are released, I don't think Varren's men will have a chance of withstanding the Raiders without Theriomorph aid. I don't know what to do."

Talos and Rosalyn solemnly looked at one another. Then Talos spoke in a hushed voice. "We have to tell you something." He glanced over at Rosalyn, who nodded.

"What?" Lluava asked, a little worried by her friend's odd manner.

"Ever since the Fall, as you call it, Rosalyn and I have been rallying supporters. Most of the Elysians who survived Yena's purging are still faithful to the crown. There are even a few Outlanders so appalled over Cronus's upheaval that we believe we could convince them to side with you."

"Me? Wait, hold on," Lluava said. Rubbing the sides of her temples, she asked, "You have been rallying supporters for Varren this whole time?"

"More like support for you," Talos corrected. "There are many who want to see Varren back on the throne, but all want to follow you, for they believe you will lead our race out of these dark times. To them, you are Issaura, the savior."

"H…How many are with you? I mean, us."

"Well…" Turning toward each other, Talos and Rosalyn deliberated. Lluava could hear numbers like "ten from West End" and "the twelve from Broad Street." Finally, Talos pronounced, "Fifteen hundred at least, and that's not including whoever's in Tartarus."

Now Lluava's pulse began to quicken. "Are there humans alive?"

"Did you think that the high priestess's people slaughtered all of them? Those who begged for salvation were locked up in the dungeons. I am certain *they* will fight to have Elysia back."

Rosalyn spoke up in her soft, harmonious voice. "Talos and I have been very cautious about whom to approach and when. I have full faith that once a rebellion starts, more will rise up and join."

"I can't believe this," admitted Lluava. "The risks you both have been taking!"

Talos smiled gently. "All worthwhile."

"There is more," Rosalyn went on. "During the Fall, I needed to find a place to hide, as I was not sure what was happening, whether the Raiders had breached the capital. I could not risk being caught in my rooms." Rosalyn crossed her arms over her belly. "I hid in the Burnt Wing, up in the tower. I found a trapdoor in the ceiling that led to another room, a vast one. Barricading myself in there, I shifted and flew up to the single, narrow window to peer out of it. The scene below was unimaginable. I was frightened and chose to stay in that room for a long while." Her hands trembled as she held them protectively over her swelling belly. "It is in that secret place where we began to meet with your supporters."

"How do you get inside the castle if the former Elysians are not allowed within?"

"Although we are not allowed to live inside those walls, we are permitted to come and go during daylight hours," Rosalyn explained. "The high priestess wants to show her faith in the former citizens. Since that area of the castle is thought to be just ruins, we have been able to meet in peace. Not only that, Talos takes small groups there every few days to train them in combat skills."

Talos added, "You will need trained fighting men on your side when the time comes."

"Does Yamir know any of this?"

"He knows enough to vouch that the clans will back anything you do," acknowledged Talos. Running his fingers through his golden hair, he warned, "But, Lluava, he is against Varren taking back the kingdom."

"I know."

"Yamir has changed," Talos pointed out grimly. "We all have. I fear his change is not for the better. Whatever you choose to do, Lluava, be careful what you say around Yamir. Looking at it from a purely military perspective, you do not want to risk losing his support."

Lluava nodded and said, "I did worry that the clans would join Yena's cause as soon as we arrived. Though I'm glad that was not the case, I wish I didn't feel like I was using Yamir for my own ends." Suddenly, she locked her jaw as emotions flooded through her.

Talos, sensing some of this, said, "Nobody likes being manipulated, especially you. Sometimes one must become partly what they hate in order for the best outcome to manifest."

Lluava stood up and said, "Take me to the hidden room."

Talos smiled. "I expected you would say that. Unfortunately, I cannot take you there right now. As we told you before, every Elysian must take part in one of the mandatory educational sessions, and I am an educator. Rosalyn and I usually attend this next one. If we are both absent, it may seem suspicious. Let Rosalyn take you while I show up at the temple."

"Thank you, Talos," acknowledged Lluava. "Rosalyn, when would you be ready to leave?"

"As soon as I grab my shawl."

***

Through the heavy double doors and the foyer with rolled-up carpets went the pair, past the sheet-draped living space with its covered frames and furniture, and up, up, and up the cut stone spiral stairwell that clung to the perimeter of the tower.

Halfway to the top, Lluava paused to peer down. The vast space still reeked of charred wood and cloth from the long-ago fire. This was as far as she had ever explored before being chased away by the Obsidian Guard for trespassing in the Burnt Wing.

She spotted several grooves made by the throwing suns that were once aimed at her. The blades had been collected by their owner before the castle was abandoned. All the time and effort spent protecting this area had been for naught, since no Outlander cared about the quarters of Varren's parents, where the young couple had met their end.

"Come on." Rosalyn's voice trailed down from above.

Keeping one hand in contact with the stone of the tower, Lluava climbed higher until she passed under a blackened frame where a door once must have stood. The room beyond was covered in a film of ash. Intricate smoke patterns now decorated the walls where tapestries once hung.

Closing her eyes, Lluava envisioned the royal bedroom of the young parents. A large armoire would have been furnished, along with a pair of cushioned chairs. A magnificent four-poster bed would have been positioned so that those slumbering could awake with the rising of the sun outside the curtained, stained-glass window. Nearby, a crib would rock, close enough that the princess would have only to reach over the edge of the bed to check on her infant son.

"Are you all right?"

Lluava blinked, and the room was once more a blackened shell, akin to the inside of a fireplace. "Yes, I'm fine," she lied as she looked up at the painted ceiling. The decorative design had mostly flecked off, leaving only fragments of color pockmarking the gray smudges. "Where's the trapdoor?"

Rosalyn shifted into her dual form. The swan flew up to the ceiling and, with a few mighty shoves, dislodged a segment of the pattern. Had Lluava not been shown where it was, she would never have discovered the door herself.

As the beautiful waterfowl glided into the hidden room and disappeared,

Lluava called after her, "How did you ever figure that out?"

Something swung down. Lluava instinctively leaped backward. The knotted rope swung back and forth like the tail of an anxious housecat. As Lluava began hoisting herself up, Rosalyn shifted and replied, "The gods were in my favor. The door was not fully sealed, and I was able to fly up. There was no rope then."

"Do you think," Lluava asked as she grabbed a higher knot, "that the Shadows..."—she inched up to the next handhold—"knew about this room?" Pausing, Lluava looked around the empty space below her. There was not a single piece of furniture upon which to climb. "Maybe that's the real reason the Guard protected this place so carefully."

Seizing Rosalyn's extended arm, Lluava clambered up into the secret chamber. Rosalyn admitted, "Possibly, though I am not sure what would be so special about this room."

Lluava recognized the answer to that immediately. "The Obsidian Guard had no knowledge of this place."

"How do you know that?" Rosalyn asked. Her voice quivered like a leveret's with hounds on the prowl.

"Because," Lluava stated as she turned in a full circle, "this is the place where the Guardians used to meet."

They were standing on the outer edge of a circular room with only one window, narrow and tall, cut high up the wall. If the trap door were closed, the room would appear to have no doors. On the floor, a massive symbol had been painted, one that she had seen before. This was the room where she had met with the masked Guardians in secret.

"What do you make of that?" Lluava gestured toward the image. Twelve rays emanated from a gigantic eye positioned in the dead center of the room. At the tip of each ray was a rune representing one of the twelve gods of the Theriomorph pantheon. "I don't think Varren's parents decorated their quarters with pagan imagery."

"We have no explanation," Rosalyn admitted, "but the gods seem to be helping our cause." She added worriedly, "There has been no sign of anyone else entering this place since I found it."

Realizing what must have happened, Lluava explained, "That's because the Guardians have replaced the High Council. They no longer need to meet in secret." Looking around once more, she added, "That's possibly why the door was left ajar. When Yena's people were overthrowing the Guard, whoever was hiding here probably hurried down to give aid."

"This would have provided the perfect cover," Rosalyn said. "Since King Thor decreed that, out of respect for his dead son, no one could enter these quarters, a room like this would have been virtually invisible, untouched by prying eyes. With Guardians like Hyrax on the council, who knows? Maybe they influenced Thor to close this place off for their own purposes."

Lluava agreed, "It is a marvelous plan, though it is hard to believe that the Guardians were never discovered by the Guard. On the other hand, they seem to be far sneakier than I would like to admit. Well, I don't think you will have much trouble continuing to meet in here. Other than the Guardians, it is doubtful that anybody else knows it exists, or even cares. And with the Shadows gone, you don't have to worry about opposition at the entry."

Grimacing, Lluava thought back on her first confrontation with a Shadow and meeting Holly. Trying to get her bearings, Lluava asked, "Which way does that window face?"

"South," Rosalyn stated assuredly.

"South," Lluava repeated to herself. Somewhere south of here, Varren was gathering his army. "Rosalyn, when you meet in here, I want you and Talos to always post a lookout. If Varren's army is sighted, I need to know immediately, no matter how far away they seem."

"Of course." Rosalyn paused. "Do you miss him?"

After musing for a moment, Lluava replied, "Of course I do, but it's different. Now that it is certain that we can never be together—romantically, I mean—my feelings for him appear to be changing."

"For the better, I hope?"

Looking down at the rune for Ullr on the floor, the image of Apex clawed its way into Lluava's mind. "Yes. For the better."

This was true. Ever since Lluava had seen Apex on her balcony, old emotions had begun to resurface. Had she made the wrong choice of men? Her question went unanswered.

Shortly afterward, the pair left the Burnt Wing and parted, for there was no need to draw attention to themselves. And Rosalyn wanted to check on Derrick and her other patients in the city. Lluava was left to mull over the concept of an uprising. This time, those she worked with would help the crown and not hurt it. At least, that is what she hoped.

Chapter 22

The Gray Time

Days slowly melted into one another like the slushy puddles on the ground. Though refusing to get warm, spring had taken hold. Trees and other plants struggled to bear their green tidings, though many smaller species began to curl up and die. The prolonged absence of sunlight seemed to stifle new life. The chill in the air did not dissipate, nor did the thick blanket of clouds.

Everything seemed gray. This growing sense of melancholy persisted even inside the stone walls of the castle. Onyx appeared weary of the capital and often slumped listlessly on his perch. Aquila had to work with the raven to get him to peck at any sort of table scraps. Lluava was surprised at how well Aquila handled his confinement. He rarely left her quarters, though he often stared out into the unchanging gloom of the sky.

She, on the other hand, was free to come and go as she liked within the castle and throughout the city. A rhythm began to form in her life, something blessedly reminiscent of the times she had trained in the Southern Camps. And she had returned to deciphering old scriptures as she practiced reading runes in one of the royal libraries.

Sometimes she would spot Hyrax coming and going with various scrolls. Lluava made it clear that she had little to say to him, so he left her in peace. However, she always took note of which rolled-up, yellowed parchments he returned; these she immediately examined.

Although most dealt with some statistical rubbish or logs on depleting stores, occasionally she would find a scroll that pertained to the pantheon or a prophecy. Skimming over one such document, Lluava read:

Direct communication with the Twelve is limited, for mortals are rarely able to hear, let alone decipher, the language of the Gods. This most highly blessed gift is bestowed upon the High Priestess of each Temple who, in turn, communicates only with the God or Goddess with whom she is associated.

The High Priestess serves as the voice of her God or Goddess. She alone knows how her deity chooses to contact the mortal world. The knowledge a deity imparts to the mortal voice has a special purpose and often pertains to that deity's attributes or sphere of influence.

Rare exceptions can occur if a mortal rises to become a hero or is selected to commune with the banished deity, for whom no High Priestess is ever chosen...

Allowing the scroll to roll back up, Lluava leaned back and stretched as she considered the importance of what she had just read. Most of this she had surmised already. Yena, serving as Crocotta's high priestess, communicated only with the Queen of the Gods and none other. And it was very obvious that Crocotta, the Goddess of Prophecy, could and did choose to show her high priestess glimpses of future events.

Yet, what was so important about the scene Crocotta kept showing Yena? It had become an evening ritual for Lluava to convene with the high priestess and discuss the vision. But nothing more had been gleaned. Neither could discern a reason for the presentation of the same image night after night.

And what was Hyrax's interest in this specific scroll? According to Lluava's understanding of him, the Guardian never did anything without a reason. Was he trying to help Yena decipher the message? That would mean she had told him about the vision. Lluava doubted she had. What, then? Why else would he research communing with the gods? What had he to say to the Twelve that they did not already know? What did he want to ask?

With a rumbling stomach, Lluava left the confines of the library to grab a quick meal before hurrying off to meet with her friends. Talos, ever cautious, never left the knotted rope dangling for long. If one were late to a session, one had to make an appropriate noise, usually pertaining to the sound one made in dual form. In Lluava's case, that would have been too dangerous. Luckily, she arrived just as Talos was preparing to pull up the rope.

"Quickly, now," he called down as Lluava shimmied to the top and into the hidden room. Sliding the trapdoor into its original position, she looked about to see who was attending today's lesson.

There were seven others. Some faces she had come to recognize, and a few were new to her. Lluava had attended the past three sessions; the fourth had had to be quickly canceled because it was rumored that the Guardians were about. After changing the meeting times and waiting two days, the training had resumed.

As usual, Talos distributed a bundle of sticks that were kept in the room. Their various lengths simulated those of swords and daggers. A rope ladder had also been affixed to the ledge of the narrow window so they could take turns at the lookout position. Before assisting Talos with the day's lesson, Lluava always took a moment to peer toward the south, ever watchful for a glimpse or a sign that Varren was on his way.

"One more time!" the Elysian soldier called out. The students would realign and attempt the respectably complicated footwork that Talos and Lluava had just demonstrated. As the pair of instructors watched, Talos leaned over and spoke into Lluava's ear. "What do you think?"

"The short one over there is a bit slow." She gestured to a man on the right. "Gregory, isn't it?" She nodded at another man on the end. "Well, he picks up the steps quickly, though he needs better form with his sword."

"No. I meant overall." Talos's eyes had not left his students. "Again!" he ordered, once they had stopped. Returning to his conversation with Lluava, he asked, "What do you think of the training so far?"

"Well, I can see the effort each man and woman is giving to this cause. But these are commoners. They have known nothing of warfare. Their chances…I don't like the odds," she finished in a whisper.

"I know," Talos acknowledged. "What they need is more time. A lot of it. I just wish I knew how much time we had."

Looking over the sweaty brows of those before them, Talos finally relented. "That is all for today. Each of you will be informed individually of your next session. If you can, practice that new footwork in the safety of your household. Until next time."

One by one, they slid down the rope and dispersed throughout the city. As usual, Rosalyn met Lluava and Talos in the lower room to help reset the trapdoor in her dual form. Lluava could not help hide her sheepish smile when she observed them kiss. Talos always leaned in to whisper something sweet into his wife's ear, and Rosalyn always blushed. Then he knelt to press his lips to his wife's belly.

"Have you thought about a name yet?" Lluava inquired, once the trio was far enough away from the Burnt Wing to feel comfortable with normal talk.

Rosalyn beamed. "We have discussed many possibilities. One of which is to name her after you—that is, if the baby turns out to be a she."

"Ah…I don't know what to say. I'm flattered," admitted Lluava joyously. Then she gently placed her hand over Rosalyn's belly. "Hello, little one," she crooned. "You have the most remarkable parents."

The three smiled at each other, knowing it was time to part. "See you around," Talos said before he offered his arm to his wife, and they made their way back to their jobs in the city.

Evening was always the most stressful time of day for Lluava. As usual, she met Yena at the foot of the temple, but this time she was invited to join the high priestess during her scrying session. Nothing had changed since her last observance, no matter how hard Lluava searched for any hitherto unnoticed differences or details.

Walking back through the oppressive darkness, she realized that there were many tunnels and corridors leading away from the one they were in. "How big is all of this?" she asked, gesturing to three entryways leading to unknown places.

"Rhadamanthus?" Yena's eyes sparkled like the fragments of the diamonds Selene adored. "It has a vast sprawl, reaching farther than the humans would have led you to believe."

"Do some of these paths extend beyond Cronus's—" Lluava quickly corrected herself. "I mean, New Rhadamanthus's walls, then?"

Yena was not upset by her slip. "The walls were a human-designed boundary. The original city had no need of them. It was open for all to enter. It was only when the humans overpowered the city that they decided to create a physical barrier."

"But are you saying that there are tunnels that extend beyond the gates?" Lluava was excited at this new discovery.

"Yes," Yena almost purred. "And, yes, we have been working to extend them far enough that an opening would not be detected by the Ocean Men. Soon, I will be able to send word to our awaiting army."

Lluava was impressed. The high priestess had plans. Logical ones. Exciting ones. As they turned a corner and entered another cavernous space, she inquired, "You have *more* men? *Another army*? Why not bring them all at once? Your army, I mean. Two waves arrived while I was here—the land travelers and those that fly; one came while I was gone, and now there is another. Why?"

"The final wave is waiting for the rest to arrive."

"Rest?"

"Those from the other Theriomorph cities. Leucrocotta is not the only one."

Had she been told this? Had it slipped by her? Lluava's mind was a whirl of excitement. "Have there been signs of Incarn in the other cities? Hendren's? Valcum's?"

Yena gave Lluava the sincerest of looks. "I know not. As high priestess of Crocotta, I was born, raised, and one day hope to die in my city. Only if my goddess commands would I choose to explore elsewhere."

The pair walked on a little farther before Lluava questioned her again. "You want to die in Leucrocotta? But what about ruling? What about this place, New Rhadamanthus?"

They were back inside the marbled walls of Cronus's former church. Gesturing to the vacant pedestal that had once held a god's statue, Yena explained, "This is not my temple. I serve Crocotta alone, and her city is not this one. I am only here to fulfill the will of the gods. Nothing more. Once the war is won and this temple restored, new priestesses will be trained. I will remain long enough to ensure that the high priestess of Giahem is discovered and consecrated. Then I will return to the temple at Leucrocotta and live out the rest of my days serving the will of *my* goddess."

"I thought…I assumed you wanted to rule. I thought that's why you did all this." Lluava followed Yena to the entrance of the temple and then turned her gaze upon the sleepy city. "I thought that's why you conquered the capital."

"I am only a servant of the gods, as we all are. One of the many who serve the few. I am here only to reestablish order in our world."

Lluava began to see Yena in a new light, one that made her far more difficult to understand. "When you return to your duties as high priestess for Leucrocotta, what will happen to the Guardians? I assumed they were to serve as the new governing body."

Taking a deep breath of the cool, damp air, the priestess said, "They will do as they have always done. Serve the gods in their own way."

"So," Lluava wanted to verify what she was hearing. "They will willingly step down from their current seats of power?"

"Yes."

Lluava wondered how true that would prove to be.

***

And so the weeks passed.

Lluava kept to her routine. Reading, training, questioning. Occasionally, she would catch sight of Selene and Luka, arm in arm, gossiping in the halls. Though Selene would offer a smile and Luka a friendly grin, Lluava always found a reason to head to a different area of the castle.

From time to time, Luka would show up at her quarters. At those moments, Lluava felt that she could relax enough to resume whatever sort of bizarre relationship she had had with her fellow Incarn. Aquila was always indifferent toward Luka, although for some strange reason he seemed to enjoy Yamir's company.

Luka wasn't her only visitor. Relaxing on Lluava's overly cushioned furniture, her old friends brought word of the many trivial happenings around the city.

The most disturbing news was that Derrick's injuries had still not healed. Yena had refused to allot any Idun to an unknown Theriomorph, even after Lluava's many requests. Yet the fierce soldier refused to give up and somehow continued to survive.

Another soldier of a different sort also took up residence in her thoughts. Maruny's presence was felt, even though Lluava rarely caught a glimpse of the young woman. Waking to the ever-changing song of a mockingbird, her heart would give a start. Once, Onyx harassed one of the gray-plumed birds in the air. Lluava could not help but hope it was the spiteful Theriomorph, even though she knew it was not.

One evening after leaving the library, as Lluava moved through the network of corridors and stairwells in the castle, her nose picked up a familiar scent. Following the trail of musk, she soon turned the corner to face Hyrax.

"Hello, Theri," he said first. He seemed to think a conversation was overdue. "How is your re-acclimation to the city coming?"

"Well, since it has been a month, swimmingly." Lluava tried to keep the note of irony out of her voice. Instead, she moved the conversation in a direction of her liking. She decided it was time to confront the former councilman about his dealings with the other Guardians. "Now that the Theriomorphs rule the city, and the knowledge of the Incarn is no longer a private matter, I want to know why you felt the need to drug me last fall and display me in front of your fellow Guardians. You once said you doubted my legitimacy. Did others?"

Hyrax gave her a look of surprise before he gained control of his emotions. "There was doubt about your legitimacy. Once I verified that Issaura's Claws were the true relics, I wanted to eradicate all other doubt before anything went further."

"How so?" Lluava asked. "Like me meeting Apex? Or did you need validation to steer the pair of us into the Outlands to find Yena?"

"I have always tried to respect the pantheon. Gods have their reasons for everything, Lluava, for creating you and setting you on your appointed path. Everything they do has meaning."

Lluava was unaware that her jaw had dropped in amazement.

Clearly worried, Hyrax inquired, "What's the matter?"

"I just realized what the gods have been trying to tell us." Realizing that Hyrax had no knowledge of what she was referring to, Lluava continued. "They weren't sending us a warning about monsters. They were trying to point us in the right direction."

Turning on her heel, she ran to find Yena and shouted in elation, "We are meant to rescue Ambassador Alcove!"

GIAHEM'S TALONS

PART II

Chapter 23

The Water Source

Yena and the other Incarn met with Lluava in the Judgment Hall. After dismissing the Guardians to ensure privacy, the high priestess took her seat upon the throne and waited.

"Crocotta *has* been trying to tell you something through the images you have seen," Lluava began. "She wants us to save the one called Alcove—the prisoner shown in your visions."

Instead of questioning why they should save an Ocean Man, Yena remained silent as she listened to Lluava's explanation.

Lluava continued. "When the first boatload of Raiders arrived in Elysia, they were led by Ambassador Alcove. We assumed that he was their military commander, but we were mistaken. During the autumn, Alcove led an attack in the North, but he was recalled by someone else, someone with higher authority over the Raiders' armies.

"I suspect the seated figure in your vision is the actual leader. The red-bearded Berserker is Sweyn; I believe he is the second-in-command. Together, they must have stripped Alcove of his status.

"I think that Crocotta has shown you this particular scene because she wants us to rescue Alcove and use him to our advantage. He could provide us with their plans. He knows their chain of command, and with that information, we would know the most beneficial targets to kill or capture. His knowledge could turn the outcome of this war in our favor."

"What then?" Yena questioned. "Why should we believe any of the information this human offers? If the war is won, then what of the prisoner? Do we keep him at our mercy? Allow this ambassador to lead his men back across the great water with no further conflict? What you are advising me is to trust the lesser of two evils. How can I know that we can trust such a man?"

Lluava expected no less from the priestess. She pointed out, "The Raiders' military commanders have not only revoked Alcove's authority but also undermined and abused him. I am sure bad blood has been building between Alcove and those other two men. Moreover, the ambassador has helped me several times in the past. During the winter, I infiltrated their camp to release captives. I believe he tried to warn me to flee before I was captured."

"What reason does that man have to save a Theriomorph?"

"I have no idea. But I believe that if there is any chance to defeat the Raiders, it is with Alcove on our side. Be it willingly or by force."

Yena leaned back against the throne. "As I see it, your suggested strategy has three objectives. First, capture the ambassador. Second, slay their militant leaders. Third, force this ambassador to order the remainder of his army back to their homeland or have them submit to us in defeat. Am I correct so far?"

"More or less, yes."

"What if we go straight to the second objective and eradicate their leaders? All three of them."

Lluava ran her tongue over her incisors as she considered this proposition. "If we killed all three, what would happen to the army left on our shores? They might flee on their own, but that is doubtful. More likely, they will continue to attack and kill our people. We would have to slay huge numbers of Raiders before they would consider leaving. And then there are the Berserkers. Although it's possible that someone else would assume command, we do not know who. No. Unless their commanding leader orders them to return to their homeland or commands them to surrender, I think the bloodshed will continue."

Yena looked skeptical.

"Why," Lluava asked, "do you think the goddess has repeatedly sent that specific image to you? If the focus was on the so-called monsters, why not show them to you? Then we would at least know what we're up against."

During this entire time, the other three Incarn had remained silent. Lluava was uncertain whether they fully understood what was being discussed. Resolutely, they focused on the high priestess. Yena seemed to be running through all viable options in her mind. At the base of the dais, Lluava was also considering possibilities. Hers, though, were centered on ways to rescue Alcove.

Finally, Yena spoke. "I will not have my people combat the Ocean Men in open battle, not after our last encounter. This enemy is far stronger than I had ever imagined. Their intelligence adds to their lethal nature. I underestimated them once, and I will *not* do so again."

"Does she know?" Although Apex's voice was husky and slow, it held a subtle strength.

Lluava glanced at the huntsman in surprise. Did he understand?

She turned her attention back to the priestess, who explained, "As I think you know, I had troops positioned northwest of here. Once New Rhadamanthus was ours, I sent a messenger to summon them to the city and strike the enemy unawares. Yet I was the one unaware of what was to come. Unable to scry anything beyond that same repetitive scene, I could not foresee my mistake.

"The enemy allowed my messenger to fly out of the city and then followed him straight to our unprepared troops. They were ambushed. Our losses were substantial. Barely any warriors made it here to safety. I will *not* permit any action that would lead to the slaughter of our people. I learn from my mistakes."

Something did not add up. Lluava spoke out testily, "I have heard conflicting information. I was told that only two messengers were sent out, and that neither survived to get help. Now you tell me that a messenger did contact troops but with dire results. And what of the remainder of your army? What is the truth? What other information are you keeping from me?"

Yena gathered her thoughts. "Our army was organized into two divisions. Each division was further divided into two strategic forces, or waves. The initial attack on New Rhadamanthus utilized both waves of the first division. The second division was held in reserve. The larger force was posted at the border to await the aid sent by the other Theriomorph cities. The smaller force, located nearer the capital, was contacted by our initial messenger. They attempted to provide aid shortly after the city was seized. As a result of the Ocean Men's trickery, this smaller force was all but decimated at the city's walls. Since then, we have sent two other messengers to contact our forces at the border. Both were aerial in form to evade the Ocean Men. Their bodies were returned to us in pieces."

Lluava recalled her conversation with Yena beside the scrying pool hidden underground the temple. "So, your remaining troops are at the border awaiting word to approach."

"Yes."

"How many?"

"Larger than the force we have here."

Lluava needed time to think about how to use this in some future advantageous plan. But for now, first things first. "We still need to capture Alcove."

"I will *not* risk any other Theriomorph lives needlessly."

"But what if those undertaking the plan were not your people?" An idea had begun to take root.

"Explain."

"You have human prisoners. I know you do," Lluava stated assuredly. "Let them do the work for us."

Luka, unable to remain quiet, questioned, "What are they going to do? Disguise themselves as Raiders and waltz right into the enemy's camp?"

Lluava's eyes widened. She looked from Luka to Apex. "That's exactly what they will do. High Priestess, if I am right about Crocotta's intentions, and we act upon the goddess's suggestion, would you be able to scry freely again?"

"That has happened."

"Would you be able to follow the movements of specific humans?"

"My gift comes from Crocotta herself. I see what she reveals to me. If I ask for a specific vision, I have usually been blessed with the ability to follow certain Theriomorphs. Humans are different from us, which makes them more difficult to perceive."

Lluava's frustration dissipated as she studied the faces before her. "Luka, you told me that our abilities as Incarn continue to grow. I have seen you create an illusion strong enough that a number of people, myself included, believed it.

"We are all Incarn. We are blessed with gifts of the gods for some reason. Let us use these gifts to save our race." Thinking of Aquila's strange aura, Lluava asked, "Luka, do you think you could make humans emanate the same essence that Theriomorphs do in order for Yena to follow them when she scries?"

"I've never tried. I've never thought about it. Truly, I'm not sure what you mean," admitted Luka. "But I've always liked a new challenge."

"Selene, you could— wait, no, that won't work—" Lluava broke off in exasperation. "When we free them, I *need* the prisoners to believe that they have escaped and are switching sides to join the Raiders. They have to be convincing, or else they will be killed."

Selene glanced at Apex, then looked down at Lluava. "I agree. In order for the humans to function the way they must, they would need to be controlled. Control is different from seduction. Lust can make a man or woman act in ways they would never normally choose, but it has its limits. Fortunately," Selene said with a thin smile, "I seem not to. I can control your humans."

Lluava forced herself to look up at the young woman she loathed. "Selene, how many men could you control at one time?"

The beautiful woman hesitated as if wanting to keep her secrets to herself, but catching the eye of Yena, she answered, "A score, maybe more."

Apex asked in a semi-lucid manner, "Won't the Raiders kill them regardless?"

Lluava responded truthfully. "That is a possibility; but if not, this provides the opportunity to find out where Alcove is being held. If the humans are able to infiltrate the Raiders' camp and Yena can scry them, we will discover the layout of the camp as well as Alcove's location. If possible, Selene could have the men release the ambassador. Once free, he will attempt to leave the camp, and we could capture him. With luck, we might even discover the enemy's plans."

No voices spoke in opposition, so Lluava continued. "If all works out, we would be one step closer to defeating the enemy. If anything goes wrong, only humans die and not our people, High Priestess."

"And how would you have us capture the ambassador?" Selene questioned. Lluava could not tell whether she was being mocked.

Unsure who might be privy to certain details, Lluava answered in the form of a question directed to the high priestess. "How is the work on your tunnels progressing? Are they long enough?"

The question hung in the air, and Lluava waited for Yena's response. "They are sufficient, although patience and more time would be beneficial."

Regarding her fellow Incarn, Lluava said, "We, I, could bring Alcove here by way of tunnels that extend far outside New Rhadamanthus's walls. The Raiders do not know of the tunnels' existence; if we are careful, they would not be aware of one or two people coming and going through them."

"Tunnels?" Luka questioned excitedly. He was not that concerned about Alcove, but this was to his liking.

Yena explained in her mother-like tone, "These are ancient tunnels that have been reopened and extended from the underground city to the outside world for the purpose of sending messages. We need an active line of communication to coordinate assistance. Yet, why volunteer yourself, Lluava?"

Lluava assumed Yena knew her reasoning, but she answered, "Because I am the Incarn of Issaura, Goddess of War, and this idea was my own."

The priestess spoke without empathy. "If you choose to leave by these means, I will consent, but I cannot allow you to return that way. The entrances to the tunnels must not be discovered by the Ocean Men. If Alcove escapes, the enemy will certainly pursue him. The entrances to the tunnels will be resealed after you leave on this mission."

Though she understood Yena's logic, a low growl of annoyance rumbled up Lluava's throat. "Then make sure the gates are ready to open upon my return."

The high priestess smiled. "You are thinking like a true goddess of war. I do have doubts, but I am only a vessel for the gods. I cannot understand their grand meaning unless they wish to share it with me. So, Lluava Kargen, Incarn of Theri, I will leave these war games to your discretion. Help us end this war."

**

After far too much time was spent getting everything in order, Lluava, Apex, and Yena waited in the temple for the return of Luka and Selene. With the ever-massing clouds above them, it was hard to tell if it was day or night. The warming winds rushed aggravatingly through the capital and the neighboring lands, whipping Lluava's platinum-blond hair into her eyes and mouth.

Would the storm ever break? Lluava anxiously fidgeted from side to side. Everything had to be in place for this to work. There were so many aspects that could go wrong. She had done everything she needed to do, and now it was up to the twins. They had been in Tartarus practicing their abilities on the twenty men selected for this mission.

So that the prisoners' escape would appear genuine, very few people knew of their release. Certain guards were forewarned, as were the keepers at the main gates. As soon as the twins arrived, Yena led the group into the caverns below the temple and entered the chamber with the scrying pool.

I hope this works, Lluava thought. She saw Luka's eyes flick about excitedly while Selene furrowed her brow in deep concentration. Even Apex's typically glazed eyes appeared more alert.

Yena began her ritual, and five faces peered into the black liquid. An image of the band of prisoners escaping from the castle manifested. The men would not remember their doors being unbarred nor the weapons placed for them to stumble upon. They would not question how they could so easily overpower trained Theriomorphs. All they would know is that they needed to seek the protection of the Raiders from the cruelty of the Outlanders. Lluava's plan was working! If only everything else would fall in her favor.

Ammit's job was to keep the Theriomorphs away from the fleeing men. Although the castle's halls were vacant, once the men were outside, a few members of the Silver Tongue Clan intercepted the humans. From the clansmen's loud, brash singing, they had been into the ale again.

A fight erupted. Most of the prisoners escaped, but one was killed and another taken hostage. The poor, abandoned human looked frightened. The drunken clansmen struggled to decide his fate. Suddenly, the human lurched to his feet. Spitting out a curse, he pulled a small vial from a pocket and swallowed. He instantly grew rigid and fell motionless to the ground.

The image changed, rippling as though someone had tossed a pebble into the pool. The fight at the main gate was like a well-choreographed dance. The Theriomorphs faked injuries and death as the humans fled through the doors as if their lives depended on it. If enemy spies were about, they would certainly be convinced that the humans had escaped on their own.

Once away from the city walls, the men seemed to recollect themselves and cautiously advanced upon the Raider's camp. Words were whispered among them as they approached the line of torches marking the edge of the enemy encampment. Where were the Raiders? They must have realized that an unfamiliar group of humans was arriving. Would the Elysians be kept alive? If not, the whole ordeal would have been for naught.

The scene began to dissolve. As soon as the water resumed its reflective properties, Lluava and the others found their voices.

"What happened?" Luka cried out. "They should still be able to be tracked."

Selene's eyes gleamed in the dim lighting. "I only sense fifteen. No...fourteen at present. I have lost touch with the others."

"They are being killed, you fool!" Lluava snapped. She was unable to contain her dislike of her fellow Incarn. "High Priestess, can you try to reconnect with them?"

Yena scrutinized the four Incarn. "The problem is that one among you is currently being charmed by another." There was no need to acknowledge Apex. "The charm is similar to the one being used for this mission. Release your fellow Incarn, or send him back to the castle. Until you do, my line of sight to the prisoners is blocked."

Lluava and the twins looked at Apex, then at one another. Finally, Selene placed her hand gently against the side of the huntsman's face. "Go, my love. Return to your rooms. I will meet you there later."

"Yes, Selene," was Apex's only reply before he left the chamber.

As soon as he had departed, Lluava rounded on the twins. Her anger at Selene's lie, as well as at this situation, was too much. "What in the seven hells happened to the human captured by the clansmen? Was that poison? How did he come across a vial of poison? They were to have only some second-rate weapons."

"Calm down, Lluava," Luka soothed, but Selene was the one who answered. "Of course it was a vial of poison. They all have one."

"For what purpose?" Lluava demanded angrily. Though the mission was her idea, she never wanted to harm any of the Elysians. Human or not, they deserved better. "So they would have a way out if captured?"

"I am sorry to disillusion you, my dear Lluava," said Selene in her sweet, syrupy voice. "The poison given to them is for a much greater purpose. The men are to pour the liquid into the source of the Raiders' water. Starting from the farthest point upstream, the enemy will fall."

"As will anything else that drinks the water," said Lluava mortified. "What of Alcove? What happens if he is killed?"

"If your plan works," Selene countered, "then there is nothing to fear, for he will flee the area. And if not, well, that is why there must always be a viable backup plan. Risks need to be taken. You did not seem willing to take them."

Heat began to bubble up in Lluava's core. She stifled a growl.

In turn, Selene's eyes sparkled under her thick eyelashes. "Why, Lluava, are you upset? Surely, you understand that removing the threat by any means is beneficial to us all. This way, we are not risking extra lives."

In truth, Lluava was frustrated with herself. Why hadn't she thought of such a simple solution? Yet her concern still remained. The poison could kill not only Alcove but also any innocent being that used the same water source. Who knew what ripple effect this would cause?

"Selene's plan has merit," Luka admitted. "Maybe this is all that needs to be done to end this war. And having a backup plan *never* hurts."

Of course, Luka would side with his sister. Lluava, unable to hide her annoyance, asked again, "What about Alcove? Why has Crocotta been telling us to save him if he is not important?"

Selene countered in earnest, "How do you know the will of Crocotta? You are not her seer."

"Children." Yena's full-throated voice silenced the trio around her. "Do not search for deceit among yourselves, for you will only create it in your pursuit. We must act together. We can work on resolving your issues at a later time, but for now I need all of you with me."

Selene suddenly looked genuinely ashamed, as did her brother. Lluava could not find it in herself to apologize, even when Selene said, "I only did what I thought was right."

Yena seemed to smile without actually doing so. She turned back to the pool. "Let us try again."

This second attempt was more fragmented. The image struggled to manifest. Looking at the survivors, now bound at the center of a group of Raiders, Lluava felt sick when she realized how few of the Elysians were still alive.

Were they all to die by the enemy's blade? Was there truly no mercy among the Raiders? Lluava wondered if she had sentenced all these men to horrific deaths, a fool's errand. Her confidence in her plan wavered as another prisoner was put to the blade.

The image went black.

"I'm sorry." Luka was the first to speak. "I wasn't able to keep up the illusion for that long. I've never attempted a prolonged experiment at such a great distance. They can no longer be traced."

"You did well," Selene soothed her brother, hugging him. "As long as my connections do not fail, the men will not speak of anything but the desire to work for the Raiders. There is hope yet."

"Did you see what was happening to them?" Lluava cried out, her voice ringing through the vault.

Still holding her brother to her chest, Selene turned to Lluava. "What were your expectations? That all would live? Of course some would die. The Raiders need to test the truth of their words. Inevitably, some were going to be tortured or killed. Our only hope is that a few survive."

"What happens now?" Lluava demanded. She was angry at everyone, including herself. Secretly she knew what Selene said was true. "What happens if Alcove is set free? How are we to know to search for him?"

Letting go of her brother, Selene challenged, "*You* created the plan. *You* figure that out." Turning to Yena, she pointed out, "I am able to control the survivors for now, but I have no idea how long my connection will last. Like my dear brother, I have never tried to manipulate so many men and over such a great distance."

"Your contribution," Yena began, "has been exceptional. As have those of all of you. Now, return to the castle. I will stay here and pray to Crocotta for further guidance on this matter."

The trio walked somberly down the mosaic-lined corridors. In a miasma of their own making, they passed the bejeweled scenes with little awareness. Shennue's anger over his unrequited love was ignored. The indestructible net he fabricated to hold anything he captured, mortal or not, was unheeded. The moment when Valcum first began his work creating weapons for the gods in his smithy was overlooked. Only when they neared the exit did Selene stop to study the image of Suada's initial seduction of Ullr.

"I know you do not approve of my actions," Selene said as she continued to stare at the mosaic. Realizing the other woman was talking to her, Lluava listened quietly. "Yet, I do not regret any choices I have made. I also know that because of what I have done, we may never be friends. For that, I am truly sorry. I will not change. For what I am, I was always meant to be."

Selene reached out her hand as if to touch Ullr's depiction. Then, turning to look at Lluava, she continued, "I say this out of the respect I bear you: the connections I have with the surviving humans are already beginning to deteriorate. Once they are free of my power, they will admit the truth, that they had no intention of switching sides. The enemy will realize our deceit, and the end result, I fear, could be grievous. Your plan has a time limit, Lluava. One that is rapidly approaching."

Chapter 24

The Storm Breaks

Something had to be done. Fast.

Without so much as a thank you, Lluava bolted toward the city. She needed to gather her closest friends immediately. Finding Yamir first, she had him send word to Talos. Then, doubling back to her quarters, she met with Aquila.

"Are you ready to use that bow of yours?" Lluava asked. Her face was flushed from running and her lungs burned, yet she felt more alive now than she had since returning to the capital. Her feet ached and her leg throbbed and she was elated.

Holding Giahem's Wings, Aquila said, "I feel I was born to shoot this bow."

"We are waiting on a few others; then I will tell you what has occurred."

The nomad was strangely accepting of this. If the situation had been reversed, Lluava would have been dying to know the reason for this summons to battle. As she forced herself to take a few bites of the cold dinner that had been left in her chamber, she could not stop fiddling with the Claws.

Finally, her door opened. Yamir entered, leading Talos and a pallid Derrick.

"What are you doing here?" Lluava asked her dark-skinned friend.

"Going to fight by your side," asserted Derrick grimly. His face showed signs of strain, and Lluava wondered if he was still in pain. "I know you are planning something dangerous, and I'm ready."

"Nonsense," chastised Lluava. "You're not recovered, and that could cost you your life."

"I'll stand in his stead."

Lluava hadn't expected Apex's gruff voice. The huntsman walked into her room, his eyes flashing fiercely.

Forgetting the others' presence, she asked, "Why are *you* here? Shouldn't you be with Selene? Waiting for her in her chambers?"

"No. To battle is my purpose. War is my calling," affirmed the huntsman. "The time for masquerading is over."

Lluava was still baffled. "Masquerading? What do you mean?"

Apex looked at her as if he expected her to answer her own questions. "I was never under Selene's influence. Her intentions were plain from the start. I knew what she wanted to do to me, what she *thought* she was able to do with me. Fortunately, Luka expressed interest in helping with this charade almost as soon as I was brought back to the castle. He made it appear as if I was under his sister's spell." The ends of Apex's lips curled in pleasure. "That way, there was no doubt whose side I was on or who I was working for. As long as Yena saw me as Selene's puppet, she never once questioned my loyalty."

Lluava's heart began to beat rapidly. She hoped no one else sensed it. "Luka helped you? Why?"

"You have a way with people. You make them like you. They seem to want to follow you in whatever you undertake. Luka is no exception."

For a long moment, Apex and Lluava stared at one another. Their connection was only broken when Talos inquired, "Why are we all here, Lluava?"

Pulling herself back to the matter at hand, she explained the current attempt to rescue Ambassador Alcove and bring him to the castle. Once done, she was left with unhappy faces.

Talos began, "You sent men, Elysians, on a suicide mission. *Knowingly.*"

Suddenly, the wrong she had committed overwhelmed her. "Yes."

"How could you?" Talos asked. "They were common people who knew nothing of war. They survived one tragedy only to be killed in another."

"I did what I believed was right," Lluava explained, though her words turned to ashes in her mouth. They echoed the words Selene had spoken earlier that evening. "Alcove must be brought here. He is our best chance to send the Raiders home."

Her comrades looked skeptical, so Lluava tried a new approach. "Think about this. Alcove has been stripped of his command and his rights, yet instead of killing him, the Raiders have kept him alive. Their ambassador has become their prisoner. Why? Because he has an "affinity" for the Theriomorph race. And regardless of their reason for imprisoning him, he has worked alongside the Berserker Legion. He has valuable information about those brutes and more. There is also a chance that if the water source is poisoned, he will die as well. I cannot allow that."

"Would that be the worst thing?" Yamir asked, unafraid to speak his mind.

"Do you really believe the poison will destroy the entire army? If the plan fails, then what? The enemy will surely be enraged and attack us. You may question my reasoning, but please try to understand. Something, whether instinct or the divine, has been telling me to rescue Alcove. I must do this, for I know, I absolutely *know*, that it is right."

Everyone but Apex had taken a seat. "I honestly don't give a rat's ass about Alcove," he said. "I don't care if the poison works or the humans are slaughtered. I'm just ready to get out of this hellhole and stretch my legs. Ullr's Fangs have been starved for too long."

"Talos? Yamir?" Lluava looked at her oldest friends. "Will you join me on yet another preposterous mission?" Though she tried to sound playful, her voice was full of concern for all that could go wrong.

"If your strategies made sense, I would doubt whether they'd work," Yamir said with a faint smile. "Let's go kill some Raiders."

"I agree with the clan-beast," Aquila asserted proudly.

The group turned to look at Talos. The young soldier appeared drained of energy and lacked the enthusiasm of his spiky-haired friend. "I cannot condone your recent actions. Lives were lost. Good lives. But I wish to prevent others from meeting the same fate. I will join you, Lluava. My sword is yours, but never ask this of me again."

Onyx, who had been slumbering on his perch, suddenly awoke. Without vocalizing, he fluttered about the room, then swooped into Lluava's bedchamber and disappeared.

Derrick struggled painfully to his feet. Looking about, he said, "Since I can be of no service this time, I will leave you to plan. It's best that I not know, so that if I am asked, my lie will be genuine."

"Thank you, Derrick. Recover swiftly," Lluava said as he hobbled to the door. Yet as the soldier opened it, he froze mid-step.

Another figure blocked his way. Ammit's massive presence caused Derrick to stumble back. Dressed in a gray-green Endun military uniform with his serrated scimitar dangling from its scabbard, Yena's thug was ready for blood. Had they been caught before they could even *try* to save Alcove?

Striding past her bodyguard with a presence that matched his, Yena emerged from the darkened hall. Lluava's forehead began to bead with sweat.

Bowing low, Yamir inquired, "What brings the pleasure of your presence, High Priestess?"

Yena's voice filled the room. "It seems, Lluava, that you were correct on at least one count: the visions have changed. The great Crocotta has shown me your intentions."

It was as Lluava had feared. They were undone. All they could do was await Yena's verdict.

Without acknowledging Derrick, the high priestess spoke. "So, the five of you wish to rescue the Ocean Men's ambassador?"

Lluava spoke for the group, "Yes, High Priestess."

"And you believe that this is the will of the gods?"

"Yes."

Yena's ghostly eyes softened. "Then I will send Ammit with you. In return, the nomad, Aquila, will be stationed on the castle rampart."

Had she heard right? "You'll allow Aquila to fight? You'll allow us to fight?"

"I will not stand in the way of the gods' will. As for the nomad, what better vantage point for an eagle's eye than from above? He says he can wield a god's weapon. Let him prove it."

Although Lluava could hear her friends readying themselves behind her, she had one last question. "Have you seen what has happened to the rest of our prisoners, High Priestess?"

"Crocotta has chosen to keep her eyes on you and you alone. I have ordered one tunnel to be opened for your departure. Achieve the gods' will, Lluava, Incarn of Theri."

***

With Yena's blessing, the group made for the entrance to old Rhadamanthus without further hindrance. When Aquila parted from them to climb the stairs of the outer wall, Ammit gave him a spyglass. The others remained quiet as the nomad departed. Their silence continued during the remainder of their trek. Though they were grudgingly grateful for Ammit's support, the Outlander's presence stifled any friendly conversation.

As they approached the temple, Lluava saw Talos glance toward a cluster of town folk. With a small nod, he touched his chest with one hand in a sign of affection. Was Rosalyn there? Did she realize what was happening? Lluava knew her friend would choose to remain behind and cover for Talos's absence. Yet now that there was no need for secrecy, would the raven-haired woman regret her decision?

Once they reached the temple's underground labyrinth and entered the tunnel, it took them another hour to reach the end of the newly made shaft. A well-camouflaged trapdoor opened inside a scrubby patch of forest. One by one, they emerged.

A groan far too loud for their liking was heard as the entrance was sealed from within by those who remained to defend the city. With the ominous presence of the capital behind them, the small party made for the Raiders' camp. Their varied military training enabled them to approach far more stealthily than the unfortunate Elysians.

Ammit signaled a halt with his raised arm. After peering through his spyglass, he passed the device to Lluava and pointed ahead. A human corpse bristling with arrows came into focus. Not far away, a second man had succumbed to the same fate. Suddenly, she wanted to vomit. These men had died on a mission she should have undertaken herself.

Aware of the large Outlander's presence next to her, the young woman forced herself to keep moving. The group made a wide arc around the enemy's camp, for they planned to penetrate it at a location far from the tunnel entrance.

Cautiously determined, Apex approached her. "The deception was never meant to hurt you."

She knew he was referring to Luka's illusion, which had tricked Selene into believing she controlled Apex. Yet Lluava had been living at Cronus for a month, and Apex had never tried to tell her the truth. He had continued the charade despite knowing how much it pained her.

Her lip curled over an unusually pointed canine tooth. "I'm sure it was a terrible experience bedding Selene, Incarn of lust and seduction," she sneered.

"I had no reason to believe that you would return," he stated gruffly. "How was I to know?"

"She's going to be furious when she realizes what you did," Lluava pointed out. She wanted him to apologize for his actions, maybe even regret his choices.

"Let her be," Apex huffed. "There is no more time for games or deception. We must fight this war, you and I."

"Oh, *I* will fight. I have not stopped doing so since this cursed war began. And I will do everything in my power to see that the *rightful ruler* reclaims this kingdom."

Apex allowed Lluava to take the lead as he dropped back among the others.

For the first time in months, Lluava saw the Raiders' encampment. To say that they had been busy would have been a vast understatement. The earth had been stripped bare of the ancient forest. A twelve-foot-high stockade of logs had been erected around the camp's perimeter, protecting newly constructed buildings and barracks.

Ammit explained that to the best of his knowledge, there were only two points of entry, and both were obviously heavily guarded. They would have to find another way in.

With senses heightened, the group easily navigated the terrain with only the minuscule light from the cloud-covered sky. Torchlight spread a warm halo around the wooden barrier. Crouching just outside the luminous circle, the party reviewed their plan. Once it was set in motion, everyone would have to move quickly and without hesitation.

Over the tense silence, Lluava thought she heard a low rumble. Thunder? Or something more ominous just beyond the wall?

Handing his pouch of quills to Talos, Yamir gave the signal, and he, Ammit, and Talos rushed to the wall. Using the braced arms of the other two as steps, Yamir hoisted himself over the barrier. Talos quickly tossed over the quills, along with a knife. Then he and Ammit pressed themselves against the wall to avoid casting shadows in the firelight.

For several heart-wrenching moments, all they could hear was the scuffle of feet on the other side of the barrier. At last, the thick cords that bound the logs together moved. Lluava watched them closely—every twitch, every moment when all seemed still. Finally, the cords slackened.

That was her sign. Shifting, she and Apex lunged at the wall. His massive, bronze-furred, dual form matched her striped feline form in power and strength. The Yorrick wolverine's metallic muzzle slammed into the logs just moments before the tigress's gilded claws bit into the bark. Heaving with all their might, the loosened logs began to list inward. Soon the incline of the wood formed an ideal ramp, and the two beasts, followed by the other two Theriomorphs, breached the enemy's lair.

Several bodies lay scattered nearby with quills protruding from throat or temple. Yamir was nowhere in sight; only his knife lay discarded on the heavily trodden ground. Lluava gestured at the blade. Talos, sword in hand, collected the knife and tucked it into his belt. Their friend seemed to have disappeared without a trace.

Cursing under her breath, Lluava was both furious and worried about her spiky-haired friend. Yamir was supposed to have waited for them. Had he been captured? Or had he rushed off due to some temperamental lapse in judgment?

They could not afford to wait. Searching for Yamir would ruin their chance to retrieve Alcove. They forged ahead, hoping only that their friend would meet up with them later during the mission. They could not risk being discovered.

Shouts erupted. Too late.

Some of the Raiders must have stumbled upon Yamir's carnage. Before anything could be done, a number of sea brutes charged. Roused from bed and therefore lacking armor, they nonetheless outnumbered Lluava and her companions ten to one.

Above, a golden flash briefly illuminated the scene. A drop of moisture landed on Lluava's muzzle.

Ammit swung his scimitar; the curved blade lashed out as the enemy hesitated before him. "Attack!" he screamed, and the shouts of men and beasts merged into one horrendous cacophony.

Another golden flash from above. This time it ended with a noise even louder than the yells from the battle. Lluava, clawing at a Raider, could not afford to risk an upward glance. The smell of charred flesh tickled her nose.

Suddenly, the heavy clouds burst open. Torrential rain poured down, blurring everyone's sight. A third flash of light was followed by a thunderous roar. Where the lightning struck, a dozen or so men were blasted into the air. The strange explosion elicited more cries from the harried sea brutes.

Another flash, and another, each followed by a cracking boom that flung men into the sky like shrapnel. The electrical currents pulsing through the air caused Lluava's fur to stand on end. Looking in the direction of Cronus, the tigress saw a new flash of light arc up from the castle's wall to explode upon the earth inside the encampment.

"Gods be good," Apex snarled as he, too, stared at the source. "That isn't lightning. Those are Giahem's Talons."

A streak of gold impaled the dark clouds before beginning its descent. Lluava sensed its point of impact before it occurred.

"Run!" she roared.

Then the whole world lit up in an explosion of scorching light.

Chapter 25

Úlfhéðinn

The crackling air told Lluava she was still alive. Had she fallen, or had the force of the Talon's explosions thrown her backward? Blinking to rid her eyes of the bright, unrecognizable shapes blurring her vision, she tried to assess the situation around her. The entire camp had awoken. Like a colony of ants disturbed by an errant footfall, the Raiders charged about angrily. Or was it fearfully?

Sounds were oddly muffled, as if blankets had been thrown over the mouths of the speakers. Sheets of rain blurred sight. Mud clung to clothes, hindering speed. Nearby, Apex clawed at a fallen marauder.

Standing up, Lluava realized she had shifted into her human form. Talos was running toward her shouting something, but she couldn't make out the words. Suddenly, the babble of voices took form and rushed toward her.

"Aquila's making a path for us," Talos declared, pointing to a road paved with charred flesh and blackened earth.

"Do you think he has spotted Alcove?"

Lluava's question remained unanswered, for in the next moment, Ammit was shouting, "Go! Go! Go!"

The Raiders regrouped quickly, though they were much more cautious. Every so often, another crashing boom rang out. This time, the results were tamer. Real lightning was striking.

Though Aquila would never intentionally kill one of their own party, nature was not so kind. Ammit, Talos, and Lluava raced toward the debris-strewn trail, while Apex slew any Raider who got too close.

Lluava paid no attention to the massive beast charging beside her; she already knew that Ullr was controlling Apex. She could sense his change, his power, his raw hunger. The Yorrick wolverine was perfectly attuned to the enemy, swiftly consuming life after life without a glimmer of fear or a sense of mortality. Ullr and Incarn were one.

Soon they reached the end of the track. Despite Apex's fearsome ability, they were no match for the immense opposition they faced. The Raiders converged upon them in a furious attempt to slay those who had dared to infiltrate their camp. Silhouettes of an entire armory of weapons loomed up with each flash of lightning.

What now? Lluava wondered, refusing to allow her dread to control her. Gripping Issaura's Claws tightly, she positioned the weapons in the most threatening way. The thing inside her stirred. "I'm ready!" she shouted to the enemy. "Come on!"

Another explosion. This one opened a path off to the side.

"Go!" Ammit ordered as he swung his scimitar, sending beads of blood through the rainfall. "Get your man!"

Understanding what he meant to do, Lluava and Talos hurried down the path, leaving the Outlander to kill as many marauders as possible. A flash of lightning illumined a fallen tree trunk with one end of a chain affixed to the wood and the other tethering a battered figure. The captive lay face down in the mud. Quickly turning the body over, Lluava looked at the shell of the man she had once known. Alcove, severely weakened, moaned pitifully.

"Get him up," Lluava ordered Talos. "I need to break his shackles."

As mighty as Issaura's Claws were, they could not slice through the thick iron. Instead, she carved into the wooden weight. The log splintered and soon released its grip on the chain.

Talos attempted to revive Alcove, but the frail ambassador was clearly disoriented from Aquila's last shot. Helping the man to his feet, the young soldier said, "We must keep moving. Other Raiders will certainly arrive soon."

Only half aware, Alcove struggled forward, but the heavy chain dragged in the mud, slowing him down. As Lluava shifted, she told Talos, "Get him onto my back. I can carry him to safety."

It took a few moments to position Alcove along the tigress's spine. For a moment, Lluava questioned whether the weight might be too much after all. Then she and Talos made for the entry point, their only hope of escape. Her friend acted as her personal guard, allowing Lluava to concentrate on carrying Alcove. Each time the ambassador or the chain slipped, she desperately readjusted them to prevent her precious cargo from falling off.

Amid the chaos, Apex roared. The unearthly ring of that primeval sound caused Alcove to shudder. Yet that same sound reenergized Lluava. Moving even faster, she heard the ambassador speak.

"How?"

Unsure what he meant, Lluava replied, "We are assisted by a great archer."

"Arrows shouldn't be able to reach us," muttered Alcove, still not fully aware.

Gesturing with her paw at a large, scorched divot in the earth, Lluava noted, "Arrows shouldn't be able to do that, either."

A bolt of lightning crashed behind them. Once again, the electrical energy caused Lluava's fur to rise. She turned to Talos. "The storm's worsening. Do you see the others?"

Squinting hard, Talos said, "There is a group of Raiders over there, but I cannot be sure whether Apex or Ammit is the cause."

Hesitating, Lluava wondered if she should search for their other companions. She had dragged them into this fray. How could she abandon them in the den of the enemy?

Talos, always levelheaded, said, "The best we can do is head for the exit. I know they would do the same."

Following the young soldier, Lluava found it oddly fortunate that so few Raiders were attempting to attack them. Yet fortune did not stay with them; enrobed in mud and sodden furs, a Berserker stood in their path.

Lluava growled.

"How do you want to do this?" Talos inquired as he raised his sword.

Alcove spoke in a voice far more like the one Lluava remembered. "Do not worry about the likes of him. With this rain, he would not have been able to smoke his horn."

The giant man approached. Lluava could now discern that the whites of his eyes were unblemished. "He's not drugged," Lluava said gleefully. "Kill him."

Talos was first to run toward the Berserker. Lluava would have followed, but a series of thin projectiles bit into the enemy's exposed arms and neck. As the Berserker's throat began to bleed, Yamir appeared and shouted, "That's the last of my quills! I don't dare shift here to collect more."

The unexpected injuries distracted the brute just long enough to allow Talos within striking range. His sword struck the giant's with a mighty clang. Yamir hastily searched for any discarded weapon he could find among the dead until Talos was able to toss him his dagger. Leaving the pair to finish off the brute, Lluava skirted around the fight. She had her mission and was determined to complete it.

Another group of Raiders cut her travel short. Snarling, the tigress lashed out. In the bedlam, Lluava had hoped the enemy's nerves were failing, but the marauders did not disband. She felt Alcove tighten his grip.

"They won't risk killing you," she said.

"With Niðingr in control, I cannot swear to that," he countered.

Before a move could be made by either party, Apex and Ammit rejoined them. The Outlander was clearly exhausted from the prolonged battle. The wolverine, still energized under his god's protection, was ready for more.

Together, Lluava and Apex let loose mighty roars. Behind them, Talos and Yamir arrived. Thankfully, they were no worse for their own struggles.

With comrades on each side of her, she prepared to meet the enemy.

A wolf howled.

Derrick? Lluava wondered. No. This came from deep inside the camp. Several other howls rose up from the same direction. Could Derrick's men have found a way inside? Not many had survived the fight by Cronus's wall. Talos gave her the same questioning look, while Yamir asked aloud, "Wolves?"

From atop her shoulders, Alcove's voice rang out. A chill colder than the storms of the tundra seemed to overtake him. "No!"

Suddenly the sound of men beating on shields arose. The Raiders around them scattered in sheer panic.

"What is that?" Yamir questioned as he and the others turned about.

A row of Berserkers approached, then stopped as if awaiting a signal. Wolf cloaks and headdresses covered bare chests. Their painted shields were aligned before them, and they bit and tore at the tops with their teeth like rabid animals. Spitting out blood and splinters, they beat their weapons against those same shields like strange war drums.

Finally, one of the men lifted up his head and let loose a howl. As he did, his skin color began to change until he was entirely blue-black, while his muscles grew visibly bulkier. When he turned toward Lluava and her friends, she saw that the man's eyes, including the whites, had turned completely black. This inhuman apparition dropped his shield and lifted a horrific-looking axe.

Alcove's breaths had become shallow. His voice wavered, as did his pulse. "Úlfhéðinn. We are undone."

Another figure howled, then another. Each one in turn transformed into the same unnatural, blackened form. Their grizzled beards and hair were all that marked them as human.

These were not Berserkers. These were something new. These were Thad's "blue monsters." In her peripheral vision, Lluava noticed that the Berserkers were withdrawing. Slowly, she took a wary step backward. Her friends also edged toward the wooden palisade. Positioning himself as a buffer for the small band, Apex raised his bronze hackles menacingly.

One by one, the line of strange beings began to drop their shields and ready their weapons. Suddenly, the line split, allowing a new figure to approach. It was the sea-ravaged man from Yena's black-water visions—the true leader of the Raiders' army, the man from Lluava's nightmares.

"Beasts, creatures, abominations, pets of Mandrun's heirs, you are nothing," the leader said slowly, in a manner calculated to make sure the Theriomorphs understood every accented word. Lightning flickered; thunder boomed. The man continued. "We have studied you, learned your anatomy. You no longer hold any mystery."

The Úlfhéðinn—growling, howling, and foaming at the mouth like maddened beasts—made false lunges toward the slowly retreating group. Their leader continued, "Your reign over this land has come to its inevitable end." He lifted a jug, and a putrid, rotting odor permeated the air. Drinking deeply, the leader smashed the ceramic vessel on the ground.

Lluava's friends retreated quickly, yet she could not take her eyes off this nightmarish man or the dark, pulsing veins of his neck as the blackness spread through his body. When he cried out, even his tongue was now blue-black.

The line of Úlfhéðinn emitted their inhuman sounds once more, then charged. The monsters from the vision had been unleashed.

Chapter 26

Conspiracy Theory

Lluava did not need the presence inside her to tell her what to do next. Before the Úlfhéðinn had taken their second steps, she was running away as fast as her burdened dual form would allow. Alcove gripped her fur with all the strength he could muster. The spear tips of fear burrowing deep in Lluava's soul would not allow her to stay to combat those monstrous beings. If the Berserkers themselves had backed off in terror, what sort of horrific abilities did these blue-black men possess?

"Faster!" urged Alcove, and Lluava drove her paws as hard as she could against the slick mud. The storm had not lessened. In fact, the rain was coming down harder.

Beside her, Yamir's gangly legs seemed to blur as he struggled for speed, but his pace had begun to slow. Not far away, a panicked stag with velvet antlers bounded ahead of them, the whites of its eyes flashing like the lightning around them. As they neared the collapsed section of the stockade wall, Ammit's scimitar bit into one of the few Raiders who refused to back away from their positions. As Ammit's victim fell, the other Raiders began to flee. What terrified them more, the bedraggled tigress racing toward them, or the line of Úlfhéðinn on the animal's heels?

"Go!" shouted Lluava, as Alcove scrambled off her back and clambered over the angled logs. In the same moment, she glanced back at the terrifying sight so quickly approaching. The gap between the Úlfhéðinn and Apex, who was no longer under Ullr's control, was far smaller than she would have liked. This was partly due to Apex's own rider. Yamir, now nestled in the wolverine's hackles, brandished the javelin of an unfortunate Raider.

Turning to look at the charging creatures behind them, Yamir threw his weapon at the nearest brute. That was when the Úlfhéðnar did the impossible: he caught the spear in mid-flight. He swiftly sent it back in his opponent's direction.

There was nothing Lluava could do. She had only moments to escape the encampment before the enemy swarm would arrive. The spear hurtled toward its mark, promising certain death.

Then the world lit up with a new explosion. The entire projectile—shaft and tip—was consumed by the scorching eruption, which flung several Úlfhéðinn into the air. Aquila had saved them again!

Their victory was short lived. Lluava had barely climbed over the leaning logs before Apex leaped next to her, Yamir still clinging to his back. As Alcove reclaimed his position on the back of the tigress, dark-fleshed monstrosities arrived at the wall.

Like the Berserkers, the Úlfhéðinn, despite their injuries from the explosion, still charged forward. Pain appeared to be irrelevant to them; relentless and driven, they focused only upon the horrific destruction of their enemy.

They growled, snarled, roared, and foamed at the mouth like beasts possessed with the Rage. While some clambered through the opening, others rammed their large bodies against the wall. The line of tethered logs began to ripple. They were breaking through!

Lluava and her comrades ran. Just as she began to pick up speed, Alcove's body lurched. The metal chain had slipped from his grasp, and its heavy weight was dragging in the mud and tangling in the underbrush. Straining just to hold on, the weakened man was unable to pull up the chain. The tigress struggled to keep up with the others.

Were the Úlfhéðinn gaining on her, or was it just her imagination? She did not dare look back. Apex slowed his pace to match hers.

"Can you grab it?" the wolverine asked Yamir.

The young clansman leaned over at a precarious angle, groping for the dragging chain. Apex moved closer; Lluava's shoulders rubbed against his as their riders worked to reel in the iron weight. Once out of the mud, the burden of the dragging chain lessened. Both wolverine and tigress, with their harried riders, resumed their speed.

The hidden tunnel having been sealed behind them, the fleeing party now had to reach Cronus's gates. The safety of the castle walls loomed up through the downpour, but the band of tiring rescuers was still too far away. Would they reach the safe radius of the castle's own archers? And if they did, would arrows and spears even slow down the Úlfhéðinn? If even one of the creatures made it inside the gate, the safety of their own stronghold would be at risk.

"What in the seven hells?" Yamir cried out as he stared over his shoulder.

Lluava glanced back and saw that half of the Úlfhéðinn were running on all fours. Their mud-encrusted, wolf-hide garments gave the impression of bestial creatures resurrected from the underworld to claim unprepared souls. Worst of all, they were closing in.

"Apex!" she cried. "They can't be allowed inside! Do you understand? They cannot be allowed to enter the city!"

Lluava sensed a change in the giant wolverine as he realized what had to be done. She was glad she would not have to fight the Úlfhéðinn alone. In order for her friends to reach the gates, she and Apex must surrender themselves to their gods. They would willingly forfeit their lives to prevent the enraged monstrosities from breaching Cronus.

Two loud crashes occurred, one natural, the other not. Aquila must still be watching, but how many shots did he have left? His finite number of arrows should be diminishing. Did the decreasing number of fired projectiles mean that he realized it and was saving each shot in order to inflict maximum damage?

"I'll help you fight," Yamir said grimly.

"No," Lluava countered. "I need you to assist the ambassador. Get him inside the gates."

Alcove remained silent. What could he say? Apologize for the inconvenience? Thank them for their aid? Lluava realized he was grateful.

Ammit had entered the perimeter of protection. Above him on the wall, archers were positioned at every parapet. The Outlander stopped and gestured toward the sky.

Above, a massive flock of birds had taken wing. Theriomorphs? No. These were very much actual birds, carrion eaters all. Had they come expecting a banquet?

No—they were flying in a specific formation. Their unnatural movements were led by a single avian. One raven, larger than those around him, cawed out commands. Like a swarm of locusts blackening the sky, the flock spread out overhead, then dove at those on the ground.

The raven's good eye looked at Lluava as he flew past. Onyx was commanding his own aerial army to combat the enemy! If told of this strange event at a different time or place, neither she nor her companions would have believed it. Wild animals were taking a stand against the Raiders from across the ocean!

Lluava felt the puffs of air as thousands of wingbeats passed. Rushing at the line of Úlfhéðinn, the birds used Thoth's iconic form of attack and targeted the eyes of the enemy. Unflinching, the savage monsters pushed forward, not even bothering to strike at the winged projectiles. Still, the mass of birds managed to slow the marauders' approach.

Realizing she had hesitated, Lluava loped toward the capital's opened gates. Behind her, arrows plummeted earthward. Though aimed at the enemy, they had inadvertently hit many of the winged helpers. The cries of birds, the shouts of men, and the rumbles of thunder created a cacophony in the cloud-choked sky.

Lluava felt her burden slip. In an instant, the chain dropped and snagged on the ground. Alcove was wrenched from her back. The muddy puddles hindered her ability to stop, and she skidded off in the opposite direction.

Motionless, the man lay crumpled on his side, entangled in chain and mud, as the wall of doom approached.

Struggling to her feet, she attempted to reach the ambassador before the wave of arrows, avians, and Úlfhéðinn collided with him. She was close. So close. Suddenly, a lone Úlfhéðnar appeared before her.

On all fours, the behemoth leapt at her as a lion leaps upon an unsuspecting buffalo. Bowling her over, the man's giant fist beat against Lluava's unprotected face. His other hand reached for the large blade strapped on his back.

Kicking him with her rear paws, the tigress drove her gilded foreclaws into the man's underbelly, gutting him on top of herself. For three long moments, the Úlfhéðnar continued his assault as blood dripped from his open mouth. But before his sword was fully raised, her attacker collapsed. The weapon fell from his hand, nicking the top of Lluava's ear.

Writhing beneath the large corpse, she fought her way out from under it. Úlfhéðinn surrounded her, blocking her line of sight to Alcove. Another explosion blasted the earth next to her. The shock wave flung her into the air and left a large divot in the mud.

Sounds rang dully in her ears. Flecks of dirt stung her eyes and distorted her vision. She was aware of people moving around her, felt hands helping her rise onto her four limbs. Her body was wracked with pain. She shifted. Arms looped under hers, and she was helped from the field of battle.

A deafening groan escaped her. Someone held a small vial to her lips. She drank the offensive liquid without hesitation. Her body felt as if it were on fire as the Idun took effect. She was inside Cronus. But where was Alcove?

Another figure offered water to help rinse out her eyes. The cold liquid stung briefly before relief set in. Blinking out soiled tears, Lluava saw that the others in her party had returned as well. Ammit was overseeing the removal of Alcove's chain. Rosalyn and Talos were tending to the ambassador's still form.

Yamir approached her. "That was a close one," the young clansman said. His left arm oozed blood.

"You all right?" Lluava asked as, together, she and her coppery-skinned friend approached the group around Alcove.

"Could have been worse," he acknowledged with a shrug. "Better than him, that's for sure. He's got a nasty bump on his head. Out cold."

Once they were within earshot, Rosalyn confirmed Yamir's assessment. "The ambassador might have a concussion. I will not know for sure until he wakes. He is unconscious now."

"But he will wake?" Lluava wanted to make sure. The memory of Varren strapped on the stretcher filled her with foreboding.

"I believe so," answered Rosalyn. "Let's just hope your burns heal as well."

Lluava finally took note of herself. She had several patches of seared flesh, although due to the dose of Idun, the pain was rapidly lessening.

From beyond the wall, a dark form flew down. Onyx perched on Rosalyn's shoulder. The black-haired woman smiled at the raven and scratched its throat. The bird muttered contentedly.

Gazing past Lluava, Rosalyn said, "Look—it seems Apex bears news."

When the huntsman strode up, he spoke to those who had ventured into the Raiders' camp. "The poison has been released. Let's hope that it works and kills many."

"Poison?" Rosalyn looked aghast. Talos bent over and said something in her ear. Glancing about once more, Rosalyn said, "I will excuse myself now."

"What then?" Talos grimly asked Apex, after Rosalyn and Onyx had gone.

"Then..." Apex began. He gave Lluava a long, if not questioning, look. "We go out and slay any who are left alive."

"Do not worry about tomorrow," Ammit joined the conversation, now that Alcove's shackles had been removed and the ambassador taken to the hospital. "Fortune has smiled on us this night. Food has been prepared in the castle. Go and enjoy your well-deserved meal."

Ammit went ahead while the others waited for Aquila to come down from the parapet. Yamir looked at the rest of the party. "Do any of you know what in the seven hells went on with those birds out there? Onyx was one of them, right?"

"Your guess is as good as mine," said Lluava.

Talos shook his blond locks. "I have no explanation. But I will be praying my thanks tonight."

"And what about your arrows?" Yamir asked the approaching nomad.

Lluava studied Aquila's face; he appeared empowered. Looking down his sharp nose, he told them, "My father told me this bow was our family's destiny. He spoke truth."

"Your quiver—it's full," Apex pointed out. Lluava noted the tinge of jealousy in the huntsman's voice. She, too, had to acknowledge that the combined power of Giahem's Wings and the Talons was something out of myth. His quiver was full as it ever had been.

"The bow will never be without its arrows again."

There was a rumble of thunder. The rain had not abated.

"Come," Talos said, "let us change out of these wet clothes and enjoy our meal. I am hungry."

"I definitely agree with that," said Yamir, grinning, as the party dispersed.

***

Having taken extra time to wash and dress, Lluava hurried through the castle toward the banquet hall. As she passed the Grand Hall, a figure called out from the doorway.

"Lluava! I see you made it back in one piece."

Selene's sweet voice seemed to coil around the pillars in the hall. Lluava paused to look at the other Incarn. Remembering Apex's news, Lluava said,

"I should congratulate you on your success. Your plan to poison the enemy has been implemented. You may have saved the kingdom from the Raiders."

With a charming smile, Selene motioned for Lluava to join her. Following the young woman, Lluava entered the vast chamber. She had never seen it so empty. The throne room had been the heart of the castle as well as the Elysian government. Here, aristocrats had gossiped and new proclamations were pronounced. On this cold marble floor, Lluava had partnered with Varren in the ceremonial Dance of Suns. And here, too, the High Council had met its end.

"Magnificent, is it not?" Selene noted as she, too, looked about the vacant chamber. Gesturing at the line of thrones, she said, "Soon we will be the protectors of this realm, to rule over it as we see fit, to render judgment when needed. We will have to make choices, hard ones, for the betterment of our people. We will have to cast aside our petty differences in order to put others first. Soon we, the Incarn, will live for the people and not for ourselves. Our own dreams will be cast aside, our emotions suppressed. We have been created for a greater purpose, you and I. In order to fulfill it, we will have to put aside the selves we now know." Sighing, the beautiful woman added, "There is little time left to act on our own before we must sacrifice our identity for the greatest good."

Thinking deeply, Lluava mused, "I don't know. How can we be sure of our grand purpose? Maybe..." Lluava thought of Varren in the south of the kingdom. "Maybe we are not meant to rule Elysia but to act as guides to help our race move into a more peaceful and prosperous era."

"Varren will never be allowed to rule again." Selene's eyes narrowed as they scrutinized Lluava. "The era of humans is at its end. He will be killed." She paused before asking, "Does it hurt, knowing that someone you love will be taken from you?"

"How can you ask that, Selene?" Lluava questioned hotly. "Didn't you admit you had feelings for him while you were by his side?"

"He was just a toy. Something to play with." Selene's icy honesty was shocking. "If he ever shows up, I have half a mind to do it again until he faces his horribly public execution."

Lluava waved Issaura's Claws threateningly in front of Selene. "He doesn't need to die."

"Oh *yes*, he does. High Priestess Yena will never allow him to live. He is the sole heir to the throne, the only surviving descendent of Landon Mandrun, the conqueror. That we both can agree on."

As much as she hated it, Lluava knew that Selene was right. The high priestess would always view Varren as a threat, even if he willingly handed over the throne and kingdom to the Theriomorphs. Still, Lluava refused to give up.

Selene offered a broken smile. "The question is, which is worse? Knowing that Varren will lose his life at some point in the future, or that one of your friends will die tonight?"

"What are you talking about?"

Running her manicured nails through her bejeweled hair, Selene explained, "As we speak, one of them is sipping from a congratulatory goblet rimmed with poison."

Lluava could not think clearly. Why? How? Who? Suddenly, she realized the obvious truth. "*You* poisoned someone!"

"Think of it more as a *venomous* bite."

Selene had to be bluffing. Surely, she was just toying with Lluava. She was not the murderous type. Well, not when the situation didn't warrant. Sweat began to bead on Lluava's brow. She had to make sure this wasn't a ruse. "What did any of my friends do to you?"

"Nothing. They are just important to you."

Panic. Lluava raced toward the doors. Maybe she could reach her friends before the celebration began. Behind her, Selene's honeyed voice spoke out, "Don't you want the antidote?"

Halting, Lluava turned around, "There's a cure? Give it to me."

As if she had not heard the demand or Lluava's voice at all, Selene asked, "Don't you want to know why?"

"If there is some remedy, give it to me, Selene," Lluava tried to sound authoritative, yet in this situation, she felt helpless.

"As someone who cares about everyone else, don't you even care why you vex me so?"

Lluava realized this was just a game to Selene. The woman was toying with her, trying to get her to play. With a friend's life at risk, Lluava had no choice but to play along.

"All right. Why?"

Quite serious, Selene also appeared thrilled and went on to explain, "Poison has always been my...*specialty*. Well, that and sex. Using both, I was able to acquire the power and position that others only dream about. I worked hard for everything I have. Struggled in ways you cannot even fathom. You did not crawl out of the muck of poverty. I did. I rose to the top. I was happy." Selene's pupils narrowed until they looked like needles. Her body quivered, and her silver pendant necklace swung like a pendulum between her breasts. "Then you stole that which was most important to me."

"Varren? Apex?" Lluava snapped. Her own fury bubbled up. "They never loved you. They were never yours. I cannot take away something you never had."

Selene paused. "No—my brother's affection. Luka was the only one who ever truly loved me." A tear rolled down her coppery cheek. "You took away something I love. In return, I am taking away something of yours."

Lluava realized that Selene had found out about Luka's betrayal. Well, betrayal might be too harsh a term, but Selene's own brother had helped Apex trick her with a scheme he had devised.

Lluava quickly countered, "Luka did not conspire against you. He never wished you harm. He loves you, Selene. Undo this."

Touching the teardrop pendant about her throat, Selene shook her head. "It's too late."

"Selene!" Lluava cried out as she knelt before the young beauty. "I implore you to stop this. Do you want me to beg? I will. To grovel at your feet? I will. If you have poisoned someone, provide the remedy. Please!"

Turning to look down at the tresses about her flowing gown, Selene seemed actually humbled. "Lluava Kargen, Incarn of the goddess of war, jewel to Yena, savior of our race, do you wish to save your unfortunate friend? You desire the antidote? If you want it," Selene's dark eyes burned as she gestured to her necklace, "you will have to take it.".

Chapter 27

Suada's Venom

"Come, Goddess of War! Take the *venom*. Save your friend." Selene's challenge was very clear. "That is, if you think you are strong enough." Lluava disregarded Luka's warning that Selene was far too powerful to oppose. If she did not obtain the pendant and the antidote it held, someone would die.

"If any of my friends die, I will kill you.," Lluava threatened in return. Selene smiled confidently. "Will you, now?"

Gripping the Claws tightly, Lluava implored one last time. "You are not trained in battle. I don't want to hurt you, but I will, to save a friend's life."

"Jusssst try."

There was a clamor at the doorway. Several noblemen entered. Lluava recognized them from her days at court. They were all from prestigious Theriomorph families.

"What's going on in here?" the youngest asked. He was no more than fifteen years of age, and his fellows were older by no more than a decade.

"She threatened me!" Selene declared as she pointed one ringed finger at Lluava. "She desires my jewels. She wishes to harm me."

"What impropriety!" the eldest replied, while the youngest said, "You must leave Lady Selene alone."

"She lies!" Lluava snapped back at those approaching her. "Selene says she has poisoned my friend. I need her to hand over the antidote." As one of the men grabbed Lluava's wrist, she continued to protest. "Didn't you hear me? Selene is about to murder someone!"

The man did not release Lluava. Instead, the others approached to help hold her down. What was wrong with them? How could they be so accusing?

Wrenching her wrist free, Lluava took several hasty steps back. "Selene's the one you want. Not me."

"The Lady Selene is the most beautiful, the most gracious—"

Without listening further, Lluava realized the situation she was in. The men were under Selene's control. They would prevent Lluava from attaining her goal. Time was slipping by. From behind her wall of defenders, her personal puppets, Selene watched, smiling.

Two older noblemen lurched at Lluava. She moved away once again. Feeling the arms of a third about her, she flung the poor man to the ground just as the fourth swung at her jaw. The impact caused her vision to blur. Lluava ducked and rolled out of the way. Then she was mobbed.

Elbows and arms, fists and feet were flung about like leaves in a storm. Lluava retaliated haphazardly—sometimes evading, other times striking back defensively. Tired, sore, and still in pain from rescuing Alcove, she could not defend herself properly.

"Get off of me!" she shouted as the four finally held her in place. With a burst of anger, Lluava retaliated. She was almost free when the whirlwind of grappling appendages harried her attempts once more.

Suddenly, there was a sputtering gasp, and the boy of fifteen fell backward. As Lluava shook off the other men, who ignored their fallen comrade, she took note of the bloodied Claw.

"He was unarmed. Jussst a boy," Selene's voice broke the unusual silence. "Your reputation certainly precedes you."

Lluava had not meant to kill the youth. How had she missed that her assailants were unarmed? It had been four to one, and everything happened so fast. What had Selene made her do? As the trio lunged for Lluava again, she shouted, "Selene, *you* should be the one fighting me. One on one. Not these pawns of yours. If you have something to prove, you need to be the one to prove it."

With a sidelong glance at the youth's body, Selene shrugged her narrow shoulders. "I have no more need of your assistance," she said to the men. Entranced, they filed out of the chamber and closed the doors behind them.

"One on one?" Selene laughed. "As you wish, Incarn of Theri."

Selene began to shift. Her form expanded, growing larger and larger until her lovely silken gown, which was not made of Endun, shredded. Bits of cloth, lace, and ribbon scattered, as countless scales stretched out in a large loop. Shhhhhh. Sssssssssss. Sibilant sounds slithered from the innumerable coils that seemed to loop and knot, twist and stretch, simultaneously.

A massive anaconda, shimmering green as a cut emerald in the sun, began to cover the Grand Hall's floor. The serpent's unheard-of size would surely have struck fear into most people's hearts.

Lluava had no time to let her own doubts take hold. As Suada's Incarn slowly slithered around the room, Lluava searched through the scraps of clothing littering the floor. The necklace had to be somewhere. The chain was too small to encircle the snake's thick neck; it must have snapped or the links broken. She had only to find the pendant.

Where was it? It had to be here. As Lluava moved to another small pile of remnants, she noticed a reflection on the polished marble floor. The anaconda had reared its head. Cold, dark-gold eyes stared down at her; the forked tongue flashed out angrily. It was scenting its prey; it was scenting *her.* A shiver ran down her spine.

The serpent opened its jaws. Two large fangs appeared, fangs that a true anaconda did not have. What made the unnatural sight even more terrifying was that these fangs were formed from a silver-hued material. How could that be? Unless—

Selene's necklace was a god's weapon: Suada's Venom. Now Lluava understood. With poison as one's weapon, there was no need for blade or bow. When Selene shifted, the pendant shifted with her. There was no way to retrieve it from her dual form. Venom coated the fangs, becoming one with the snake just as Issaura's Claws became one with the tigress. Lluava would have to combat the anaconda in order to force her to shift into her human form. That was the only way to attain Suada's Venom.

Lluava was not prepared to make the first move. She kept her back to the anaconda. Once she let Selene know that she was aware of the serpent's large head looming above, the snake would strike. A bead of sweat rolled down the side of Lluava's face as she readied herself to spring aside. Just a moment more.

As soon as Selene struck out at her, Lluava dove away. There was a grating sound as metal scraped stone. Taking advantage of the jarred serpent shaking its pained mouth, Lluava looked about her.

The anaconda's colossal form encircled the perimeter of the room; the massive green walls of its coils were tightening and closing around its prey. If Lluava couldn't find a way past the snake, she would become ensnared in Selene's fingerless grip.

Getting a running start, she leapt onto the second tier of coils, digging Issaura's Claws into the scaled flesh. There was a dry, gasping sound. In a flash, the gigantic serpent bunched into a ball, writhing on the ground.

Lluava was almost over the emerald wall when the flailing tail knocked her back down. All about her, the towering coils knotted up. Each time she surmounted one writhing coil, another slammed down from above. In desperation, the two forms struggled with each other. The serpent involuntarily reacted to the pain. Although Selene was not purposely attacking her fellow Incarn, Lluava could feel the anaconda's strong, muscled form and sense the danger. She was unable to match the snake's haphazard ferocity; if she did not escape, she would surely be crushed.

Lluava shifted. In her larger dual form, equipped with tooth and claw, she was able to heave herself out of the emerald cage. Once free, the opponents reassessed each other.

Fortunately for Lluava, the Claws' surprising pain had caused Selene to react instinctively. When balling up, the serpent was unable to coil around her prey. But the glimmer in Selene's golden eyes held a warning: the snake was preparing herself for a second round.

"I told you," Lluava said, "you have no combat training. If one cut caused you such pain, what is going to happen when we go head to head?" She allowed Selene to consider her words before adding, "Give me Suada's Venom. I will return it to you after my friend has been saved. We can move on from this. We must."

Although Lluava was doubtful, she would say anything to prevent this battle from continuing. What good could come from a fight between two Incarn?

The gargantuan serpent lifted its long neck and began to scale the wall. When it reached the lip of the ledge that ran behind the seats where the High Council had once perched, the anaconda slithered over the top. Lluava's heartbeat quickened. She had allowed her opponent to hide. Far from being over, the fight was just about to begin.

One seat near the front of the room teetered. Another, close to the royal dais, was shoved back completely. Selene's huge form stretched the length of the room. The question was, where was the head?

"Did you think thisssssssss would be easssy?" Selene's voice arose from no place in particular. "I haven't felt ssssuch pain in a long while. I'd forgotten how invigorating it can be. Yet, doling out pain to others issss ssssssooo much better. You might call me a ssssadisssst."

Lluava's lips curled up and she emitted a low growl. There was no movement indicating where or even how Selene had positioned herself. What were the anaconda's weaknesses? Her vertebrae. If its spine were snapped, the snake would be helpless; yet Selene herself would be paralyzed. That would not do. This was just a game—a sick, twisted game that Lluava was forced to play. One innocent youth had already lost his life. Selene should not lose hers, too. What about the base of her skull? If Lluava grabbed hold of her there, the snake could not bite her, but could it strike her with its tail?

"Mossst of the woundsss I deal are not of the physssical kind. Where emotionsss run fassst, pain can be..."

A scraping sound caught Lluava's ear, and she turned around. The enormous body of the anaconda arched over the doorway, its head having already disappeared among the raised seating on the other side of the room. In the blink of an eye, the lengthy form had hidden once again.

"I am to be Varren'ssss executioner." Selene's voice rose, again from seemingly nowhere. "At firssst, I wanted him to die quickly. Call me temperamental, but based on the way thingssss have recently played out, I've changed my mind."

Another rumble escaped Lluava's lips.

"As a fellow Incarn, I may not be allowed to kill you, but I think it will be enjoyable to sssee you sssuffer as each of those you hold dear die around you."

Was Selene trying to bait her to climb after her? Was the snake going to wait in ambush until Lluava was nearby? Time was passing and could be wasted no longer. Something had to be done.

Unfortunately, nothing seemed to happen in Lluava's favor. The tigress felt the prick of a blade at the base of her tail. The men had returned, this time bearing weapons.

"You said one on one," snarled Lluava as she split her attention among the new players. "A fair fight."

"A fair fight is what I am giving you, Incarn of Theri," Selene's voice reverberated throughout the hall. "I admit that I know nothing of warfare. These men do."

Without hesitation, the first man attacked, and the other two mirrored his actions. Lluava was unable to avoid a confrontation. Slashing out threateningly, she tried to scare them off. Her tactics were futile; Selene's pawns refused to stop. The tigress defended herself against the charging nobles down the full length of the chamber. Blood flowed from her wounds as well as from those of the men.

Weak as she already was, this proved trying. The presence inside her implored release, yet Lluava wanted no more blood on her hands.

Only after the sickening snap of a leg did all three men suddenly seem to be released from the spell. Bewildered, they looked in horror at the blood-splattered tigress before them and their deceased comrade on the floor. Dropping their weapons, they withdrew as fast as the two could carry the injured man. The corpse was left behind.

"There goesss your reputation," hissed Selene from above. "Pity."

Summoning the will to continue their horrid game, Lluava scanned the chamber and wondered where the snake would appear next. She did not speculate long. The anaconda struck from above. Lluava worked hard to evade the snake's quick reflexes.

Selene was unlike any opponent she had ever faced before. Every inch of the serpent was deadly, for every inch could contort to constrict its prey. Its wide maw sported abhorrent, venomous fangs, lethal daggers ready to puncture vital arteries or tendons. Its jaws could unhinge to swallow her entire form. The creature could climb, coil, and spring. With its great size, it could lash its tail almost the full length of the hall. There was nowhere to retreat, no place to hide.

Lluava had to keep ahead of the gaping mouth and lethal coils. Surely her own endurance was greater than the serpent's. Moreover, the anaconda was not designed to give chase. Yet, as Selene continued to lash out again and again, Lluava's defensive tactics were weakening.

Incarn were not meant to kill one another, that was clearly understood. Yet if Lluava could not inflict severe harm on Selene, how could she overpower the serpent? How could she gain Suada's Venom and save her friend?

Then Lluava realized she couldn't.

If Selene lived, her friend would die. If she harmed Selene, how would that affect her own destiny? Weren't all Incarn supposed to unite for one great purpose? When, she wondered, had she begun to believe in the power of fate? This was *her* life. Hers. Why should she give something or someone else control over it?

Distracted by her thoughts, Lluava lost her focus on the serpent's long form. Abruptly, the thick green tail slammed down in front of her. She crashed into it and then fell backward.

The power of the attack knocked the wind out of her. Gasping for breath, she realized she had been perfectly positioned for Selene's purpose. A second later, the tigress was wrapped in the anaconda's coils, her life slowly being squeezed out.

The strength of Selene's dual form was incredible. Suada's Venom could not be taken by force, that was clear. Yet with each tightening sinew, Lluava questioned Selene's actual motive. What if the woman's true intent had always been to kill her?

Releasing a furious roar, the tigress concentrated her energy and forced each digit of her forepaws to curl, then drove her gilded claws into the muscular body of the snake. Opening her own mouth, she tore into the scaled hide, tongue and teeth ripping and slashing at the snake's flesh.

In response, Selene's muscles tightened further. Lluava's sight began to waver. Her lungs burned. As her own grip slackened, images of family and friends flashed before her. Was she dying?

The fire in her chest spread through the rest of her body. From whiskers to tail, a hot energy coursed through her. Suddenly, Lluava was able to thrust free. Tigress and serpent stared at each other, puzzled. Several open wounds on the anaconda oozed blood. The room became so silent that the drip, drip, drip of the crimson droplets splattering on the marble floor echoed in the cavernous space.

Locking eyes with the serpent, the tigress prepared to make her next move. But move she could not. This time, invisible coils enveloped her, squeezing out air. She could not breathe. She could not cry out. She could not blink. The huge, golden-eyed gaze held hers in an intangible grip. Lluava was under Selene's control.

The foreign force began to pervade her own form even as her mind struggled against it. *Kneel.* The order was understood, though no voice had uttered it. Lluava's forelimbs lowered. Her mind grew hazy. Reality faded in and out.

Suddenly, another fiery wave seared through Lluava's body, causing her eyes to tear with pain. She was back in control. In that moment, she could have asked for the antivenom. She could have implored Selene to stop this madness. Instead, her fiery anger seethed.

"Luka did not choose to help Apex deceive you because of his feelings for me. You drove him away. He did what he did because you are cold and heartless."

The snake struck so quickly that Lluava did not feel the twin punctures in her shoulders until after the serpent had retracted its large head. Was that a flicker of doubt in Selene's eyes, or was her own sight wavering once more? As intense pain shot through her, Lluava shifted to human form. Crying out, she stumbled away from the emerald anaconda. Whether the bite was intentional or instinctive, Selene's posture altered.

Lluava's entire body began to convulse, and she struggled to remain standing. Meanwhile, Selene's jaw began to unhinge. First one side dropped lower followed by the other. In a slow, practiced movement, the snake's mouth opened to a gigantic hollow. Would the giant anaconda swallow her victim, thereby erasing any trace of the battle?

The poison coursing through Lluava had a secondary effect. She could feel her other self and knew that the goddess's grasp on her was slipping away. Lluava must deal with the unfolding events on her own.

Sweat dripped into her eyes, further distorting her vision. I will not die tonight. Lluava willed herself to believe it. I will not die *this* night. With slippery palms, she gripped Issaura's Claws tightly.

Stumbling away from the serpent's approach, Lluava fought the drowsiness weighing down her aching body. She felt herself slip, and her knees hit the ground before she sensed her full collapse. All was pain.

A massive shadow rose above her. Lluava wanted to roll over, to lash out with her weapons, yet her body was leaden. Calming her mind, she focused on harnessing the remaining scraps of her energy. She would make one last effort.

"What is the meaning of this?"

Lluava heard the coils shift position as a distorted voice rumbled through the vaulted room. At the edges of her vision, everything was growing gray. The sound of whispered voices fluttered about her ears. Chat? Horus? Austro? Gramps? The dead were calling her, telling her to follow.

Wait, she wanted to shout out, not yet!

Biting her tongue, Lluava tasted her own blood as it slid down her throat. A stirring arose, an overpowering fury. Leaping to her feet, Lluava charged at the one thing that filled her vision—the emerald anaconda.

The beast was facing away from her. In a single leap, she thrust Issaura's Claws deep into the flesh at the base of the creature's skull. The serpent writhed briefly, sending Lluava crashing to the floor, and then the great, limp body collapsed beside her.

The gray haze in Lluava's peripheral vision continued to mass like storm clouds. Crawling on her stomach, Lluava approached Selene's form as it reverted to a naked body sprawled in a pool of blood. Reaching around the woman's throat, Lluava grasped the item she desired.

Strands of black hair entangled in the chain were ripped away as Lluava grasped the teardrop pendant, Suada's Venom. If anything could save her, it was this god's weapon. But how?

Fighting to keep her eyes open, Lluava felt her body tremble as she inspected the pendant carefully. There was no line or latch to suggest that this object was a container of any sort. Rounded on the bottom, the top ended in a needle-sharp point. With a whisper of hope, Lluava drove the pointed tip into the palm of her hand and pierced her flesh.

The entire world went black.

Chapter 28

Origin of the Beasts

In an explosion of sensation, Lluava was jarred into awareness. She felt the pressure around her hand before she registered what she saw.

Apex was trying to pry her fist open. Lluava realized he was attempting to get the pendant, Suada's Venom. She lurched to one side, accidentally cutting his hand with the Claw. Hesitating, she tried to figure out the huntsman's motives.

"For a moment, I thought—" Apex began, then his worried features changed. "Lluava, it's me. Apex. Do you recognize me?"

Her mouth refused to function. Unable to speak, Lluava nodded warily. Why was he after the Venom? Why hadn't he gone for help? Trying to scoot back farther, she slipped in the liquid around her. Selene's blood had become a large puddle that was being absorbed by the clothing of both women.

Selene was dead.

The Incarn of Suada was no more. Her unblemished skin seemed drained of the hue that only life endows. Her nakedness unashamedly dared anyone to deny that she was created for the goddess of lust and seduction.

Apex looked at the body with a grim expression. "She was speaking to me when you struck. She wanted me to reach out to you so that she could give you the cure. However misguided Selene was, she never wanted a fellow Incarn to die."

"She's poisoned someone, one of my friends," Lluava spat out. Her voice was barely audible. "I needed the cure." The hand that held Selene's necklace stung, but not as much as her shoulder, swollen where the serpent's fangs had dug in.

As she struggled to stand, Apex assisted her. "The banquet hall. I need to get there." As Lluava began to make her way out of the throne room, she realized that she was the only one leaving. "Apex?"

"Go," he said roughly. He gestured toward the bodies of Selene and the youth. "This needs to be dealt with."

Not wasting time to argue, Lluava staggered to the nearby hall, from which the smell of mulled wine and braised boar wafted down the corridor. After what seemed like an eternity, Lluava finally arrived at the banquet hall's doors.

There was a clatter and a shout.

Shoving the door open, Lluava yelled, "Stop drinking!"

The first thing she saw was Talos, wiping spilled wine from Rosalyn's gown. The startled onlookers turned to gape at Lluava whose Endun clothes were covered in blood. Realizing that she probably sounded crazy, she hastily explained, "There is poison in one of your cups. I don't know which one. Who drank anything? I have the antidote."

"No one," Talos told her, still holding his handkerchief. "Nobody drank anything."

Rosalyn spoke up. "We were waiting, but we had just decided to toast the safe return of all of you. That was when your bird flew at me."

Yamir jumped up and pointed. "Look at Onyx." The raven was sprawled on the ground, feathers dripping with red wine. His small body shuddered. "You don't think—?"

Lluava hurried to the bird and pressed the sharp tip of the pendant into its leg muscle. She stopped only when she saw beads of blood bubble up.

"Are you all right, Rosalyn?" she asked her friend, as she carefully watched the raven's chest rise and fall.

"Yes. The wine spilled mainly on my dress."

"Let's get you changed. Quickly," urged Talos, now quite worried. His concern for his wife and their unborn child was obvious. The couple gave their friend a grateful glance and hurried home.

A second, trembling voice spoke up. Luka asked agitatedly, "Whose blood is on you?"

Lluava suddenly felt nauseated. "Luka, it couldn't be helped. If you knew what she tried to do—"

Selene's brother did not wait to hear her explanation. He strode over to Lluava, snatched the necklace with the Venom, and raced out of the room. Only she knew where he was headed.

"What happened?" Aquila asked, his eyes scanning the room, on the alert.

Still monitoring Onyx, Lluava shared everything with the few who remained. Derrick, Aquila, and Yamir listened intently. When she finished answering their questions, she inquired, "Where is Ammit? I thought he would be here as well."

"He chose not to eat with us," said Yamir. "I think he might not be comfortable with those whom he does not know...or trust."

Ammit, scared? Not likely. Lluava guessed that he had gone to deliver to the high priestess the news of their return. Before she could wonder further, a tall, lanky Outlander entered the room. His eyes sought Lluava with an expression that masked his personal thoughts.

"Finish your meal later, Theri. The Ocean Man has awakened."

Lluava's stomach heaved. Yamir said, "After all this, I wouldn't be able to eat." Heading to the door, he continued, "I'm going to check up on Rosalyn." With a fleeting smile, he added, "And then see what food they have at their house."

Handing Onyx to Aquila, she said, "If you want, go with him. I know you're hungry as well." With no chance to change clothes, Lluava followed the Outlander through the corridors. He stared suspiciously at the fresh blood on her but said not another word.

Alcove was propped up in a bed. Though alert, he looked dreadful. Skin hung loosely on his arms and face. His jawbones were more pronounced than ever. Still, there was very little sympathy in Lluava's tone when she asked, "How does it feel to know that the den of your enemy is now your salvation?"

"God works in strange ways," he answered weakly. His thick accent made his words almost impossible to decipher.

"I never thought you were religious."

"On the contrary, religion is my highest motivation."

Even now, Lluava felt as if Alcove had the upper hand. Was it the way he spoke? Or the glint in his sunken eyes? "Are you going to tell us what we want to know voluntarily, or through other means?"

Adjusting his pillow, Alcove countered, "What is it you want to know?" Would he actually work with them without demanding something in return?

"Everything."

"Where do I begin?" he chortled before grimacing with pain. Clearly, Yena had not prescribed Idun for the ambassador.

Lluava had little compassion. "The giants and your monsters would be a good start."

"How do I explain in a way that you would understand?" Alcove mused to himself.

Insulting as his statement was, she waited patiently for the answers.

"The Berserkers came first, I suppose. Those large men you call giants. Actually, they are not giants but our engineered soldiers."

"What do you mean?"

"Well, you must understand about breeding beasts to enhance a characteristic, like creating large udders on cattle. When you have a cow with a large udder, you breed it. If you have one that does not, you do not let it breed. Then you take the offspring of the first cow, judge them when grown, select the one with the largest udder, and breed her, et cetera, et cetera. Soon, your entire herd will have large udders and thus produce more milk."

"I know this already," Lluava said, for she had grown up in the country. "But we are not talking about cattle."

"No. We are not. But we *are* talking about selective breeding." Alcove shifted a leg to get into a more comfortable position. "In the empire, we have bred the strongest, tallest women to the strongest, tallest men. Over the centuries, we have created people who are known as the Berserker Legion. They are, in fact, our soldiers. Their unusual height and strength is due to the traits we have selected. They have been trained in warfare since childhood."

This astonishing concept caused Lluava to shiver. The Raiders had designed their warriors for that sole purpose. "If the Berserkers are your soldiers, what about the regular Raiders, or whatever you call your army?"

One corner of Alcove's lips curled up. "They are nothing. Rubbish. Cutthroats. Vandals. Scum. They are men who made a choice between a life of imprisonment and one of freedom if they enlisted and helped us conquer new lands. All are branded with a mark on the inside of the lower lip." Alcove pulled his own down, though his was not tattooed. "It is a physical sign that they have been, and will always be, convicts. They are the colonizers, our initial settlers, when we claim new territory. Or in this case, reclaim what is rightfully ours.

"Unfortunately, they are uncouth and poorly trained. Usually, their brute force and tenacious drive is all we need. Yet in some cases, such as this one, our true soldiers must be summoned."

"Thus, the Berserkers," Lluava stated, now comprehending last year's events.

"Thus, the Berserkers," acknowledged Alcove. "We have used selective breeding for many occupations, yet our military program is clearly the most advanced."

Choosing her next question with care, she asked, "And your monsters? Those men that scare even the Berserkers? And scare you. What are they?"

"Soldiers. An elite group of warriors, far stronger and fiercer than the Berserkers themselves. They are known as Úlfhéðinn or, individually, as Úlfhéðnar. Though of the same build as the Berserkers, they are selected for other qualities as well."

For a moment the ambassador's eyes glazed. Then he resumed his explanation. "Though the Berserker Legion is naturally strong and fierce, they smoke a drug—"

Lluava cut in, "Which makes them immune to pain and increases rage to the point that they will cut down anyone in their path."

"Very good," noted Alcove. "Well, the Úlfhéðinn's drug is much stronger. Known as Óðr, it is a liquid brewed over several weeks. The contents and the process are known only by the Úlfhéðinn. Once drunk, it quickly spreads throughout the body. The drug not only provides the extraordinary strength of the Berserkers, but it also activates muscles in new ways for increased speed and lightning-quick reflexes. Their body type is enhanced as well. However, the drug strips them of their humanity. "The most visible and strangest side effect is the temporary alteration of skin color, which I'm sure you noticed. The potion is so potent that many who train to become Úlfhéðinn die the first time they consume it. This is why only the best physical specimens are selected for their regiment."

Lluava thought of the blue-black skin of the Úlfhéðinn that had pursued her earlier.

Alcove finished by saying, "In fact, the potion is so powerful that the average Úlfhéðnar risks dying if he takes it more than ten times."

"The man who leads the Úlfhéðinn. His neck veins remained dark. Is that because of the potion?"

"General Ivar Niðingr . He is the only Úlfhéðnar to have drunk the potion almost twice the survivable number of times, yet he still shows no ill effects other than his veins. They are stained that color."

"Outside of Níð…whatever…and his veins, is there any way to detect the difference between your monsters and the Berserkers when they're not under the influence of the potion? You all dress in furs…" Lluava's mind was working rapidly, "but the monsters seem to wear a particular type of cloak."

"Again, very good. The Úlfhéðinn don cloaks of wolf hides. They believe that they gain some of their violent and bestial nature through their close identity with those animals. The cloaks are awarded to them at their initiation."

"I see they have stripped you of yours."

"I was honored by the Emperor with an Úlfhéðinn cloak. However, Niðingr did not deem me worthy."

There was a bad feeling building inside of Lluava. The information was coming too easily. "Why are you telling me all of this?" She wanted to add *willingly*, but that was understood. "Why are you betraying your own men with such little disregard."

"You chose to rescue me for some purpose," acknowledged Alcove. "I assume it would be better for me not to stand in your way. Furthermore, as I see it, we both desire the same outcome, at least for the moment.

"In my empire, we have certain rules that should not be broken. Niðingr did so as soon as he chained me. This action proves that he has renounced the authority of the emperor; he must be stopped at all cost. As the royal ambassador, I must be present during all dealings with representatives from other kingdoms. I am here to make sure the correct protocol is observed when new lands are conquered. Niðingr holds higher authority over the military, that is true. But when dealing with politics, I am his superior.

"Only once in our history has a military figure so blatantly flouted the emperor's wishes: your very own Landon Mandrun. Of course, his reasoning is now very clear. He desired unquestionable power of his own. He set himself up as the ruler of this foreign land. My hope is that this and nothing more is also Niðingr's intent. Yet, if someone in his position disregarded the authority of those of higher rank, what would happen if he chose to return home? If he has utterly dismissed my authority, what of our emperor's? He holds the entire army of Úlfhéðinn under his control and thus the Berserkers as well. Niðingr is a dangerous man. A very dangerous man. He must be stopped."

"And if he is killed, what then?" Lluava asked skeptically.

"Sweyn Surtur, Niðingr's second, could possibly lead the army." Alcove paused before continuing. "But without a leader, there would be chaos. Both the Úlfhéðinn and the Berserkers know only how to follow orders. That has been their training since the beginning. Without someone in command, they would be uncontrollable."

"You have only two military officers? Isn't that poorly planned?"

"There has never been a need for more with Niðingr in command. Most believe that he is unstoppable. I pray that *most* are wrong."

"And who would be the next leader? The one the army would turn to if there were no commanders? You?" Though Lluava knew the answer, she waited for Alcove's response.

He looked at her complacently for an extended time. Was he considering her question, or the reason behind her inquiry? Maybe he did not have an answer.

Before Lluava could speculate further, Alcove simply stated, "Yes."

Whether her instincts were right or she had received a message from the gods, somehow she had known this was the case. Nevertheless, she needed to know more about Alcove's own intentions. "What would you do if you became their leader? Destroy our people? Slaughter more innocent lives?"

"End this fight."

"Why? Why not finish what you started?"

"Because we were wrong about this place. We were wrong about your kind, Theri."

It was always unnerving to hear a Raider refer to her using the goddess's name, yet she looked past that. Alcove seemed to understand her confusion. His wan smile held more power behind it than Lluava had thought possible.

"When sent out on scouting missions, the ambassador must determine the value of the natives to our empire's cause. On rare occasions, we have concluded that the native population is better served as an ally and not as a forced member of our society. I had deemed this to be the case with Elysia."

The blood on Lluava's skin had begun to dry. The thickest clumps flaked off when she moved. Remembering the first time she had observed Alcove and the slaughter he had caused, she replied, "You came to Elysia intending to wipe out my race. Clearly, I cannot condone that."

"Nor would I, if I were one of you. Fortunately, your race has proven itself much more worthy. You are far more human-like than we originally thought. Far less bestial. Far more intelligent. From my point of view, far more intriguing."

"What changed your mind?"

"You did."

Once again, everything pointed back to her. Though Lluava wanted to know more about that, her mission was to gain information about the Raiders and find a way to stop the war. In his weakened state, Alcove needed to rest—but not before she confirmed what she wanted to believe. "You would end this bloodshed if you were to regain control? Is that what you are telling me?"

"I promise you that I will cease this attack on your city and return to our ships."

"And sail home?"

"And sail home."

That was what she had hoped to hear. This was the reason they had risked so much to rescue him. He had confirmed her hopes. Now, all she had to do was—

"That matters little now."

Alcove's attention was drawn to the speaker behind Lluava. Ruire Thoth, purple turban still wrapped around his short red hair, stood in the doorway. Lluava blinked several times, for she had been all but certain he was dead. "The Lady Selene's plan has indeed worked. We have already observed a number of Ocean Men clawing at their throats, gasping as they stumbled away from their encampment before they fell. In turn, I have sent our fighting men to slay any who have survived."

"So quickly?" The flutter of excitement inside Lluava was immediately stifled.

Alcove's threat was almost casual. "If you do not call them back, your fighting men are as good as dead."

"They have already left."

Lluava caught her breath as Alcove continued, "Niðingr is very intelligent. Your humans did not contaminate the water. He knew foul play when he saw it. Ivar discovered the poison before the plan unfolded."

"Lies!" spat Thoth.

Lluava reluctantly stood up for the ambassador. "If Alcove is lying, how did he know we were going to poison the water? None of us told him that."

Thoth glared down his sharp nose. "Then why did those Raiders emerge from their camp and display clear symptoms of poisoning?"

"You do not know Ivar Niðingr," Alcove spoke out, exasperated. "In order to win a war, he would willingly sacrifice a few of his own men. Any Raiders who died were used only to deceive you. He has set a trap. And you, my friend, have just fallen victim to it."

Lluava knew that Alcove, in this moment, told the truth. Hurriedly, she asked the ruire, "How many of our fighting men did you send?"

"All of them."

Chapter 29

Flame in the Storm

How can that be?" Lluava cried out. "You couldn't have known that the poison had had any effect until recently. And we have just returned."

Testily, Thoth countered, "Did you think we would loll about during your mission? I was gathering the Warrior Caste before you even left. The clans joined us as well. As soon as we had confirmation that the poison was working, I readied our troops to attack. The enemy could not be allowed to escape." He glared down at Alcove. "Not a single one."

"And what about those who came back with me? Yamir, Talos, Aquila?"

"Gone as well." Thoth's sharp features became rigid. "They encountered Ammit and me by the entry gates to the castle. When they heard what was happening, the stag and the porcupine headed off with Ammit to follow the army. The nomad returned to his post on the wall."

"And Rosalyn?"

"Returned to her home, I would assume."

How could her friends have left so soon? Yet with Talos's determination to protect his growing family and Yamir's hatred of the Raiders, could she have expected anything less? Aquila's rationale was not as clear, but all three were willing to battle once more. This time, however, they were heading straight into a trap.

The presence inside Lluava stirred angrily as if some wild thing were clawing its way out. She felt wave after wave of an unexplainable intensity rock her like the storm-tossed fishing boats of her seaside village.

"The ambassador is telling the truth," she said, vouching for Alcove. Somehow, as with the Raiders' plans, she was certain of it. "If the army does not turn back, our troops will be slaughtered. New Rhadamanthus will be defenseless."

The young woman recognized an emotion in Thoth's eyes for the first time—present, perhaps, due to her assertion or to his own warning instinct. The ruire was afraid.

With no time to confer with the high priestess, he made a decision. "The Twelve have not abandoned us. They have given us the Incarn of the gods of war. You and Apex must call the army back. Head to the gate; I will find Ullr's Incarn."

Lluava left quickly and focused on conserving her waning energy. Dawn was only hours away; there would be no rest this night. She hoped the goddess would endow her with the strength and power she would need to succeed.

As she jogged down the hall, she saw Rosalyn approaching, a pair of unlit lamps in her hands.

"I was about to look for you in your quarters," Rosalyn said shakily. "Talos has left again—with the others. Even though I asked him not to."

"I know. I'm going after them."

"Something…something's not right about this."

Lluava placed a hand on Rosalyn's slim shoulder. "That's why I'm going to bring them back."

Rosalyn spoke in a whisper. "Lluava, while you were away, I went to the tower to see if I could spot Talos. The window faces due south, so the angle was wrong, but I thought I saw movement in the distance. I cannot be certain what I observed, for that was when the storm broke, and the rain blurred everything."

Was Rosalyn suggesting that more Raiders were coming? Before Lluava could reply, her friend asked, "What if it is Varren?"

Varren. Could he have arrived so soon?

Raising the lamps, Rosalyn added, "I was hoping to find you, to tell you that I am going to the tower. If I am able to determine what I saw, I will light these as a signal: one if it is Raiders, two if it is Varren. Lluava, bring Talos back, bring the others back, and maybe—just maybe—bring our king back as well."

Lluava's concern was obvious. "The storm is still raging out there. With all the wind and rain, what if you can't light them? Worse, what if you're caught?"

"I have to try."

***

Before leaving the city, Lluava saw Thoth waiting at the gate to bid them farewell. Unable to hide her anger at the ruire for risking her friends and their last hopes on a poorly thought out endeavor, she brandished the Claws and remarked, "Clearly, you do not have a head for warfare. Next time you think about commanding an army, think again."

Even though this man had recently risked his life for hers, she had an aversion to him. Maybe the goddess was influencing her. Maybe it was his cold demeanor, or her own recurring hot temper. Maybe it was an aftereffect of battling and slaying a fellow Incarn.

With impassive face and expressionless voice, Thoth presented a pair of items to the duo. "With respect, Incarns of Theri and Ullr, these will enable you to signal the army to retreat. Give five consecutive blasts within earshot, and the troops will return to the city without question."

The ruire handed Lluava and Apex two small silver whistles. Though simple in appearance, the pair recognized them as something more. When blown, the resulting high-pitched trill could be heard only by Theriomorphs. The sound, though grievous to their own ears, would allow them to signal their army before the Raiders attacked.

"Thank you," Lluava said sincerely, though she was not ashamed of her prior statements. Thoth bowed briskly in response.

Rain continued to pour down and mingle with the blood of Lluava's saturated attire. Red lines formed and dripped over her exposed arms like vermilion stripes. Apex, already drenched and obviously agitated, grunted, "Let's go."

The gates swung open, and the pair of Incarn headed toward the Raiders' encampment. Well before reaching the warped wooden palisade, they encountered fresh corpses. Dead Raiders. Everywhere. With skin the color of gangrene and eyes protruding from their sockets. Hands of the stricken still clutched throats that had gasped for breath as they died. This poison was meant to inflict pain, suffering, and revenge. Selene's choice of venom was as foul as the woman herself. Yet Lluava still struggled with the question of whether or not Suada's Incarn had deserved to die.

As they proceeded, they encountered more and more corpses, until they found themselves treading carefully over the bodies. Why sacrifice so many of their own men? Lluava could not fathom the reason. Was Alcove wrong? Perhaps the enemy had indeed been poisoned.

Apex, taking the lead, kept the pace steady and cautious but far too slow. The rain continued to assault the drenched earth, and deep puddles impeded their progress.

As they approached the wooden wall, Apex whispered, "There are no Berserkers among them."

Looking about, Lluava saw that he was right. All the dead on the front lines were of the smaller variety, those who had not been raised as warriors. The pawns, the trash, as Alcove seemed to think. If the Berserkers were not dead, where were they? And where were their monstrous wolf-men?

Approaching the gaping hole in the wall, Lluava could see some of the Outlanders and clansmen prodding the dead with their weapons, ensuring that none would rise up in a deceptive strike. That was smart. What wasn't right was the fact that the worst of the enemy were nowhere to be seen.

The whole area looked abandoned. Barracks and buildings appeared empty. Tents bent under the weight of pooling water. Clothes and supplies were unguarded. The half-finished shells of their siege weapons listed sideways in the mud.

Joining the ranks, Lluava spied Talos and Yamir talking with several

Outlanders. She hurried toward them. "You must go back," she implored as they turned to her.

An extremely tall and gangly Outlander sniffed. "Not you as well. Can't you see that they are all dead?"

Ignoring him, Talos broke in. "Lluava, there are no Berserker corpses. Not even one."

"I know," she said. "It's a—"

The jarring shrill of Apex's whistle caused everyone to cover their ears. There was little reprieve in this action, and they could clearly hear the five sharp blasts. Their heads throbbed from the noise as the tall Outlander noted, "That's the call to retreat."

"Yes," Lluava acknowledged, as the Outlanders obeyed the signal. The clansmen followed suit.

"Gods! I hate that sound," exclaimed Yamir as he rubbed his temples.

"That sound might be our salvation. Let's move!" ordered Lluava as she joined the retreating troops.

The warriors of Leucrocotta headed back to the capital without question, just as Thoth had said they would, though it was clear they had no idea why their mission had been called off.

Rounding the side of the deserted compound, however, the army halted.

Ahead of them, the Berserker Legion had combined with the Úlfhéðinn to form a massive wedge that was now attempting to force the capital's gates. The sound of battering rams splintering sections of reinforced wood was heard over the thunder and wind of the storm.

Arrows, like black rain, were shot from the top of the wall—though to little avail, Lluava knew. Exasperated, she cried, "Why isn't Aquila shooting at them? They're going to break down the gates!"

"He can't," said Apex. "The Talons' blasts are too large. They could destroy the gates or the wall itself. You saw the power behind his shots."

"We have to stop them before they break through!" Lluava stated determinedly. Lacking defenders, once the walls were breached the high priestess and the ruire would be forced to capitulate.

Yamir scowled. "They would make mincemeat of us. You know how strong they are. Our army would stand no chance."

"Where is Ammit?" Talos questioned, peering around.

Standing next to Apex, the swarthy man's wide mouth was contorted in a grimace. He must have understood what needed to be done.

All around, expressions changed from shock to determination.

Ammit shouted, "In whatever form you will, attack!"

The Outlander warriors and the clans charged. Lluava and her companions did the same.

She and Apex shifted as they raced toward the rear line of Berserkers on the leftmost flank. Sinking her fangs into flesh, Lluava realized how fortunate they were. The continuing rain had prevented the Berserkers from smoking their drug, which would lessen the initial losses of their allies. However, the Berserkers were trained warriors, and they were still a formidable enemy.

The giant brutes deftly swung their weapons with their full might. Harbingers of death, they laid low many who attempted to oppose them. The tall Outlander, now in his dual form of a giraffe, slammed his long neck into one of the enemy, knocking him to the ground, only to have his own neck severed moments later.

The wind was picking up again, as was Lluava's inner presence; the goddess thirsted for the blood of the human horde before her. With every crack of the battering rams, Lluava's heart raced faster. With each thrum of pain from her swollen shoulders, she fought more violently. Soon she would let the goddess take control. With her eyes trained on humans, Issaura's savagery would be undeniable.

Nearby, Lluava thought she glimpsed the sharp, graphite silhouette of Maruny's mockingbird form. Of course, she would be here; she was one of the Warrior Caste. In appearance, she looked ill-suited to battle, yet Lluava could not help but be impressed by her fiery determination.

The Outlanders made progress as they carved their way through the rear lines, yet neither side could claim the upper hand. Lluava knew the time had come. As color began to drain from her vision and the world shifted toward a blue-green tint, a strange, flickering light caught her eye. High in a castle tower, a lantern was lit. One light. One single flame, signaling calamitous news.

Light another, Lluava willed. *Light another, Rosalyn.* If there were only a single flame, all was lost. The Outlanders stood no chance of withstanding the enemy reinforcements.

As she focused on the flame, Lluava's senses returned to normal. She needed to be fully in control to explain the warning signal to her troops and not get caught up in blood lust at the castle gates.

"Theri," a Berserker grunted as he charged. She turned to lash out with her gilded claws, prepared to take on the behemoth. But the fight was cut short as a simple arrow ended the Berserker's life. Had Aquila changed weapons, or had a lucky stray shot aided her? She was too far from the wall for the skill of an ordinary archer to protect her.

Then another thought took hold. How were her friends faring? Between the sheeting rain and the oppressive darkness, it was almost impossible to tell. With each slain Berserker, the Theriomorphs drew closer to the raging Úlfhéðinn. With every crackling boom, the Úlfhéðinn were closer to forcing Cronus, and thus Elysia, to its knees. In war, when one is forced to kneel, one often never rises again.

"Apex!" Lluava roared, for his hulking mass was easy to spot. "Others approach from the south!"

As the giant wolverine muscled his way next to her, awareness returned to his eyes. Momentarily, his god relinquished control. Apex snarled, "Others? How can you tell?"

"A signal. There." Lluava gestured at the tower with her wide paw.

In the solitary window, the flame was fighting its own battle, with the storm itself. Its meager attempt to give light foretold the awful truth: the last of the Outlander warriors would soon perish. They had no chance.

Was this the end? Had everything come down to one final battle? What purpose did she or any of the Incarn have if they were only to die tonight? Had she really believed she was meant for some great purpose? Lluava felt her strength draining away. Maybe it was time to let the goddess take control. At least, she would deliver the Raiders a grievous blow.

Scowling at the pathetic flame, Lluava wanted to curse the light and its message. Would it have been better not to know?

Then, something changed; a second source of illumination appeared. Two lanterns had been lit. Varren's army was approaching.

A sense of calm washed over Lluava, and her spirit was revitalized. They still had a chance. The war was not over.

Another Berserker approached. Snarling, Lluava affirmed, "Time to end this."

Chapter 30

Powdered Rain

A maul slammed into the large puddle in front of Lluava, sending mud upward like a geyser and forcing her to shield her face from the onslaught before she could make her move. Suddenly, a massive bronze form collided with the Berserker in front of her.

Lluava leaped to assist Apex, and the two beasts brought down their prey. Coated in mud and pelted with rain, the tigress roared over the cooling corpse. In the near distance, the two lanterns continued to flicker in the storm.

The blood-smeared muzzle of the Yorrick wolverine tilted toward the flames. "What aren't you saying?" Apex's red-flecked eyes seemed to bore into Lluava's soul. "What's this signal mean?"

Should she tell him? There were so many times the huntsman had helped her and, in doing so, had helped Varren and Elysia. Suddenly, the image of Apex prying her hand open to get Suada's Venom flickered into her thoughts. Moreover, he had deceived her for an entire month upon her return to Cronus. If he had aligned himself with Yena, he might hinder Varren's reentry into the capital.

"Can I trust you?"

The wolverine's fierce expression changed to one of confusion and pain. "My life has been yours since the time we spent together in the Pass. Everything I've done…for you. Don't you know this?"

Lluava could no longer deny what she felt for Apex—felt not merely at this moment but during the months prior. Perhaps they were indeed meant for each other. He was the only one who understood her internal turmoil with the inner presence, her fear of losing herself to the darkness, and her terror of what would happen when their destiny was fulfilled.

More Berserkers were approaching. Apex turned and snarled; his hackles raised. Without benefit of their drug, the behemoths were clearly more cautious and hesitant.

"Apex," Lluava began. The wolverine's ears told her he was listening, though he kept his eyes trained on the enemy. "Varren's army is arriving. That was the signal. The Outlanders must not attack his men."

Without warning, the air crackled with electricity. Lluava's fur stood on end with the intensity of the charge. Could that have been Aquila? If so, what had he shot at? Unless—

"Go!" ordered Apex. He moved toward the enemy to prevent them from following her.

Hoping she would not regret her decision, the tigress hurried southward. Aquila should recognize Varren and his men, but if he did not, the damage he could wield with Giahem's Wings would be devastating. She needed to help lead the Elysians toward Cronus's gates. Of all of them, she was the only one who could unite the two armies against the greater threat.

Lluava did not have to search long. Marching into the clearing were hundreds—no, thousands—of men. Moss-green and gold banners snapped in the wind. The rows of soldiers parted as three riders approached the tigress and then halted.

Varren was flanked by two men: the redheaded Lieutenant Vidrick, attired in age-old chain mail, and Regin, dressed in his black bodysuit. Varren wore a soldier's uniform. A simple silver circlet was affixed to his metal helmet. This humble crown was the only symbol that identified him as the one true ruler of the kingdom. A black panther, Ojewa's dual form, stretched at the feet of the king's mount.

"It sounds like you are in a bit of a scrape," Varren said above the din of battle. Though he did not smile, Lluava could sense his spirits were high. And why shouldn't they be? A vast army stood behind him that comprised trained soldiers, the Obsidian Guard, volunteer patriots, and the like.

"There is little time." Lluava spoke quickly. "Berserkers and even worse monstrosities are beating at the gates. The Outlander army has been trapped outside the walls, and their numbers are falling far too fast." The three mounted men talked in hushed voices among themselves for a moment before Lluava broke in again.

"But, Varren, I have not been able to ensure that the Outlanders will switch their allegiance to you." Although the king's face remained unreadable, she could see the dismay on Vidrick's. Lluava continued, "Regardless, do not consider them enemies, not just yet."

Varren did not appear distressed. Hushing the military leaders beside him, he tossed down a small pouch and said, "We come bearing gifts."

Before Lluava could shift, Ojewa resumed his tall, ebony-skinned form and untied the pouch for the feline. Reaching inside, he scooped out a handful of powder as black as his flesh.

"Flashbang!" Lluava exclaimed, hope now rekindled.

"That and much more," repeated Varren. "It seems our old friend Berkley has been mass-producing it since the battles by the sea. It is water resistant and explosive, and it may help us again."

"There is a problem," noted Vidrick. His voice had become hollow since Lluava's dealings with him in the North. "We have no way of positioning it around the enemy. It must be in place before we ignite it."

"Surely we can figure out a way," insisted Lluava. For the sake of these nearby friends, the tigress resisted her desire to shake the excess rainwater from her sopping fur.

Varren seemed to sense Lluava's discomfort. "Go on," he said as he nudged his horse to step back. Lluava relieved herself of some of the water weight while Varren explained, "We have been trying to conceive the best way to position the Flashbang among the enemy. So far, nothing seems plausible."

"There is an alternate plan," Vidrick reminded his king.

"As I said before, I will not consider that."

Lluava eyed the redheaded lieutenant. "What's the other plan?"

"Send men in," Vidrick began, "who know full well the sacrifice they would be making."

"You mean, allow a few people to die in order to kill many of the enemy." Lluava hated to agree with the benefit of this approach. This is what the Raiders had done to trick the Outlanders. This is what she had done when she sent the Elysians into the enemy camp. Had she become so cold? Did lives no longer matter to her?

Two more figures approached. Byron was dragging a bound captive dressed in gray with her head covered by a sack. "We discovered this woman skulking about in another regiment," he explained before removing the cloth and exposing a sorry-looking Maruny.

"Friend of yours?" questioned Regin coldly, as he readied several throwing suns.

"Traitor!" the small, young woman screamed as she cast her smoldering eyes on Lluava. Maruny's platinum-blond hair stuck to her face in dripping cords. An Endun collar strapped around her neck was securely held by Byron to ensure that she would not shift and escape. Lluava wished she had thought about one of those before. There were several people she would prefer to see tethered. As Byron reached for a gag, Maruny hissed, "That's what you have always been. Claiming friendship. Do you ever speak anything but lies?"

Byron paused as Lluava responded. "I was her friend," she said to Regin, then turned to Maruny. "I *was* your friend. I know you do not believe me, but I really was."

This was a great understatement. As Lluava spoke, she felt her words turn to ash in her mouth. Though what she said was true, the fact remained:

Maruny had killed June. Lluava did indeed desire revenge.

Maruny spat on the ground. "The high priestess will have your head once she hears of your betrayal."

Could she have discovered what Lluava had done to Selene? No. The Outlander must be referring to the discovery of Lluava conversing with Elysia's king, the high priestess's enemy.

Maruny finished her threat. "I pray that I'm the one to give it to her."

Lluava could see Regin preparing to throw his weapons if the girl made even the slightest move to fulfill her desire. Byron, in turn, shoved the gag into her mouth while tightening the bindings. Maruny tried to scream, but only a muffled wail escaped.

"What should be done with her?" Byron asked.

Vidrick eyed Lluava doubtfully. "You said not to view the likes of her as the enemy. That hardly seems possible."

Before them, the clamor of battle raged on. Above, more winged carrion-eaters flocked toward the city. Lluava felt a silent and overwhelming need to return to the front lines. A decision had to be made.

"Release her," she uttered, at first to herself, then to the others. Even Maruny stared at her with puzzled eyes. Lluava needed all of them to see things her way. "Maruny, hate me though you will, it is clear we are fighting a losing battle. The enemy forcing entry *will* destroy us. You have seen what is happening. Once the Berserkers enter the city, we are all doomed. There is no place for Theriomorphs in the world these Raiders wish to create."

The Outlander glared at her with contempt, refusing to acknowledge the truth of the tigress's statement. Lluava continued cautiously, "This blood feud—this war, or whatever you wish to call it—between your people and those who follow King Varren matters little when we both face adversaries such as the Raiders. I do not expect your hatred to diminish, nor do I expect to regain your trust. I can only implore you to put aside these feelings and work alongside the Elysians until this threat is dealt with."

There was a moment of silence as Maruny eyed Lluava suspiciously. After receiving a nod of approval from Varren, Byron removed the gag to allow his captive a chance to speak.

"I will never work for humans!" snapped Maruny as she kicked at Byron. He gave her a strong backhanded slap that split her lip.

"I never said 'work for humans.' What I am asking you to do is work for *your* people. The Warrior Caste has no chance of defending the gates alone. They need help. These men behind me, this man right here—" Lluava gestured at Varren, "They *all* are willing to battle the Raiders. In order for you to defend the city, you need the assistance of humans, if only for a short time."

The crackling boom and groans of the shattering gates battered their ears. Maruny's eyes darted from Lluava to the humans to Cronus. Then, wiping her lip on her shoulder, she asked, "What do you propose?"

***

"They are almost in place," Vidrick announced as he squinted through his spyglass. "They are lining up perfectly."

Lluava did not need the aid of the small device to see that the flying Outlanders were beginning to drop parcels of black powder across the enemy lines at a specific distance from the city's walls. Once the archers on the wall shot their flame-tipped arrows, the resulting explosions would provide the signal for Varren's army to attack. Maruny had kept her word.

The Obsidian Guard gathered about Varren and prepared for their greatest mission yet.

Vidrick counted. "Three." His horse pawed in agitation.

"Two."

Lluava hoped that the rain would not douse the flaming arrows too early.

"One."

The night sky was illuminated with brilliant light. The resulting noise of the numerous explosions caused many a man to pray to his god. Lluava did not need to resort to prayer. This was no holy intervention but the unfolding of a masterful plan.

"Attack!" roared Varren, and those of station, rank, or reputation repeated the order until the entire army thundered with war cries.

Lluava envisioned what the scene must look like from above. A human-led army from the South rushing to combat the Raiders' horde just as the Theriomorphs resumed their attack in full ferocity. Archers and spearmen rained down their projectiles from the wall as lightning illuminated everything in quick flashes.

"Make for the gates!" roared Lluava. Still in her dual form, she forced herself to keep pace with those on horseback.

Vidrick's stallion whickered as a spear launched at its chest found its mark. Horse and rider were sent sprawling to the ground. Leaping over the lieutenant, the tigress collided with the flailing equine and received several sharp kicks in her side. At least one broke flesh.

The scream of sword biting sword reverberated above Lluava as she scrambled to her feet and away from Vidrick's opponent. Now in the midst of the fray, she took note of the enemy. Though not nearly as deadly as their larger kin, these ordinary Raiders were clearly causing enough havoc of their own. Once Vidrick slew his assailant and Lluava disemboweled another, the pair pushed on. Ahead of them, Varren's band of black guards hewed their way forward.

Large, charred craters had been gouged into the ground inside the battle zone. Near the gates, obliterated battering rams had been reduced to smoldering kindling. Remnants of victims among the blackened fissures were all but indistinguishable. Lluava wondered if they were Berserkers or Úlfhéðinn. As she had feared, several bags of Flashbang had indeed been ignited too close to the walls, which were now pockmarked from the powerful explosions. So far, no hole had been blasted through.

Nearing Cronus's gate, a new wave of aerial Theriomorphs flew overhead, bearing more parcels of death. As the flock began to drop their packets, Vidrick pointed out, "They're not stopping."

This was true. The flying Theriomorphs were releasing the bundles of Flashbang closer and closer to Varren's army. They wouldn't try to destroy the Elysians, would they? Yet Lluava was not convinced. Yena was in charge of the Outlanders. She would not risk placing either Ullr's or Theri's Incarn in danger. As long as Lluava stayed near Varren, he would not be harmed. Yet, with Maruny coordinating the attack, who knew if an "accident" might occur?

Joining the ring of Obsidian Guard, Lluava shifted and approached the gates warily. Behind them, a new series of explosions erupted as flaming arrows flew past and ignited the powder. The enemy had abandoned the gates. Were the Raiders retreating? Maybe some greater power actually was smiling on the defenders.

Reaching the doors, the massing number of soldiers waited. The numbers of Theriomorphs and Elysians continued to multiply, yet the gates did not open.

"They are leaving us to die!" a human shouted.

"What of our agreement?" cried another.

Outlanders, clansmen, and Elysians looked at each other with great distrust. If the Raiders did not resume their attack, fights would break out among the three tenuously allied parties.

Flashbang exploded closer and closer to the gates. Fear in those who awaited entry caused many to force their way toward the fractured doors and bang futilely at the splintered wood. Lluava was jostled by all the bodies pressing close together. Like a fly stuck in molasses, she could neither move nor lift her weapons.

Suddenly, someone shouted, "They are returning! The giants are attacking!"

The crushing weight of the people crammed against the walls was suffocating. Desperately, Lluava tried to heave others aside to make room for defensive maneuvers. But there were too many bodies. She was at the mercy of the mob—one that had given way to fear.

"Move back!" someone cried. "They are trying to open the gates!"

The words went unheeded. With the Berserkers approaching, the panicked mob pushed harder toward the doors, which prevented them from being opened. If they remained closed, those outside were inviting certain slaughter.

An internal heat flared within Lluava. Snarling, she shifted once more and charged through the confusion. Reaching the gates, she could see the gaping wounds that reached the metallic center of the doors. Rounding on the men about her, she let loose the loudest roar she could muster. Impressive though it was, the crackling explosions and cries of the warriors nearly drowned out this display.

Still, those near her took notice. "Back!" they shouted. "Move back!"

After several moments of confusion, the men at last cleared sufficient space for a small arc that allowed the gates to swing open. The entry was not large, but it enabled a flood of soldiers to rush through like water spouting from a cracked dam.

Lluava was carried along in the crush of bodies. Once inside the walls, she struggled to break free of the mob. Taking note of her surroundings, she saw the throng of black Shadows encircling their mounted king.

Many of the men had moved deeper into the city, opening up space for others to spread out a bit. This helped, and she finally reached her former partner.

"Varren!" Lluava called as she returned once again to human form.

The young king's blood-splattered face alarmed her. "It is not mine," he explained, as he wiped off what he could on his sleeve.

Lluava released a breath and shivered. If Varren had been harmed, what would she have done? She couldn't bear the thought. Something in her would break if he...if he...

Regin, now on foot, asserted, "We must make for a meeting point farther in. There is too much chaos here."

Thinking quickly, Lluava replied, "The castle is not safe. For all we know, Yena or her followers could prevent us from entering the gate at the curtain wall. Another landmark?"

"The Church," decided Varren.

Before Lluava could counter that idea, there was a loud groan as the gates began to close. Outlanders and Elysians were still pouring through, yet it was clear the doors would be sealed before everyone was safely inside.

"It's the enemy." Lluava recognized the familiar female voice. Holly stepped next to her. "They are following us in."

"No," corrected Varren. The elevated seat atop his mount gave him a better view. "They have already forced entry. Berserkers are inside Cronus's walls!"

Chapter 31

Observation Tower

M ake for the church!" ordered Regin. "We must protect our king."
At their leader's command, the Shadows began to flood the
roadways like a black wave.

"What about the Raiders?" called Lluava over the cries of the dying. The
rain was finally tapering off, and she could smell wisps of tainted smoke.

"They are drugged." But how could they have lit their horns in this weather?

"The soldiers will fight them," Holly explained tersely. "Our mission is to
keep King Varren safe. Stay here or come with us. We will be at the church."

Everyone scattered into the labyrinth that was Cronus. Remorsefully,
Lluava looked back at the fighting. Was Apex there? Were her friends inside
the walls, or were they caught up in this new battle? As much as she wanted
to join them, she knew she needed to be at Varren's side.

Lluava watched in awe as Shadows climbed up the walls of the homes
and shops lining the narrow passageway. Leaping from rooftop to rooftop,
they expanded their defensive radius around their ruler.

Moments later, a crashing sound came from inside one of the humble houses.

Weapons were aimed toward the apparently vacant building just as a
window shattered outward. Before them, an Úlfhéðnar leapt out and landed
on all fours. His blue-black skin was clothed in wolf hides matted with blood.
The whites of his eyes had turned completely black, and he glowered at them
like a creature from the seven hells.

"Go, Your Majesty!" Regin shouted as he prepared to combat the fiend.
As one of the closest Guards to the monstrous Raider, he knew what must
be done. "Flee!"

Inside another house, a low howl erupted. The Úlfhéðinn did not know the complex layout of the city, yet that did not matter. Boring holes and tunnels like maleficent moles, the creatures were devising their own routes—right through the buildings.

A small band of elite Shadows broke away and ushered Varren onward. Lluava followed horse and rider, positioning herself by the king's side. Meanwhile, a storm of black-garbed Guards descended upon the Úlfhéðnar as Lluava and Varren rushed toward their final destination.

The city seemed to be falling around them. The combined weight and aggressive moves of several clansmen battling a huge monstrosity on the second floor of a storefront caused the weight-bearing beams to collapse. Lluava sensed that Varren wanted to stop and help.

She dissuaded him. "Your life's more valuable. Don't risk it."

Varren's jaw twitched, and he pointed at several of the Guard. "You, there! Give them aid." The Shadows obeyed unquestioningly.

The king turned onto another narrow road. Weaving through the city was far from easy. When more Úlfhéðinn emerged, a detachment of Shadows attacked the adversaries. Their party was shrinking. None of the Shadows seemed to rejoin them.

"Do you sense someone following us?" Lluava asked after a hesitant pause.

Holly's emerald eyes darted about, but before she could respond, howls echoed ahead of them. She looked at Lluava, her green irises aflame. The Guard was clearly torn, and Lluava knew why. If the female Shadow left the king to attack an enemy well out of striking range, the young ruler would be vulnerable to an attack. On the other hand, staying by Varren's side might risk a close-up mishap if confronted by an Úlfhéðnar.

Holly made her choice. "Protect King Varren. Get him to safety. It's up to you now." With that, she left the pair and led the rest of the Shadows to the top of a nearby building in hope of hindering the progress of the approaching enemy.

Lluava felt the hairs on her neck stand on end. She realized this must be what a leveret tracked by hounds feels like. Varren also appeared worried. There was no need for words; both immediately understood. They must keep moving, for standing still was the equivalent of giving up.

Moments later, as they approached another crossing, Varren pulled on the reins to halt his horse. He seemed to be listening for something, although this part of the street was quiet. Despite Lluava's heightened senses, she could not discern any problem.

"What's wrong?" she finally asked.

"Look there."

She followed his pointing finger. Many of the structures looked like they had barely made it through an earthquake. Windows were shattered, walls cracked; most ominously, they seemed vacant. Not one person, friend or foe, could be seen.

How had the Raiders come so far so quickly? Had they moved on? Slowly, the pair trekked ahead, eyeing the molested structures as they moved past.

Varren stopped again. Breathing heavily, he asked, "What's that noise?"

Listening, Lluava heard the long, low moan. A support beam of the building next to them gave way. A memory of the collapsing tunnel that had engulfed her and Varren caused Lluava to act. She slapped his mount, and it leaped ahead as the front section of the structure began to fall.

With the king out of range, she dodged splintering wood and disintegrating stone. The entire façade fell, and Lluava was forced back. The rest of the building groaned from the gaping wound. It could not remain standing, and she would not be able to cross over the debris before the structure gave way.

Varren had regained control of his horse and now turned toward Lluava. "The church!" he cried out, realizing her dilemma. "Head to the church!"

The building shuddered and collapsed, taking down a secondary structure with it.

Once the stone and rubble settled, Varren shouted over the impromptu divider, "Lluava!"

"I'm fine! I'll meet you at the church!"

She had to get to Varren quickly. Though he was a more than capable fighter, he would have only a slim chance of survival if he went head to head with an Úlfhéðnar. It was her duty to defend him if he was discovered by those brutes. She might not be his military partner, but it was her responsibility as an Elysian. Moreover, Holly had left the young king in her care. Lluava would do whatever she could to protect him and, if need be, die for him.

Using the gap left by the fallen buildings, she clambered over to a secondary street. Where did this one lead? Cronus was a maze; there was no straight path to her goal. She picked her way forward with extreme caution. Who knew where other Úlfhéðinn might lie in wait? The vacant structures loomed threateningly. From their height, she knew she was halfway to the center of the city, because the larger homes of the nobility were closer to the castle, as was Varren's church—the former Theriomorph temple and their meeting spot.

Should she have risked making her way over the debris to reach Varren? If the stone or mortar had shifted, she might have been seriously hurt or killed. That would have been equivalent to handing over her life to the enemy. Yet now he was on his own. The thought caused Lluava's heart to flutter with an excruciating terror.

Treading as fast as she dared on the cobblestone road, Lluava was thankful her Endun shoes had soft soles and muffled her footsteps. She advanced on one street and doubled back on the next as she tried to find her way among the convoluted roadways.

Something flew overhead.

Ducking, Lluava sprang next to a wall to protect her back.
The small pebble bounced off a cobblestone before skittering down the road.
"Psst. Over here!" hissed a roguish voice.

In an alley on the far side of the street, Lluava recognized the massive
silhouette of a Berserker, his horned helmet distorted by the flickering light
from a wind-rocked lantern. Lluava's insides knotted and she stepped back.

The speaker swore. "Wait!" he called, as loudly as he dared. The voice
changed pitch, lower to higher. "Just a moment." Soon, Luka's lanky
silhouette replaced that of the brute. Her fellow Incarn waved his hand for
her to approach. As she did, she saw Luka tuck his slingshot into his belt.

"What are you doing here?" she asked.

Luka peered about warily as he answered, "I don't want to be here in
this mess. Where's Apex?"

"I don't know. I last saw him at the gates. I was heading to the temple."

"Right..." Luka poked his head around the corner.

"That trick," Lluava remarked, still astonished at the capabilities of her
fellow Incarn. "That was amazing. I really thought you were one of them."

Distractedly, he waved to her to follow. "This way, then."

Lluava trailed her friend as he led her in several winding loops. Finally,
she was able to see the castle towers rising above the destroyed buildings that
had hindered her ability to recognize where she was.

"Luka, about Selene." Lluava understood this was not the time or place
to offer her explanation of his sister's murder, yet she might not get another
chance. But what should she say? He knew they hated each other. He knew
of Lluava's impulsive decisions. Nevertheless, he had to have known that she
had never desired Selene's death. "Things should have ended differently."

The youth hesitated briefly. "That they should." He gestured for her to
continue as he pushed open a door leading into one of the larger houses.

Luka moved purposefully. Like his shadow, Lluava crept up the first
two flights of stairs.

"Why are we inside?" she asked as they progressed through the
abandoned building. "And how did you know this door was unlocked?"

Luka put his hand on her arm as if to lead her. Feeling a small sting,
Lluava stepped back. "What —" she began, and then she felt her whole body
go numb. Luka caught her as she fell. She would have cried out, but her
tongue was immobilized as well.

"I forgot how quickly that one worked," he said aloud. Looking at
Lluava's wide, rolling eyes, he added, "Don't worry. The effects are only
temporary." He began to drag her across the room. "You will be back to your
old self," he said with a heave, "soon."

Able to move only her eyes, Lluava was prevented by her angle of vision
from seeing where Luka was taking her. She heard him kick open a door as
he struggled to pull her outside. They were on a balcony. A light but steady

rain splattered her face.

"You have to understand," he began, almost slipping in a puddle as he lowered her to the ground, "I never wanted to do any of this. I would have liked things to be different, too."

Luka left her for a short time before returning with pillows in hand. "You have family, a brother, a sister, a mother. You understand. You might not be related by blood, but your feelings, your connection—*that* is real." He propped pillows under her head. "Selene was my sister. Self-centered, I know. But she was my family, and *that* was real."

Throwing a blanket over the immobilized woman, he carefully tucked her in, leaving her head exposed. "I don't want you getting sick out here. The rain is merciless." Beads of water dripped off his white-spotted hair. One landed on her cheek, and he wiped it off immediately. "Okay." He looked her over. "I'll be back."

What was happening? Lluava wondered in sheer fear. Unable to move or cry out, she was at Luka's mercy. He did not seem to wish her harm, but why place her in this position? The Raiders would be different. If a Berserker found her, she was as good as dead.

***

Although the rain had lessened by the time Luka returned, Lluava's blanket was soaked through. After replacing the sopping cloth with a dry one, he anxiously peered over the balcony and sighed.

"It shouldn't have ended this way. Yet family ties are so strange. Here we go…"

Squatting down by Lluava's head, Luka tucked more pillows behind her until she was propped up on her side. Now she could look through the decorative gaps in the balcony's balustrade. What was all this for? She could see the roofs and walls of the neighboring homes; curtains were drawn at most windows. As she looked, one distant building crumbled and collapsed.

The sound of shouts and the clatter of weapons could be heard from multiple sectors around the city, yet the loudest seem to come from directly under them. Luka muttered, "Oh, wait." With one more adjustment, Lluava's face was pressed close to the gap at a new angle.

In the street below, illuminated by torchlight, she could see two figures in combat. Varren was fighting for his life. His opponent threatened him with every move. What was happening?

Varren's enemy couldn't be real. This must be one of Luka's tricks. Apex was attacking the king without mercy. The fury of Varren's sword fended off the threatening twin blades of Ullr's Fangs. They were both out for blood! This was no game but a fight to the death—and only one man would come out alive. But why?

Luka appeared to read her thoughts. "This is what becomes of men when they are stripped down to their base natures. No inhibitions. Pure emotion." He moved to the other side of Lluava and stared at the men below. "Those large Raiders, the Berserkers, are just the same. It sickens me, but that's the way it seems."

Lluava wanted to speak but was unable to. She could only watch as each man attempted to release the other's soul in death. This was not possible. Why this fight? Was Apex siding with the Outlanders? Or had Varren assumed he was?

Once again, Luka seemed to understand the utter confusion written on the young woman's features. "They are fighting over *you*. Base instincts. Testosterone everywhere. Stags in rut. Both desire you; both loathe the fact that your affections have wavered between them. Whom will Lluava choose? The king—the epitome of sophistication, honorable, overly righteous? Or the huntsman—crude, rough, far too physical for my taste, but an Incarn like yourself? Which one? Which one?

"I only had to, well, act as a sort of catalyst to help enhance their anger, their lust, each one's desire to make you his own. Strange what a simple trick of the mind can do." He paused, listening to the clamor of weapons. "They are on their own now. You have a front-row seat to watch this final climax. I know I'm forcing a resolution on this matter, but you were never really going to decide. So much drama. Too much, really. Especially when there are far more important issues at hand."

Stop this nonsense! Lluava wanted to scream. Yet her tongue remained limp in her mouth. Her body was useless. Neither Apex nor Varren had any idea that she was observing this wretched show of brute strength, this fabricated duel for the right to her heart.

There was no satisfaction in Luka's hushed voice. "Do not worry. I have ensured that neither Varren nor Apex will be disturbed. Even the Obsidian Guard will be of no consequence. Their pathetic minds will not tell the king apart from a certain common foot soldier." He waved his hands in front of her face, and for a moment, Lluava could have sworn Varren was stooped over her. "I bet that poor bastard is wondering why he deserves their royal protection. Ha!"

From below, Apex yelled, "You don't deserve her! You couldn't even resist Selene's charms. You are weak in both mind and body. Lluava deserves someone strong. Someone who is her equal match."

Varren countered Apex's attack with respectable ease and responded between thrusts and parries, "I have loved her since the beginning. I have never, could never, conceive of hurting her. But you," Varren said, striking at the huntsman, "you tried to rape her. You who preferred to swim at the bottom of a bottle or sleep with any whore you could afford. You even admitted to killing a child, taking an innocent life. You are vile. Loathsome. Grotesque."

With an animal roar, Apex slashed at Varren with the Fangs. "I might be all those things, might have done those things. But who are you to judge?

I have paid for my sins. The boy should not have been there that day. Killed in crossfire. I buried my sorrow, my remorse, in a blind stupor for years. I never sought redemption. It was fate that ripped me free of that life. That same fate drives me toward Lluava, yet you are too small-minded to understand that."

As their battle continued, Luka spoke again, and Lluava sensed his own heartbreak. "This is a bit much, I understand. But it needed to be done, finished. You killed Selene, my beautiful sister. That hurt. What also hurt was knowing that no matter how much I helped you, you would never look at me the way you look at either of those two." From the corner of her eye, Lluava could see Luka pointing to the pair of men below. "My poor sister. She saved me."

Lluava could hear the curses doled out as the men fought.

"Then again, she *was* a bitch. Controlling, conniving, manipulative. I guess, in a way, you set me free."

Varren cried out as a line of red appeared on his soiled white shirt. Nearby, Apex faltered from an injury of his own.

"So I am, in a way, doing you a favor and freeing you from this unending drama of the age-old romantic triangle. Please try to understand. I don't hate you." There was another pause before he spoke in a very thoughtful tone. "Now, perhaps my sister's soul can rest in peace."

As soon as Apex received a matching wound from the king, he shifted into his dual form. The beast with blood-matted fur snarled as Varren chastised him. "You're pathetic. You cannot even fight me like a man. Your savagery comes out. How could Lluava ever love someone so dishonorable?"

Responding to the goad, Apex retorted, "And you would not use any means possible to cut me down? You lie to yourself if you think otherwise. We are the same in this."

Varren stumbled away from Apex's lunge.

Luka continued to speak. "This is my exit. Out of respect for you, you will never see or hear from me again. Through the darkness I go, until I reach the light. In new lands will I seek my home. Long life, Theri, Goddess of War."

At the edge of her field of vision, Lluava watched Luka shift into a black jackal, pause to look back at her one final time, and then lope off.

Apex's voice boomed, "Lluava told me what happened to Thad. She killed him. In front of you. How can you openly admit to yourself that you can forgive her for that? You would harbor the seed of hatred within you. It would grow and fester until it tore you both apart. Lluava deserves someone who accepts her in all her forms, along with all the choices she makes."

Varren held his sword positioned between himself and the massive animal and replied, "She deserves that. I fully agree. But you misjudge me. The anger I hold is not for her."

"Liar!" roared Apex. He shook off a layer of tinted rainwater in all directions. Several of the muddied droplets hit Varren's face and blurred his sight. The king desperately swiped at his eyes to clear his vision. Before the wolverine could lunge, Varren shouted, "Thad murdered his wife!"

Apex hesitated. Varren continued, "When the Outlanders turned on the humans, Thad thought the Raiders had breached the walls. It was a grave misunderstanding. In response, Thad stabbed his wife several times and watched her bleed to death in front of him. I arrived moments later. He was hysterical. He said he had murdered her out of *mercy*. That death was better than being in the clutches of the enemy. I told him to never speak of it again, and I took him with me. I needed to save him, to save something, when all else seemed lost."

The two men circled one another suspiciously while Varren continued, "Lluava was right to kill him. He was a danger to himself and others. And to me. I knew it, but I was compelled to take that risk. I refused to lose him. I did not have the courage, even though I knew, I *knew* he... Lluava is stronger than I."

"On that, we can both agree," Apex snarled.

Varren lowered his sword. "Lluava is better than both of us. Just look. Look at us. What are we doing? We should be concentrating on Elysia and this godforsaken war. We have made—are still making—poor choices, selfish ones. Lluava puts others first; she desires only what is best for her comrades, our people, and the kingdom."

For a long moment, Apex considered Varren's words. He was skeptical of the human's intentions. Clearly trying to expose this as a bluff, Apex stepped closer, "What greater good?" He spat into the king's face. "To the seven hells with your babbling! We have a fight to finish."

"No. That is where you are wrong." Varren sheathed his sword. "Not everything should be resolved through bloodshed. We cannot duel over Lluava as if she were an object. She is not a prize to be won. She has the right to choose between us, if either one is what she truly desires. I will let her have that choice." The young king turned away.

Apex's pain intensified his rage, and Lluava could sense his fury from her prostrate position.

"Don't turn your back on me, coward!" Shifting to human form, Apex jeered, "Fight me like a man! If that's what you want, I will show you that I am the only one worthy of her! Right here, right now. Fight me!"

Speaking over his shoulder, Varren responded calmly, "No. I have a *war* to fight, to win."

The roar of frustration following Varren's departure echoed down the street. Before Lluava could observe which way Apex was heading, she felt huge, leathery hands grab hold of her. She had been discovered! But by whom?

Chapter 32

Entering Nott's Embrace

Lluava's limp body was lifted up by the strong form. She was carried away from the balcony, down flights of stairs, and into the streets of Cronus. Friend or foe? She yearned to turn her head and see who held her.

Instead, her head bobbed up and down with each long stride. Once again, Lluava was trapped—this time, inside her own body. Her heart raced with the awareness of her lack of control. She could not lash out, scream, or utter a single sound. Her body was a cage, and she was locked within.

If this man was a Raider, why hadn't she been killed on the spot? Yet if he was a friend, what then? What would he do if the Raiders charged them? Would she be discarded like a decoy to die at the hands of the enemy? How could this man defend them both, when carrying her prevented his use of any weapon?

She could see the overturned carts of street merchants that had displayed brightly dyed fabrics and large spools of yarn. Smeared with dirt and rubbish, the wares were scattered over the cobblestones. An alley cat slapped at an abandoned birdcage. The colorfully plumed creature inside it cried out and beat its wings at the far side of its prison. The powerless woman identified with the poor avian's feelings. She could almost taste the fear, so like her own, emanating from the feathered animal.

Lluava felt herself slip. Rough hands gripped and shifted her dead weight to a different position. Now her head tilted at a new angle, rolling to the other side. She could finally see her abductor.

Ammit's expression was determined. His wide mouth curled in something akin to a grimace. His vigilant dark eyes darted in all directions. Lluava knew the Theriomorph's small ears were alert to every sound.

Unable to ask him where they were going, she tried to soothe her thrumming heart and reassure herself that she was in the arms of a mighty warrior. The Outlander was as fierce as any drugged Berserker. Lluava had dealt with him firsthand not that long ago, in an arena where she expected him to kill her. How far they had come since then!

She was certain of one thing: wherever Ammit was taking her, Yena was sure to be waiting. He was her servant, her strong man, her unofficial champion. The Outlander was following the high priestess's command. Lluava was thankful that she would at least be carried to safety.

That safety soon loomed over them. Ammit's stride changed as he climbed the temple's steep stairs. Lluava looked over his shoulder as they crossed the columned porch and entered the temple. As they approached the sanctuary, a new concern assaulted her. Apparently, neither Varren nor Apex had arrived. Although Ammit's echoing footsteps made it sound as if they were not alone, the whole building appeared empty. What had happened to everyone else? Others should have been here by now.

Lluava's sight began to blur. Tears bubbled up, distorting her vision, but she could not wipe them away. A few rolled down her face; others obscured her chance of glimpsing the king's arrival.

She realized they were descending into old Rhadamanthus, but she was unable to orient herself during the journey into the depths of the ancient city. Finally, she was lowered onto something cold and hard—a stone block or perhaps the floor. Ammit gently wiped her eyes. Although Lluava still could not control her neck, she began to feel a tingling at the very tips of her toes and fingers.

Time dragged on as, one by one, her muscles slowly regained feeling. Finally able to prop herself up, she recognized the underground chamber that contained the black water pool.

Someone was approaching.

"My child, how are you feeling?" Yena's husky voice asked kindly. "When Ammit informed me that you were still paralyzed, I was worried that you would not recover. I am glad your enemies had not the chance to inflict any more damage."

The high priestess raised her gaze to the third person in the room. "Here...."

Lluava felt Ammit lift her once again but this time only to her feet.

Yena studied her fellow Incarn with a quizzical expression. "I sent Ammit to find you. I have received visions." The priestess glanced at the pool. "They all seem to be connected to you. I know you are weak and exhausted, but Crocotta herself desires your presence."

The high priestess's assumption was correct; Lluava was struggling to find strength, and she was hungry and tired. Though part of her exhaustion could be attributed to Luka's treachery, most was simply due to lack of rest over the past few days. As her tongue still felt like lead in her mouth, she nodded in acknowledgment.

"Will you help me interpret Crocotta's message?"

Again, Lluava nodded, and Ammit assisted her to the edge of the pool. "I am always humbled when I scry for the goddess," Yena continued. "Crocotta has the power of prophecy, yet I, her mortal instrument, can only do so with her blessing and the black water. The irony is that this liquid is found only in the eleven centers of Nott's worship."

The high priestess studied Lluava's confused expression. "After Nott's affair with Giahem, she was banished and sent to rule over the underworld. Although a goddess, she was never permitted a patron city. Yet death is everywhere, and the goddess of death needed to be worshiped.

"Every Theriomorph province has a coliseum associated with the goddess where those of might or ill will, in competition or in punishment, depart the world of the living. The eleven great cities also created underground realms that mirrored the upper world. These were cities for the dead, and specific chambers were dedicated to Nott.

"Offerings for the goddess are left in the black water. Our people believe that when an offering is dropped into the liquid, the blackness absorbs it completely and sends it to the seven hells. The pools of black water are thought of as gateways to the other side."

Yena's hands hovered over the pool. "I have always found it strange that I, Crocotta's Incarn, receive her visions by means of the black water inside places of worship dedicated to Nott—the goddess whom Crocotta despises. Yet, who am I to question such things?"

She gave Ammit a signal and he left the room. Lluava gripped the lip of the pool for support while considering the new knowledge. The high priestess began her preliminary ritual. This time, Lluava was by her side.

Multiple images manifested in no discernable order: First, a pair of hands groped at a gaping wound in a torso. Spurting blood, the wound meant certain death to whomever suffered it. This boded ill for Lluava. Was the tragic vision a signal that the war would be lost? Soon, the image changed. Varren's face appeared and turned a hideous shade of blue, his eyes bulging as the light in them began to fade. Was he the one injured? No; he looked as if he were struggling for breath.

The image grew faint, then reformed into that of Head Councilman Themis holding the pale hand of Odel as he led the boy away from the Verta Mountains and Erebos. In the distance, the setting sun seem to set the mountain range ablaze. What had happened to Themis since he had departed southward? Lluava had not seen him among the soldiers. Had he returned to the City of Shadows? Stayed at Amargo? Or was he here at Cronus?

The water rippled as a panorama of blood and decay filled the entire pool. Skeletal wolves rose from red puddles to slaughter the few poor unfortunates that still drew breath. This was a little more obvious to Lluava: the wolves were the Úlfhéðinn. They were killing everyone, with no end in sight.

The scene was slit into thirds as if one of Issaura's Claws had sliced through the image. Once the panorama faded into darkness, an image manifested against the black backdrop: the golden weapons dripping red pearls, a limp snake lying skewered on its tips. Lluava's stomach twisted. Did Yena understand what this meant? Before she could wonder further, the vision reformed a final time to show an aerial shot of silver and white forms in combat. They spun and spiraled around a black pond.

She barely had time to look around when the crack and snap of Crocotta's Hackles broke the heavy silence in the room. Yena's eyes burned as her silver whip flicked in the air. Leaning against the ledge, Lluava struggled to lift Issaura's Claws in defense.

She knew. Yena had understood it all. The priestess had brought Lluava here not for assistance but to charge her with the crimes she had already committed. Unfortunately, the younger Incarn was in no shape to defend herself.

The high priestess's voice rose, its cadence transformed into something unearthly. "And the twelve Incarn of the gods are to unite, righting the past wrongs." Yena cracked the Hackles again, and the tip of her weapon unwrapped to reveal nine barbed ends lapping at the air.

"The golden era of the Theriomorph race will begin."

The whip snapped; its hooked ends shot forward. Lluava had no time to react as one barb stopped just short of her left eye.

"Leading them into this light is the one birthed from the life blood of Issaura."

Yena allowed the Hackles to settle. "I am only the mortal instrument, flawed as all mortals are. I was wrong." The priestess trailed one ebony hand down the whip's handle. "You are not Issaura's Incarn. You were not made by the gods. I wanted you to be. I believed you to be. I *needed* you to be. You were supposed to be the sign we were all waiting for." Taking a shaky breath, she continued, "*I was wrong.* When I saw that first vision of Apex and you, I thought it was you—but it was Apex, the whole time it was Apex. I placed upon you a burden that you did not deserve, and for that I repent." A single tear slid down her cheek.

Lluava awkwardly clutched the ledge of the pool as she tried to keep her knees from buckling. She focused on the sensations rising through her body.

Yena sighed. "In a way, I am partially at fault for this, our race's undoing. All the Incarn were supposed to unite. All of us. Now, one is gone. You killed the Incarn of Suada. You destroyed the chance for our golden future. No Incarn was ever to raise arms against another. Now, as punishment, *I,* Incarn of Crocotta, sentence *you* to death."

"You don't understand." Lluava's voice sounded thick and muffled. Her tongue seemed to roll around on its own accord. "Selene was the villain, not me. She was going to poison my friends. I was only trying to get the cure from her, and if it hadn't been for my bird—"

Yena shook her head dismissively, then looked up quickly. "Bird?"

Lluava realized that the high priestess had no knowledge of her pet—but how could she not have known? Yet Onyx had never been in Leucrocotta. What about afterward? They must have crossed paths in Cronus.

"Yes. Onyx, my raven."

Gazing at the black water, Yena muttered to herself, "Strange. Another sign that you are Issaura's Incarn, but—"

"What do you mean?" demanded Lluava. She didn't care about the signs, but she had to stall Yena. Too weak for combat, she needed time to run through possible escape strategies.

The priestess was clearly struggling; something was bothering her. "Your bird...the dual form of Theri's mother, Nott, is a raven. Yet you cannot be Incarn. You are an impostor." The priestess flicked Crocotta's Hackles again. "You are false! You must be killed for your sins!"

The whip's ends ripped through Lluava's soiled shirt and bit into flesh, tearing out chunks on its recoil. The Hackles never tangled, and each time they lashed out at her, she retreated lest she be pierced by more barbs.

Although Lluava swiped at the Hackles with Issaura's Claws, another section of her flesh was peeled from a knuckle. Would Yena skin her alive, or bleed her to death? Stumbling on wobbly legs, Lluava's tactics changed abruptly when the Hackles ensnared one of the Claws. Glowing runes appeared on both weapons.

Yena attempted to wrench the Claw from Lluava's weakening grip. Instead, the barbs reacted to the jerking motion, untangled themselves, and recoiled. Lluava's body moved sluggishly, but she made her way around the perimeter of the room.

A gale of laughter erupted behind her. Turning, she saw the priestess expertly sling the Hackles over her shoulder, allowing the long cords to wrap around her own torso several times before the barbed ends hooked into the flesh of her back. Yet she did not flinch, and the laughter of a hyena burst forth once more.

Then Yena shifted. As the silver-furred creature snarled, a line of metal-coated hair stood erect down its back.

"I will fulfill the will of the gods. You will never leave this place, dear one. Relinquish Issaura's Claws, and I will end this quickly."

"I am Theri's Incarn," Lluava responded. Her voice slowly regained its normal tone. "Issaura's Claws are mine."

Yena charged, hysterical laughter trailing behind her. Lluava barely shifted in time. When the tigress collided with the hyena, the gilded claws nearly knocked the smaller animal off course. However, Yena's metal-infused fur pierced the tiger's hide like needles. The tigress slashed at the hyena. Both animals attacked in full ferocity.

With Lluava still weakened, Yena's strength was proving to be a substantial threat. For the first time, the younger Incarn could not sense the presence of her goddess. Theri seemed to have abandoned her, leaving only an internal void. On the other hand, Lluava questioned whether Yena's overpowering force was all her own, or if she was blessed with divine help. Regardless, the tigress was losing this battle.

Returning to human forms, the pair continued to fight. Now, the contest was far less physical, as Lluava desperately tried to keep out of range of the whip. Her body bled from countless wounds, though thankfully none too large.

Yena was unharmed but for a gash on her right arm from the tip of a Claw, which did not slow the high priestess down. Lluava knew this chamber would become her tomb if she could not escape. Hoisting herself onto the lip of the raised pool, she made for the door. If she could reach it, maybe she had a chance of escaping.

Suddenly, multiple sharp pains stung her calf, and she fell. Slamming onto the ledge, Lluava almost rolled into the black water. She quickly turned and tried to loosen the whip that encircled her leg. Then she changed her mind, grabbed hold of the cords, and tugged hard. The Hackles slipped from Yena's grip.

Lluava was able to untangle herself. As she stood and locked eyes with the high priestess, the worst pain she had ever felt tore through her torso. Looking down, she saw a simple stone dagger embedded in her abdomen.

Grabbing the hilt, she pulled out the crude blade and threw it to the floor. Fiery tendrils of pain attacked her body. Her hands were gloved in blood; she pressed them against her stomach to stanch the bleeding. The taste filled her mouth.

Spitting red, she asked, "What of the prophecy?"

Yena stood at a distance and did not move to pick up her weapon. "I pray that it can still come to pass with Issaura's true Incarn. Yet with one of the Twelve dead...maybe this is not the pantheon's second coming. Or maybe we were being tested and have proved unworthy of saving."

The priestess retrieved the stone dagger and placed it on a narrow shelf, carved into the wall with such subtlety that it was barely visible. At the same time, the image of Varren's straining face came into Lluava's mind. She had to warn him of what she had seen. If this was the last thing she did, let it be the one thing she could accomplish! She needed to save the king from the fate shown in the vision.

Lluava stumbled along the narrow ledge toward the far end of the pool. When she reached it, Yena was already there. The priestess turned toward Lluava and seized her wrists as if trying to keep the wounded woman from falling backward.

"Our people believe that when one dies, she or he is brought into Nott's embrace. This is most fitting for you, for you have represented yourself as Nott's daughter." There was a long, reverent pause. "I wish you well as you enter Nott's embrace."

With lightning speed, Yena shoved Lluava into the pool. Issaura's Claws remained clutched in the priestess's hands.

The black water flooded around and over the dying woman, enveloping her body, penetrating every part of her being. She could not struggle. The thick, syrupy liquid weighed her down, pulling her toward the bottom.

A bottom that did not exist, for in this surreal state, there was no sense of gravity, no discernible edge, just darkness. Unable to breathe, Lluava's chest burned until she was forced to gasp and swallow mouthfuls of the liquid.

Blackness encroached upon everything. It coated her eyes, flowed up her nostrils and into her mouth, filled her wounds and her lungs. It seemed to fuse with the very essence of her soul and consumed her final thought as her heart beat its last.

Chapter 33

The One

The chamber was drenched in black.
Inky droplets trickled down walls, dripped from the ceiling, and poured off of the form that slowly rose from the depths of the pool. As if braided through the platinum-blond hair, dark rivulets ran down her head. Out of her ears and eyes, the liquid drained.

Suddenly, Lluava breathed. There was no coughing, no gasping for air; the black water in her lungs had been absorbed by, fused with, her very being. A slow, calm inhalation was followed by an equally languid exhalation.

Shoulders emerged, followed by arms and torso. Wading to the pool's edge, Lluava lifted herself from the black abyss. The pitter-patter of black water falling on stone was audible throughout the chamber. Added to the sound was the cascade of droplets that slid from her body.

Strange, she thought, as she sensed herself moving. Everything felt new, yet oddly familiar. The bizarre sensation was reminiscent of being caught between the realms of sleep and wakefulness. All her exhaustion, hunger, and pain had dissipated, leaving a sense of fulfillment. Dreamlike, everything about her was brighter, more defined. Or maybe more like the clarity of wakefulness after a long sleep.

The shallow carving of the raven by the door seemed to shimmer. Moving closer, Lluava reached out to trace the design. The arm that rose was hers, yet as the black liquid slid off, golden stripes were exposed on her olive-hued flesh.

Examining her body, she discovered that her entire form displayed golden stripes. Tiger's stripes. Returning to the pool, she looked at her reflection in the rippling surface. This was her face, her slitted green eyes, her lips exposing the tips of fangs. Her skin revealed more of those golden ribbons. This was her face—the face of Theri's Incarn.

As Lluava left the chamber, a vision crept into the back of her mind, a dream borne on black wings. Blurred at first, it gradually took shape, and she recognized the Grand Hall. Ammit was beating Varren, whose hands were tied behind his back. One ear bled from an uppercut; an eyebrow dripped scarlet over his bruised face. Receiving a kick to his stomach, Varren crumpled into a ball on the marble floor. Ammit shifted into a snapping crocodile. He was going to kill the king. Yet before he could attack, Apex intervened for the young sovereign's sake...

Swiftly yet calmly, Lluava moved through the city before that dream fled her mind. The vision had been sent to her, just as all her dreams had been sent for the past year. A gift from a goddess not her own. A chance to see things in a way that others could not. This understanding came to her as naturally as that first breath out of the black water.

Upheaval.

The capital exuded a restlessness, a partially metamorphosed version of panic. The undercurrent of Cronus's emotions soured on her tongue like turned milk. Humans and Theriomorphs were at odds, neither able to conceive of the possibility of unification. The heart of the kingdom was faltering, dying. Yet Lluava was not deterred. They would all listen to her soon enough, that she knew. There was an order to be followed. Certain steps to be taken.

When she entered the Grand Hall, everyone was where they should be: four pawns in place. Apex stood next to Varren, while Ammit faced them angrily, his yellowed teeth protruding over scaly lips. Perched on the central throne, the high priestess stared down. On her face was a mixture of shock and fear.

"You can't—" she began, rising. The others turned to look at Lluava as well. Yena's voice shook. "You died."

"I died..." Lluava mused over those words. "Yes. So the prophecy could be fulfilled."

"No. No. No," Yena countered, not daring to leave her vantage point. "You were not the one. The child. The offspring of Issaura's and Ullr's love. Our savior—"

Lluava looked tenderly at the priestess. "Leading them into this light is the one birthed from Issaura's life's blood. I was the representation of Issaura on earth. From my life's blood, the blood I spilled, the life I cast away, I was able to be reborn. It was my life's blood that enabled me to become the Incarn of Theri. I am part of her, as she will forever be part of me. United for eternity."

Although aware of the awestruck expressions on the others' faces, Lluava focused on Yena. "Do you understand now?" she asked serenely.

The high priestess radiated uncertainty. Her eyes grew wide. Blinking away tears, she asked, "What about the other prophecy? The part where the

Incarn allow the gods to undo past wrongs? Selene—"

"That has been happening all along." Lluava answered Yena's questions with her new-found knowledge. "Think of your sacred texts. Luka had an opportunity to turn against me. However, he assisted me by creating the illusion that Apex was under Selene's control and loyal to you. This offset the slight when Shennue trapped Issaura in the unbreakable net after she failed to reciprocate his affections. His Incarn has more tests to come.

"Apex," said Lluava, looking at the huntsman, "did not allow himself to be seduced by Selene. Thus, Ullr did not fall victim to Suada. You chose to encourage me toward my destiny, reversing the animosity between Crocotta and Theri. Selene was the only one who forsook her true purpose. She chose the wrong path, wished me ill, and paid for it with Suada's mortal life."

"If this is true, *you*, and no other, are the savior of our race."

"It is true," Lluava began. "I have risen in order to protect our people from destruction."

Descending the dais, Yena stood in front of Lluava in awe, sensing changes both great and small in her counterpart. The high priestess sank to her knees and placed an ebony hand over her heart. "Blessed be the will of the gods."

"I hold no ill will toward you," Lluava acknowledged earnestly. "You did only what you believed was right."

"And I will continue to do so," noted Yena, her throaty voice rumbling. She summoned her attendant, who had shifted back to human form. "Ammit, find the ruire and bring him here. Also, send a healer to deal with young Mandrun. I sense he will not die this night."

Yena retrieved Issaura's Claws from the throne. "These belong to you," she said as she handed Lluava the golden weapons.

Having accomplished her goal, Lluava moved toward Varren, who still lay on the floor. Severing his bindings with her Claws, she helped him to his feet. The young king's clear blue eyes stared at her as if seeing her for the first time. Behind him, Apex did the same.

The men's emotions muddled the air. There was confusion, uncertainty, and more than a little fear. Focusing on Varren, Lluava sensed his pain and inquired, "Can you stand on your own?"

"Yes," he said. He seemed to want to say something else, but whatever it was, he held back. He ran his thumb over a stripe of gold on the back of Lluava's hand, then lowered his hand to his side. She felt a tingling sensation come and go with the touch.

"You're so strong," Apex said, still too hesitant to approach. "So powerful. I can feel it, even from here."

Behind them, Yena explained, "She is one with her goddess. More connected than either of us. In time, may we all be so unified. For now, Lluava is blessed over all other Incarn."

"Do not be afraid," Lluava told them, although there was a hollowness in her voice. "I am as I should be. Now, it is time to change the course of the war. Now is the time to *end* it."

Lluava was not bothered by the three sets of eyes trained on her. Why shouldn't they wonder about her transformation? She looked obviously different. Her movements were different as well, and even the way she talked had changed. It was logical that they would need time to process the alteration that had occurred.

In truth, all her personal opinions, prior emotions, previous connections with these people had been washed away by the black water. They were still important to her, but the bonds had been diluted.

Lluava knew that someone was headed their way several minutes before the door heaved open, allowing the healer to enter, a Theriomorph she did not recognize. Already well informed, the older man began inspecting Varren's extensive injuries. After giving him a dose of Idun, the healer applied salves and poultices to the wounds.

Save an occasional moan from Elysia's king, the Grand Hall was silent. When the doors reopened, Thoth approached with Ammit. Bowing to Yena, the ruire inquired, "Why have I been summoned?"

He was understandably worried about the large number of Elysian soldiers that had accompanied Varren and were now inside the city. Suddenly, he looked at Lluava and took a step back.

Yena spoke. "It seems you have answered your own question. I need you to tell the entire Theriomorph citizenry that we are supporting the Incarn of Theri and will follow her to the war front."

"Is she—?" Thoth was unable to take his eyes off Lluava's golden markings. "She is."

They would observe her command. No matter what she ordered, it would be done. In battle, her word would be obeyed. Such was the nature of things.

Thoth bowed before Lluava, a bit stiff from his recent injuries. She cocked her head at the gesture, finding it curious.

"What is your command?" the ruire asked.

"Summon every leader, from clan chiefs to those who oversee the Warrior Caste, and bring them to the Lesser Hall. Invite the Guardians to attend as well."

"As you wish," consented Thoth before leaving to fulfill his duty.

Ammit, standing nearby, nodded toward Varren. "And what of Mandrun's humans?"

Varren spoke out. "We will back Lluava as well."

Adding to the young king's pronouncement, Lluava said, "The heads of Varren's military factions are also invited to the meeting."

"Yes, of course," agreed Yena. "Ammit, release those you have captured."

"Ammit," Lluava clarified. "Release *all* your Elysian prisoners from Tartarus. Every one."

Inclining his head, Ammit left.

Lluava addressed those who remained. "We will meet in one hour to discuss the war's end."

Yena, Apex, and the healer filed out, though a little reluctantly. Only the human remained.

"Lluava." Varren looked deeply at her, his eyes searching hers.

"What is it you are looking for?"

"You."

Reaching out, Varren touched her cheek. Again, a strange tingling caused Lluava's heartbeat to quicken, while she sensed his doing the same. Pulling back, the human closed his eyes and breathed out very slowly. "You are still here."

As soon as he stepped away, the emotional connection lessened, and that new detachment filled the void. Lluava followed him out of the Grand Hall to the now empty corridor, where sconces flickered. Once again, she sensed other presences approaching.

She spoke with certainty. "Your Shadows are here." Turning around, she added, "You don't have to hide, Holly."

The female guard stepped into the light. Then the entire corridor was filled with the black-clothed figures.

"Varren will be fine," Lluava told them. "He has made peace with the Outlanders. We are to fight the Raiders together."

"Is this your wish?" Holly asked the king.

"This is my command," Varren affirmed. Looking at Lluava once more, he invited Holly, "Come. Help me find the others."

Like animated darkness, the Obsidian Guard followed Varren down the hall, leaving Lluava alone.

The question now was what to do for the next hour. Sleep was not a necessity. Lluava did not consider returning to her former chambers, for they were no longer hers, not really. She would not need food for a while. Besides, others needed nourishment more than she.

Choosing instead to wander the corridors, she leisurely strolled about the castle. Everything was so familiar, yet so foreign. This sensation was strange but not unpleasing. As the time drew near to meet with the others, she recognized two approaching figures: Hyrax, followed by Rosalyn. The pair halted rather abruptly.

They must think I look strange, Lluava thought with a smile. She said, "You are wanted in the Lesser Hall, Hyrax."

"Lluava, what happened?" Rosalyn quickly asked. At the same time, Hyrax said, "You look—"

"All in good time," said Lluava. "For now, I must ask Hyrax to come with me."

There was a moment of hesitation before the Guardian stepped to her side. As they turned to leave, Rosalyn blurted, "There is a woman around our age with hair like yours. She trapped me in the tower."

"Maruny," Lluava stated.

"I do not know what she is called, but she discovered my signal and blocked my exit. Even in my dual form, I could not get out the window. If Councilman Hyrax had not heard my cries…"

"I must thank you, Hyrax, for saving this woman."

"Anything for you," the Guardian said as he continued to stare at Lluava's golden-striped flesh.

Rosalyn, shaken up and motivated by fear, asked, "Did they…did they make it?"

Lluava looked kindly at the raven-haired woman. "Varren and his commanders are gathering in the Lesser Hall as we speak." Glancing at the former councilman, she continued, "That is why your presence is needed, Hyrax."

"And Talos?"

"I do not know his current whereabouts, but I am certain he is inside Cronus." Somehow, Lluava could sense Talos's presence still on this plane of existence. "Go and find him."

Rosalyn did not have to be told twice. She ran past the pair to search for her husband.

Next to Lluava, Hyrax remarked, "So, you have finally come into your own."

"It seems I have."

"I always knew you were the one."

"Indeed."

Chapter 34

Siege

luava cocked her head and listened. A loud blast erupted somewhere
far above. Hyrax had heard it as well, for he was looking at the ceiling.
Another rumble caused the walls to tremble ever so slightly. If one
had not been paying attention, the minute shifting would have gone
unnoticed. Lluava knew exactly what the cause was. She had heard this sound
before. A low growl clawed its way up her throat. "Let's head to the Lesser
Hall. There is much to discuss."

Lluava led the way. She could not help overhearing the conversation
within the room well before she reached the door. The raspy voice of the
oldest Guardian retorted, "That's preposterous. It was to be her child!"

Stepping through the doorway, she confidently pronounced,
"Prophecies are misinterpreted all the time. Is it so incredible that this one
was misunderstood?"

The dark-robed Guardians wore their Obsidian masks, which caused
strange whistling sounds when they inhaled through the carved fissures. One
by one, they lowered those relics, revealing aged faces with mouths agape.
The last one to remove his mask was so ancient that he needed the assistance
of the Guardian next to him.

Hyrax entered behind Lluava and took a seat on the perimeter of the
room, as all the chairs around the table were filled. The Guardians occupied
most of them. Yena sat at the head of the table, flanked by several
Outlanders, including Thoth, Ammit, and another who smelled of caribou.
Each clan was represented by one person; Yamir had taken Father's place
upon his death. Holly and Jigo stood on either side of Varren, who was
seated. Near one wall, Vidrick and Colonel Ojewa stood with two people

Lluava had not expected to see: Admiral Merrow and Colonel Skipe, commanders she had served under in the Southern Camps. Apex sat not far from where Lluava stood.

The Razor Backs' clan leader offered his seat to the young woman. Those seeing her transformation for the first time were stunned into silence. It was clear that no one would oppose her. All for the better. They waited for her to speak.

Claiming her position, Lluava began, "This war will end and soon. It is up to those of us in this room to ensure that the outcome is in our favor. This is the turning point. Have you been listening?"

Pausing, she allowed the others the opportunity to focus on the rumbles from above. Though the humans were unable to distinguish any unusual noise, many a Theriomorph's eyes darted about.

"Yes. We are under attack as we speak. The castle and presumably the outer wall are being bombarded by projectiles from the Raiders' siege weapons. If not stopped, the enemy will decimate our final defenses. We will be helpless and will fall victim to their cruel and ruthless behavior."

"How do you know that is the case? Did you observe catapults at work?" one Guardian questioned. Across from him, another suggested, "It could just be thunder." A third added, "It was reported that their construction had not been completed."

Lluava calmly replied, "Go and look for yourselves, if you must. We will let you know what has been discussed upon your return."

Several Guardians arose, though there was no need; a breathless Theriomorph burst through the door.

"We are under attack!" he gasped, then bent over to gulp air like a fish out of water. "Trebuchets! Many of them!"

A clan chief inquired, "Can any projectile reach the castle? We are in the center of the city."

Still breathing heavily, the sentry stated, "They can, and they are."

"Are the external walls holding?" asked a Guardian.

"Fairly well against the stone orbs, but their other projectiles concern us."

"What are they?" Varren asked. He looked at Lluava. She knew he was remembering the initial attack on the Southern training camps. The pair had watched in horror as projectiles coated in flames tore through two of the camps, burning them to the ground.

The messenger explained, "Glass containers are filled with acid. The containers are wrapped in cloth soaked in oil. They are set on fire and aimed at the walls, and now at the castle. When they strike wood, fires start. The glass containers break on impact, and the acid dissolves the stone and mortar."

The silence was broken by shouts, exclamations, and questions; everyone seemed to be speaking at once.

Apex silenced them with his wall-trembling roar. "The trebuchets must be destroyed. Until that happens, the enemy has the upper hand."

"I agree," Varren said. "We still have a small supply of Flashbang, the explosive that helped us wreak havoc upon their army. If an aerial attack were to target the siege weapons, we could destroy them without incurring significant troop losses."

"That can be done," agreed Thoth. "Though after the last mission, I know my troops are near exhaustion—as, I suspect, are most of the other warriors. Those who fly will not have the strength to help further until they rest and recover."

Faint echoes of the outer explosions continued.

"My men also need rest," Varren admitted; Ammit added, "As do ours."

Lluava regarded the weary faces about her. The idea of rest at this crucial time in the war was now alien to her. Yet all living things needed rest and recuperation. Not everyone could survive without sleep.

"Well," said Yena, "the first step seems clear. Those who can fly will destroy as many of the siege weapons as possible. If they accomplish their mission, we might gain a reprieve long enough for the rest of our forces to recover before we attack."

"And what would happen next?" Yamir questioned. Lluava noticed that the youth refused to look at Varren or the Shadows. "Launch one army against another?"

"That would not be wise," interjected Lluava. She quickly assessed various approaches of attack. "Even with the trebuchets destroyed, the Raiders might still have vast stores of this acid. They would find other ways to use it to their advantage."

Grunting, Apex said, "I have to agree. We must discover where their munitions are stored and destroy their supply. Then we can focus on eliminating their leaders. Until then, we need to minimize our losses. That is the only way to survive a threat like theirs." During the entire conversation, his gaze never left Lluava.

The young woman made a decision. "Rest will have to wait. The Raiders' siege weapons and ammunition must be destroyed immediately." Though several individuals were clearly disgruntled, none dared counter the goddess incarnate.

"All able-bodied fighters are to be divided into three factions. The aerial Theriomorphs will start first, by bombing the trebuchets with packets of Flashbang that will be exploded with the aid of archers. Next, a small number of ground troops will infiltrate the enemy camp and attempt to discover the location of the acid. If they can destroy the stores on their own, they will do so. If not, they will use our whistles to signal to the aerial troops where to deploy the last of the Flashbang."

Lluava scanned the room. "Finally, the remainder of our army will stand guard at the walls to defend against the surviving enemy. Minimizing entry into the city is of the utmost importance. I need not remind you what damage just a few Úlfhéðinn can inflict."

There was a pensive silence after she had finished speaking. Although some people might perceive Lluava's ability to influence others as a god's gift, she felt it had always been part of her essence.

"How are we to leave Cronus?" questioned Vidrick. "Surely not by the main gates."

"There are other points of exit," she noted, glancing at the high priestess.

Yena inclined her head toward Lluava and spoke. "All of which will be opened for your cause. I will back your plan and, in doing so, volunteer to help destroy the weapons stored outside the walls."

"Do you think that is wise?" Thoth asked the high priestess.

"I believe this is the reason the Incarn of the goddess of war is here. So, I will join her on the battlefield."

The ruire bowed his turbaned head and pronounced, "I will lead the aerial Theriomorphs in their attack." Before anyone could ask about his injuries, Thoth added, "This is *my obligation* to my people as ruire."

"Who will then take on the defense of our city?" Yena questioned, with unusual restraint.

Lluava noted that Varren's eyes darted between her and Apex. "I will," the young king stated. "I know this city well. I know her strengths, her weaknesses. I will protect her and her people with everything I have."

Yena scrutinized the king. Was she questioning her decision? Could she actually entrust New Rhadamanthus to this man? Finally, the high priestess said, "That is the wisest choice."

Next, the discussion focused on the division of the ground army. Aquila was an obvious choice for the defense of the walls. He would target not only the trebuchets with his arrows but also any oncoming projectiles that came within his incredible range. Apex would join Lluava and Yena on the front lines with a small band of volunteers. Using the tunnels, they would emerge somewhere between the Raiders' encampment and the trebuchets. With luck, they would not be observed. Varren would lead the remaining forces inside the city walls. Those unable to fight would seek safety behind the inner curtain wall that protected the castle.

Once the meeting was adjourned and the participants moved toward their assigned stations, Lluava approached Holly. "Where is Regin? He should have been at this meeting."

"He would have been, if we had been able to find him."

"Is he not still in Cronus?"

"I can't say for sure. Not yet." The tone of Holly's voice left a dark implication in the air.

Lluava paused for a moment, but she could not detect the missing Shadow's presence. There was no need to push further. "You must protect Varren."

"With my life," the female Shadow replied, then left to follow her king.

***

Near the temple, a respectable group was forming. Yamir, along with several clansmen, joined a number of Yena's men and even a few Elysian soldiers. Ammit stood watch as Lluava approached Apex's side. They knew their objective was to breach the walls of the Raiders' encampment, yet this suddenly changed when Colonel Ojewa left his position on the wall to raise an alarm.

"The Raiders' entire army appears to be on the battlefield. Be warned."

Yena's eyes glazed over for a moment before she spoke directly to the other Incarn. "If the enemy attacks us when we leave the tunnels, as I believe they might, the two of you must take it upon yourselves to destroy their camp. I will remain with the others and prevent the enemy from following you." Turning to Ojewa, she added, "Make sure the tunnels are destroyed after we leave." Ojewa, along with Apex and Lluava, nodded their agreement, and the order for the ground troops was modified.

Aerial warriors had gathered near the front of the city, ready to take wing at Thoth's command. Meanwhile, Yena led Lluava, Apex, and the volunteer troops into the underbelly of the old city. There they split into several smaller bands of warriors and headed down their respective tunnels to await a signal from the whistle. The sharp trill would permeate the passageways despite the distance and underground positions.

Once each individual group reached the end of its tunnel, the signal was given; the camouflaged openings were shoved wide open simultaneously. Lluava and Apex were among the first to clamber out. Looking to the sky, she saw the aerial Theriomorphs swooping over Cronus's wall. Amid the disparate flock, she glimpsed a swan gripping a parcel of Flashbang in her webbed feet.

Wingbeats thrummed in the air as explosions began to rock the walls, and deadly projectiles flew through the skies. There was a stunted screech as the first of the aerial troops collided with a trebuchet's orb. Soon, the archers let fly their initial wave of flaming arrows, targeting the siege weapons and setting off a new cacophony.

It was time for Lluava's band to make its move toward the encampment of the enemy. As they approached the palisade, she glanced back at the battlefield. In the scorched swath of land leading to the castle gates, large siege weapons were aligned. Several rows of trebuchets and catapults continued to sling their lethal weapons at the stone fortress before them. Even as flames fed upon their oaken limbs, they hurtled fiery projectiles of doom in systematic order.

The trumpeting of a war horn alerted Lluava and the others that they had been spotted. A small detachment of Raiders at the rear of the lines turned and headed in their direction. Yena cried out, "All from Leucrocotta, the Clans, and Elysia, follow me! We feed on Ocean Men tonight!"

The high priestess looked at Lluava and Apex and said, "You must destroy their munitions. Here," she handed Lluava a bag of Flashbang to add to the two she already carried. "I will try to keep them at bay." Lluava inclined her head slightly in a sign of gratitude.

As Yena led her men toward the approaching enemy, she untethered Crocotta's Hackles. With a flick of her hand, the coiled silver whip emitted a cracking sound far louder than should have been possible. How many of her followers understood they were striding to their deaths?

"Onward!" Lluava roared as she moved toward the remnants of the Raiders' stronghold. Apex followed a few paces behind.

As they angled away from the main battle, Lluava felt alert and oddly composed. She was in control and could sense everyone on the field of battle. Her ability to foresee her opponents' upcoming moves enabled her to avoid them, and she had no need for caution. Her boldness did not go unnoticed.

Apex jerked her to the side. "What in the seven hells is wrong with you?" he snarled, as an arrow flew past and sank into the ground where she had been standing. "Do you desire to be killed?"

"I was not going to be shot," she replied flatly. Seeing the frustration and anger in Apex's eyes, she tried to appease him, "But I thank you for your concern."

"What's happened to you? I stayed out of Varren's way so he could have a chance to find out. It was my way to make amends... He and I, well, we are at an impasse for now. But I need to know what happened!" Apex barked after Lluava, who had started toward the broken fence line. "Lluava? Lluava!"

There was little time to reason with the disgruntled man. The stores of acid had to be found and dealt with immediately. She heard Apex's rapid approach but chose to disregard it. Once again, he yanked her back. The heat inside her flared up at his rough handling.

As she turned to face him, he shoved her abruptly away, and a clang resounded overhead. One of Ullr's Fangs had parried a strike from an enormous axe. Spinning around to see the attacker, she recognized the twin braids of Sweyn's red beard, but this man had turned into a monstrosity with blue-black skin, devoid of all humanity.

Apex swung at the Úlfhéðnar with both blades. "What are you waiting for?" he roared at her. "Go! Go! Finish what you started!"

The smell of freshly welling blood in the air caused Lluava to salivate. Jerking her thoughts back to the mission at hand, she left the pair to battle to the bitter end.

Lluava reached the stronghold without further interference, although now she was alert to any sign of unexpected attack. Steadily moving around the wreckage of tents and half-constructed longhouses, she passed the row of snarling, dragon-shaped hotboxes. The charred remnants of burned-out fires had left the metal underbellies as cold as Lluava's compassion for the foreign men who had brought the cruel devices with them.

Divots of earth and parts of dismembered corpses were strewn around the ground from Aquila's earlier unholy lightning strikes. None of this affected her purpose. She searched every structure without success. There was no sign of acid, not even a small pile of their stone projectiles, and there was not a single guard. Lluava halted.

Was this it? This scattered rubbish? That meant that all the Raiders able to fight were on the field of battle, as well as all the remaining munitions. Was this the Raiders' final push before claiming victory, falling to a dire fate, or retreating to more fruitful territory? Regardless, if the Raiders did not conquer Cronus soon, they would be forced to leave. They had no food, no weapons left. This was the Raiders' last stand.

Scanning the area again, Lluava began to sprinkle the black powder from each parcel around the stronghold's buildings. When she had moved away from the encampment, and only then, did she pull out her tinder and flint and begin to strike. Once…twice…

A sparking line of flame hurtled over the collapsed wooden posts that had once formed a mighty palisade, and jumped toward a mound of debris and the Flashbang. In the next moment, the stronghold erupted in a raging inferno. The initial explosion sent Lluava flying backward to crumple on the muddy ground.

A deep sense of pleasure burned through her just as the fire burned through the camp. Columns of flames soared into the sky as if hoping to join the stars before dying down to a blazing bonfire.

A dark form emerged from the intensely hot wall of light. Sweyn shrugged off his smoldering clothes of singed fur and crackling hide. His unnaturally hued flesh had been blistered by the fire's kiss.

Lluava's eyes were riveted on his solid black gaze. Slowly, he lifted a blood-splattered fist into the air as if presenting a gift. In his grip was a large swatch of long bronze fur and oozing flesh.

The victim's name slipped past Lluava's snarling lips. "Apex."

Chapter 35

Void

Sweyn dropped the swatch of fur as though he'd forgotten it. For a moment, he looked as if he were trying to speak, but his smoke-infused mind failed to form the words. Instead, he stuck his swollen tongue between his teeth and bit down until blackened blood oozed onto his ruddy beard.

The scent of the onyx droplets stirred the presence inside Lluava that awaited release. She felt her pupils narrow instinctively as her body prepared to shift.

The dark-skinned Úlfhéðnar swung the axe he held in his other hand. Sweyn seemed to have no reaction to the metal heated by the conflagration he had just walked through. Lluava's lip curled in agitation. What had this creature done to Apex? Was the huntsman alive? The Incarn was not meant to be slain on *this* field of battle.

Around them, flames hissed and spat. Like summer's fireflies, embers fluttered into the sky to merge with the twinkling of stars hidden behind the veil of clouds. Neither figure moved, even when hot cinders bit into their skin.

Something was wrong with this man, this monstrosity before her, but Lluava could not determine what it was. It was not his odor, which was akin to the smoke of the Berserkers. It was more than the unnatural hue of his flesh.

Sweyn's black eyes looked at her critically. Was he capable of thinking? He took two long steps toward her but never reached his destination. At the same time, an empowered being lunged into the space between the would-be combatants. The huge bronze Yorrick wolverine snarled menacingly at the Úlfhéðnar before attacking.

So, the huntsman had not been killed. That boded well. Lluava took a moment to observe the two nightmarish creatures as they assaulted one another. The open wound on Apex's mid back exposed mutilated muscle. She could sense his pain as well as his fury.

The sound of screaming metal hammered their eardrums as the large axe slid down the wolverine's metallic muzzle. Apex went on the offensive as Lluava continued to watch them. She noted how the wolverine emanated energy. Although Lluava could sense everyone else around her, including Apex, she could not detect this Raider, this creature. Instead of leaving an imprint that she could discern, Sweyn did the exact opposite. In the space filled by the Úlfhéðnar, there was only a void, an emptiness. Was this a side effect of their drug? If so, this would indeed hinder her plans.

Irritated, Lluava snarled as she shifted into her dual form and prepared to help her fellow Incarn. And she would have, had not a multitude of Raiders begun to approach. Roaring, Lluava struck out at the first of the oncoming enemy. As the creature's life was torn from him, she felt his energy dissipate.

Without looking at the Raiders surrounding her, Lluava allowed her vision to slip into its blue-green state. Like a master of Kings and Crowns, she was able to foresee all the enemies' upcoming moves. The boundaries between herself and the goddess had been transcended. She was unstoppable.

Glimpsing the carnage she left in her wake, Lluava spotted Apex. Looking away, she continued to feel the strain on his physical vessel as it combated the living void. The huntsman had not reached full transcendence with his god. His body was weakening, and that realization disturbed her.

The tigress moved to aid the Yorrick wolverine. As she did, a sharp, icy sensation ran up and down her side. Glancing at her ribcage, she saw a thin line of red on the mud-smeared white of her fur. The feeling of ice turned into a ribbon of fire. This was pain. *This* was unacceptable.

A second Úlfhéðnar had arrived. Lluava chastised herself for not being aware of his presence. That was also unacceptable. That was not part of the larger plan. Her whiskers flared out, then pressed tight against her face. This man had no palpable essence, either; he, too, read as a void. Was this true of all Úlfhéðinn? She would need to be extra careful. Her pain was proof of that.

Apex would have to battle on by himself, at least until she could remove this grievance. Lunging at the Úlfhéðnar's weapon, the tigress nearly lost an ear. The sword had been brought down at an unsuspecting angle. How could that be? She should have foreseen his movements. Unless…

It was that void, that lack of perceptible essence. The Úlfhéðnar was as unpredictable as any opponent she had faced prior to her transcendence. The inability to sense danger from them and respond would slow down her intended victory. This would hinder many things.

Lluava drew upon all the knowledge she had gained from her training in warfare and combat. Once again, she relied on her quick thinking and her skill in recognizing the physical tells of upcoming moves.

The Úlfhéðnar drove his sword forward again and again. Lluava narrowly avoided the volatile end of the blade. Her enemy was before her, above her, to the side of her. His looming form would have been threatening had she been able to feel fear.

The fringe of the man's wolf-hide cloak dragged in the mud. Clumps of soggy earth clung to the speckled gray fur like minuscule weights. Dodging his swinging of his sword, Lluava clawed red gashes in the bare-chested form. His black blood oozed onto his dark-hued skin. The demonic man struck out again.

Meanwhile, Apex fought on. It was hard to tell which of the pair had the upper hand. Although Sweyn was impervious to any pain inflicted upon him, Apex, with his god now forcibly controlling his Incarn, was more energetic. Unfortunately, the huntsman's level of transcendence only allowed a fraction of Ullr's capabilities to manifest. Úlfhéðnar and Incarn were well matched, but only one would live.

"Lluava, help!" Apex's voice bellowed as another Úlfhéðnar came to Sweyn's aid. Lluava resented the distraction. She was fully engaged with an enemy of her own. Apex was an Incarn and should be able to rise to this new challenge.

Once more, he cried out, "Lluava!"

The tone of his voice triggered a memory, a feeling. The last time she had heard him call out like that was in Tartarus, when the cavern caved in. Apex had needed her then as he needed her now. On that occasion, if Varren had not held her back, she would have crossed the narrow bridge and been impaled by the falling stalactites. Varren had nearly died saving her.

The rage of war was forced aside by her fear of losing someone she cared about. There was no time to wait.

With a gigantic roar, the tigress disemboweled the Úlfhéðnar before her and sprang at the wolverine's second attacker before the brute had time to strike. In turn, Apex was able to focus solely on Sweyn, who was a far more adept fighter than other Úlfhéðinn.

Time dragged on; yet none of the combatants could gain the upper hand. Finally, Lluava executed a maneuver that enabled her to bite her Raider's exposed neck. Simultaneously, Sweyn forced Apex to the ground. The massive form of the wolverine was on his side, breathing heavily.

No! Lluava thought, but she had to make sure her Raider was dead before she assisted Apex. Bones snapping in her jaws, she could only watch as Sweyn grabbed Apex by the scruff and yanked his head back to expose the Incarn's throat.

As life slipped from Lluava's prey, she leapt to Apex, but she was too late. Sweyn was driven backward by the impact of the single Fang protruding from his chest. The other Fang was in Apex's now human hand. The huntsman thrust the twin blade next to its brother.

She wondered if Sweyn realized what was about to happen. Quickly, Apex torqued the two pommels together like a gardener snipping weeds. The

Raider's heart was sliced in two, and Sweyn fell limply to the ground.

"I'm glad you're alive," Lluava said. She shifted, and for a brief moment, she felt relief, happiness, and a muddle of other emotions. Soon they would be veiled by the goddess's will, but for now, Lluava gave his arm a squeeze.

Apex offered her an understanding nod before asking, "To Cronus?"

"To Cronus."

The huntsman wavered. His foot slipped on the saturated earth. He reeked of blood.

"Can you make it?" she asked, eyeing the gaping wound on his back once again. His bronze Endun shirt had been ripped and torn, exposing the lacerated flesh. Somehow, the wound appeared more serious in his human form.

"Have I a choice?"

Lluava glanced about them. Although other Raiders were nearby, they gave both Incarn a wide berth. Many eyes were cast upon this pair who had fought with such otherworldly power and ferocity. Apex faltered again, and Lluava pressed close to the huntsman. She knew she needed to protect him, but she could not openly assist him. If the enemy realized how weak he was, they would surely attack.

The sounds of war had lessened. The explosive booms of Flashbang had ceased. The shattering impacts of the trebuchets' missiles had abated. Only two of the heinous siege weapons were still working, but one was listing so badly that it would soon topple of its own accord.

Shifting into their dual forms, Apex inquired, "Do you want to pull down the last one?"

Lluava sensed Apex's body fighting hard to keep him moving. With each beat of his heart, he lost more blood. "No. We must head back to Cronus and the others."

Apex did not argue. This was both a blessing and a curse, for with his strength went his determination and his headstrong opinions. He would need all three to combat any opponents along their route.

Many Raiders ran in terror at the sight of them, though a few made ill-fated attempts to attack, which resulted only in death as they were felled by Lluava's teeth and claws.

Yet Raiders were not the only ones who approached. Yena, with what remained of her troops, joined them. Together, they would have to fight their way to the city's gates.

Suddenly, an explosion of sound and brilliant light surrounded them. Aquila shot the Talons, targeting the enemy to the left, right, and rear of the returning party, leaving only the Raiders directly in their path. The nomad could not risk the integrity of the wall to slay those foes. Instead, a barrage of arrows from the archers on the castle parapet dispatched many of the brutes near the gates. Without hesitation, Lluava's party rushed into the fray as arrows and projectiles whizzed past. Several of their group were accidentally killed in the onslaught from above.

The Raiders, focused on slaughtering the dwindling ground troops, did not notice that the gates had been opened just enough to allow Varren and his men to rush out and attack them from the rear. The sudden and unexpected assault caught the remaining enemy unprepared. They ran pell-mell about the battlefield. With most of their siege weapons destroyed and no sign of their commanders, the Raiders were incapable of making decisions. Their confusion enabled Lluava and her allies to slip inside the capital.

Just before the doors were shut and sealed, she had the eerie sense that she was being watched. Looking back through the door as it swung shut, she spied Níðingr. Although his skin had reverted to a normal hue, black veins snaked down his arms and up his neck. He stared at her coldly.

Yena addressed the troops who had fought on the land or in the air or defended the walls. "I thank you for the great sacrifices you have made. Those we have lost will be rightly mourned at the appropriate time. For now, all must rest and recuperate. The war is not over, though today victory was ours."

Not stopping to listen to the high priestess, the pair made their way to the castle in human form. Lluava slid her arm under Apex's and tried to keep the huntsman on his feet. He was sturdily built, with barrel chest and heavy musculature. He outweighed her by a good bit.

"Let me help." Lluava looked up to see Varren take Apex's other arm. Together, they half carried the huntsman through the city.

Varren nodded at Apex's wound. "How did that happen?"

She could not answer, for she did not exactly know. Looking far too drowsy for her liking, Apex responded, "That damn blue-skin had a grip on me when the encampment went up in flames. In the explosion, we were flung away from one another. That part of me went with him."

Lluava blanched, a strange feeling indeed. She had lit the Flashbang, thus causing his injury. "I'm so sorry," she hurriedly replied.

"Not your fault," Apex affirmed through gritted teeth. "You could not have known."

Several Outlanders ran to assist them and took Apex off to their healer. Hopefully, Idun would speed his recovery. As he was carried away, Lluava gave Varren a worried glance.

The young king consoled her. "He will be all right, Lluava. Apex is strong, like you are."

"I hope so." Her voice came out oddly strained.

"You are more like yourself, I see."

Lluava was about to inquire what he meant, but then she understood. Though the goddess was still with her, the immortal's influence was subdued. The sudden awareness of all her emotions, feelings, and thoughts over the past few hours flooded her senses, and her knees buckled. Before she could fall, Varren grabbed her.

"I have you," he said gently into her ear. "It is okay." After making sure she had regained her footing, Varren bent down and looked her in the eyes. "You need rest. Sleep. We all do." The statement was only partially true. Everyone else needed sleep. Lluava was mentally drained, but she was not physically tired.

Talos approached, looking sick with exhaustion. Byron and Rosalyn, weary as well, were not far behind him. Once they entered the grand foyer of the castle, Talos's hoarse voice rasped out, "We need to decide our next move."

Byron agreed with his military partner. "The enemy is in a panic. We must attack them now, before they regroup."

Lluava's head was beginning to throb. The muffled noise of the intermittent missiles bombarding the outer walls did not help. The goddess inside was irritable, as if she, too, were tense with the thought of oncoming evil.

"A decision should be made, but not without full representation of all those with authority here," Varren replied. "I will not make that decision alone."

"You are the king, Varren," Talos reminded him tersely. "No one has more right than you."

"That may be true," Varren replied. "But not all here view it that way. We need the support of the Outlanders' high priestess and the clan chiefs."

"We are wasting valuable time," Talos countered impatiently. "Who knows how long it will take to gather all of them? We do not even know how many are left."

"I am sorry, my friend," Varren began, placing his hand on Talos's shoulder, "but this is the way it must be. And right now, *all* need time to rest. We have pushed ourselves beyond the point of exhaustion. We must recover our strength, or we will be in no shape to defeat our enemy."

Another trebuchet blast exploded closer to the castle. Rosalyn placed a hand on her swelling belly and worriedly eyed the direction of the sound. "That weapon is sending projectiles inside Cronus. How are we to rest?"

"Stay in my quarters," Lluava offered. "Use my bed. It would be safer than your house. Farther away from that weapon."

"Thank you," Rosalyn replied, obviously relieved. Talos was still unhappy. "That weapon won't stop wreaking havoc while we sleep. It is still reaping lives."

"Where is Aquila?" Lluava inquired. "He could destroy the trebuchet with Giahem's Wings."

Rosalyn gave Lluava a sad look. "He was injured. Not seriously, but badly enough that he had to be brought down from the wall."

"I meant to tell you," Varren confessed. "One of the trebuchet's orbs fractured the parapets near him. He fell backward and hit his head. He is being treated for a concussion."

Lluava chewed her bottom lip. "Well, my offer still stands. You can use my room, Rosalyn. You too, Talos. Byron, you are welcome as well."

"We should be out there, Varren," Talos argued. "We *should* be out there." "We will be soon enough."

With her own anxiety growing, Lluava added, "Talos, go with Rosalyn. I will let you know once a decision is made."

Together, the couple left. Byron held back for a moment before speaking. "I apologize for Talos. He is exhausted. We all are. I know you are right about resting, but…" Byron sighed. "He wants what's best for you. For Rosalyn. For Elysia."

"I know," Varren acknowledged. "I have never doubted that."

On the far side of the foyer, Talos and Rosalyn had stopped, caught up in their own conversation. Rosalyn was clearly trying to urge her husband up the stairs. Talos was holding back, still dissatisfied with Varren's decision or lack thereof. They took a couple of steps in the direction of Lluava's rooms before Talos paused, turned, and shouted in a much calmer manner, "Varren, just know—"

High above, glass shattered and fell like razor-sharp hail as one of the trebuchet's small glass containers broke through. The jar burst on impact with the rim of the window. In the space of a moment, acidic rain poured down on the young couple below.

Chapter 36

Kamikaze

A woman's screams sliced through the foyer. Lluava's vision was instantly blue-green. A focused blood thirst pulled her toward the doors, the city, the threat. An odd sense of calm about what she was to do compelled her.

Then Varren cried, "Oh, god! To them! Hurry!"

Abruptly, Lluava's vision reverted to normal. Her friends were hurt. Seriously hurt. She ran toward them. Others appeared, following the sounds of explosion and screams, as Theriomorphs and humans alike made their way to the injured couple. Even a Shadow or two appeared. A barricade of onlookers blocked Lluava's view.

Rosalyn was crying hysterically, making unidentifiable sounds. The hiss of the smoking acid was drowned out by barked commands. Lluava glimpsed Byron in the center of a circle of onlookers, trying to pull someone away from the corrosive puddles.

"Move aside," Lluava snarled, as she and Varren forced their way through the helpless bystanders.

Byron had laid Talos on the ground, away from the slow spread of the liquid. Ignoring the burned splatter marks on her face, Rosalyn was crawling to him. She had not stopped screaming.

Lluava rushed to her side. Seeing the acid's damage on the left shoulder and sleeve of Rosalyn's gown, she pulled the raven-haired woman to her feet and began to tear off sections of the contaminated cloth. Beside them, Byron quickly tugged off his shoes while Varren assisted Talos.

Rosalyn's words began to take shape. A single word, repeated over and over. "Talos," she cried, "Talos. Talos. Talos."

Continuing to inspect the mangled dress for any other sign of damage, Lluava asked, "Did any get on your belly?"

"Talos," was the only word that escaped the trembling woman's lips.

Fumbling among the pleats of Rosalyn's dress, Lluava demanded, "Did any touch the baby?"

Eyes wide with terror, the pregnant woman shook her head no. Tears streamed down her face, now more than outwardly scarred by the attack. Lluava inspected the blistering marks on Rosalyn's pale features. She was relieved that her friend had not sustained more burns.

The acid appeared to have splattered when it hit the ground. Nasty inflamed marks were clustered on Rosalyn's neck and under her chin; a few peppered her cheek and brow. Her eyes had been spared; one ear had not.

Behind them, people moved hurriedly. A middle-aged woman, a Theriomorph whom Lluava did not know, brought clean, wet cloths.

"Let me wipe your face, dear," she cooed. Rosalyn, unmoving, let the stranger tend to her burns, all the while repeating her husband's name.

At last, Lluava had a chance to look at Talos, who had been moved farther away. His body lay convulsing on the floor while Varren and Byron struggled to keep him still. A third man stood over them and repeated, "Hold him down. Hold him down."

Lluava glared at the useless "assistant" as she headed toward them. One of the Shadows shouted, "A healer is on his way!"

Talos's clothes had been stripped from his body. Wet cloths lay discarded on the floor. Picking one up, Lluava stepped closer. Varren and Byron's struggles prevented her from seeing how badly Talos was hurt. As she moved to help, she glimpsed a face, or what used to be one, under the shadow of Byron's shoulder. Some of the acid must have landed directly on Talos's head.

"Keep her away," Varren ordered. His voice was menacing.

At first, Lluava thought the command was intended for her, but then she heard Rosalyn approaching. Quickly turning, she blocked the distraught woman's view.

"Let me get you out of here," Lluava said, as she reached for her friend's slender arm. Her thoughts were on Rosalyn's stress and her unborn child.

"Talos," Rosalyn replied trying to peer around Lluava.

"Where is the damn doctor?" Byron shouted.

"Talos!"

Somebody asked, "Isn't she a healer?"

Given Rosalyn's emotional state and the horrific situation, the woman surely would not be able to function in any beneficial form. She continued to cry, "Talos, Talos, Talos!"

"Let me—" Lluava began.

Rosalyn darted around Lluava, only to collide with Byron's torso. He had released his partner in order to keep Rosalyn away from Talos's flailing form. Gathering her in his arms, Byron carried her away from the area. The young soldier had an obligation to protect his partner's wife and unborn child, and he would fulfill it. But as he passed her, Lluava saw the terror in his eyes.

Someone shouted, "The healer! Where is the healer?"

There was another explosion. This time, the vile projectile landed just short of the castle.

"Everyone, get away from here!" Varren commanded. Turning to the Guard, he ordered, "Help the others to safety!"

A stranger questioned hesitantly, "But the man?"

"There is nothing to be done."

Varren's words made Lluava's stomach heave. Solemnly, she looked at her friends. Talos's body continued to twitch. Varren, still seated on the ground, had at last let go of him.

With another explosion, the remaining people vacated the foyer to seek refuge deeper within the castle.

Lluava could not bear to look at the ravaged face. Sinking to the floor next to Varren, she held Talos's hand in hers, feeling his ragged pulse. She stared at her feet, at the broken window, at anything but her injured friend. Varren put his arm around her shoulder. And so they waited.

By the time the healer arrived, Talos had died. He had taken his last painful breath a good ten minutes earlier, yet Varren and Lluava had not moved from his side. With the healer's assistance, they carried their friend's body into a nearby room before the healer hurried off to see to Rosalyn's burns.

"Should we have allowed Rosalyn to stay here with Talos?" Lluava questioned. She was thinking how devastating it would be to die without partner or lover nearby.

Varren, distraught as well, admitted, "I ... I don't know what we *should* do anymore."

"Was it right for us to send her away?"

"I do not know."

"Byron should have been here."

"Perhaps."

Their tears of grief and overwhelming loss were interrupted by Yena's roaring voice.

"What in Giahem's all-knowing mind was he thinking?"

The priestess's voice had never sounded so uncertain, so unsure, so afraid. Stepping into the foyer, Lluava saw Yena fuming at Ammit. The priestess looked as if she wanted to strike the tall man. "It was not an order given to him. He directly disobeyed me!"

The next explosion was extraordinarily loud; the vibrations rattled windows, and a few more broken shards of glass shattered on the floor.

Yena wavered as if she were about to faint. Her face was pale in comparison to her typical obsidian hue.

"It is done," Ammit stated.

"What is done?" Lluava asked. Varren had joined her at the perimeter of the room.

Yena slowly raised her gaze. Lluava realized it took every ounce of the priestess's will power to do so.

As Ammit steadied the shaken woman, he explained. "The Ocean Men were going to smash through the gates. We had run out of arrows. Ruire Thoth gathered the last of your Flashbang. In his dual form, he flew with it and a lit torch, and dove at the last trebuchet."

Lluava hesitated before asking, "Are you saying he sacrificed himself?"

"Yes, to destroy that weapon," Yena confirmed. Her voice was once again in control.

Lluava felt numbed by the loss of so many people. "His life saved other lives and has bought us time," she said with gratitude.

Ammit's exaggerated grimace showed he did not agree. "The gates will fall. The damage is too severe."

"Tomorrow..." Varren began. His features conveyed his utter exhaustion, though his voice remained strong. "We must all convene in the Lesser Hall and discuss what is to be done next. Tonight, everyone must rest, if they can. Do you agree, High Priestess?"

Yena faced toward the main gates, her eyes glazed. "Yes. Tomorrow."

After a formal bow to the priestess, Varren escorted Lluava to her quarters. They found Byron slumped on the couch. It was clear he knew his partner had died. Whether by the length of time, the severity of Talos's injury, or something the healer had imparted, he knew. But where was Rosalyn?

Before either could ask, the weary soldier nodded toward the alcove. "She is in there. The healer left a little while ago. The baby will be fine, as long as she avoids further extreme stress. The healer left us medicine." He passed Lluava a vial of Idun. "But she refuses to take it."

"I'll talk to her," Lluava said. She wished the little vial could alleviate the pain Rosalyn must be feeling, both physical and emotional.

"Where is Talos?" Byron asked solemnly.

"Downstairs," Varren responded, "in a room adjacent to the foyer." As tired as he was, he chose not to take a seat. "I will return shortly. Someone must inform Yamir."

"Let me," Byron said as he rose to his feet. "Talos was my partner."

"The Obsidian Guard are nearby. They can come with you, if you wish."

"No, thank you."

The men gave each other a strong hug before Byron headed off. Lluava left Varren in the outer room and went to Rosalyn. The heartbroken woman lay on her side in the bed, half-covered by silken sheets. She was silent and did not acknowledge Lluava's approach, though her eyes were wide open.

"I have medicine," Lluava said soothingly.

Rosalyn did not respond. Finally, she uttered, "No."

"It will help you," urged Lluava. She moved to the side of the bed. "It does wonders with scarring."

"He protected me," Rosalyn's voice was barely a whisper. "Our baby. And he... and he took the worst of it." Tears rolled down Rosalyn's porcelain skin, though not as many as before.

The parallel actions taken by Talos and Varren to protect the women they loved did not go unnoticed. Without taking the time to bathe, Lluava changed clothes and slipped into the bed beside Rosalyn. She gently smoothed some of the dark, tangled hair from her friend's face. Then the pair lay next to one another, just as Lluava had done with her sister only a year before, and their weary bodies at last obeyed the command of sleep.

***

When Lluava awoke, she noticed that although the sky was still riddled with ominous clouds, the sun was out and high in the sky. However, it was not the bright light that had awakened her but a small tapping at the window. Outside, Onyx perched on the sill, steadily pecking at the glass with his beak.

Carefully getting out of bed so not to disturb Rosalyn, she unlatched the window. The raven flew over Lluava's head and into the main room. Following the bird, she noticed several slumbering bodies sprawled about.

Aquila was stretched out near the balcony door. Giahem's Wings and the quiver of Talons were clutched in his hands; a bandage was wrapped around his head. She was glad that his injuries were not severe, but she was also disappointed. He could have destroyed the trebuchet. Byron snored on the couch, his clothes still smeared with blood. Varren was slumped in one of the wing chairs. Yamir was not with them. She did not know if that had to do with Varren's presence or with an obligation to be with his clan.

Onyx cawed once and received a quick frown from Lluava. She watched the raven cock his head and shift his stance on his perch.

"You must be quiet while they are sleeping. Understand?" she asked the ratty bird. Onyx bobbed his head rapidly as if nodding.

With Issaura's Claws in hand, she made her way to the baths. Relishing the steam of the heated pool, she gingerly stepped in. How she wished that all the evil that had occurred could be washed away as easily as the scum that coated her skin. Lluava could sense a numbing detachment growing between herself and her prior emotional strain and knew that her goddess was ever aware.

By the time she had dried off and untangled her hair, she felt somewhat refreshed. That changed as she was returning to her quarters and saw Hyrax about to knock on her door.

She cleared her throat and he turned toward her. He held a large, covered tray of food and something that smelled like hot herbal tea. "I was just bringing this to you. I have some medicine for your unfortunate friend, the woman who lost her husband."

Lluava eyed the offering suspiciously. "How did you know that?"

"I have the knack of hearing things." Hyrax gave a half-smile. "And this tea is infused with herbs that will help relax her, calm her nerves."

"Why do you care?"

"Because you do." Offering Lluava the tray, he added, "There is food here for you. It might not be what I call a lavish meal, but it was all I could scrape up."

"Leave the tray by the door," said Lluava, as she pondered the Guardian's kindness. "Have you heard how Apex is doing?"

"Do you wish me to take you to him?"

"I would appreciate that."

Hyrax led Lluava to the room designated as the Outlanders' medical ward and pointed to Apex's cot. She had expected the huntsman to be griping at the attendants. Instead, he was in a deep sleep, having received an extra-large dose of Idun. A healer explained that this was a precaution, as another patient had disrupted the entire ward when he left against orders, shoving the healer aside and knocking down an attendant.

The Guardian stayed with her the entire time. When Lluava was satisfied that the Incarn would recover, she asked the former councilman, "When will the discussion of our plan of action begin?"

"This evening. It was determined that every person needed maximum rest. It is critical that everyone be able to think clearly and make sound decisions."

"So, we have a little more time till then?"

"What do you need, Lluava?"

"I need to talk to our prisoner."

***

Alcove no longer lay in bed. Though still grizzled in appearance, he looked much more like himself. For some reason, that made Lluava uncomfortable. As soon as he noticed her physical transformation, Alcove's mouth twisted into a smile, although his eyes were wide.

"I want you to tell me how to kill Níðingr."

The blunt request did not seem to affect the man. "Some believe he cannot be killed."

"Sweyn was killed." Lluava made sure to observe Alcove's reaction.

The hint of a smile touched the ambassador's face. He inclined his head subtly, as if acknowledging a great feat. "Sweyn was a great warrior; however, Níðingr is far greater. Was it a good death?"

The question baffled Lluava. What made a death good? "He was slain on the field of battle. Swords to his heart."

"God will be pleased."

Now Lluava was not only confused but also disgusted. What sort of god did the Raiders believe in who demanded such a blood sacrifice? A good death? Was being killed in battle something to be esteemed? Was that why they never balked at war?

Shaking her head to clear her thoughts, Lluava asked once again, "How can Níđingr be killed? Tell me. If you want control of the Raiders, of your men, tell me."

"He is mortal," Alcove admitted. The swatches of silver hair over his ears had grown long and now swayed as he slowly paced in the confinement of the small room. "Beyond that, I am not sure I can offer much help. I cannot assist you on the field of battle until he is slain. If I am to regain authority over the army, my people must not see me engaging in traitorous actions. As long as they trust me, I will be able to ensure that they stay within the perimeters of our empire. You and your kind must kill Níđingr on your own."

Chapter 37

The Final Council

Lluava observed Alcove. Was he studying her reaction, or just staring at her golden stripes? Did he expect her to question his usefulness? If she did, he would certainly have a counter-argument. Could he even be trusted? Lluava's expression gave nothing away. As she began mulling over various scenarios, the ambassador added, "There is one more thing that must occur if you want me to be able to do my part."

She knew he was trying to lure her in, like an expert fisherman ensnaring an unusually large bass. "What is that?"

"I need the horn that Niðingr carries with him. He is never without it. This horn is unique, from its carvings to its distinctive sound. I need that horn to prove that Niðingr has been killed and that I am now in command."

Lluava was annoyed that Alcove would send her on an errand like some low-born page. "Anything else?" she replied snidely. "Want me to find your falcon and feed it for you? Retrieve your lost cloak? Polish your helmet?"

Alcove refused to rise to the bait. "The cloak and helmet have been stripped from me. My bird has most likely been killed."

Was he mocking her? Judging her emotional outburst? No. Yet, once again, he appeared to expect something more from her. For a few minutes longer, the pair discussed the delicate plan to hand over the horn to Alcove without arousing the Raiders' suspicion of his treachery.

When she finally left, Lluava headed back to see whether her friends had awakened. As she walked, her personal emotions faded, distancing themselves. A harsh clarity took their place. The battle was to begin anew, and she could not allow anyone or anything to impede her ability to make difficult decisions.

***

As Lluava entered the Lesser Hall, the grim faces of the survivors turned toward her. Apex was not present; he was still recuperating from his blood loss. Derrick, however, had returned and looked far more like his old self. Even Byron had attended, although he seemed preoccupied.

The room grew silent in anticipation of the high priestess's initial remarks, yet Varren was first to speak. "The Raiders' second-in-command has been slain, and their siege weapons have been destroyed. For the moment, it seems that we have a reprieve from battle, yet the war is not yet finished. The enemy is still under the command of their leader. From the report I received a few minutes earlier, the Raiders' units are reforming and will attempt to breach the gates. Their resources are low as are ours. The question remains: what is our next move?"

Yena recognized Ammit, who added, "The gates are severely damaged. The Raiders could break through shortly."

"Then fortify them," stated Derrick. "That does not seem like a question."

Yamir, representing the Cloven-Hoofed Clan, added, "There is plenty of debris from the damaged buildings; we could use it to patch or pile up behind the doors."

"If we do that," Varren asked, "how would we confront and fend off the Raiders, once we have barricaded ourselves inside? Moreover, the enemy will continue to poke and prod Cronus's defenses until they find a weakness."

Yamir shot the king a dark look. Varren had meant only to spur the generation of ideas, but the young clansman must have assumed his suggestions were being demeaned. More proposals were presented. Lluava could hear every murmur, every whisper, around the room. Although she was mildly amused at the actions and reactions each idea received, time was short, and none of the plans would succeed.

Lluava's voice was emotionless. "The Raiders will find a way in. That is certain. They will attempt to break open the gates. *We* are going to let them."

Whether due to the utter certainty of the way she had spoken or the unearthly power she emanated, not a single argument was raised. She was the Incarn of the goddess of war, and this was why she was here. Sensing doubt and fear, Lluava explained her reasoning.

"This city was designed as a labyrinth in the event of enemy infiltration. Once the gates fall, the Raiders will enter, presumably in large numbers. The narrow roadways will quickly become overcrowded and cause bottlenecks. We will block certain routes and set traps that will further isolate the enemy. Our fighters, positioned on the rooftops, will be waiting. Yamir, I need you to lead the clans in these preparations."

Yamir's oval eyes sparkled. "I can think of a few ideas that might work, depending on where you want these booby traps."

"Good. You and I will talk more later. Now, to the main point," Lluava continued. "We must split the Raiders into as many small groups as possible. This will help our odds. We do not need to kill all of them. We only need to separate their commander, Ivar Níðingr, from his men. Once he is slain, the enemy forces will be left in chaos. Níðingr carries a special horn that we must obtain; it will signal the Raiders that their leader is dead. With the loss of their military commander, we will be able to defeat an army that is no longer organized and disciplined."

Lluava did not reveal her source of information or Alcove's future role in assuming command of the Raiders' army. "I will admit that there are concerns. One issue involves the strength of the buildings themselves. Many have been damaged by projectiles; others were compromised when the Berserkers and the monstrous Úlfhéðinn entered the city."

She paused to see if anyone would suggest a solution; if Elysia were to prove itself worth saving, its people must make their own choices.

Colonel Ojewa stepped forward. His accent matched Yena's. "I will form a team to see what can be done. I am sure we can strengthen a few of the weaker structures or, at the very least, tear them down to create barricades."

Lluava inclined her head slightly in acknowledgment. "Whatever we do, we must keep the enemy away from the castle. Those unable to fight will continue to take refuge within these walls. Children, elders, and the injured will be moved to the innermost area. Barricades must be erected outside the castle's inner curtain wall. Ammit, will you work on this? Vidrick?"

Ammit responded, "If it be your command, Theri, I will do so gladly." He would never challenge the goddess incarnate.

Vidrick hesitated. He looked at the large, intimidating Theriomorph, then nodded. The redheaded lieutenant added, "I will always do what is asked of me."

Varren spoke next. "Then I must ask that none of you challenge the Úlfhéðinn in hand-to-hand combat unless specifically ordered to do so." He spoke as a leader, with the voice of authority. "I do not wish to demean anyone's ability, but we must ensure minimal losses. The Úlfhéðinn are vicious, murderous monsters and extremely dangerous. Moreover, the rain has finally stopped. This means that the Berserkers will be able to smoke their drugs. So be wary of large Raiders. Any encounter should be considered life-threatening."

Lluava could sense the discomfort and fear permeating the room. The corner of her mouth twitched, as her tail would have done had she been in her dual form. The mood in the room was heavy with emotions and men's sweat.

Varren glanced at Lluava. "If the primary goal is to separate Níðingr from his men, we must decide where and how to lure him. Even if our intended strategy does not unfold the way we wish, a plan must be made so that men and traps are aligned accordingly, to force them back on the correct paths."

"The temple." Yena's voice was heavy with sorrow. "On the temple steps. I have seen it. That is where your last stand with that abomination will occur."

"Did you see Níðingr being killed?" one of the Guardians questioned.

"No," acknowledged Yena. Her white irises flashed fiercely in the dimly lit room. "But the battle that will determine how this ends will occur on the temple's steps."

The young king respected the high priestess's vision. "Then let us ensure that Niðingr is led to his doom."

Lluava felt a low vibration throughout her body, and she smiled; the goddess within was pleased. Those around her took no notice as they continued to strategize.

There was a newfound harmony among the diverse groups as they collaborated on a shared goal. Together, they worked to fine-tune the plan, allocate jobs and responsibilities, and set the plan in motion. When the meeting was adjourned, many moved into the dining hall for a late supper. The rest headed off to begin their new tasks.

Lluava did not crave nourishment—at least, not until Varren handed her a platter containing tenderloin on the rare side. Her favorite. In short order, the sloshing of goblets and chewing of food tapered off as people left to make preparations.

***

In the early morning hours, well before the light of day, word came that the Raiders were on the move. Although the allied forces quickly moved into position, the city remained quiet. They did not wish to alarm the enemy.

Outside in the cool spring air, Lluava was ready and waiting. Varren was next to arrive, followed by Yena, brandishing Crocotta's Hackles. They were joined by Aquila, who had strapped on a second quiver. Giahem's Talon's were positioned on his right shoulder, while a cluster of battered common arrows filled the quiver on his left.

"That is all we could salvage," he stated, as he adjusted the strap of the tattered leather quiver. "Once I have run out of these, you must decide whether I am to shoot the Talons."

Lluava nodded as she considered the damage radius surrounding a single shot of a golden arrow. In such close quarters as Cronus's streets, they might do more harm than good. There was no need for such sacrifice at this time.

"Everyone ready?" Varren asked.

The four of them looked at one another: male and female; Theriomorph and human; Elysian, Outlander, nomad; different religions, different gods. Together, every person for whom they were fighting was represented. And they were about to fight for everyone they loved, everything they knew, and everything they believed in.

A loud boom was followed by a groan that was lost in the cracking and shattering of wood and metal. "It only took one hit," somebody shouted down from a rooftop. "The Ocean Men have breached the gate!"

Yena was oddly calm. Gesturing, she said, "Into that house, the second one on the left."

Once inside, the small party climbed onto the roof, using a ladder that had been carefully propped up on the ledge of a fourth-floor balcony. Quickly adjusting to the roof's steep angle, Lluava looked around. Nearby, the castle rose above them. While the commoners' dwellings lined the inner perimeter of the city, the grand homes of the nobles, built shoulder to shoulder, surrounded the castle and extended outward from it. The city's design was not only a visual indication of wealth; it also provided a secondary defense against intruders, for the roofs provided vantage points for archers as well as an aerial roadway.

Yet now this same construction hampered the mobility of the defenders. So, for this final fight, ladders had been positioned from rooftop to rooftop over the narrow streets, and ropes and pulleys had been rigged to enable quick movement from higher to lower levels. Nothing was set up that could not be cut down or pulled away if the enemy breached these makeshift aerial highways.

Lluava's team carried the ladder with them and used it as a less than secure bridge to cross over passages and alleyways until they reached their specified position. Though the wind was not strong, an occasional gust caused one or another to almost lose their balance and cling to the wooden rungs for dear life.

They made their way to the top of a large manor house in clear view of the temple, where they could reassess how the plan was working elsewhere in the city. Under the silver gaze of a sliver of moon, the sun had begun to rise.

Varren peered through his spyglass, while Lluava allowed her senses to heighten. On various levels, small groups of people moved about busily. It seemed that almost all the clansmen were there, as well as a respectable number of Outlanders and Elysians. Some monitored existing barricades; others pulled down weakened buildings and created new barriers from the debris.

The wreckage of lumber and rubble slowed the Raiders' approach and forced them to split up. Some of the allies pelted the brutes from rooftops with sharp or heavy objects they had collected. Others used polished metal shields and even large silver platters to indicate the locations of the enemy. The metal reflected the sun's strengthening rays, and the pattern of the bursts of light signaled specific information.

Other than the ongoing rumble of falling debris and occasional shouts from small skirmishes in the distance, Lluava could not detect the sound of significant battles. Based on the carefully planned movement of their troops, as well as the signals they flashed from the rooftops, everything was going according to plan.

Suddenly, a glaring flash caused Lluava to blink. That was their cue. Nídingr was heading their way. The next signal that glinted came a little earlier than expected. The third came far too soon. The pace at which the defenders were moving continued to increase. Lluava released a low growl.

Had they separated Ivar from his troops? If Nídingr and his men were moving at such a rapid pace, could the clansmen set their traps quickly enough? If not, Ivar would arrive with company. That was something they had hoped not to deal with.

"Can you see him?" Lluava asked Varren, for she could spot no movement below.

Varren was scouring the roadway in front of them. "No. He is still out of sight." Another series of flashing lights.

"Did that just say—?" Aquila began, as Varren confirmed, "Yes. Niðingr is heading in the wrong direction."

They were not the only ones to receive the news. Band after band of men left their posts throughout the city to scramble into new positions. The plan was altered in response to the enemy's movements. Their unused blockades and unsprung traps were abandoned like a child's forgotten toys.

"I see…" Yena mused to herself before speaking to them. "We need a better location." She gestured at the others on the roofs. "They will attempt to maneuver the Ocean Men back to the temple using a different route. Our current position is futile."

"Yes," Varren agreed. "If they head here on the wrong route, they might encounter a dead end. We need to provide an accessible path for Niðingr to reach the temple and ensure that he arrives alone."

Carrying the ladder, the band made its way toward the pandemonium. Their progress was painstakingly slow. At one point, the ladder was too short to reach a higher level. Yena leaped from the top rung to the ledge of the adjacent roof and hoisted herself up. Once there, she assisted the others. The ladder was left, wedged at a precarious angle, until they needed to move elsewhere.

From this new vantage point, Lluava was able to observe some movement in far-off streets. Yet, she could not spy Niðingr. Looking at Aquila, who was perched on the ridge of the rooftop, she saw the nomad swing his strung bow in her direction. Glancing behind her, she noticed an approaching band of Raiders, a score or more.

They were not Niðingr's party but another group that had advanced far into the city. With so many eyes trained on Ivar's men, this rogue group had slipped through. If these Raiders arrived at the temple first, there would be too many to fight. Aquila could shoot the riggings and set off the trap, which would cause a blockade of stone to seal off the route. But if he did, Niðingr would not be able to reach the temple.

In mere seconds, Lluava mentally ran through a host of scenarios, but there was only one viable solution. At that same moment, Aquila barked out, "Down!" and she pressed her body close against the slanted roof.

An arrow whistled over her head.

With a thwunk, it sank into its mark. A second and a third flew past. With his salvaged collection of arrows, Aquila was picking off the entire band of Raiders. How many arrows did he have left? Were there enough?

Lluava's position limited her line of sight. From the corner of her eye, she could see the Raiders collapsing like sacks of barley. Aquila never missed a shot. Yet one of the brutes, probably the most intelligent of the lot, held his shield in a way that protected his front, while the wall behind him safeguarded his back.

"He is going to break through!" shouted Varren. His words mirrored her thoughts.

One last arrow whirred by. This one skittered off in the wrong direction. Skimming against the building's stone wall, it ricocheted off the decorative metalwork around a doorway—right into the unprotected side of the Raider. Dropping the shield, the unfortunate victim stumbled over a companion's corpse, fell upon it, and impaled himself on the protruding shaft of another arrow.

They were all slain.

There was no time to rejoice. Yena had not noticed Aquila's feat of marksmanship, for she had climbed to the peak of the roof and was facing the opposite direction. "Niðingr has been separated from some of his men, but he is still heading the wrong way."

Varren and Lluava clambered up to see where she was pointing. Looking through his spyglass, the king concurred. "The only barricade left to be sprung is now unmanned. Those stationed there must have changed their positions earlier. If it is not released, Niðingr will head to the castle. If it is triggered, he will be forced to follow the planned course." Looking at the nomad, the young king said, "You can set that off. Do it."

That was the most logical move. Lluava would have made the same choice, even though a good dozen of their men would be killed by the blast of the Talons. Aquila, his blond-streaked auburn hair flowing in the wind, looked pensive. He also realized that lives would be lost. "I could aim for Niðingr. End him now."

Although the option was appealing, Lluava realized that the end result would be failure. "You could, but you would destroy his horn. We need the horn to signal to the rest of the Raiders that their leader is no more. Killing Niðingr that way would mean greater losses afterward."

Aquila pulled out one of the golden arrows and shot it at his target.

For a moment, the whole world gleamed white. The explosion that followed shook the very building they stood on. The vibrations sent Lluava and Varren tumbling down. She dug Issaura's Claws into the tiles of the roof. Clay shrapnel scattered everywhere. With one Claw serving as an anchor, Lluava grasped the king's arm with her other hand.

While Varren regained his footing, Yena reported, "The entire building has collapsed. Niðingr is alive and moving onto the correct path. At the rate they are moving, he and his men will arrive at the temple well before we can get there." As the foursome slid down the roof toward their waiting ladder, Yena admonished them, "Hurry, or all will be lost!"

Chapter 38

Upon Rooftops

Splinters bit into her flesh as Lluava slid down the ladder—sharp, stinging reminders of the far worse pain they would all feel if they failed. Following the others, she moved as quickly as possible to return to their initial position.

Varren hastily lowered the ladder to the next rooftop. The loud crack caused all to wince as the ladder slipped out of his grip. Had the enemy heard? Would the Raiders suspect what they were planning? While the others took a moment to regain their calm, Lluava led the way across the chasm.

The ladder was almost horizontal. This should have made the crossing easy, but wind gusts were picking up. Instead of walking across upright, Lluava chose to crawl on all fours. As she moved, she sensed that certain sections were weakening, and she avoided placing too much pressure on them. The eighth rung was the worst.

Reaching the other side, she steadied her end of the ladder as Yena crossed, followed by Varren and Aquila. The group made steady progress until they encountered a drop trap that appeared to have been set off on its own. On closer inspection, Yena noted, "The ropes were not tethered well. Someone rushed their work."

"The Raiders' path is still open," Aquila remarked, as he examined his last regular arrow. The sorry-looking thing had tattered fletching, though he must have deemed it worth holding onto.

"Yes," countered Varren, "but *our* path has been affected. Look."

Stony debris had fallen on the rooftop opposite them. The uneven surface and weakened structure would not be safe to cross.

Lluava grew impatient with the others; decisions needed to be made.

255

"To another building, then. If the Raiders can alter their routes, so can we."

They veered off in the direction of the approaching Raiders and their leader, Niðingr. As the homes of the wealthy increased in size, Lluava and her companions picked their way around chimneys and climbed over steep peaks. At last, Yena raised a hand, signaling the others to slow down; she suspected they were near Niðingr's location. The roadways were empty, households deserted. Everything was eerily still.

Varren scanned the panorama with his spyglass. The others relied on their keener sense of sight. Niðingr had disappeared. Nothing they saw indicated an oversight in the plan; all the pathways had been altered, and there had been only one route to take. The enemy should be here. But they weren't.

So, where were Niðingr and his men? What could she have missed?

Beside her, Lluava noticed that Varren held his breath. The Incarn's unnatural calm did not allow fear to enter her thoughts. Let the young king worry. Or the nomad. She had no time for such petty things.

There was a sound of crashing and cracking.

"That was under us," Varren stated, his eyes wide with understanding. They rushed to the edge of the roof and looked down. Suddenly, a large bay window directly below them shattered. Shards of glass flew into the cobblestoned street. Peering over one side of the building, Lluava saw a blue-black-skinned Úlfhéðnar climbing up the sheer wall of the building.

From the other side of the house came the sound of more glass breaking.

"There is another Úlfhéðnar over here!" hissed Yena, as she uncoiled Crocotta's Hackles.

"One here as well," snapped Aquila, as he let loose his last ordinary arrow. The weapon must have struck its mark, for a sickening thump was heard as the victim hit the ground. "I'm out," said Aquila as he backed away from the edge. He could not use the Talons at this close range.

The former asset had suddenly become a burden. Now Lluava would be forced to watch over this helpless cub. She backed over to the nomad's side as the first Úlfhéðnar attempted to climb onto the roof. Varren dispatched the Raider's head with his sword, though the young king warned, "More are coming."

Yena's Úlfhéðnar had avoided initial decapitation and was threatening the high priestess's life. She snapped her whip as if awakening the Hackles from their slumber. The crackling sound that followed was paired with an electrical sensation in the air. Lluava felt the fine hairs on the back of her neck stand up as if on command.

Aquila recognized Lluava's intent to protect him. He glanced over the wall, past the Úlfhéðnar climbing to the roof, and focused on the dead corpse sprawled unnaturally on the ground. "He has arrows."

The nomad was right. His victim had been carrying a large crossbow. The full quiver was positioned under the Raider's naked shoulder.

"Don't do it," Lluava warned, as she saw Aquila searching for the best way down.

Slinging Giahem's Wings over his shoulder, Aquila said, "I am not like you, she-beast; I cannot change my skin. But I can help with those arrows." Without another word, Aquila began to descend the wall, as he had done in Erebos. "I will be back!" he shouted, just as an Úlfhéðnar rose up in front of Lluava.

Blue-black skin glistening with sweat. Tattered wolf-hide cloak pinned by a brooch under his Adam's apple. Pale blond beard and hair matted with blood. Eyes glinting like flecks of obsidian in the sun.

Lluava tilted her head to the side, considering the monstrosity before her. She calmly observed the Raider as he unsheathed his longsword. Issaura's Claws felt cool against her palms, as if they, too, were unthreatened.

Around her, Crocotta's Hackles were carefully filleting the exposed chest and back of Yena's Úlfhéðnar. Varren's sword was swung expertly to deflect a giant axe's blade. In the distance, a raven cawed. The bellowing roar of Theriomorphs met the furious shouts of men.

In a world wavering blue-green, Lluava was both Theriomorph and something more extraordinary. She knew when to spring aside. The Úlfhéðnar thrust his sword at her, but she was already scaling the roof, using her Claws to pull herself upward. The giant Raider raced after her once he realized his mistake. On all fours, sword between his teeth, the savage brute was rapidly catching up.

Reaching the peak, Lluava spun around and dropped down onto her back, her head now lower than her feet. Bending her knees, she planted both feet firmly against the slanted roof and pushed off. Allowing gravity to help accelerate her, she slid directly toward the approaching enemy. With her arms stretched over her head like an arrow, she turned her Claws so that the sickled blades faced the Úlfhéðnar. She raised them at just the right moment, and they collided with the behemoth's sword. The impact forced the blade backward, slicing off the top of the Úlfhéðnar's skull.

Her body continued to slide, picking up speed. She quickly tried to catch hold of the roof with her weapons. Shingles shattered with each bite of her Claws. Suddenly, one dug in and caught; her body was wrenched to a stop at the edge of the roof, with her head dangling over the side. She looked down at the street. Aquila had apparently retrieved the quiver, but there was no sign of him.

A mixture of sounds—clattering, thudding, scraping—assaulted her ears. Raising her head, she saw the corpse of her recent victim sliding in her direction. She scrambled to her feet and vaulted out of the way just as the Úlfhéðnar rolled over the edge.

Lluava moved to help her comrades. Although Yena had already killed one of the creatures, others hoisted themselves onto the angled battleground. Two Úlfhéðinn readied their weapons before her. The high priestess caught

Lluava's eye and shouted, "Head to the temple!" She had only a moment to point to a rope that led to another household. The high priestess shared a final vision from Crocotta: "I was never meant to be at the fight by the temple. Only you two! Go!"

The priestess shifted into the silver hyena with metallic hackles. Emitting a nervous laugh, the creature lunged at its first opponent. Lluava was busy assisting the young king in the midst of his own battle.

Collecting the faulty wooden ladder, Lluava swung it at Varren's Úlfhéðnar. The monstrosity instinctively reached out and grabbed hold of the impromptu weapon, then jerked both the ladder and Lluava toward himself. Though his reflexes were anything but normal, the creature was momentarily distracted and unable to block Varren's sword.

Although the weapon severed the spinal cord and the Úlfhéðnar collapsed, the brute continued to cling to the ladder while swinging his axe at Varren and Lluava. Between them, the Úlfhéðnar soon drew his last breath.

"To the rope," Lluava stated calmly while Varren panted. Infused with the goddess's power, she would never be weary from battle.

Varren glanced at their mode of escape. "What about the high priestess?"

She did not look at the other Incarn. "Níðingr is getting away. Yena said to leave without her."

Lluava sensed the human's uncertainty and dismay, but she responded firmly, "We need to move, Varren."

Reluctantly, the young king grasped the rope. He used his hands to pull while his legs, crossed over the cord, helped shimmy him forward. Once he was a good body-length out, Lluava followed.

The rope was hard to negotiate with two bodies causing it to swing from side to side, but it was their only option. Even if the ladder had not cracked from the Úlfhéðnar's abuse, the other building's roof was too far away.

The wind continued to be more burden than blessing. Varren almost lost his grip. Once secured, he glanced back at her. They were three-fourths of the way up, and there was no turning back.

Suddenly, Varren warned, "Watch out!"

An Úlfhéðnar's sword was spinning through the air at Lluava. Drawing upon her inborn strength, she hauled herself up one length farther just as the blade severed the cord by her feet.

Human and Theriomorph clung to the rope as it swung to the far side, where they collided with the stony wall of the other building. The jolt caused Varren to lose his grip, but he grabbed hold of a window ledge. A fall from that height would surely have killed him.

Lluava's body jerked and she slid down the rope. There was no time to find footholds. Her fingers slipped past the frayed end, and she was free-falling to the ground.

Shifting, the enormous felid landed on all fours like a housecat. The impact was staggering. Her entire body was momentarily in agony, before another force took over and the pain faded away. The world was a vivid blue-green.

Sparkling red droplets splattered on the cobblestone from a cut on her shoulder. It was ill-placed but not deep. No major veins or arteries were affected. She would be able to continue with relative ease.

Varren had pulled himself onto the wide ledge, broken the window with the hilt of his sword, and entered the building. Lluava knew he would make his way to the street. She would have waited to take action, but action found her first.

The tigress turned in the direction of the road's curve, around which figures were emerging. Níðingr and his men had arrived.

He caught sight of her. A low rumble escaped her lips. Her whiskers flared; her tail twitched. Her ears pulled back against her head.

In the sunlight, Ivar's dark auburn hair and beard were no less threatening. His eyes, like his flesh, were that blue-black hue, yet they seemed to coruscate with a piercing, almost consuming, quality. About his shoulders was a hide cloak—not the tanned pelt of a wolf but the flesh of a man, a Theriomorph. Lluava instinctively knew it was one of Derrick's comrades. There was no mercy in Níðingr.

There was no mercy in Lluava either.

An overpowering urge to fight him consumed Lluava's emotions. She could kill him now. Who cared what happened to her afterward? Her comrades would win this war without her if Níðingr were dead.

The Úlfhéðnar, seeming to understand her desire, appeared to smile without doing so. He approached at a steady pace. His men, like hounds looking to their master for a command, followed at his heels, eyeing the white tigress viciously.

She would kill him, Lluava decided. She spat and snarled, her gilded foreclaws grating on the cobblestone. She would know what his life tasted like.

"Don't do it," said a man's voice. It was not Varren but Apex.

The huntsman had loped up behind her in his dual form. The massive bronze wolverine, muzzle encased in metal, stood just as tall as she. Shoulder to shoulder, the two beasts watched as the Úlfhéðinn continued their steady approach. Apex's presence reminded Lluava of her original purpose. She would fight Níðingr, but not with his men, and not alone.

"Where are the others?" Apex asked quickly, for time was running out. The wound on his back had not healed and was still raw and open.

Lluava had no time to answer. Although she had not observed him doing so, Níðingr must have given a signal. Without warning, his men lunged onto all fours and charged. Half of them bounded along the narrow roadway; the others nimbly climbed the walls in an inhuman manner, as if gravity had no hold on them. All had but one intention, to slay the pair of Theriomorphs standing in their way.

Chapter 39

The Last Stand

alf stumbling out the door behind Lluava, Varren was already preparing to fight. If he was surprised by Apex's unexpected presence, that thought was all but forgotten by the sight of the advancing Úlfhéðinn scaling walls and sprinting down the cobblestoned road.

"Move back!" The presence that was Lluava was surprised at how quickly Varren had recovered from the visual shock and given the order. Humans were proving to be adaptable. "To the church," he shouted as he began to run, although his speed was the slowest of those involved in this race.

Lluava shouted, "Climb on!"

Without hesitating, Varren swung up behind the tigress's withers as though mounting a horse. With Apex loping beside them, the trio desperately tried to gain ground and stay ahead of the enemy.

"What's the plan?" Apex grunted. Lluava realized that he had not been present for the decision-making. She wondered how he had known where to find them in the labyrinth of roadways.

Varren responded, "We must lead the Úlfhéðinn toward the last rigged trap before springing the device. This final blockade could help separate Níðingr from the rest of those monstrosities."

Lluava added, "We must be far enough beyond the trap so that when the debris falls, we are on the temple side along with Ivar—assuming he is not killed by the debris itself. All other routes into the temple grounds have been sealed. He will be forced to fight us and die."

Apex glanced back, then said, "Níðingr is not among the forerunners, though he is following."

"Let us hope that changes," stated Varren grimly. He clutched Lluava's fur tightly enough to hold on but not enough to hurt her. At the moment, she would not have cared either way.

The last trap came into sight. Beyond it stood the temple in all its glory. "Damn!" Varren exclaimed.

The human's anger caused Lluava to scan the area. It was impossible for her to have missed something or someone. The only thing of note that she could see was the ever-nearing trap and the white marble of the columned temple.

"What?"

"Everyone left their posts, remember?" Varren said, his voice strained with worry.

"So…" Apex began, then griped, "there is no one to set off the trap. We have led the band of Úlfhéðinn into a dead end."

They would need a new plan. Lluava knew that the road wrapping around the temple was one of the widest in the city. It afforded greater maneuverability, which was good for battle. She quickly calculated how she could combat multiple Úlfhéðinn. With the goddess in her, she could accomplish what others believed impossible.

Feeling Varren tighten his grip, she wondered what good the human would be. And what of Apex? The Incarn had a god of his own, but he had yet to fully connect with Ullr. Lacking that bond, he was far weaker than she, and there were too many Úlfhéðinn.

"Thank you."

Who was Varren talking to? From the corner of her eye, Lluava saw the wolverine veer away. He was going to charge the pack of Úlfhéðinn! The probability that Apex would survive was nil. He must realize this was suicide. Another Incarn would fall. So be it.

A cold resolve swept over Lluava. She would neither turn around nor go after him. Not this time. The temple was their goal, and that was where she headed. The sound of mythic beast battling mutant monstrosities caused Lluava's ears to flick back, but her eyes remained focused straight ahead. Why look upon the devastation behind her? What would be the point? If Apex chose to sacrifice himself, the very least she could do would be to keep her own mind collected and clear for the fight still to come.

Counting the strides left before they passed the overloaded trap, Lluava eyed the bulging net that would never release its burden. High up, where the rooftop met the cloud-studded sky, there was movement. A figure appeared. Squinting to recognize the person against the harsh sunlight, Lluava recognized Yamir. He was preoccupied with severing the taut rope with a knife. The entire load jolted, as if it were about to drop too early.

Was Ivar behind them? How many Úlfhéðinn were on her heels? Would the trap hold long enough?

Picking up speed, the tigress leaped into the clearing in front of the temple. She sensed a slight vibration, which quickly grew from a low rumble to a thunderous explosion of sound. As she skirted the clearing to face the collapsing pile of rubble, she felt Varren jump from her back. Stone and mortar, timber and iron—all crashed onto the cobblestones, sending a cloud of dust into the air. Glimpsing the top of the pile through the settling debris, Lluava realized that the barricade was only three stories tall. Any Úlfhéðinn remaining on the far side could easily climb over.

All at once, more clansmen appeared. They began to hurl javelins and spears at the enemy. With that worry abated, Lluava waited to see whether Ivar had been crushed or had made it past the barricade.

The dusty cloud began to dissipate, exposing the giant silhouette of an Úlfhéðnar. The man stepped forth defiantly. It was Níðingr. Unfortunately, he was not alone; two Úlfhéðinn had crossed with him. The helmet of one had been knocked off by the debris, and a deep gash in his head bled heavily. Lluava was able to calculate the moment he would die from loss of blood, and so disregarded him as a threat. The other seemed unharmed.

Without hesitation, Níðingr moved forward. His minions waited as a sign of respect. Lluava knew it would take both Varren and herself to kill Ivar. With one brute certain to die on his own, the other monstrosity remained to foil their hope of slaying the Raiders' commander.

Suddenly, there were five ear-piercing whistle blasts.

Varren and the Úlfhéðinn were not affected, but the clansmen began to abandon their positions. Lluava wondered who had given the signal to retreat, and why. This situation worsened their likelihood of success. At any moment, more Úlfhéðinn would climb over the barricade.

Without warning, the temple grounds shook with another explosion, closely followed by a third. The two accompanying Úlfhéðinn were flung into the air, while Níðingr was thrown to the ground. Behind them, the pair of buildings that bordered the makeshift barrier collapsed, creating an enormous barricade that would be virtually impossible to cross.

Giahem's Talons had saved them again. But where was the shooter stationed? Lluava turned to the issue at hand. The remains of the pair of Úlfhéðinn were scattered about. Níðingr had righted himself. He almost looked impressed, if such an evaluation could make its way through his drug-infused mind. Ivar's jet-black eyes cast their menacing gaze on Lluava and the human standing beside her.

"You and me," Varren said. His voice was calm, though he emanated nervous energy.

"You and me," Lluava heard herself say. Herself. Not the goddess. She was back in control for the moment.

Níðingr dropped to all fours and charged, the cape of tanned hide rippling behind him. Roaring, Lluava readied herself to strike out at the oncomer. Varren held his sword before him. Several yards out, the giant Raider sprang to his feet and pulled his weapon from his sheath. The longsword was serrated on both sides like the teeth of an alligator ready to snap at its prey.

Lluava's dual form presented too large a target. The tigress leaped aside while shifting back to human form. Somersaulting onto the ground, she saw Varren's sword hook Níðingr's. The serrated edges caused the king's weapon to dislodge at an odd angle. Untrained against such a weapon, Varren slowly edged backward toward the temple.

Lluava's mind was calmed by her blue-green state. As if by instinct, she understood the maneuvers she would need to take. Nevertheless, both Varren and Lluava found it surprisingly hard to stay ahead of this brute's strikes. Like all Úlfhéðinn, this man was a void, thus unpredictable and extremely dangerous.

Time slowed, enabling Lluava to envision the angles and trajectory of Níðingr's weapon. His sword was ribboned with red, a color that stood out brightly in her altered vision. This red was not the blood of prior victims, but more like veins under flesh. It was as if the sword had a life of its own.

Unwilling to feed the weapon's clear hunger, Varren and Lluava were forced back against the temple's unusually large steps. They could not turn to run inside, for exposing their backs would mean certain death. Where else could they go?

A bird cawed fretfully above them. Onyx? Or a repugnant scavenger waiting for its next meal?

Clearing her thoughts, Lluava identified a moment to strike out. Her Claw carved divots in the back of Níðingr's dominant hand, which gave Varren an opportunity to scramble up the stairs to the temple's large, open doors.

Leaping after Varren, Lluava barely missed a strike. A loud crack resounded as Níðingr's sword cut deep into the marble step. After a small tug to remove his weapon, he was after them again.

There was no time to use the higher angle to her advantage once Lluava reached the top, for the massive Raider was only a step behind. Leaping to Varren's side, she brandished Issaura's Claws.

Everything was happening so fast, even for Lluava's hyperacute senses. One moment they were battling in the doorway; the next they were backing up into an interior room of the temple. Lluava received a superficial cut to her thigh, but Varren delivered a matching mark to Níðingr—the first real hit on the brutal opponent. Once again, she shifted, and the white tigress gave a mighty roar.

"What do you think will happen if you kill me?"

Níðingr had spoken. Slowly and clearly, making sure that every word and syllable was identifiable.

How could that be? None of the Úlfhéðinn had been able to formulate rational thought while in their drugged state, much less communicate it. If Níðingr was able to do this, he was far more powerful and dangerous than

Lluava had imagined.

Varren also looked stunned. This was not good. Níðingr took advantage of their momentary confusion to swing his serrated sword at the young king, who was slow to register the Raider's intent.

Lluava refused to lose her partner. Biting down on Varren's arm, the tigress jerked him toward herself, pulling him out of range of the blade's swing. She tasted the coppery warmth of his blood as it oozed between her teeth, and felt his veins pulsing with every heartbeat.

Varren cried out from a combination of shock and pain yet clung to his sword. That was good, she thought, for he would need it in the moments to come. Unwilling to dwell on the injury she had inflicted upon Elysia's king, Lluava lunged at Níðingr.

The brute would have cloven her head in two had she not instinctively skirted the move. The cracking sound of shattering marble reverberated among the stone walls. Lluava and Varren were forced to retreat farther into the temple.

Entering the inner sanctum, they cautiously circled their massive opponent. Níðingr spoke again, this time to Varren. His voice was as cold and merciless as an ocean storm. "More'll come. More'll always come, 'til th' land is under th' rightful rule."

Sword in hand, Níðingr dropped to all fours and charged Lluava. The tigress crouched and sprang over the living battering ram before he could mow her down. With a burst of extraordinary energy, he ran a third of the way up the side wall, pushed off, and flipped backward over his two opponents, landing on his feet to face the perplexed expressions of Varren and Lluava.

Once again, Níðingr spoke to Varren, as if Lluava were too bestial to understand language. "When the emperor gets word of what happened 'ere, more'll be sent, in far greater numbers."

This news boded ill for Elysia. Lluava hissed, "So you aren't the only commander of your empire's armies—there are others. Berserkers and such." Partly assuming, partly trying to tease out information, Lluava waited to see if Níðingr would respond.

He did, but not to her. Níðingr's eyes never left the king. He refused to acknowledge Lluava in any manner. "You'll be brought down and beaten, and those that survive'll be enslaved. Your pets'll all be butchered. Emperor Einherjar'll not stop 'til he has reclaimed this land. Nor'll I."

Lluava took a steady breath and shifted back. She could hear droplets of blood splattering on the polished floor and various heartbeats. Thump-thump. The tang of sweat tickled her nose, along with the pervasive odor of incense burned here days ago. Thump-thump. She ran her tongue over her sharpened teeth. Thump, thump. Her slitted pupils registered everything around them.

Thump. Thump.

Níðingr swayed slightly from side to side. His gaze finally focused on Lluava and her gold-ribboned skin. The massive void was unreadable to her, unpredictable. Nonetheless, she formed a plan. Well…more like various plans. Almost as if she had double vision, Lluava could see every possible move and its outcome simultaneously. Each result birthed other possibilities. Endless choices. Lluava moved toward Níðingr, not with a specific path in mind but with every option open. She knew what would happen if Varren struck first, or if she did. She foresaw every variation of movement that Níðingr could conceive, spun from innumerable beginnings. Even if she did not know which course of action would be taken, she would still be able to control the outcome.

In a blur of weaponry and skill, the three figures met at almost the same time. Brilliant light poured through the open doors and the small windows that clung to the roofline, casting impressive shadows on alcoves that had once held relics and statues.

There was no flow of movement, no back-and-forth motion like the rocking of the sea, yet a choreographed pandemonium ensued. Chaos to the point of perfection. Varren's sword just missed the Úlfhéðnar's Achilles tendon as the king, lying flat on the ground, rolled out of the way of a counterstrike. Lluava's platinum-blond hair swirled around her eyes as she bent backward to escape the swinging, serrated blade. Níðingr skewered only the shadow of a woman turned tigress turned woman again.

Ivar strode forward and Varren retreated. The Úlfhéðnar kicked the weakening man, who stumbled toward the rear of the room. Varren lurched behind the large, three-foot high pedestal that had once held the statue of Giahem, but the giant Raider effortlessly vaulted onto the base and then jumped down on its far side.

Considering the speed of Níðingr's attacks and Varren's limited maneuverability, Lluava foresaw that all scenarios would end the same way— with the king's death. What was she missing?

With Varren in the Úlfhéðnar's line of sight, Lluava could not hesitate. She sprang onto Níðingr's back and dug Issaura's Claws in deeply behind his shoulder blades. Black liquid oozed from the wounds and soaked into her clothes. Still, the outcome had not changed.

Lluava pulled back on the right-hand Claw, causing Níðingr to step back as if pulled by an invisible force. He tried to shake her off and lunged toward the king. Using all her strength, she ripped the left-hand Claw free of the dark musculature. The Úlfhéðnar's attack slowed, but not fast enough.

There was a clatter as Varren dropped his sword; the useless weapon rocked slowly to a stop. He extricated his wounded arm from the Úlfhéðnar's serrated blade. The king had not been killed, not yet, but he was bleeding freely, and his fighting arm was all but useless. There was no time to retrieve his weapon. The Raider's free fist caught Varren on the jaw so hard that he crumpled to the ground.

With a roar, Lluava transformed, clawing and biting her victim. But this creature did not react like other prey. Ignoring his wounds, Niðingr reached around with both hands and grabbed hold of Lluava's large, feline form. His ugly weapon fell to the stone floor. In mere moments, the tigress had been dislodged and thrown backward, slamming into the pedestal. The sharp angle of the marble edge cracked her ribs, then her body slid over the smooth surface.

With thunderous steps, Niðingr leaped atop the stone block. Did he have his weapon? Lluava couldn't see from her angle. There was only one viable option. She sprang up just as the brute reached her; the tigress's body collided with his, and they both fell. Lluava's felid form struggled to pin Niðingr down.

The glint of a sword was accompanied by the slashing sound of a blade slicing through flesh and cutting through bone. Blood spewed into the air. In the sudden stillness, only the spurting of the horrific wound was heard with each beat of the heart.

Chapter 40

The End of Honor

The bloody puddle grew. Twitching twice, the Úlfhéðnar accepted his fate. The survivors watched, grimly awed.

Varren had severed the head of Níðingr from his shoulders. It rolled off the pedestal and into a dark corner of the room, eyes still glaring at a victim never to come. The corpse's blue-black flesh began to regain its normal hue, revealing black tendrils of stained veins.

Slowly, the tigress moved off the body. Her vision returned to normal, and she shifted.

Lluava stepped closer to examine the heinous weapon left on the pedestal. It took all her might to lift the weighty handle and gruesome pommel of the skeletal sword. Níðingr would not take this with him to his hell.

Varren, pale from loss of blood and shock, leaned against the pedestal for support as he struggled to retrieve his blade and wipe it down.

In that moment, the goddess failed her.

Without warning, Níðingr's hands were at Varren's throat, choking the life from him. In a single fluid movement, Lluava thrust the monstrous sword straight into Níðingr's chest, obliterating his heart. The corpse fell limp for the final time, a blood offering on a makeshift altar.

Varren doubled over, gasping for air and gripping his bleeding arms. Seeing him wracked in pain, Lluava suddenly felt her own. She cried out and almost collapsed onto him. Her shoulder, thigh, and broken ribs were serious injuries, but she had survived the horrid attack.

However, the battle was not over. Beyond the barricade, the Raiders continued to fight, unaware that their commander was dead. More lives would be lost before the war could be ended. Lluava knew what she had to do.

First, she assisted Varren. The large gash in his right arm was severe and would need to be looked at immediately. She tore lengths of cloth from his shirt and applied a tourniquet to the wound. It was hard to tell whether his shirt had been originally red or white. The fang marks on the left arm were not as critical, but she had been responsible and was concerned.

Next, Lluava sheathed Varren's sword, then found Níðingr's horn. It was ridged and curled like that of a ram's but far larger. Tiny images had been deftly carved into the surface: monstrous wolves consuming men. Death and blood and doom. On the end of the horn were a golden mouthpiece and a link for attaching the leather shoulder strap.

Together, Varren and Lluava left the temple and began to search for a way to the castle. The temple grounds had remained undisturbed, sealed off from the rest of the city. Although this had worked for their original plan, their current confinement was a problem.

Lluava considered the king's injuries. His continuing blood loss would be fatal if he did not receive proper care soon. Along with pain, she felt fear take root in her mind—the fear of losing this man who meant so much to her.

"Can you climb?" she asked, as she stared at the wall of debris.

"I can try," he replied. His determination had intensified with the death of Níðingr.

After several failed attempts, Lluava realized that plan was pointless. Without the use of his arms, Varren's mobility was too limited. What to do? While she pondered her unvoiced question, he asked, "Why not use stairs?"

Turning around, Lluava remembered that most of the barricade was composed of buildings. The simple solution was right in front of her.

Laughing, Lluava nodded. "Stairs it is."

She selected a building based on its location. The entrances and windows had been boarded up in case any Úlfhéðinn had sought a quick escape route or an easy entry point. Lluava shifted. Using her claws, the tigress peeled back sections of wood until the opening was wide enough for Varren and for her, in human form, to slip inside.

The interior was dark. Little light made it past the shuttered windows. Lluava's hyperacute eyesight allowed her to steer Varren to the stairwell and ascend to the top floor. They had to get on the roof, where there would be less chance of encountering Raiders. Flinging open a window, she craned her head upward, trying to devise a plan to get the injured man onto the roof.

"Stay here," she said, as she carefully climbed onto the window ledge. "I'm going to try to signal for help."

Varren did not complain. Lluava wondered if that meant he was weakening. In a very risky move, she jumped up and grabbed hold of the edge of the roof. The tiles were loose but did not slide off. Hoisting herself up, she scrambled to the peak and pulled out the silver whistle she had been given. Scanning the horizon, she observed various parties of men moving about on rooftops. She blew her whistle as loud as she could and waved her arms, pain wracking her body. Surely someone would see her.

Someone did.

Lluava felt something seize her leg and wrench her downward. She cried out and used the Claws to catch hold of anything to stop herself from slipping off the roof. There was no danger of that. Standing over her were four Úlfhéðinn with weapons in hand. They could have easily killed her already; why did they hesitate? Then she understood. They were all eyeing Niðingr's horn. Did they realize their leader had been slain?

The moment did not last. Abruptly, they fell on top of her. Literally. Lluava felt the wind being squeezed out of her as the weight of the giant men—no, their corpses—crushed her, for each had an arrow protruding from his eyes or chest. Struggling to move, she was helplessly pinned underneath them.

Another figure stepped into sight. With the sun behind him, it was hard to make out who he was, but Lluava could sense him. Aquila squatted down and said, "As I promised."

After shoving the dead brutes off her, the nomad helped hoist Varren to the roof. The pallor of the king's face and his reddening bandages indicated that there was no time to waste. Following a route of makeshift rooftop bridges, the trio headed back to the castle and the waiting Obsidian Guard.

Leaving Varren under Holly's protection, Lluava headed off to perform her final task.

***

Alcove's room was empty, as she had expected. The ambassador had said he would not need help leaving the premises, and he was right. Unfortunately, that had resulted in two Theriomorph corpses in the hall. If only his guards had known to be somewhere else.

Grimacing, Lluava limped back out into the city and headed toward the prearranged meeting point. The chosen house was one of the taller buildings and easily viewable from Alcove's window. That vantage point was crucial to the staged production about to take place.

The ambassador was waiting for Lluava in a room on the top floor. The space had been used for storage; furniture and chests were stacked one upon the other. After years of neglect, only a single pair of tracks had disturbed the dust.

"I see you have the horn."

Alcove's statement startled Lluava. The goddess within had gone dormant after Niðingr was killed, and Lluava's emotions and actions were her own. She responded by lifting the horn.

"I knew you would be the one," Alcove stated calmly. A cloud temporarily hid the sun, catching the ambassador's interest. It was clear he wanted to wait until the light returned.

Lluava used the moment to her benefit. "You told me before that I, specifically, had changed your mind about Theriomorphs. What was it about me that did that?"

"What you are."

"And what am I?"

"*Glorious.*"

Lluava did not comprehend his meaning.

Alcove explained, "I am human. Being human, I have personal interests and passions outside my occupation. As ambassador, I have been privileged to travel far and wide to meet and observe many different peoples and experience varied cultures. This is perfect for me, for I have always been fascinated by the mythologies of others."

Moving around the room, Alcove picked up a four-barred cross representative of the humans' religion. After looking at the tarnished item, he set it back down. "I collect religious artifacts. Upon each successful mission, Emperor Einherjar allows me to keep any relics I discover."

Lluava began to understand where this was headed. She inquired, "I ask you again, what does that have to do with me?"

"Because of what you are..." Alcove looked upon Lluava fondly. "Your people, your belief system, is unlike anything I have come across before. In all my years, I have never found a *living* relic. Sculptures, medallions, sometimes even sources of water, but never a living, breathing being. I have watched you, seen what you are able to do, what you have become." He eyed Lluava's golden-striped skin. "You are magnificent."

The sun returned. Alcove walked to the window, where a rope, the other end of which was attached to a chimney, swayed slightly in the breeze. "It is time."

Lluava watched him climb up to the roof. A nauseating feeling stirred inside her. Had Alcove saved her, let her live, only so he could add her to his collection of oddities?

Rubbing her eyes so hard she saw spots, Lluava forced herself to follow Alcove. This final act was a trial in itself, as her pain had not decreased. The light was brilliant, the sun almost directly overhead. The remaining cloud cover had relinquished its rule over the sky. Lluava barely had Issaura's Claws ready when Alcove made the first strike. He smiled at her playfully.

This was all for show, she reminded herself. A sham. Observers would see Alcove battle Theri's Incarn, supposedly kill her, and take the horn of Niðingr. He would blow the instrument and signal the Raiders. They would look to the sound, see the ambassador with the horn, and understand that he was in charge. Then Alcove would collect his men and leave. That was the plan. Right?

With each strike, Lluava felt her body tiring. Her injuries aggravated her movements; the worst were her ribs. She was in no condition to continue the charade, but that had been her agreement with Alcove. If this worked, the war would end.

By comparison, Alcove had regained his strength and was aggressively testing his skill. Several times, Lluava lost her footing and barely escaped falling to her death. The ambassador could not move to help her, for that would ruin the entire plan.

As they fought, Lluava tried to distract herself from her pain. She confirmed the terms of their agreement. "After this," she said, dodging a thrust of Alcove's sword, "you will take your men home."

"With myself in command," Alcove responded as he swung at Lluava again, "these men will be forever stationed inside our empire."

"What of the other armies? Nídingr said there were others."

Without a moment's hesitation, Alcove affirmed, "There are others. Nídingr was not the only military commander at the emperor's disposal, but he was the most vicious." Alcove must have noticed the worry on Lluava's face. "Remember, Theri, I am the ears and eyes of the emperor. All that he will know about this voyage will come from my lips. I will make sure he is well aware of Nídingr's treachery."

The moment had arrived. Alcove drove his sword at Lluava, sliding it between her side and her far arm. From an observer's point of view, it would look as if he had driven his weapon right through her body.

Alcove pulled his sword back, and Lluava crumpled to the ground without moving. Her assailant bent over, tugged the horn away, and pretended to shove her body off the roof. She slid down the castle-side ledge. Although she was out of sight of those fighting on the ground, she could watch the ambassador to see whether he would keep his word. If only she could keep hers.

As Alcove brought the horn to his lips, Lluava lunged and drove both of Issaura's Claws into his back. He sputtered, dropping the horn. His sheathed sword would be of no use to him now.

She felt Alcove try to move, but the sickle-shaped blades of her Claws gripped him tightly. She whispered into his ear, "In a way, I can respect your honor. You were not lying to me. You only said half-truths. You *were* going to keep your word and have these men stay in *your* empire. But your emperor, and I also suspect you, believe that Elysia is already part of your empire by right. You were never going to leave with your army, because you believe this land is yours."

Alcove tried to form words, but only gurgling sounds were heard.

"If your intent was to leave and return home, you would meet with your ruler. He would be told about us and what happened here. Other armies would be sent. Other wars would begin."

Speaking almost to herself, Lluava admitted, "I cannot let that happen. It would be better if your emperor believed that the mission failed, that this land was never found, that all were lost. It would be better for him not to know."

The full weight of Alcove's body caused Lluava to sink to her knees. As a trickle of blood dribbled from the corner of his mouth, she laid him on the rooftop and closed his eyes for the final time.

Some might have seen the ambassador's brutal end, but many did not. Below her, the war was still being fought. Carefully easing her aching body down the slanted roof, she picked up the discarded horn. It was surprisingly light.

Ascending to the peak of the roof, Lluava inhaled deeply and blew into the instrument. The resounding noise sent a shiver down her spine, and her body seemed to vibrate. Throughout Cronus, everyone paused and looked toward the sound. In one final act of showmanship, Lluava blew the horn again and followed it with a mighty roar.

***

In the following hours, the tide turned. Raiders were corralled like cattle, their weapons and armor stripped, drugs confiscated. Many faces, both enemy and friend, looked to Lluava for some indication of what would happen next.

A passage was cleared so that enemy survivors could be escorted to the temple grounds. Lluava stood deep in thought as she watched the prisoners pass by. Sensing a presence beside her, she looked up.

"I will ask *how* in the future," she said with a hint of a smile.

"I will answer that Ullr is mighty indeed," Apex responded.

Ammit approached and stepped in front of them. The Outlander had been overseeing the capture of the enemy. "That is all of them," he confirmed.

Apex leaned toward Lluava's ear and asked, "What now, Goddess of War?"

Lluava's steely control of her emotions was mirrored in her voice. "The Raiders must die. Every. Last. One."

Chapter 41

Hail and Farewell

The order was followed quickly. No one questioned the goddess incarnate. Through it all, Apex never once looked at Lluava disapprovingly. He understood. He *always* understood. She valued that greatly.

Upon the bloody completion, the pair picked their way through the barricades, which were being disassembled. Yena greeted them on their return to the castle. She had bathed and dressed in flowing, silvery-sheer garments.

"You survived." Lluava stated the obvious.

"The gods are not finished with us yet." Casting her glance through the open doorway, Yena noted, "You killed them all."

"You knew I would."

"You are Incarn of the Goddess of War, the Daughter of Death. It was preordained. Come," she said, gesturing, "you must have your wounds tended. There is ample Idun in your chamber for both you and the king. He awaits you there."

Yena's choice of words was surprising. Had the high priestess acknowledged Varren's right to his throne? Did she intend to return to Leucrocotta after all?

Entering her rooms, Lluava heard Holly talking to Varren, who was lying down on the couch. "He is still missing."

The pair looked at Lluava, who walked straight to the vials of Idun set out on the table. "You may continue," she said, then gulped the putrid liquid. Instantly yearning to vomit, Lluava collapsed into one of the wing chairs. "I do not know which I hate more, the smell or the taste."

When no one spoke, Holly gave Lluava a slight nod and stepped away from the king. Although the Shadow did not leave the room, she allowed

Varren and Lluava their privacy.

Still nauseated, Lluava turned to the injured man. "How're your arms?"

Varren looked down at his bandaged limbs and his pristine white clothes. "The bite will mend. My other arm…well, it seems I should not attempt to fight with swords again."

"You were never *that* good anyway," Lluava teased. Her humor had returned, as had her disgust at the aftertaste of the Idun.

"That is why I have you." Varren offered a slight smile before furrowing his brow. "I heard what happened. I know what *you* ordered." Lluava glanced at Holly as Varren continued, "You did not have to do that. We could have taught them, changed them, converted them. Allowed them the opportunity to become Elysian subjects."

"No, Varren. *You* could have. *I* could not."

There was a prolonged silence before Varren spoke again. "Everyone has a weakness, Lluava. If compassion is mine, I am glad of it. But as a ruler, weaknesses are ill advised. This is why I want you to stand by me as my advisor. I wish to reinstate all titles that have been stripped from you. I need someone near me whom I can trust. Someone who will be brutally honest. Someone who is not afraid to see things from a different perspective."

Lluava felt her mouth gape. She quickly closed it.

Varren finished by saying, "I do not always agree with your choices, but I respect your reasons for making them."

As much as she desired to say yes, she said, "Let me think upon this. With everything considered…"

"Take all the time you need." Varren adjusted his position on the couch before continuing. "The high priestess spoke with me earlier. She is renouncing all claim to Elysia and will return to Leucrocotta. She desires to open the borders so that the Theriomorph communities can work jointly with our kingdom. In turn, I am reinstating the Temple of Giahem. It will no longer serve as the church. Moreover, other temples will be erected throughout the kingdom in accordance with your people's beliefs."

"This all just happened…?" If this was true, then Yena had foreseen the outcome of the war and had known that victory was at hand.

Varren allowed Lluava time to consider this information before adding, "The high priestess is even allowing Ammit to remain at the capital to help with the unification of our peoples. He will be installed on the new council, where a seat will be held for you if ever you are ready."

"What about Themis? What happened to him?"

"He was not allowed to travel with me to Cronus, in case I failed. There had to be someone who could step up as leader if I were slain."

"Will he return?"

"He will," acknowledged Varren. "But his time on the council is over. A new era is beginning. I need councilors who are open to new ways. We must change—all of us—and move forward."

"Wow. Is *he* in for a surprise." Lluava wondered how Themis would react when he realized he no longer wielded power. It was a rather pleasant thought. "He will be summoned from Erebos, where he has been in hiding, and informed upon his return." Varren was far too logical to act petty in this situation. Lluava, on the other hand, could be as petty as she desired.

"Can I be the one to tell him?"

"I think it would be best if I did the explaining."

"Fine," Lluava grumped. She was already feeling better, though she was not sure if it was from the Idun or all the news. Regardless, she would fully heal over the next few days.

***

Orders were given to gather all the dead, and a huge ceremonial funeral was planned. On the muddy battlefield, large pyres were erected from some of the debris removed from Cronus. Holly found Regin's trampled body. He had died near the gates of the capital. Lluava was suspicious that Ivar Níðingr had killed him, though nobody could be sure. Vidrick had also died during the final fight. Lluava looked upon the redheaded lieutenant one final time before Aquila lit the pyres with Giahem's Talons. The resulting blaze quickly consumed everything in the span of an hour. Lluava hoped that Vidrick would find peace with Illia, his love.

***

Changes came rapidly now. Themis was summoned from Erebos, along with one other at Lluava's specific request. Holly was installed as head of the Obsidian Guard, with Jigo as her second. Ojewa, now a general, left Cronus along with Colonel Skipe and Admiral Merrow, to rebuild the southern camps. Maruny had vanished from the city, as had Luka. Lluava discovered that Domar's son, Daniel, had survived the Fall and had been fighting with a group of rebels. Returning to the capital, he assumed his father's position as weapons instructor for the new castle guards. She was curious about how the mute would teach, but one thing was certain, Daniel was an expert with the sword. Most importantly for Lluava, her nightmares ceased.

A few days later, on a lazy spring morning, the entire capital was thrown into an uproar. An approaching army had been spotted. Yena was summoned to the Grand Hall from the temple, where she had been training the new priestesses.

Varren sat on the main throne. Lluava, unsure of the protocol, took Themis's former chair. Yena strode into the hall past everyone to stand before the king.

Without hesitation, Varren asked, "High Priestess, why are armed Theriomorphs marching upon us?"

Yena's angular features added to her stern, imposing appearance.

Unexpectedly, she burst into peals of high-pitched, staccato laughter. "Because I summoned them."

"Why?"

Those watching waited impatiently for the priestess's response. What was her purpose for calling this army? Did she wish another war? Hadn't enough people perished already?

"At the time, we were still under attack," Yena spoke in her throaty way. "You will remember that I had tunnels built, exit routes for messengers. Using those means, I contacted the rest of my forces to assist us. I was not certain whether they would arrive on time, but at the very least, they could have eradicated the enemy—that is, had we not done so already."

"What plans do you have for them now?"

Yena raised her gaze to the ceiling, then lowered her eyes to the young ruler. "They can be the forerunners of our new borderless community. Humans and Theriomorphs, Elysians and us, your so-called Outlanders—we have no war among ourselves. Not anymore."

Varren thought for a moment. "Then, all will be welcomed once their weapons are collected."

"As a sign of peace," Yena smiled, "we will present those weapons as a gift to you, Your Majesty."

The high priestess kept her word. Varren opened the gates and greeted many of the arrivals personally. The armory was more fully stocked than it had ever been.

Along with this change came another. The clans returned to their traditional territories within the kingdom. When the Cloven-Hoofed Clan was ready to depart, Rosalyn, Byron and Derrick gathered to say farewell. Varren chose to stay in the castle, a choice of which Lluava disapproved.

"This is senseless. You should say goodbye to your friend."

Varren shrugged. "If Yamir wished to see me, he could have done so during these past few weeks. His anger has not dissipated, and I do not wish to taint anyone else's farewells."

Hating to agree with him, Lluava chewed on her lip. Varren looked at her bemusedly. "After you see Yamir off, come find me in the gardens. I would like to talk to you. And, if you can, wish that rascal well for me."

Lluava headed to a field outside the city. Horses were being harnessed to new wagons and lined up. At least, the clans had accepted Varren's gift, though the wagons' gold-and-green covers had been stripped and burned.

Yamir stood proudly as he watched the clan assemble. With spiked hair, piercings, and now several tattoos, he had fully accepted his new position. And it suited him perfectly. He was speaking to Rosalyn, who was just beginning to appear in public after Talos's funeral. Her scarred skin was a visible reminder of the husband she had lost. She had chosen not to hide her injury, so that none around her would forget the war with the Raiders.

Yamir looked at her swelling belly. "You know, if you chose to name the baby Yamir, I would not be upset."

Rosalyn cracked a weary smile. "If it be a boy, I will follow Talos's request and name the child Argon, after the man who helped train all of you. Yamir might be considered for a middle name."

That seemed to please their spiky-haired friend. He grinned wolfishly, although not as wolfishly as Derrick, who stood nearby. Derrick looked at the clansman. "Once again, my men and I are ever grateful for your aid, Yamir."

"You are always welcome to stay with our clan," Yamir stated. The two men gave one another a firm handshake.

"We will miss you, my friend," Byron added. He placed his hand on Rosalyn's shoulder. He had taken care of the young woman since Talos's death, and Lluava suspected that he would continue to stay by her side in the times to come. Actually, somehow, she *knew*.

"As will I," said the clansman.

With a quick wave of his hand, Yamir smiled at Lluava.

She responded with a strong hug. "I'm going to miss you. Are you sure you cannot stay?"

He gestured to the rest of his clan. "We refuse to follow a king. The clans' ideals have never changed. The kingdom should be run by the people, not by a crown."

"Will you go to Leucrocotta or one of the other Theriomorph cities?"

"No. This is our home. We will live in Elysia, but not anywhere near the capital. The government is poisoned."

Lluava tried one last time. "But Varren—"

Standing eye to eye, Yamir's oval eyes met Lluava's green ones. They flashed with a fierce passion. "I will never bow to Varren or to any of his lineage."

A small boy approached meekly. "Father, your horse is ready," he said, and scurried off.

Yamir smiled after the child, then turned to gaze upon Lluava one last time. "You will always be a friend of ours, Theri. You will always be a friend to me." With that, Yamir turned, mounted his horse, and rode away, leading the Cloven-Hoofed Clan home.

***

The wagon train had disappeared from sight some time ago. When Lluava finally turned around to head toward the castle, she saw that Aquila stood watching her. Had he come to observe Yamir's departure? They had seemed to approve of each other.

"And will you, too, be returning home?" She wondered how many people were dispersing now that the war was over.

"Yes." Aquila's hazel eyes looked keenly about. "I want to show my people the Talons now that the bow and arrows are united. These arrows were stolen from my father's house long ago."

"You have houses? I thought you were nomads."

"We are. Father says he used to have a grand house, long ago, from which he ruled. It was destroyed by Mandrun's people."

As they walked back toward the castle, Lluava's mind reeled as an intangible idea took form. "Where did he live?"

"Your people were not the only ones who called this land home before Mandrun's ancestors arrived."

Lluava's head began to hurt. "But that was centuries ago! Your father couldn't possibly have lived here before Elysia was formed. He would have had to be as ancient as—"

She froze in mid step as everything fell into place. She scrutinized Aquila's features while he curiously stared back at her.

"Are you well, she-beast?"

Lluava blinked. Could it be true? Right here, standing before her, and she had been blind to it the entire time? Aquila's father was a Theriomorph. That's why the nomad had traces of Theriomorph about him, in his blood. It was the telltale sign of an interracial offspring. More importantly, his father had to be Giahem's Incarn. That's why Aquila could control the Talons and wield the Wings! The blood of an Incarn ran through his veins.

"Aquila," Lluava began once she found her voice. "Take me to your father. We have much to discuss."

Chapter 42

Odyssey

M y father hates Theriomorphs," stated Aquila firmly.
"I'm sure that's not *exactly* true," Lluava countered.
"He will kill you."

"Maybe…" Lluava implored the nomad again, "You will take me to him. Won't you?"

"Yes."

"How much time do I have to prepare?" Lluava asked.

"I can give you three days."

Lluava returned to her quarters to consider what must be accomplished before she left. As she was busy choosing some items and discarding others, there was a knock at her door. Moving to open it, she saw that Onyx's perch was empty. The bird must have found a way out again.

Yena entered with a scroll in hand and Apex at her heels with a listless expression on his face. Recently, the high priestess had come by a few times to share a religious reading with the other Incarn. Sometimes they were interesting, other times not, but Lluava had always been agreeable. Not today.

"Can we do this another time?"

Yena smiled and pleasantly inquired, "You are leaving?"

The disarray in the room was answer enough. "I am going to meet Giahem's Incarn."

"You know where he is!" Apex exclaimed eagerly.

Surprisingly, it was Yena who answered, "Haven't you figured it out? Aquila is Giahem's son."

"That can't be…" Although Apex was shocked at this revelation, Lluava was stunned. "You knew this whole time?"

279

"I was suspicious," Yena admitted. "You just confirmed it."

"How?" Apex asked, clearly unhappy about being the last to know.

"Only a god can wield a god's weapon," Yena explained. "We are Incarn. Each of us has been created from the blood of our respective god. That is why we can use their weapons. Aquila is not an Incarn, but the blood of Giahem is in him; he is a son of the Creator."

"But Aquila is human."

"Half human," Lluava corrected. In fact, not every child born of both races was able to shift. Some could pass as full-blooded humans, with only their lineage to reveal the truth.

Apex was slowly catching up. "Then Aquila's father, the chieftain of his people, is actually Giahem, or at least his Incarn."

Both Lluava and Yena nodded.

"Aquila is going to take me to his father," Lluava explained. "If I'm right, then…well, I don't know what then."

"I will go with you," Yena began. "I had foreseen a journey, though I knew not where. We have Crocotta's blessing."

Apex added, "In that case, I will come as well. It's time for a little reunion."

"You don't have to come," Lluava pointed out. "Neither of you does."

Yena smiled. "This is our destiny."

"Very well," Lluava agreed. Her confidence was increased by the knowledge that she would be accompanied by the two Incarn. "We leave in three days."

With a graceful bow, Yena left to begin preparations. Before Apex could follow her, Lluava asked the huntsman, "Are you at all afraid of what we might find?"

"No."

Apex's assured response caused Lluava to eye him closely. He appeared to be in earnest, and she did not sense any hesitation. An emptiness gnawed at her. "Are you ready to become one with Ullr? Are you not afraid of losing yourself, of whatever it is that makes you, you?"

He looked at her gravely. "I cannot lose something that I do not have. To be finally complete, fulfilled—that is not something to be feared. Look at yourself. Lluava the Elysian is still present."

"At times," she acknowledged.

Lluava trusted Apex's judgment. Turning toward the window, she asked quietly, "Did I make the right decision? They had already submitted to us."

"You made the same decision I would have made."

She turned back to her unkempt room. The day was late, and there was much to be done.

Apex inquired, "Need any assistance?"

"I just wish I knew where my dratted bird keeps disappearing to." Lluava sighed once again as she looked at the empty perch. Part of her hoped that Onyx had not followed Yamir. Part of her wished he had.

Apex grunted and stretched. "She probably flew off to breed. It's that time of year."

"She?"

"Yes. Her instinct probably told her it was time to mate. To nest."

"Wait. He's a she?"

"Of course, she's a she. I can stake my claim as a huntsman on that. Female ravens of her particular species are larger than males. And that raven of yours is the largest one I've seen." Apex moved over to the window and looked out. "Actually, Onyx is a rare species. I haven't caught sight of one like her in a long while. Not since my childhood, in fact."

"Apex," Lluava said very slowly, as the image of Nott's empty eye flashed before her. "You don't think my bird is—?"

She did not have to finish her question. Apex picked up on her train of thought. "No. No. *No.*"

"But her eye, her strange behavior—could she be?"

Apex closed his eyes and rubbed his temples. "There are too many Incarn in this world already. Your bird's just another bird." From the way he said it, it was obvious the huntsman was now doubtful.

Lluava looked out the window, searching for black wings in the sky. If Onyx was a female Incarn, why didn't anyone sense her as a Theriomorph? How could she stay in her dual form for so long? No. Apex was right. The raven was just another bird.

"She'll come back," he said, leaving the young woman to her wild fantasies.

Lluava was unable to concentrate on organizing her belongings. She kept stepping onto the balcony to watch for her bird. Giving up, she went in search of the one person she had to tell about her upcoming journey.

Varren was sitting on a bench in the royal gardens; night was just upon them. Nerve damage had left the fingers of his right hand clumsy, and he had been trying to train his left to write with some sort of elegance.

"Do you have a moment?" she asked. "I know it's far later than you might wish."

He smiled at her, and Lluava felt her heartbeat quicken.

"Of course. Take all the time you need. Would you like to sit down?"

"No," Lluava admitted. She didn't know how to begin. After a few moments of silence, Varren moved the parchment with its illegible lettering to one side. He pointed to a thick book that had been left on the path several steps away from the bench where he sat. "Would you get that for me? There is something in there that I hope you will want."

Picking up the book, she sat down next to him and rested it on her lap.

"Flip to page one hundred."

The yellowed pages felt pleasant under Lluava's fingers. She thumbed through until she found the page. In the center of the page was a small, diamond-shaped cutout; hidden inside was a piece of jewelry. She pulled out a platinum ring set with a brilliant emerald. Her eyes widened as she inspected the beautiful gemstone, then looked up at Varren.

The young king stood and quickly knelt down on one knee. Lluava couldn't speak. Fortunately, that was not Varren's problem. "I may not be worthy in your eyes, but I will try to do everything I can to be the man you desire. I love you, Lluava. I cannot picture a life without you in it, beside me. Will you—"

"I must leave Elysia again." Her words hung in the air and felt heavy on her tongue.

Varren slowly stood up. His face had lost its earlier glow. "We have had this conversation before."

"Yes. But this time, I can let you know what I am going to do." Lluava began to babble. "I believe I know where Giahem's Incarn is. Of all the Incarn, he would be the one with answers. He would be the one to tell me why we are here. Clearly, we were not all needed to win the war. If not that, what other purpose must we serve, if any? When will I ever be able to control my own life? My own destiny? Without that...without that, I can never fully give myself to anyone."

Lluava's voice caught as the tears gathered and fell. "I need to do this, Varren. I must do this. I have to *go* if I am ever to be able to *stay*."

Varren had listened quietly. "I want..." he began, then collected his own thoughts. "I want you to stay with me, but commanding you to stay would be wrong. I do not have that right. My purpose is clear: to govern my people, to rebuild Elysia. Your purpose—only you can discover that."

Lluava handed Varren the ring. Her voice shook. "I do love you. I will always love you. Ever since this," she said, gesturing at her golden-striped skin, "I have felt myself, my humanity, waver. But whenever I'm with you or think of you, you bring me back. Me. Not the goddess." Taking an unsteady breath, she continued, "You are the only man I want to be with, but I must go with Yena, with Aquila, with Apex. I need to search for the other Incarn."

"When are you leaving?" Varren asked, his voice cracking. He was looking at the ring he held in the palm of his hand.

"In three days."

"So soon?"

"Yes. We need Aquila to take us...to find his father..."

Lluava tilted her face, now striped with tears, toward his. Taking her hand, he gently led her to the garden seat and waited until her tears abated.

Brilliant green eyes gazed into sorrowful blue ones. "I have a gift for you," she breathed. "I wish he were here now; I'm worried he won't arrive before I leave."

"You're giving me a person?" Varren seemed both perplexed and amused at the same time.

Regaining her composure, Lluava looked directly at the man she loved.

A smile played upon her lips. "I thought you liked people."

"I do," Varren chuckled. "I love one in particular." His fingers tightened around the ring, and he studied his hands. Lluava felt her heart breaking.

Taking several breaths, she said, "Themis will be arriving with a boy."

"Yes. Odel. The one you asked for."

"Varren," Lluava said, "Odel is your son."

Silence.

Lluava felt Varren's gaze upon her. She matched it with her own. "I know things now, after—" Again she indicated her golden stripes. "Things that I could never have known otherwise. Odel is only seven, far too young to have been selected by the Shadows during the last Call. Random children are not brought to Erebos. When the girl you impregnated all those years ago had her baby, Themis hid him with the Obsidian Guard, a precaution lest something happen to you and your grandfather. The child has royal blood in his veins, and Themis would not dare destroy that. Odel has been with them since he was born."

Varren's eyes were wide with disbelief. Lluava felt he needed more convincing. "I met Odel in the kitchens, where I worked alongside him. When Themis saw us together, he had me removed. At first, I believed he did it to spite me and my happiness. But that was not the case. He did not want me associating with Odel. I don't know if he thought I would find out or corrupt him. But he looks like you, Varren; his hair, his eyes. And he's smart."

Lluava realized Varren had been caught completely unaware. She paused to give him time to absorb this news.

"I…I have a son," Varren stammered.

"Yes. You have a child, and that is my gift to you. That is the only child I can ever give you." Lluava touched her lower abdomen. "When Yena attacked me, I was badly hurt. I will never bear offspring. I knew immediately. No amount of Idun will change that. I am truly the Incarn of Theri, the Virgin Goddess. She was never to bear a child, nor will I."

Varren remained quiet. Lluava filled the void by saying, "When Themis arrives, I am certain he will admit what he did. If not, ask Holly. She is privy to that information as head of the Obsidian Guard."

"Thank you."

Lluava had not expected those words from Varren. "For what?"

"For giving me everything I desire. Your love. A family. A new and better future for the kingdom. Without you, all this would be lost." He waved his hand at the plethora of greenery and vibrant splashes of flowers. Nearby, a butterfly danced above a stalk of Theri iris, and a lizard skittered on the ground.

The pair continued to sit in the garden, holding hands and listening to mockingbirds sing and dragonflies whir by. The evening was hot, though not as hot as the year before, when a young girl had left her small seaside village in search of her destiny.

Epilogue

A moving shadow flitted over parched, cracked ground. The form was small compared to the vast expanse of desolate territory, yet it flew determinedly, farther into the desert's heartland. The creature that cast the shadow cared little for the dried-out tongue that rattled in its clenched beak. Its destination beckoned on the horizon like a mirage.

Heat from the sun beat down on ebony plumage. Wings grew ever wearier with each flap. Energy to continue ebbed.

A small tree, bare-limbed, appeared in the distance. With rest now a necessity, this oncoming perch was the only appreciable source of safety from the vipers that slithered over the sandy earth below.

Something else presided on one of the dead limbs, an avian much larger than the one seeking shelter. An eagle, whose feathers glinted golden in the overhead sun. There was no hope of an alternate destination. The smaller bird alighted on a branch alongside the raptor. Shrinking down and lowering its head, it appeared to give a sign of respect.

Neither bird moved. No action was taken to indicate malicious intent. Together, they perched, surveying the harsh wilderness and the struggle to survive within it.

A large-eared mouse darted from a hole under a stone. Scampering across the ground, the eagle took no note of the minute creature. The other bird twitched its head and scrutinized the little animal until the rodent retreated to its hideaway.

Without a cloud in the sky, the bright blue expanse showed no sign of dulling. Time was marked only by the slow movement of the blazing orb above them. At last, the eagle turned to stare at its exhausted visitor. Cocking its glorious head, it seemed to consider the other bird for the first time.

"It is done." A woman's voice emanated from the smaller bird's beak. "She is more spectacular than we had ever hoped." The raven tilted her head and regarded her companion with her one good eye, as if awaiting a response.

The golden eagle turned and fixed his steely stare out over the arid desert. In a voice like thunder rumbling from its gilded shell, the raptor pronounced, *"Now we wait for our family to be united once more."*

APPENDICES

APPENDIX I

Diagram of the Theriomorph Pantheon

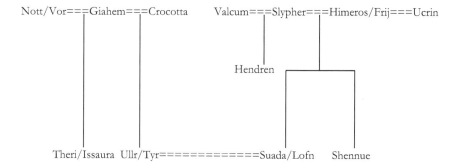

APPENDIX II

The Theriomorph Pantheon

Name	Sex	Divine Realm	Dual Form
Giahem	♂	King/ Husbands/ Fathers/ Heavens/ Males/ Sky	Gold Eagle
Crocotta	♀	Queen/Wives/Mothers/Prophecy/Mating Rights	Silver Hyena
Ullr/Tyr	♂	Young Men/ Inception of War/ Sun/ Courage	Bronze Wolverine
Nott/Vor	♀	Night/ Sleep/ Dreams/ Death/ Underworld	Black Raven
Theri/Issaura	♀	Young Women/ Cessation of War/ Moon/ Wisdom	White Tigress
Ucrin	♂	Ocean/ Water/ Wind	Blue Whale
Valcum	♂	Fire/ Volcanos/ Blacksmiths	Orange Orangutan
Slypher	♀	Earth/ Seasons/ Song/ Dance	Pink Parakeet
Frij/Himeros	♂♀	Love/ Beauty/ Hermaphrodites	Purple Peacock
Hendren	♂	Knowledge/ Virtue/ Health	Scarlet Panda
Suada/Lofn	♀	Lust/ Seduction/ Desire	Emerald Anaconda
Shennue	♂	Mischief/ Mayhem / Illusions	Black Jackal

APPENDIX III

Pronunciation Guide

Alcazar	AL-ca-czar
Alcove	AL-cove
Amargo	a-MAR-go
Ammit	AH-mit
Apex	AA-pecks
Aquila	a-KEY-la
Austro	AWE-strow
Berserker	bur-ZERK-er
Cherin	CHEER-in
Cronus	CROW-nus
Crocotta	crow-COT-ta
Durog	DURE-og
Einherjar	ane-HAIR-yar
Endun	EN-dun
Elysia	ee-LAY-szuh
Erebos	ear-A-bos
Giahem	GUY-a-hem
Hyrax	HI-racks
Idun	EE-dun
Incarn	IN-carn
Issaura	i-SAR-a
Ivar	EYE-var
Jigo	JIGH-go
Kargen	CARG-en
Karmasana	CAR-ma-SAW-naw
Kido	KIGH-dough
Leucrocotta	LEW-crow-COT-ta
Lluava	you-AA-va
Maessa	MAY-es-sa
Maruny	MAR-ou-ne

Mandrun	MAN-drun
Níðingr	KNEE-ding-gir
Odel	OH-dell
Óðr	OH-der
Ojewa	OH-jay-wa
Okeanos	oak-EE-a-nos
Regin	REEG-in
Rhadamanthus	RAD-a-MAN-thus
Rosalyn	ROZ-za-lin
Ruire	RUE
Selene	sa-LEAN
Shennue	SHEN-new
Skipe	SKY-p
Surtur	SUR-tur
Sweyn	SWAIN
Talos	TAL-ows
Themis	THEE-miss
Their	TH'AIR-ee (like Carrie)
Therial	TH'AIR-ee-al
Theriomorph	TH'AIR-ee-OH-morph
Thoth	THAWTH
Tyr	TEAR
Úlfhéðinn	OOLF-he'ed-in
Úlfhéðnar	OOLF-he'ed-nar
Ullr	OU-yer
Varren	VAIR-en
Vidrick	VEE-drick
Virisinu	VERE-i-SIN-ew
Yamir	YA-mear
Yena	YEN-ah
Yorrick	YOUR-ick

APPENDIX IV
Elysian Military Ranks

Terra Divisions
    Private
    Corporal
    Sergeant
    Warrant Officer
    Lieutenant
    Captain
    Major
    Colonel
    General
    Chief General
    Master Chief (General)
    Grand Master Chief (General)

Aerial Divisions
    Private
    Airman
    Sergeant
    Lieutenant
    Captain
    Major
    Colonel
    General
    Chief General
    Master Chief (General)
    Grand Master Chief (General)

Marine Divisions
    Private
    Seaman
    Petty Officer
    Warrant Officer
    Ensign
    Lieutenant
    Commander
    Captain
    Admiral
    Chief Admiral
    Master Chief (Admiral)
    Grand Master Chief (Admiral)

THERE IS ALWAYS MORE TO COME...

Although The Incarn Saga is at its end, I am currently working on independent novels and novellas as well as new series. Keep an eye out for upcoming works in the young adult, new adult, and adult categories. I hope that you will continue to support me as I reveal worlds and kingdoms beyond Elysia and expand upon the limitless universe that is Fantasy. I can't wait to share some of the strange and mystical places that I have already begun to explore.

NOTE FROM THE AUTHOR

As an author, writing the story is just the beginning. Next come revising, editing, formatting, proofreading, and marketing. Surprisingly, marketing requires a huge amount of time. If you enjoy an author's work and want her or him to publish more in a shorter time span, you can help! Spread the word on social media and by word of mouth. Post reviews on Amazon, Goodreads and other websites. Believe me, I would much rather write a new book than spend time promoting the one I have just finished. So go ahead—pin, tweet, post, review, and like. Thank you, my dearest fans!

ABOUT THE AUTHOR

Katharine Wibell's lifelong interest in mythology includes epic poetry like the Odyssey, Ramayana, Beowulf, and the Nibelungenlied. In addition, she is interested in all things animal whether training dogs, apprenticing at a children's zoo, or caring for injured animals as a licensed wildlife rehabilitator. After receiving degrees from Mercer University in both art and psychology with an emphasis in animal behavior, Wibell moved to New Orleans with her dog, Alli, to kick start her career as an artist and a writer. Her first literary works blend her knowledge of the animal world with the world of high fantasy.

LEARN MORE

WWW.KATHARINEWIBELLBOOKS.COM

Issaura's Claws ~ *Ullr's Fangs* ~ *Crocotta's Hackles* ~ *Giahem's Talons*

Made in the
USA
Lexington, KY